D1761114

THE SOLDIER'S RETURN

Kate Channer is settled in London, helping half-sister Naomi as housekeeper while the Great War rages on. When Naomi's brother Ned is sent home seriously injured, it's up to Kate to manage the household as well as Ned's rehabilitation. But with the growing workload, she struggles to keep everything running smoothly and yearns to return to Woodicombe House. And with no word from her husband Luke, fighting in France, it's becoming increasingly difficult to stay positive. Hard times are ahead for Kate and her family — when the realities of war land on their doorstep, can Kate find the strength to keep going?

ROSIE MEDDON

♦

THE
SOLDIER'S
RETURN

Complete and Unabridged

MAGNA
Leicester

First published in Great Britain in 2019 by
Canelo Digital Publishing Limited
London

First Ulverscroft Edition
published 2020
by arrangement with
Canelo Digital Publishing Limited
London

A catalogue record for this book is available
from the British Library.

ISBN 978-0-7505-4752-9

Published by
Ulverscroft Limited
Anstey, Leicestershire

Set by Words & Graphics Ltd.
Anstey, Leicestershire
Printed and bound in Great Britain by
T. J. International Ltd., Padstow, Cornwall

This book is printed on acid-free paper

Spring 1918

1

The Telegram

Kate Channer let out a long sigh. Her afternoon at St. Ursula's had been a busy one and now, standing beneath the porch of number twelve, Hartland Street, hunting about in her handbag for her door key, all she wanted to do was sit down somewhere quiet with a nice cup of tea. Quiet? Huh. Little chance of that! The moment she stepped over this threshold, all hope of even a moment to herself would go *straight* out of the window.

Finally locating her key, she opened the door and paused to listen. Sure enough, from along the hallway came shrieks of delight and towards her hurtled a blur of rose-sprigged pinafore dress and dark ringlets that only halted when it smacked — ouf! — straight into her legs.

'Aunty Kay! Aunty Kay!'

With a warm smile, and reaching over the little girl's head, Kate deposited her handbag on the hall table. Oh, to be so full of beans. 'Yes, hello there, Esme.'

'Swing, Aunty Kay! Swing!'

There being no point refusing, Kate gave up unbuttoning her jacket, scooped the child up from the floor and then whirled her around in a circle. 'There,' she said, setting her back down again, 'big swing for my favourite girl.'

Disoriented, and clearly giddy, the child teetered about for a moment before turning back to grasp Kate's skirt. 'Again, Aunty Kay! Again.'

This time, Kate shook her head; one turn at that was quite enough for both of them. 'No, no more, lovey. That's all for now.'

As it usually did, the commotion of her arrival brought Naomi through from the drawing room. 'Esme, darling,' she said, moving to smooth a hand over her daughter's hair, 'poor Aunty Kate's tired. She's been volunteering at St. Ursula's all afternoon.'

'No! Not tired. Aunty Kay come play.'

With Esme now tugging at her skirt, Kate nevertheless finished unbuttoning her jacket, slipped it off her shoulders and then reached to hang it from its hook.

'Esme, please let go of Aunty Kate's skirt,' Naomi chided. 'There's a good girl.' Then, turning back to Kate, she asked, 'Busy afternoon?'

'Busy and then some. Marjorie was at the War Office again, hoping to nab someone about these latest delays to the widows' pensions, leaving *me* to go about things in a manner of my own devising.'

'Hm. One can only hope that *this* time, the War Office listened to her.'

'Can only hope they see fit to get off their backsides — forgive my language — and *do* something, more like.'

'Well, *my* thoughts on the matter have always been plain,' Naomi said, bending to peel her daughter's fingers away from Kate's skirt. 'Had it been *men* waiting to receive payment for the loss of their *wives'* incomes, then this whole business would have been resolved years ago.'

Kate couldn't disagree. The state of affairs was pitiful, families who'd lost their breadwinners were faced with having to get by on handouts and charity. 'And what about *your* afternoon?' she asked, reaching to peg her felt hat over an empty coat hook.

'Oh, nothing out of the ordinary. A certain little girl refused to go up for her nap again, asking instead to go the park.'

Hm. When it came to Esme — and what she did or did not want to do — Naomi always seemed rather swift to give in. But it was easy, one step removed, to criticise; *she* hadn't been through what Naomi had. Suffering that miscarriage, especially with Mr Lawrence being away at the front, had really knocked Naomi for six. Such a blessing when they'd been brought an orphaned newborn to fill the void — and so soon afterwards, too.

Almost disbelieving at how things had turned out, she let out a little sigh. Hard to believe all that business was three years ago now. Hard to think Esme had ever been that tiny. Or that Mr Lawrence should instantly have taken to her, too. To see them together now, no one would ever imagine that they she and Naomi weren't naturally mother and daughter. Esme even mimicked Naomi's pout when she didn't get her own way. Look at her, the little madam.

'You're very naughty, Esme,' she said, affecting mock displeasure and staring down at the little face looking sheepishly back at her. 'You must do as your mamma says.'

'Anyway, I told her,' Naomi picked up again, 'that if she wants to be treated like a big girl, then she must act like one and, at bedtime, must go straight upstairs — no whining and no fuss. In fact, another five minutes and I'll take her up and get her washed — she does look awfully tired.'

Was it that time already? She glanced to the grandfather clock. Heavens, yes, it was almost six. Where *had* the day gone? Turning to the cupboard for her apron, she reckoned a list of her chores; foremost being those she hadn't got around to this morning while Naomi had been out doing her own volunteering, driving an ambulance for St. George's hospital. 'All right,' she said. 'And as soon as I've seen to the dusting in the drawing room, I'll pop down and make a start on supper.'

Nodding her understanding, Naomi returned her attention to her daughter. 'Five more minutes, young lady, and then it's bath time.'

When Esme scampered back to the drawing room, and Naomi followed, Kate let out a weary sigh. Given the afternoon she'd had, the last thing she felt like doing was dusting. But, for one reason or another, this morning she'd got all behind. So, although her feet were throbbing, and, in her skull, it felt as though a dozen blacksmiths were forging enough horseshoes for an entire cavalry regiment, there was no way around it: she had to get on. Naomi might be her half-sister — and treat her as such for most of the time — but she also employed her to run her

6

home. And household chores did *not* see to themselves.

Rappity-tap-tap.

Neither, sadly, did people knocking at the door.

She shook her head in dismay; pound to a penny it would be children again, daring each other in a game of Knock Down Ginger. Coming along the street just now she'd spotted a couple of ragamuffins up to no good behind the knife grinder's barrow; more than likely it was them larking about, the little devils.

Rap-a-tap-tap.

Yes, yes, patience, for heaven's sake.

Having fastened the strings of her apron about her waist, she reached to open the door. On the other side was a small boy with dark-ringed eyes and an ashen face. Bringing her hands to her hips, she tutted. Hadn't his friends told him that the point of the game was to rattle the knocker and then run away as fast as your legs would carry you?

On the point of giving him short shrift, though, something stopped her. Glinting on the collar of his navy-blue jacket was a brass badge. Oh, dear Lord, this was no street urchin: this was the telegram boy. And the only news that came by telegram these days was the sort every wife dreaded.

Meeting her stare, the child offered an envelope towards her. 'Telegram for Mrs Lawrence Colborne.'

She exhaled heavily. *Mrs Lawrence Colborne.* *Not* Mrs Luke Channer. It wasn't about Luke.

7

No, but it *was* about Mr Lawrence.

Her heart thudding in her chest, she released her grip on the door frame. 'Wait there,' she said to the child. 'W-wait right there.'

With the sensation that her legs might buckle beneath her, she lurched towards the drawing room and peered in. On the rug was Esme, her toy tea-service set out in front of her, several of her dolls propped up nearby. Poor love: still short of her third birthday and yet already so many people had been taken from her. Well, if it turned out that something *had* happened to her new papa, then at least she was probably too young to understand it. Or even to properly miss him.

Sadly, the same couldn't be said of Naomi; *she* was going to be devastated.

'Right then,' Naomi chose that moment to rise from the sofa and say, 'come along Esme, it's time for your — good heavens, Kate, you look as though you've seen a ghost.'

Kate closed her eyes. *This was it.* No matter how carefully she chose her words, nothing was going to soften the blow. 'There's um . . . a telegram . . . come for you.'

In an instant, Naomi was pushing past her, the heels of her shoes clack-clacking upon the tiled floor of the hallway as she ran to the door.

'Mrs Lawrence Colborne?'

'Yes, yes. I am she.'

'Telegram for you, ma'am. Will there be a reply?'

Back along the hallway, grasping the door frame for support, Kate straightened up. A

8

reply? The boy wanted to know if there would be a *reply?* Then it *couldn't* be as she had feared, because telegrams starting with the words *Deeply regret to inform you* bore a special mark on the envelope to warn the delivery boy that he carried bad news — the sort for which there couldn't possibly *be* a reply. Yes, Marjorie Randolph had told her that. And she was never wrong about anything.

Exhaling with relief for the second time in as many minutes, she sank back against the wall. Well, if it wasn't bad news, then what was it? What else could be so urgent as to necessitate the sending of a telegram?

In the doorway, Naomi was still attending to the delivery boy.

'No. No reply for the present,' she heard her say, her tone giving away nothing of her thoughts as she reached into the bowl on the side table for a coin, pressed it into the child's hand, and then closed the door.

Watching her slit open the envelope and pull out the message, Kate held her breath. But, when all Naomi did was stand and stare down at it, unable to wait, she leant across and snatched the chit of paper from between her fingers.

LT EDWIN RUSSELL INJURED.
MOUNT EDEN HOSPITAL DOVER.

Ned. It was about Ned. He was in a hospital in Dover. Dover: why did she know that name? Oh, yes: the ambulance train at the Victoria rest station that day — that had come from there.

9

Instantly, the scene from that morning, with all of its horror and its gore, came flooding back to her, the groaning from the wounded men and the stench of their blood and vomit as vivid now as it had been then.

'Ned,' she breathed, the news slow to register. Not Naomi's husband at all, but her brother.

'Yes,' Naomi whispered. 'Ned.'

Staring down at the telegram, she found her eyes drawn back to the word that had first caught her attention. *Injured.* How was it possible for a word of so few letters to cause so much alarm and yet, at the same time, say so little? Was he, for instance, *badly* injured? Were his injuries mortal, or had he just suffered a few bumps and grazes requiring little more than ointment and bandages? As his next of kin, were they, or were they not, to fear for his life? This curt little missive told them next to nothing.

'At least he's alive,' she said, trying to swallow down the panic that was tightening her throat.

Beside her, Naomi stiffened. 'Mamma and Papa!' she exclaimed. 'I must go and tell them . . . and telephone this Mount Eden place — find out what happened . . . find out how he is.'

Oh dear, yes, of course. When Ned had joined the Royal Flying Corps, rather than give his parents as his next of kin he had given his sister, meaning that poor Naomi now had the task of going to tell Mr and Mrs Russell.

'Yes,' she said. 'You must go.'

'Yes. Look . . . can you see to Esme for me?'

''C-Course,' Kate replied, attributing the

10

chattering of her teeth to shock. 'And I'll keep something warm for you.' Catching sight of Naomi's frown, she went on, 'In case you're hungry when you get back.'

Uncertainly, Naomi nodded. 'Yes. Very well. Although I can't say when that will be . . . '

'No matter.' Poor Naomi, she looked as though she'd had all the stuffing knocked out of her, her face blanched to the colour of linens dipped in blueing. 'I'll make sure to keep something for you anyway.'

Seemingly unable to decide what to do next, Naomi stood, glancing about the hallway. 'Look, if I go up and fetch my mac and my handbag and what-not, would you go along to the corner and flag down a cab for me? I shall be no more than two or three minutes at most.'

Relieved to have something to take her mind from speculating about Ned's condition, Kate nodded. 'I'll go dreckly.' On her tongue lingered the words *and try not to worry*, but where was the point in uttering something as half-baked as that? Until Naomi learned the extent of her brother's injuries, she was bound to fret. And, she, Kate, would do the same. Ned might only be her half-sibling but she still loved him dearly. So, all she could do for the moment was try to remain calm, try to make things seem normal for Esme, and then pray that when Naomi returned with news, it wasn't of the sort she had begun to fear.

★　★　★

'Now, take care, the pair of you, and don't worry about us. We shall have a lovely day, shan't we, Esme?'

It was early the following morning, and at the kerb outside of the house in Hartland Street stood two hackney cabs. On the pavement beside them, Kate was trying to persuade Esme not to keep skipping about, while Naomi was giving Aunt Diana yet more last-minute instructions.

'I'm sure you will both have a wonderful day, yes. But please, Aunt, don't overdo the treats. One small i-c-e in an afternoon is quite enough.'

'One i-c-e. Understood.'

'Too many sweet things cause her to come over quite silly.'

'Yes, dear. Now do go on with you or you'll miss your train. Give my love to Ned and we'll see you this evening.'

'We shall be on the four-thirty from Dover.'

'Yes, dear. You said. Twice.'

'Very well.'

With their cab eventually pulling away and turning towards Victoria, Kate felt her insides beginning to knot. Already it had been a fraught morning and still ahead of them lay a railway journey of two hours. Two whole hours with nothing to distract them from the fact that they were going to see Ned, with no real idea of what to expect when they got there.

Late last night, Naomi had returned from Clarence Square, weary and tearful, to relay what she had been able to find out, which was, in essence, that Ned had been flying a reconnaissance mission over Belgium — during which he

12

had been shot at by German guns — when, on his way back, part of his aeroplane had stopped working. With no choice but to attempt to bring it down in a field, he had landed heavily, injuring both of his legs.

Picturing his narrow escape had made Kate feel sick. And when Naomi had gone on to announce that she planned to travel to see him — asking her to go with her — she had been left longing for a way to excuse herself, fearing for how harrowing it would be. But, for Ned to have survived at all was a miracle. And, these days, miracles were things to be celebrated.

'Did you say that Cousin Elizabeth is going to try to get him brought to London?' she asked now, unable to banish from her mind a picture of Ned's aeroplane smashing into the ground.

Naomi nodded. 'To the new hospital in Bryanston Square, yes. As I understand it, it was set up specifically for patients from the RFC and has a specialist surgeon there. Unfortunately, it has just twenty beds. And, even were one of those to be available right now, the doctors there would still want to assess his injuries in order to be certain that it is the right place for him to receive treatment.'

Ned's situation sounded grim. After all, if a specialist hospital wasn't the right place for him, then where was? 'I see.'

'You know,' Naomi went on, her tone a little brighter, 'Elizabeth was really rather brilliant. She must be a real asset to the Voluntary Aid Detachment. She dropped everything, instantly, and made goodness-only-knows how many telephone calls to see about getting him brought back here. Apparently, the hospital where he is at the moment is little more than a country house, graciously loaned by someone with no use for it but only ever intended as a convalescent home. It just happened to be close to where they took him after the crash.'

Kate nodded. 'I see.'

'And she said that today, she will do everything she can to get him back here and into the proper RFC hospital. She even said that if necessary, she will commandeer an ambulance from the VAD and drive it there herself.'

'Goodness.'

'Of course, it had already gone through my mind that I *could* go and fetch him myself. But then it occurred to me that I might not be up to the task — you know, that once I saw him, I should become too upset. And that's before considering the likelihood of my becoming lost en route. Dover really is miles from anywhere, you know.'

The thought of Ned in the back of an ambulance with Naomi behind the wheel, driving around in circles while struggling to make sense of a map, made Kate want to giggle. She could only put it down to her nerves.

With Naomi falling silent, Kate turned instead to look out through the window of their cab. Notwithstanding the number of missions Ned had flown without incident — missions during which he could easily have been shot down by German guns — her fear had always been that something would go wrong with his aeroplane and bring him crashing to earth, his frail little craft ending up as little more than a pile of firewood and matchsticks. And now, seemingly, her fears had come true. According to the little Naomi had been able to glean, he had come down in a farmer's field, barely a mile inland from the coast. But oh, what a fortuitous mile that had turned out to be! Any earlier and he would still have been out over the sea. And then all the consoling on God's earth wouldn't have helped Naomi to get over the loss of him — not ever.

Once settled into their compartment of an otherwise empty first-class railway carriage, and with the terraced houses and factories of south-east London flitting past their window, Kate tried to picture this Mount Eden place. What would it be like? How would Ned look? What would she say to him? The safest thing would surely be to say nothing. After all, what *did* you say to someone who had crashed their aeroplane and injured both of their legs? 'Multiple fractures' were the actual words Naomi had used last night. *Lucky to be alive.*

Of course, the greater truth was that they were *all* lucky: somehow, for all the awfulness of this war, everyone within her little circle of family and friends — apart, now, from Ned, of course — had so far managed to avoid coming to harm. Oh, and apart from Mr Lawrence's brother, Mr Aubrey — but then it had never been entirely clear whether or not *his* wound had been genuinely gotten in the first place. From time to time, she still found herself wondering what had

15

eventually happened to him — where he had found somewhere to go so as never to be found. The police sergeant was convinced he had fled either to America or to Canada but, as far as she had been able to tell, that was only supposition, no firm indication of his whereabouts ever coming to light.

Continuing to stare out through the window, she sighed. Of greater importance was that, somehow, Luke had managed to remain unscathed, as had Mr Lawrence. Indeed, towards the end of last autumn, just after he had returned to the front following a week's leave, Luke had been made up to the rank of corporal, and Mr Lawrence to captain. Somewhat *less* happily, Mabel's letters from Woodicombe continued to relay details of losses suffered by families in Westward Quay — boys who had been in her class at school, like Tommy Narracott, whose sheer size had always made her wary of him, and little Joey Braund, always the first to get up to no good, both of them blown to pieces on the first day of the Battle of the Somme almost two years ago now. But, other than desperately sad incidents such as those, and despite, at times, the whole business of war still feeling oddly unreal, it had also come to feel horribly normal — the hardships and the suffering simply things they all got on with as best they could.

As best they could. Sometimes, she was minded that the only reason she continued to manage without Luke as she did, was because, from the outset, they'd had so little time together as man and wife. Folk often said you couldn't miss what you'd never had. And, by the looks of it, it was true. Nevertheless, not a moment passed when she didn't long for the war to be over and done with, and to have her husband back by her side.

In the absence of any proper memories of being wed to him, the pictures with which she comforted herself varied according to her mood. Sometimes, the two of them would be strolling arm-in-arm around Hyde Park, his fair hair and good looks drawing covert glances from other young women. Other times, they would be riding an omnibus on their way to the theatre — oh, how she longed to go to a theatre again and, from the delightful darkness of the auditorium, mouth the words to a musical spectacular! Other times still, she would picture them simply sitting by the fire, Luke engrossed in something he was reading in the newspaper while she sat darning a rent in one of his shirts, her foot keeping up a ceaseless rocking of a cradle in which lay the first of their children. Her yearning for that last miracle was new, and something she could only attribute to her increasing involvement in caring for Esme, and the astonishing speed with which the little girl was growing up. Either way, sometimes, the fierceness of that particular longing tugged at her insides more forcefully than anything she had ever known.

With the warm and orangey hues of that last picture in mind, she closed her eyes and settled back into her seat. Already, the rhythmical clacking of the rails and the rocking of their carriage was making her feel sleepy — a situation not helped by the fact that she had spent yet another night restless and wakeful. That said, she would resist the urge to doze. According to Naomi, unless you were a very young child, falling asleep in public was inexcusable.

When the next thing she became aware of, though, was a deafening roar, she lifted her head from where it had fallen forward and, raising a hand to rub at the back of her neck, tried to make sense of where she was. The light inside their compartment had turned an odd grey-green colour, while beyond the window everything was pitch black — seemingly, they were hurtling through a tunnel. And, despite her resolve, she had been asleep.

With that, a shriek of the locomotive's whistle coincided with their return to daylight. Dazzled by the brightness outside, she screwed up her eyes and stared out. Away to the left, through a break in the clouds, sunlight was flashing onto a featureless silvery sea, the squawking of seagulls audible even above the rumbling of the train. *The sea.* Then they must be nearly there.

Across from her, Naomi was sitting with her hands in her lap, the pearl buttons at the neck of her eau-de-nil travelling jacket unfastened and her magazine closed on the seat next to her.

Catching her eye, Kate stretched out her arms. 'Sorry,' she mumbled. 'I hadn't realized I was so tired.'

To her admission, Naomi responded with a light shrug. 'It's all right. I shouldn't have minded a nap myself.'

Running her tongue around the inside of her parched mouth, and sensing that they were slowing down, she directed her eyes back out through the window. Running alongside the railway track was a long terrace of houses, behind them a steep hill. As they began to slow further, the houses gave way to railway sidings, and then to the platform of the station itself, where, with a series of jerks, they juddered to a halt.

Just beyond their window, a station official stood holding a flag. 'Dover Priory,' he called out. 'This is Dover Priory. Passengers for Dover town, please alight here.'

Following Naomi's lead, she got to her feet. They had arrived.

★   ★   ★

'Begging your pardon, Matron, but I have some ladies come to visit Lieutenant Russell.'

Mount Eden Hospital, when they reached it no more than fifteen minutes after arriving at the station, was just as Naomi had suggested — a moderately-sized family home, set in sloping grounds on a rise just outside of the town.

Once they had gone in through the porch, the porter who had come out to meet their cab ushered them into a room whose light colours put Kate in mind of having once been a morning room, or perhaps a lady's sitting-room. Now, though, beneath the daintily-patterned stucco ceiling, and standing on strips of jute matting laid over the carpet, was an oversized teak desk

19

— ugly in the extreme — along with a washstand, a trestle table stacked with assorted medical equipment of indeterminate purpose, and a couple of tall but non-matching cabinets, each with four drawers.

'Ah, yes,' Matron said, setting aside the papers she had been reading and getting to her feet, 'someone telephoned yesterday evening. Welcome, ladies, to Mount Eden Hospital for Convalescing Officers.'

Despite the rustling of her starched uniform, Matron struck Kate as homely rather than clinical.

'Thank you,' Naomi replied. 'And yes, it was our cousin, Elizabeth Newsome, who telephoned. I am Mrs Colborne, and this is Mrs Channer. We are Lieutenant Russell's sisters. I do hope our coming isn't an inconvenience, but my mother is beside herself with worry, and eager that I came *poste-haste* to ascertain our brother's condition.'

With that, Kate noticed Matron glance between them. People often did that upon learning they were sisters.

'It is no inconvenience. We are a small hospital — just the twelve beds — and so I try not to have rules for the sake of them. Of primary concern is the well-being of the men in my care and, since most of them are convalescing as opposed to undergoing treatment, I try to be as accommodating as I can — a visit from family being as beneficial to a man's spirits as almost anything medicine has to offer.'

Beside her, Naomi nodded. 'Well, thank you

for receiving us anyway.'

When Matron smiled, Kate smiled back. Perhaps this wouldn't be so bad after all.

'Well, you've come a long way, so let's take you straight up to your brother. Then I'll let Doctor Chilton know that you're here.'

'Thank you,' Naomi replied.

'I should perhaps point out,' Matron picked up again, 'that even should your brother be awake, he is likely to be drowsy from the morphine.'

Standing beside Naomi, Kate stiffened. Morphine? People were given morphine for pain, which could only mean that Ned was in quite a bad way.

'We understand,' Naomi said. 'Just being able to see him will be a relief.'

'I'm sure. But perhaps try to keep your questions to him to a minimum.'

'We will do that.'

'No sense being a drain on his strength.'

'No, of course not.'

Once back out in the hallway, Kate glanced about. What little of the décor was visible beyond the paraphernalia of a hospital showed signs of a woman's hand having been at work. The walls were painted a spring-like shade of pale lemon, the door frames and skirtings were ivory. And she guessed that beneath the heavy coverings lay floorboards of polished elm to match the elegant bannisters. What a shame that every inch of such a lovely house should now smell of carbolic — even if that was preferable to the stench of vomit and blood.

'This way,' Matron directed, turning to the left

21

at the top of the stairs. Reaching the end of a short corridor she then stood aside, gesturing Naomi into the room ahead of her.

'Ned!' Kate heard her exclaim as she went in.

'Please, do go on in, Mrs Channer. I'll fetch along another chair so that you can sit down.'

Despite doing her best to raise a smile, Kate hung back. *Come on*, she urged herself, *no matter your nerviness, you have to go in at some point.* And so, drawing a breath, she forced herself across the threshold.

Once on the other side, she looked quickly about. Centred against the far wall, taking up almost all of the floor of the cramped little box-room, was a bedstead, its cream-coloured paint chipped away in places to reveal the bare iron beneath. Upon it, and beneath a blue coverlet, lay Ned, his eyes closed, his breathing barely disturbing his chest. Above the turned-back sheet, his arms lay motionless by his sides. On one of his cheeks was a series of fresh scratches, on his other a gauze bandage. With the front of his hair swept to one side he looked unusually vulnerable. And so young. And the grey tint to his complexion made him look ill. But then he *was* ill, she reminded herself. Mortally so, from the look of him.

What she was trying *not* to look at was the contraption of metal rods and fabric ties holding his feet to the top of the bedstead and, thus, his legs up at an angle from his body. Although nothing much of the device itself was evident — his legs covered by the blanket — she could think only of an instrument of torture.

On the far side of the bed, Naomi was lowering herself onto a chair. 'Oh, Kate,' she said softly, 'how is it possible for him to seem so peaceful and yet, at the same time, so pitiful? I mean . . . look at him.'

But, for her part, Kate was finding it hard to even remain in the room. More than anything, she felt as though she shouldn't be there — as though she was intruding upon Ned's right to lie injured and convalescing without being ogled by visitors — even if those visitors were members of his family.

'Here you are, Mrs Channer,' Matron returned to say, a folding wooden chair held out in front of her. 'There's room enough — just — to squeeze it in along the other side of the bed there, if you'd like to.'

Looping her handbag over her arm, Kate forced her lips into a smile and, with some difficulty in the confined space, carried the chair around the end of the bed and set it down. With no choice but to then sit with her knees pressing against the iron frame of the bed, she tried — but failed — to wriggle herself comfortable.

Once Matron had left them, Naomi looked across at her. 'I wasn't expecting him to look so . . . so *frail*.'

It was an observation Kate shared. 'No,' she whispered back.

Last summer, granted a brief spell of leave, Ned had turned up at Hartland Street. And, before he had taken Naomi out to lunch, Kate had spent a few moments chatting with him. Since then, whenever his name came up, she

23

pictured an immaculately-uniformed young pilot, bronzed by the sun and grinning broadly. By contrast, today, he looked as though every last ounce of life had been sucked from his body.

'But what was I expecting?' Naomi went on, once again echoing her own thoughts on his appearance. 'He was hardly going to be in rude health, was he?'

'No,' she said again, wishing she could summon a few words of comfort. But how on earth did she do that when Ned could barely have looked worse had he been at death's door?

Behind her, the lower half of the sash window stood slightly raised, and through it was coming the smell of mown grass, and the sound of house sparrows chirruping. How unjust that while Ned lay here lifeless and still, beyond this little room with its simple wooden crucifix above the bed-head, the business of the day continued precisely as on any other. If nothing else, it felt disrespectful. And wholly unfair.

With that, Ned's fingers twitched. Startled, Kate glanced to his face; was he stirring?

Across the bed from her, Naomi was clearly wondering the same. 'Ned?' she whispered.

With some difficulty, Ned opened his eyes. 'Min? Min . . . is that you?'

'Yes! Oh, Ned . . . ' When he tried to raise his head from the pillow to look around, Naomi grasped his hand. 'Try not to move,' she urged. 'Try to lay still.'

'What . . . time is it?' he wanted to know.

Naomi glanced to her wristwatch. 'Almost midday.'

'Ah . . . '

'Tell me, how do you feel?'

' . . . groggy . . . '

'I think that's to be expected. Matron said they're giving you morphine.'

'And is that . . . Kate?'

Dumbly, Kate nodded.

'Yes,' Naomi answered for her. 'We've travelled down together.'

'To *Dover*,' he said, as though trying to make sense of his circumstances.

'Yes. You're in a hospital called Mount Eden — '

'I remember.'

'You do? Well, that's good.'

'Had to ditch . . . in a field — '

'Yes, they told us.'

' — engine cut out. Fuel line . . . I suppose. Bit of a skirmish earlier. Took fire.'

'Please, Ned, just rest,' Naomi urged her brother.

Across the bed, Kate sat with her heart racing. His condition was considerably worse than she had hoped.

'Aimed for a . . . haystack. Fell short.' With that, his lips seemed to soften as though trying to smile. 'Managed . . . to miss . . . the poor chap's barn, though.'

'Ned, please, why don't you — '

'I say,' he began, struggling once again to lift his head from the pillow. 'Have you seen Rowley?'

In response to Naomi's puzzled frown, Kate shrugged.

'Rowley?'

'Ellis. Ellis Rowley-King. *Rowley*.'

'Shush. Stay still.'

'My photographer. We'd been . . . artillery spotting. When we had difficulties . . . I told him . . . I told him . . . once we get close to the ground . . . jump for it. Did he? Did he jump clear?'

Again, Naomi frowned. 'Um . . . I'm afraid I've heard no mention of him.'

Struggling in the confined space, Kate got to her feet. 'Perhaps Matron would know,' she said, careful to keep her voice soft. 'I'll go an' see if I can find her and ask.' If nothing else, leaving the room would allow brother and sister some privacy.

'Kate's Devon accent,' she heard Ned say as she went out through the door. 'Nice to hear.'

Surprised to feel herself flushing, Kate went along the corridor and quickly down the stairs, where she stood for a moment to draw several long breaths. How was it possible that Ned Russell still had the power to make her blush? All that nonsense . . . all that *business* between them . . . was four years ago. Granted, she'd barely seen him in that time, what with him joining the RFC, but honestly, surely by now she should have got over her embarrassment — recovered from the mortification of what happened. Everyone else, Ned included, had forgotten it.

Feeling a little less flustered, she peered beyond the open door to Matron's room and, seeing her seated behind her desk, tapped lightly.

'Mrs Channer, how may I help you?'

26

'Lieutenant Russell is asking after the photographer who was with him in his aeroplane,' she said. 'Mr Rowley-King, he called him.'

'Lieutenant Russell is awake?'

'Yes, ma'am. I mean Matron.'

'That's good. But I'm afraid I know nothing of his colleague. Where he was taken for treatment would have depended upon his condition. There's a surgical ward at Belle Vue — although that's really only for minor injuries. And I happen to know that in any event, they're full to bursting. You could do worse than speak to that young woman from the VAD — the one who called here about your brother. I daresay she has the means to find out where he is.'

Despite nodding her understanding, Kate was disappointed. She'd been hoping to go back to Ned with some news — anything, really, to set his mind at rest. But, having drawn a blank, all she could do was report Matron's suggestion that Naomi speak to Cousin Elizabeth.

'And the doctor,' she thought to say. 'You said earlier you would tell him we're here.'

'Doctor Chilton, yes, and I have. I'm sure he'll send me to fetch you shortly.'

Not much later, the doctor did indeed send Matron to collect them.

'Your brother,' he said, once they were seated with him in another of the downstairs rooms, 'was fortunate — fortunate that his aircraft came down over England and that, quite by chance, he was taken directly to a hospital with an orthopaedic surgeon who has become something of a specialist in fractures of the leg.' Sitting alongside Naomi, Kate listened intently and, when Dr Chilton looked between their faces, she nodded her understanding. 'Had he sustained his injuries in, say, Belgium or France, then in order to save his life, it is likely that both of his legs would have been amputated.'

Beside her, Naomi gasped, while, before her own eyes, the ink-stand on the doctor's desk seemed momentarily to blur. Discreetly, she pressed her hands onto her lap. She mustn't get all teary. And she definitely mustn't faint.

'Then, what a narrow escape,' Naomi murmured.

'For several reasons,' the doctor agreed.

Shifting her weight, Naomi went on, 'But, as it turns out, both of his legs are still — forgive me, Doctor, I have no idea of the correct medical terms — are still *intact*?'

As though caught in a draught, Kate shivered. These were things she would rather not have to hear. But what choice did she have? She was there to support Naomi.

'They are . . . yes.' *But?* From his tone, Kate could tell that the doctor was wary. 'But, as one would expect,' he went on, 'the impact of landing in such a manner caused multiple fractures, to both femurs — his thigh bones — as well as to the tibiae and fibulae — the two bones below each knee.' Seeing Naomi shifting yet again, she reached out a hand and brought it to rest on her lap. This was as harrowing to hear as she had feared. 'Now, the latest method for treating fractures to the femur is a device called the Thomas Splint, which, in layman's terms, consists of metal

28

rods, fastened about the patient's hips and applied so as to allow for the limb to be put into traction. Although a relatively simple device, its application requires the utmost accuracy. In unskilled hands, the bones stand little chance of being properly aligned once healed — '

'But they *will heal*?' Naomi interrupted the doctor's explanation to ask.

In response, Dr Chilton raised a hand. 'I feel it only fair to explain to you, Mrs Colborne, that medical opinion is divided — divided, that is, over whether this particular form of traction is appropriate for fractures of the bones to the *lower* leg, or solely to that of the thigh. However, in Lieutenant Russell's case, and with the assistance of X-ray photographs, it was the surgeon's opinion that the use of traction *was* appropriate. The healing of the femur being more critical than the risk of delayed bone-setting in the lower legs. Better, if you will,' he said more carefully, 'than loss of use of the legs in their entirety.'

Feeling tears welling, Kate blinked several times. What, precisely, did all of that mean? To her, it was just a string of words that didn't even seem to answer Naomi's question.

And Naomi seemed of the same mind. 'So, does that mean . . . that he *will* be able to walk again?' From the sound of her voice, she, too, was on the point of tears.

'Mrs Colborne, while one would wish nothing more than to answer you in the affirmative, I am not a man to sow seeds of false hope. So, if one were to strip out all optimism and deal only in facts, then my answer would be that, at this stage, I simply cannot say. I do concur with Dr . . . ' At this point, he peered down at the papers on his desk. 'Dr Kenwood's assessment of the risk, and also with his subsequent decision to place Lieutenant Russell's legs in traction. In addition, your brother has the benefit of being young, and otherwise fit and healthy. Thus, since you press me for an opinion, I would say there appears to be every chance that the fractures to his femurs will knit perfectly well. Will that be to the detriment of his lower limbs? That is something we will not know for a good while yet — possibly for as long as another four or five months.'

'Four or five months. I see,' Naomi responded.

Four or five months, Kate reflected. And, if she understood correctly, that was only until they knew whether he would *heal* — not until he would be up and about again, and back to normal. *Normal*. Was that even going to be possible?

'But even with the most favourable of outcomes,' Dr Chilton was continuing, 'I doubt your brother will walk as freely as he did previously. At best, I imagine he will suffer a limp and will require the use of a stick.'

Dear, brave Ned — with all of his life still ahead of him — now seemed destined to walk like an old man. Or a cripple. But she would not cry. No matter how unfair it was, she would *not* cry.

Drawing a long breath instead, she looked back up. Beside her, Naomi had further questions.

'I see. So, what happens next?'

'Well, in front of me I have a request for the patient to be transferred to the RFC hospital at Bryanston Square. I'm given to believe it's close to the family home.'

Both women nodded.

'It is, yes.'

'Then subject to there being a bed available, and to suitable arrangements being made for his conveyance, it is a request I would be inclined to authorize.'

Inclined. Presumably that meant yes. Uncertainly, Kate looked to Naomi.

'Thank you, Dr Chilton.' The relief in Naomi's tone was reassuring. 'It will be a weight from my mind to have him close by.'

'I'm sure it will be. And perhaps, in three or four weeks, he will be well enough to undertake the journey.'

'Three or four *weeks.*'

'Mrs Colborne, one would not wish to set back his recovery unnecessarily.'

'No, no of course not,' Naomi quickly conceded. 'Of course not.'

'Now, I learn from Matron that you have travelled this morning from London.'

Again, Naomi nodded. 'We have, yes.'

'In which case, may I invite you to stay and take luncheon with us? It won't be *haute cuisine*, but, by dining here with us, you will be able to sit with your brother again before you must leave to commence your journey home.'

'Thank you for the most considerate invitation,' Naomi said. 'We gratefully accept.'

'Yes,' Kate echoed Naomi's reply. 'Most kind

of you. Thank you.'

Feeling the stiffness slowly leaving her shoulders, Kate allowed herself a little sigh. At least they now knew the worst. Seemingly, the next few weeks were going to be tough on all of them, but at least they could see that Ned was in good hands. And, given what had happened to him, that had to be about the best for which either of them could reasonably hope.

2

The Patient

'Thank you for agreeing to come with me.'

Alighting from a cab onto the pavement outside of Queen Alexandra's Hospital, Kate could tell from Naomi's face that, despite being nervous, she was also relieved. And she could see why: the appearance of the building alone — a vast four-storey red brick edifice with ornate gables and an elaborate portico for an entrance — immediately instilled confidence. Ned would be all right here — she could tell.

'I wouldn't have let you come on your own,' she acknowledged Naomi's remark, watching as she fished about in her purse for the coins to pay their fare.

'Well, thank you anyway. I did feel terribly mean telling Mamma that Ned wasn't arriving for another couple of days but, had I not done so, she would have been here waiting for his ambulance to draw up at the kerb, demanding to be allowed to see him forthwith. And that wouldn't have been fair on either him or the nursing staff.'

All too aware of Pamela Russell's impatience, and her habit of finding fault with just about everything, she could see Naomi's point. It did seem sensible for the two of them to come here first. 'No,' she said. 'You're not wrong there.'

'At the very least, one imagines the journey must have made him weary — certainly too weary for him to want to face endless questions from Mamma.'

'Yes. Whereas this way, once you've seen him, you will be able to allay her fears.'

'I will,' Naomi agreed. 'I shall also be able to gauge whether the hospital as a whole is up to a visit from her. It must surely be in everyone's interests not to have Mamma waltzing in and criticising everything before Ned has even had the chance to get settled!'

It was now more than three weeks since the two women had first travelled to Dover to visit Ned, during which time, and in the absence of any word from Cousin Elizabeth, Naomi had grown steadily more and more impatient to hear from her. Then, finally, a couple of mornings ago, the postman had brought a letter to say that Ned was being transferred to the Queen Alexandra Military Hospital in Millbank. Initially, Naomi had been put out, complaining that Ned was supposed to be going into the RFC, where the doctors were specialists in the types of injuries suffered by pilots.

Specialists or no, Kate's own reaction had been that at least he would be nearby, which, surely, had to count for something. 'For certain this other place will be just as good,' she had remarked. 'And just think how much easier it will be for you to visit him there — every day, should you be so inclined.'

To an extent, the realization had seemed to mollify Naomi. 'Yes, of course,' she had gone on to agree. 'I'm sure his care will be perfectly acceptable.'

And, now that they were here, Naomi seemed happier still.

For her own part, Kate was just glad that Ned would now be close by. Had it been Luke who had been brought home injured, she knew she would have wanted him as close as possible, in whatever hospital could find a bed for him. Fortunately, she reminded herself, it *wasn't* Luke. *Un*fortunately, he was still far away in a foreign land. And oh, how desperately she longed for him not to be. How sorely she missed him!

Unsurprised to feel tears welling — these days, the least thing seemed to set her off — she straightened up and blinked them away. She would *not* feel sorry for herself. Women everywhere had the same worries — some, far worse. Moreover, since her first day of volunteering at St. Ursula's, she had learned to be grateful for small mercies: better that Luke be far away and safe, than back at home and — dare she even think it — facing the prospect of spending the rest of his life as a cripple like dear Ned might yet have to.

Their cab fare settled, they made their way across the pavement to the entrance, the door held wide for them by a liveried concierge.

'I must say, it all looks quite new,' Naomi remarked as they went inside.

It was true: the place looked modern and shiny and clean and, for a moment, Kate stood glancing about the vast marble-floored foyer, taking it all in, her eyes eventually coming to rest upon a noticeboard on the wall. On it were the names of the wards and their corresponding floors. When she went to scan the list, though, none of the names looked familiar. 'Where did you say he is?' she turned to Naomi to check.

'C Ward.'

She scanned the list a second time. Alexandra Ward, Victoria Ward . . . Edward . . . She read all the way down to the bottom. 'I don't see it here.'

'Neither do I. Most peculiar. Well, look, that sign over there says Visitors, and it's pointing up that staircase. So, let's go up, shall we? We can always find someone to ask once we're up there.'

Thinking Naomi's suggestion sensible, she nodded her agreement. 'All right.'

Ascending the curving staircase, the clicking of their heels on the marble tiles echoing around the stairwell, they arrived at a broad galleried landing, from which a corridor led away in both directions. Spotting a nurse further along, Naomi headed towards her. In the meantime, peering in through a nearby doorway, Kate found herself looking into a spacious ward. Unnoticed by anyone, she pushed the door wider, quickly counting sixteen beds — eight against each of the long walls. Flooded with light from a half-dozen tall sash windows, and with a high ceiling hung with two fans, the room felt calm and airy and cool.

'Apparently, we're in the wrong building.' Coming towards her, Naomi had a frown on her face. 'Wards A to C are in the annexe, which, I am informed, is located on Manston Street.'

'Far from here?'

'Immediately next door, apparently.'

Together, they turned for the staircase.

'It seems a nice place,' she commented, following Naomi down. 'That ward was very bright. Peaceful, too.'

'Yes, I will admit to being impressed.'

'Perhaps not as cosy as Mount Eden.'

'Perhaps not, no, but rather more modern and fit for purpose.'

'Yes.' Yes, she reflected, Ned would be well looked after here, on that score they need have no concerns.

Back outside, and with the clouds overhead threatening rain, they turned left and walked briskly along the front of the hospital. At the corner, a sign on the wall of a narrow alleyway proclaimed, Manston Street, followed underneath by the words, No Thoroughfare. Apparently thinking the same thing, they both drew to a halt.

'Oh.'

Sharing Naomi's dismay at the sight before them, Kate nevertheless determined not to become disheartened. Yes, the buildings looked distinctly older and less well-kept than where they had just been. But that was no cause for alarm. Inside, the wards were bound to be just as orderly and calm.

'Do you know which building it is?' she asked — not that any one of the facades looked more inviting than the next. Deliberately not turning to Naomi for her reply, she instead cast her eyes to where, not much further along, the street came to an abrupt end at a blank brick wall, several storeys high.

'First entrance on the right, those were the

nurse's instructions.'

Her heart sank. Of all the buildings, the first one looked to be in the worst repair of all. Even so, she still wouldn't worry. It would be just fine.

Arriving at the entrance in question she pushed open the door but, once inside, stopped dead. She was standing in a square vestibule where the light was dim, the décor well-worn, and the air thick with the smell of carbolic. At least it spoke to a certain level of hygiene, she found herself thinking.

Hearing Naomi follow her in, she stood glancing about. In the wall to their right was a hatch, through which she could see a porter, his dark jacket hanging unbuttoned and his tie loose about his neck.

In that same instant noticing her presence, he leapt to his feet, stubbed out a cigarette in the saucer of a green pottery cup, and set about re-buttoning his uniform. 'My apologies, ma'am,' he mumbled as he approached the hatch. 'You've caught me on me tea break.'

'Well, I'm sorry for that,' she replied, sensing that her own embarrassment was greater than his, 'but we've come to visit Lieutenant Russell in Ward C.'

'Third floor,' he said, gesturing with his head beyond the next pair of doors. 'You'll find Sister Morgan on duty up there.'

Having thanked the man in the tiny office, she turned back to Naomi. She looked distinctly uncomfortable. 'Third floor.'

'Yes. I heard.'

'You know, it might be better upstairs,' Kate

said quietly, holding open the next door and trying not to look too closely at the curls of grey paint peeling from its surface. After the reassuring grandeur of the building around the corner, this wasn't at all what she had been expecting.

'Well, one way or another,' Naomi replied, 'we are about to find out.'

Having climbed two sets of steep and creaking stairs, they paused on a small landing for breath — not that it did any good; this far from the door to the street the air was a good deal warmer and danker, and not something she felt inclined to inhale too deeply.

A floor further up, where a small window on the landing appeared to no longer fit snugly into its frame, the odour seeping through the resulting crack made her think of cabbage cooking.

'We must be above the kitchen,' she said.

'Vile,' Naomi replied, shielding her nose with her hand.

From this last small landing, a narrower staircase led on up to what she guessed were rooms in the attic. Of the only two doors on this level, one bore a notice proclaiming, Nursing Staff Only. To the other, someone had inexpertly nailed a wrought-iron letter C, such that it hung, askew, its attitude that of a crescent moon.

Drawing a breath, she reached to turn the handle but then, thinking better of it, raised her hand and knocked — after all, who knew what might be happening on the other side?

From beyond it, footsteps approached. Then

the latch clicked, and the door creaked open.

'Yes?'

At the sight of a tall and wiry nurse, Naomi stepped forward. 'Good afternoon. We have come to visit our brother, Lieutenant Edwin Russell. We have been informed that he is in this ward.'

The nurse stood aside. 'End bed. Though you've left it late, I must say. You've just fifteen minutes until the end of visiting. The hours are plain enough, and I make no exceptions.'

Not wanting to get off on the wrong foot with such a stern-looking woman, Kate forced a smile. 'We understand.'

'And keep the noise down. My other patients need peace and quiet.'

'Of course,' she acknowledged the sister's instruction. But honestly! Did this sour-looking woman truly think they looked raucously inclined — the sort of women to come in and cause trouble?

Naomi, meanwhile, was heading straight across the room — floorboards squeaking under her weight — to the farthest of just four beds.

'Oh, my dear Ned,' she heard her greet him, and then saw her bend to kiss his cheek.

Deliberately, she held back. Might it be better to wait outside? Space did look rather cramped and it *would* allow Naomi and Ned to talk more freely. On the other hand, she didn't want to appear uninterested in his well-being — or even unsupportive of Naomi.

She glanced in turn to the patients in each of the other three beds. Only one of them had a visitor — by the look of it his wife, her head bent as though to conceal that she was weeping. The patient, bandaged heavily about his head, appeared to be asleep — although he could just as easily have been unconscious.

Turning away, she decided that she *would* go and sit with Ned. And so, looking about, she lifted a chair from the foot of one of the other beds and carried it towards him.

'Kate,' he greeted her with a smile.

She smiled back. 'Hello.'

'You look well.'

'And you look . . . better than when we saw you in Dover.'

'I feel it.'

'That's good.'

'I did ask that you be transferred to the RFC in Bryanston Square,' Naomi made a point of saying to her brother, her tone still heavy with her disappointment.

'I know. There was a big fuss,' Ned replied.

'There was? Why?'

As best he could, given that the lower half of his body was being held rigid by the contraption of metal rods, Ned appeared to shrug his shoulders. 'Can't say for certain. Something to do with Cousin Elizabeth setting cats among pigeons, I think. How's Father?'

'What? Oh, much the same. Working too hard again.'

'And Mamma?'

'Waiting for me to report back on your condition — '

'Please don't let her come and visit, Min.'

'I'm not sure I will be able to stop her — '

'Please, Min,' Ned urged. 'I don't need the fuss with Sister Morgan. You know how Mamma can be — she would come in, criticise everything, rub everyone up the wrong way — '

While Ned and Naomi continued to discuss the wisdom of allowing Pamela Russell to visit — or not — Kate glanced about. Although not in the attic as such, the ceiling was, nevertheless, unusually low, and sloped down at an angle towards the top of the windows — of which there were only two in the entire room, neither of them having seen a chamois leather and bucket of water for several years. They did have curtains drawn back to either side but, being of mean and flimsy cloth, as well as too short by several inches, they struck her as entirely unsuited to the job for which they were intended. Slowly, she took in the rest of the room. On the wall that accommodated the four beds — each separated from the next by a small nightstand — the covering of paint might once have been white but was now what any honest person could only describe as grey. The linoleum on the floor was grey too, with a high shine, but so ancient and brittle that in places it had cracked, creating long fissures. By the door stood a desk, at first glance too bulky to have passed through the frame, let alone been manhandled up that narrow staircase — although, clearly, at some stage it must have been. Behind it, her papers illuminated in a pool of light from a desk lamp, Sister Morgan sat writing, her expression set with the same displeasure it had borne when she had opened the door to them.

'Well, I make you no promises,' she heard Naomi say; before going on to ask, 'What about the food here? How is that?'

'Desperately bad. Either boiled to oblivion or else mashed to a pulp. I can't seem to make anyone understand that though I might lack the use of my legs, I still have my teeth and they chew just fine.'

'Mount Eden was better?'

'Infinitely. Back there, those chaps not on morphine could have a glass of wine.'

To Kate, Naomi appeared to wring her hands. 'Oh dear. Was I wrong to have you brought here? Only, now I've seen what it's like, I'm beginning to wish I had left you in Dover — and I daresay you feel the same. Though of course, when I arranged it, I thought you were coming to the RFC.'

With that, Ned reached to take one of Naomi's hands. 'You weren't to know, Min. At least this way I'm closer to all of you.'

'And what about the doctors? What do they say?'

'Haven't seen one yet.'

'What? But you've been here — '

'The doc in Dover said he thought I would be in traction for another month at least. He said only then will we know how I stand. Or how I don't! Ha!'

Despite giggling, and receiving an appreciative wink from him in return, Kate noticed that where Naomi was concerned, Ned's attempt at humour went unnoticed. 'How was your journey?' she decided to ask him.

43

'Long,' he said flatly. 'And dreadfully uncomfortable. Wouldn't want to do it again, even dosed up with morphine and drowsy as hell.'

'No,' Naomi observed. 'Well, the good thing is that you won't have to.'

'Thank Elizabeth for me, won't you?'

'I shall thank her when she gets you into the RFC,' Naomi replied tartly. 'And you have my word that I shan't rest until she does.'

'Seriously, Min,' he said, wriggling his shoulders as though trying to get comfortable. 'It's fine. Whether I'm stuck in a bed here, or across the road, it doesn't make much difference to me. Although, I suppose the food might be better.'

At the far end of the room, Sister Morgan scraped back her chair. 'Time to leave, ladies. Visiting hours are over for today.'

Suddenly, Naomi grinned. 'Across the road the nurses are prettier.'

'Well, that's done it,' Ned whispered back and then pursed his lips into an identical grin. 'Get onto Elizabeth forthwith! I demand to be moved!'

Getting to her feet, Kate smiled. At least he hadn't lost his sense of humour. And thank goodness for that because, from what she had seen today, it would appear that he was going to need every ounce of it.

Travelling home afterwards, she glanced at Naomi. Since leaving the hospital, her manner had been one of preoccupation. It was understandable, of course: the conditions in which they had left Ned were hardly ideal. But at least he was back in London. At least he was back in *England*. If reports in the newspapers were to be believed, very few *enlisted* soldiers with injuries enjoyed such a luxury.

At that moment, and without saying anything to her first, Naomi spoke to the cab driver and asked him to take them to the post office.

'I'm going to telephone Cousin Elizabeth,' she said once they had arrived and she was alighting onto the pavement. 'You may prefer to wait here. I shan't be long.'

Sitting alone in the cab, Kate could only imagine that Naomi's plan was to plead with her cousin to get Ned moved. Her expression, when she returned less than five minutes later, suggested she'd had no joy.

'Did you get through to her?' she was forced to enquire when Naomi seemed in no hurry to speak.

'What?'

'Cousin Elizabeth. Did you manage to speak to her?'

'Oh. Yes. I did. Although I have to say, she was not overly helpful.'

'Oh?' From what she'd heard of this Elizabeth, it was unlike her not to be obliging. The picture painted of her by both Naomi and Ned — and even by Aunt Diana — was that of a purposeful and determined woman with a knack for making things happen. With Naomi unusually tight-lipped, though, all she could do was wait and see whether she would elaborate.

'She was sympathetic enough,' Naomi eventually continued. 'About Ned's plight in that awful place. But when I asked how long it would be before she could find him somewhere more suitable, she became quite sharp with me. She said that she couldn't just conjure a bed from nowhere. Supposedly, with all of the main hospitals full to bursting, and with Ned being in traction, we were fortunate she was able to find a bed at all.'

'Goodness.'

'She did promise to keep an ear to the ground for any change to the situation, but also cautioned against getting our hopes up.' With that, Naomi turned to look directly at her. 'But I *have* to hope, Kate. I *have* to. I can't bear to think of Ned being in that miserable little room for a moment longer than is absolutely necessary.'

Although able to understand Naomi's distress, she could also appreciate Cousin Elizabeth's point: no one could produce a bed from thin air. Perhaps, when Ned no longer needed to be in traction, it might become easier to accommodate him elsewhere. In the meantime, surely the good thing was that they didn't have to journey down and back to Dover just to see him — something they had only been able to manage twice after that first time. And anyway, perhaps, when they went to see him tomorrow, things there wouldn't seem quite so bad. Perhaps some of their disappointment stemmed from the shock of seeing the place for the first time, and to comparing it with the lavish new building around the corner. Had they not seen *that*, would the ward in Manston Street still have seemed so grim? Perhaps not quite so much, no — not that she would ever

46

persuade Naomi to see it that way.

Returning to visit Ned again the following day, though, Kate realized that she had been wrong: the ward was no better and the experience no less depressing. The smell of food being cooked still lingered in the stairwell, Sister Morgan was still unnecessarily sharp with them, and the room still felt utterly gloomy — despite the fact that outside, the rest of London was enjoying a bright spring afternoon. No, Naomi was right, she thought as she studied afresh the dreariness of it all. Surely, any man injured in the service of his country deserved better than this? Confined to his narrow little bed by the traction device Ned might be stoic, but that didn't make such conditions acceptable. And, the more she thought about it, the more she could feel her jaw tensing with frustration. There had to be something they could do to make things better for him — but what?

Listening to Naomi relaying to Ned the bones of her conversation with Cousin Elizabeth the previous afternoon, she looked along the short row of beds. The only other patient who was awake was the young man in the bed closest to the door. Aware that Sister had chosen that moment to look across at her, but determining not to lose her nerve, she got up and walked towards him. When he looked up at her, she gestured to the empty chair at his bedside. 'Would it be all right if I sat and talked to you for a moment?'

'Absolutely,' came the reply as the young patient manoeuvred himself more upright against the head of his bed.

Belatedly hoping that she hadn't raised his

hopes in some way, she lowered herself onto the small wooden chair and placed her handbag on her lap.

'We're visiting Lieutenant Russell,' she said, realizing too late how that was glaringly obvious. With a glance to Sister, whose head was now bent back over her work, she tried to smother a laugh. 'What I mean is, he's our brother. I'm Kate and that — ' she went on, turning to gesture back along the room, 'is Naomi.'

'Dickie Jupp,' the young patient replied. 'I didn't have you two down as sisters.'

Feeling her cheeks colouring, she bowed her head. Better to change the subject than become mired in explanations. To that end, she asked, 'Do your family live in town?'

Dickie Jupp shook his head. 'No, worst luck. They're down in Sussex. We keep hoping a bed will become available down there for me — you know, nearer home.'

'Yes, I understand. Ned was in Dover. Having him here is . . . ' She hesitated. She had been going to say *better* but that wasn't strictly true. ' . . . more convenient.'

'I should think so.'

'What happened to you?' she asked. From the little she could see of him, he appeared uninjured. He certainly didn't look old enough to be u pilot. But then he didn't really look old enough to be fighting a war in any shape or form. His messy dark hair and smattering of freckles gave him the look of someone about to leave school.

'I'm — I *was* — Air Mechanic 1st Class, and part of a crew testing newly-delivered aircraft arriving into Farnborough — you know, before they are handed over to go into service. A couple of weeks back, the prop on one of them didn't do quite what I was expecting. Infernal thing caught my sleeve and next thing I know, my hand was gone.' While she was still struggling to comprehend what he had just said, from beneath the bedspread he withdrew his other arm, the sleeve of his striped pyjama jacket cut off above the elbow, the remains of his forearm heavily bandaged. There could be no mistaking that he no longer had a hand at the end of it. Forcing herself not to turn away, she tried to swallow down a gulp for air. 'Fortunately, on that particular day there was a doc on site carrying out medicals, otherwise I wouldn't be here at all — you know, too much blood lost. Instead, here I am, alive to tell the tale, albeit without my right hand. Won't be back on the test crew, that's for sure. Rotten shame, that. I enjoyed it immensely.'

Still reeling with the shock of what had happened to him, and awed by the calm way in which he could speak of it, she felt lost to know how to respond. In coming across and sitting down, she'd been intending merely to draw him into conversation about conditions on the ward. But how could she do that now? What an unimaginable thing to happen to someone so young. Unlike Luke or Ned, he hadn't even been anywhere near the firing line and yet, in that split of a second, his life had been changed for ever.

'Are your family able to visit you?' she asked, hoping that he saw something of them at least.

'They come up on the train once a week.'

She contained a little sigh of relief. 'That's good.'

'They're hoping that in due course, I can get into one of the convalescent homes down on the south coast. Then, once I'm well, we're all hoping I can get into some sort of rehabilitation.'

She glanced across to Sister Morgan at the desk. 'How long have you been in here?' she asked, careful to keep her voice low.

'To be honest,' he said, also making a quick check towards Sister Morgan, 'I've somewhat lost track. Started off in a surgical ward across the street, but they said I couldn't remain there because I was taking up a bed needed for an officer. But about three weeks, I suppose.'

She lowered her voice further. 'And what's it like in here?'

'The truth?'

She nodded. 'Please, do be honest with me. Our brother was supposed to be going in to the RFC on Bryanston Square but it's full up.'

'I suppose it could be worse. It is reasonably peaceful.' With his voice so quiet, she was forced to lean closer. 'Sister Morgan,' he mouthed and nodded towards her, 'is by far the starchiest. None of the other nurses are nearly so sour. Unfortunately, she's the one who always seems to get the daytime shifts.'

Just their luck, she thought. 'Ned said the food isn't very good.'

He shook his head. 'It isn't. By the time it gets all the way up here, it's stone cold. My mother brought me a cake she'd made but, once she'd left, Sister Morgan wouldn't let me have it — took it away. Said it was unhygienic to have

50

food sitting about on the ward.'

She glanced again towards the desk. Unhygienic indeed! The dust on the skirting was far more unhygienic than a few slices of any homemade cake could ever be. What a mean and heartless woman!

'And what about the doctor? What is he like?'

Dickie Jupp shrugged. 'Haven't seen one since they moved me over here.'

'What? Not even once?'

Slowly, he shook his head. 'Sister Morgan said he's an important surgeon needed in theatre to do operations and can't be spared to come up here to see someone who's already been taken care of. She also said that anyway, all they can do for me now is change the dressings and keep a watch for infection.'

And then what, Kate wondered? What if they found an infection? What would they do then — watch some more? She looked along to where Naomi was sitting alongside Ned's bed. Unusually for her, she was slumped rather pathetically, and Ned appeared to be looking beyond her towards the far wall. Neither of them seemed to be speaking.

'Well, thank you for being direct with me,' she said, starting to get to her feet. 'But I had better go and say goodbye to Ned. Our time must almost be up.'

'Nice to talk to you,' the young man replied, sliding lower under the covers.

By way of return, she smiled, arriving back beside Naomi just as Sister Morgan got to her feet.

'Visiting time is over.'

Already getting up, Naomi bent to kiss Ned's cheek. 'I'll be back again tomorrow.'

Looking between them, Ned nodded. 'Thanks, Min. Thanks Kate.'

She smiled back at him. 'Yes, see you tomorrow.'

Nodding to Dickie Jupp on the way past, Kate followed Naomi out onto the landing and reached to close the door behind them.

'I can't bear leaving him there like that,' Naomi whispered, her irritation plain from the lines on her forehead. 'Do you know, he still hasn't seen a doctor. Can you believe that?'

'Neither has the young man I was talking to — and he's been here a couple of weeks.'

Beside her, Naomi stiffened in astonishment. '*A couple of weeks?*'

'Shh!' she cautioned.

'Why is he in here?'

Clutching the handrail, Kate started down the steep staircase. 'He lost a hand while doing something to an aeroplane.'

'He lost a hand and he hasn't seen a doctor for *a couple of weeks?*'

Turning back over her shoulder, she shook her head. 'No.'

'Right, then I'm going to see someone about this. Such conditions are simply not acceptable — not for Ned nor for that other young man.'

Continuing on down the stairs, Kate wondered what Naomi had in mind to do. The last thing they needed was for her to upset someone in authority and make matters worse for Ned. Or for Dickie Jupp and the others.

Waiting until they were out on the street and beyond being heard, she reached for Naomi's arm; she had to prevent her from marching back around the corner and doing something she might come to regret.

'Naomi, please,' she said carefully. 'I beg you, don't go doing anything in haste. Why don't we just stop for a minute and — '

Coming to a halt, Naomi swung back to face her. 'Stop for a minute and what?'

'Stop and think,' she ventured rather more uncertainly. 'Only, going at this like a bull at a gate and demanding things of people in a place like this, well, might it not make matters worse? Matters for Ned, I mean.'

Having been about to respond, Naomi instead pursed her lips. She did at least appear to be considering the point.

'Hm.'

'Might it not be better,' she continued equally carefully, 'to go home for now, work out what it is you're most unhappy about and then . . . oh, I don't know . . . I've not the least idea how these places work, but, maybe, make an appointment to talk to the doctor and . . . and find out what he's minded to do next for Ned.'

'Hm.'

Glancing quickly back to the main street, Kate determined to continue. 'I mean to say, if you could get the hospital to change one thing, what would it be? The ward he's on? The food they serve him? Only I doubt you'll bring about a change to either of those things. Nor to that sister watching over him, either. But there might be something else that — '

'Don't muddy the waters,' Naomi cut in. 'Is that what you're telling me?'

Unsure how that applied to Ned's circumstances, Kate frowned. 'I suppose. I just think it might be better to have the doctors and nurses on our side rather than have them look upon us as trouble. And to pick the thing you think you stand most chance of getting changed.'

Her lips still pursed, Naomi appeared to be considering her suggestion. 'I suppose you're right,' she said, her tone one of resignation. 'Come on, then.' Turning back towards the street. 'Let us go and see if it is possible to make an appointment with the doctor. And then we will go home and work out what, precisely, it is that I want him to do.'

Turning aside, Kate exhaled a long stream of breath: heated confrontation avoided. But oh, so narrowly. 'Yes,' she said, setting off alongside Naomi. 'Let's do that.'

★　★　★

'Kate? Kate! Are you in?'

Down in the kitchen, Kate murmured her disappointment. From the manner in which the front door had just banged against its frame, and the tone Naomi had used to call to her from the hallway, she could only imagine that the appointment with Ned's doctor hadn't gone well. Indeed, when she arrived upstairs, it was to witness Naomi yanking out her hat-pin, tugging

54

off her hat, and plonking it down on the hall table. Feeling something inside of her plummeting, she drew a breath and braced herself. 'Did it not go well?'

'If by 'well', you mean that the doctor was instantly understanding, helpful and reassuring, then no,' Naomi replied stiffly. 'We did not get off to a very good start. If, on the other hand, you mean that eventually, after considerable persistence on my part, we agreed upon a plan for Ned's care going forward, then yes, I suppose it went well. I just wish that dealing with people in authority wasn't always such a struggle — that one didn't have to dig in one's heels, threaten a scene.'

Moving to help Naomi from her coat, Kate frowned. 'No.'

'Anyway, the long and the short of it is that in about two weeks' time, Ned is going to be brought *here* to convalesce.'

Folding Naomi's mackintosh over her arm, Kate stared back at her. '*Here? Here in this very house?*' Surely, she had to have misheard. How could Ned come *here? This* wasn't a hospital. The two of *them* weren't nurses. 'I don't — '

'On my way home, I went to see Papa, my first thought being that Ned should be taken *there*. I mean, as Papa was to point out, Clarence Square would be far more suitable. But then I realized how Mamma would be unable to refrain from interfering and telling everyone what to do, which would hardly be restful for Ned. He would quickly become utterly exasperated. And so should I. But, on the point of abandoning the idea altogether, it occurred to me that we could have him brought here. So — '

Growing steadily more agitated by what seemed to be Naomi's blindness to certain facts, Kate could hold back no longer. 'But Naomi, he needs proper care — '

'He does. Although, as it turns out, not as much as you might think. You see, the doctor told me that one of the reasons he doesn't go to see Ned every day, is because for a good while yet, there is nothing to be done. The bones in his legs must knit back together and heal, which takes time. And, apparently, that contraption he's in, is helping to bring that about.'

'So, he just has to lay there and . . . wait?'

'He does. And once I understood *that*, I thought to myself well, surely, he can lay in traction in a bed anywhere, can't he? So why not bring him here? Don't you see? It's perfect.' For a moment, all Kate could do was stare back at Naomi, imagining her to have taken leave of her senses. 'He can be kept nice and warm — or indeed, cool. He can have decent and nourishing food. But, most of all, he can have company. All of which, taken together, ought surely to help him mend that bit quicker.'

'And the doctor,' she ventured, hoping to piece together exactly what had gone on, 'agreed to this . . . this idea of yours?'

'He did. His only proviso is that we provide proper nursing care.'

'Nursing care? *Us?*'

Finally, Naomi relaxed her expression. 'No, you ninny. Of course not *us*. That would be

56

ridiculous in the extreme. No. Ned shall have a nurse, night and day. I discussed it with Papa and he is quite happy to cover the cost. He told me to do whatever it takes. And so, I shall. Ned shall have the very best care Papa's money can buy.'

Standing in the hallway, Kate tried to blink back her incredulity. Somehow, the idea appeared both perfect and yet, at the same time, utterly mazed — riddled with the sort of pitfalls that were surely beyond them to even imagine until after they had stumbled headlong into them.

Slowly, she shook her head in disbelief. 'I see.'

It was clear, though, that Naomi didn't share her qualms. Turning about and spotting the day's post on the side table, she was already heading into the drawing room, examining the handwriting on one of the envelopes as she did so.

'I don't suppose there's any chance of a cup of coffee?' she called back over her shoulder. 'Although, please, do only bring me one if we still have some of Mamma's decent stuff. If that's all gone, I'll make do with tea.'

Left standing in the hallway, Kate continued to shake her head. Ned was going to be brought here, to Hartland Street. Well, it was certainly one way to remove their concerns about his welfare. But could it be made to work? And how? Where would they even put him? And his nurse? And what about the upheaval of it all — who was going to deal with all of that?

Still reeling, she turned about and began to make her way downstairs. Hang the upheaval! This was Ned they were talking about

— Naomi's twin, and her own half-brother. What better use could there be of Mr Russell's money than to take care of his son? And what better place could there be for Ned but with his family? Yes, the more she thought about it, the more it seemed not only the obvious solution, but also the right one. Somehow, between her and Naomi — and the nurse she would engage — they would find ways to cope. After all, thanks to this wretched war, coping was something at which they had become reassuringly good.

3

Upheaval

'Ta-ta, then, love. See ya tomorrer.'

Stepping out through the door of St. Ursula's, Kate smiled. She never had managed to fathom how Nell always remained so cheerful. Four years of dealing with the hardships and the suffering of a new set of women at their wits' end every day was enough to fill anyone with despair. But, no matter the harrowing tales and the wretchedness of the women and children who turned up to plead for help, Nell went through the day with a smile on her lips. And Kate was grateful that she did because it was Nell's cheeriness that kept her going, too.

'Just so long as the Kaiser don't send no more of his bombs, you will,' she replied now to her friend's observation.

'Yeah, worse when they come at night, ain't it?'

Briefly, she held Nell's look; she wasn't wrong about that. For the last few nights, and after the largest enemy bombing raid so far, Kate had found it hard to fall asleep for fear that a German shell would come hurtling out of the night sky, smash through the roof, and send the house up in flames. According to reports in the *Daily News*, German bombs had killed forty-nine people last week alone. And injured

59

almost two hundred more. She never would forgive them for killing those poor little children in their school over in Poplar, nor for destroying an entire wing of Chelsea Hospital. Nor, for that matter, for what they had done to St. Pancras railway station.

'Much worse,' she belatedly replied to Nell's observation, 'though the government would have us believe we're better protected now than ever — always going on about how we shouldn't be alarmed.'

Standing in the doorway, Nell gave a dismissive shake of her head. 'Spare me! Ever since them new guns of ours started shooting down their Gothas, all the Germans have done is give up coming daytimes to come after dark instead. They might not speak English but that don't make 'em stupid — they know as well as anyone how once it's night-time, we can't see to shoot 'em down.'

Nell was right about that, too. It had to be more than a week now since any bombs had fallen during the hours of daylight. Distractedly, she agreed. 'No.'

'Anyway. Don't let me keep you standin' about here when you ought to be gettin' home to your tea — '

'I did ought to be, yes,' Kate replied, going down the steps to the pavement.

' — and to your Mrs Colborne and her little Esme. Ooh — and your Ned, now, too.'

She let out a sigh. Ned, yes. By now he should have arrived from the hospital. 'Well, sleep tight then,' she said to Nell, looping her handbag over her arm. 'And I'll see you next week.'

Pulling the door closed behind her, Kate set off along Wharf Street. From what she could see between the tops of the buildings it had been a nice afternoon — the perfect blue-sky sort of weather for taking Esme to the park, there being nothing the little girl enjoyed more than toddling about pulling daisies from the grass and feeding the ducks. Sadly, these days, finding the time for outings such as those had become nigh on impossible. It had become hard enough to fit in time for St. Ursula's — what with everything there was to do at home, and with Naomi's shifts driving for St. George's. Only the other day Naomi had remarked how they had become like ships in the night, handing over responsibility for Esme as they passed in the hallway or, on increasingly rare occasions, as they sat down to take luncheon together in the kitchen. And now, with Ned installed, time was bound to become more precious still.

Halting at the kerb while the number thirty-six omnibus lumbered past, and then weaving her way between two horse-drawn delivery vans in order to cross over Edgware Road, she smiled. The first time she'd made this trip on her own, she'd teetered at the kerb, too terrified of the traffic to step off. Three and a half years ago, that must have been. Heavens, how she had changed. How *everything* had changed. If you'd told her back then that this godforsaken war — a business they had all been assured would be over and done with inside three or four months — would still be dragging on now, she wouldn't have thought it possible. Nor would she have believed that having been married to Luke for that same amount of time, she still wouldn't truly think of herself as a wife. After all, how many women, married for so long, would still be childless? Yes, this war certainly had a lot to answer for — including the number of boot soles she had worn through traipsing to and from Wharf Street!

When she'd got up this morning, she'd been in two minds about bothering with St. Ursula's at all today. With everything going on at home, it had seemed beyond her to summon the wherewithal. Indeed, if it hadn't been for Naomi bullying her into it, she would almost certainly have cried off. As it turned out, she had spent a particularly fruitful few hours helping at least a dozen women with their problems. And of that, she felt proud. Now drawing closer to home, though, that sense of achievement was slowly losing out to concerns about what lay ahead for Ned — well, for all of them, really. She was pleased for him, of course she was, but she was also wary of just how much disruption might be about to descend upon them. In particular, she was worried about the effect it would have upon Naomi; already, she had suggested that she was going to cease volunteering for St. George's. Added to that, earlier this week, she had also mentioned something about trying to find a governess for Esme so that — to use her actual words — a couple of mornings a week, she would *have time to breathe*. It had struck Kate as the daft sort of a thing Pamela Russell would say. After all, what on earth did poor little Esme need with a governess?

Thinking about it again now, she shook her head in dismay. Sometimes, Naomi showed all the signs of turning into her mother. And not in a good way, either.

Letting herself in through the front door, she was surprised to find the hallway silent: none of the bustle or hospital paraphernalia she had been expecting, and no Esme bounding up to greet her, either. Wary of what might be happening upstairs, she resisted the urge to call out, instead removing her gloves, unbuttoning and removing her jacket, and then unpinning her hat.

The first person to eventually appear was Naomi. 'Ah, you're home,' she said. 'Did you have a good afternoon?'

'I did,' Kate replied. 'And what about you? Has Ned arrived?'

Continuing towards her, Naomi nodded. 'He has, yes. The upheaval seems to have been rather an ordeal for him, but he's here now.'

'And he's all right?' she asked, thinking Naomi's tone rather flat.

'One can only hope so. His nurse is getting him settled and, as a consequence, has forbidden visitors until tomorrow morning.'

'And Esme?' she asked, craning to look around the doorway into the drawing room and finding it empty.

'Camped out on the landing, hoping she'll be allowed in to see him. She won't be, of course, but she's doing no harm — especially since she is obeying the nurse's instruction to keep absolutely quiet.'

'Makes a change.'

'Quite.'

'And this nurse, how does *she* seem?' Kate asked, bending to unlace her shoes.

'Nurse Hammond? Much like nurses everywhere, I suppose — *nursey*.'

'*Nursey*?'

Glancing towards the stairs, Naomi smothered a laugh. 'You'll see for yourself soon enough.'

'I suppose I will. Any road, I'd best go up and change my skirt and then get on with seeing to supper.'

'Yes. And I ought to check on Esme — just in case.'

In her bedroom moments later, though, the sound of creaking floorboards told Kate that, for some reason, Naomi had followed her on up. Presumably, she had something on her mind. She peered out onto the landing. 'Everything all right?' she asked, seeing Naomi arriving at the top of the stairs.

'Perfectly. Esme is sitting there as good as gold.'

'Well, there's a thing.' Picturing the mountain of chores awaiting her downstairs, she withheld a sigh. Clearly, Naomi hadn't gone to the bother of climbing the stairs just to report that all was well. So, what was on her mind? Reaching to the back of the door for her apron, she tied it about her waist. Whatever the matter, she did wish Naomi would get on with it.

'You know, I do regret that you've had to move back up here to this little room.'

This again? In her frustration, Kate groaned.

She had been perfectly happy to move back up to her old room and wasn't in the least put out. Sometimes, she'd felt like a fraud anyway, all on her own in that big room down on the first floor.

'I've said to you that I don't mind,' she said. 'And truly, I don't.' To support her assertion, she pulled open the door of the tiny wardrobe. 'Look,' she went on, indicating her garments hanging from its short rail, 'my dresses and jackets fit in here just fine.' Closing the door again, she gestured to the adjacent chest of drawers. 'And my under things, and my nightgowns and pinafores, are all in there. Truly, Naomi, since I've no more belongings now than when I slept up here at the beginning, it's no bother whatsoever.'

And anyway, she reflected, there had been no alternative; Ned needed a room large enough to take his hospital-style bedstead, and his nurse needed plenty of space around it to care for him. So, giving up her room had been the only possible answer.

'Well, please know that I regret the inconvenience to you nonetheless,' Naomi replied, moving across to stand on tiptoes and peer out through the dormer window. 'It is so very dark up here. And terribly cramped.'

Unable to help it, Kate sighed. She would say it one final time. 'Naomi, this room was perfectly all right when I first came to live here, and it will be fine again now. It's not as though it will be for ever. Once Ned is no longer in traction, then it will be as you said the other day, he'll be admitted somewhere for reha — , reha — , dear

65

Lord, what the dickens is that word? I never can seem to get my tongue around it.'

'Rehabilitation.'

'Yes. That. And, once that comes about, we can put things back the way they were. You said yourself that bringing Ned here to convalesce was always going to mean upheaval. But me having to sleep back up here is no hardship at all and doesn't alter the fact that bringing Ned here was the right thing to do.'

Turning back from the window, Naomi gave an appreciative smile. 'It *is* the right thing, isn't it?'

Reaching to put her hand upon Naomi's arm, Kate nodded. 'It is. But now, I really must get downstairs and make a start on supper — we don't want this Nurse Hammond thinking we run the sort of household where meals are served when-so-ever we feel like it. Best not give her the idea we're all a-kilter before we even get going!'

No, she reflected, smoothing a hand over the front of her apron and following Naomi out onto the landing, there was no need for anyone else to know that at all!

★   ★   ★

It was going to be all right, Kate decided, allowing herself to relax a little; Nurse Hammond wasn't the stickler she had been fearing. In fact, over supper that first evening, they learned quite a lot that made both her and Naomi warm to the woman. Divulging that she was the youngest of three daughters, her father was a retired doctor, and that, originally, she came from a small village in Hampshire; Nurse Hammond turned out to be as mild-mannered as her rounded face suggested. Neither short nor tall, slim nor fat, there was something about her homeliness that put Kate in mind of her own grandmother, Mabel — albeit Mabel was at least twenty years older.

'I've cared for the sick all my life,' Nurse Hammond replied to an observation from Naomi. 'It's all I know how to do. When it comes to cleanliness and following doctor's orders, you won't find fault. But it is also my belief that where a patient's recovery is concerned, it's good to show them some warmth, too. Their wounds might need nursing care but, as often as not, their hearts and minds need tending, too.'

'I can see her and Ned getting along perfectly well,' Naomi whispered later, when they were clearing away the supper things.

And Kate agreed. In fact, the moment Nurse Hammond had hinted at a fondness for the occasional glass of Mackeson Milk Stout — purely for its nutritional value, she had added with a wink — she had warmed to her. Having someone stiff and starchy in their midst would have forced them onto a constant state of alert and would have required them to mind their ways but, with this Nurse Hammond, it seemed as though they would be able to carry on almost as they did on any other day.

'Yes,' she agreed with Naomi's assessment. 'I think we'll all get along just fine.'

And, in which case, Naomi's crazed idea to

bring Ned home to Hartland Street *might* just turn out all right after all.

★ ★ ★

'Please, Min. I wouldn't have let you bring me here had I thought that's what you were going to do. You assured me I wouldn't be disrupting anything.'

Standing beside her brother's bed, Naomi signalled her disagreement with a shake of her head. 'You're not. I've already told the organizer at the VAD, and she quite understands that all the while you are here, I shall not be volunteering for any further shifts. For the foreseeable future, your well-being and recovery come first.'

It was after breakfast the following morning and, having been permitted to do so by Nurse Hammond, Kate and Naomi had gone in to see Ned. And now, while Naomi disagreed with her brother over her decision to cease volunteering as an ambulance driver, Kate took the chance to study the many changes to her former room. For a start, every piece of bedroom furniture now stood in a corner, covered with dustsheets. In its place had appeared a pair of simple metal trestles, one stacked with towels, bedsheets and linens, the other laid out with items of a more medical or surgical nature. Gone from the centre of the floor was the rug, which, according to Naomi, had immediately been decreed a hazard to health for both its propensity to harbour dust and for the likelihood that someone would trip over it. From the ceiling had disappeared the

68

light fitting — in its place an overly large electric light bulb — while on a metal stand to one side of Ned's bedstead was a reading lamp. This morning, with the curtains fastened completely clear of the window, there was no need for either, the natural light of the day sufficiently bright.

For his part, Ned looked little different from when they had last seen him in Manston Street. The lower half of his body was still in traction, his feet, in thick grey woollen socks, fastened to the rail at the bottom, the metal rods holding his legs in place disappearing under the grey blanket. Seeing him confined to such a position raised so many questions. Wasn't he uncomfortable? Didn't he long to move — or at least wriggle about from time to time? What happened if he got an itch? And how did he . . . well, no, she wouldn't even contemplate such things; concerns of that nature the business of Ned and Nurse Hammond alone.

'Min, please stop being so stubborn,' Ned urged Naomi. 'Ambulance drivers are few and far between — St. George's needs you.'

Kate agreed. Now it was clear that Nurse Hammond was competent — and that Ned was in safe hands — there was no need for Naomi to even be within earshot of her brother, let alone keeping vigil at his bedside.

She glanced to what she could see of Naomi's face. 'It's true,' she piped up, bringing both of them to look in her direction. 'You're of more value there than here.'

Turning away, Naomi gave a thoughtful sigh.

69

'Let me think about it, both of you. Let us see how we manage over these next few days.'

'Thank heavens,' Ned said, sending Kate a look of gratitude. 'Now, please, Min, do go and get on with something. I'm more than used to being left alone. Besides, today I have the luxury of a different ceiling to stare at.' With a shake of her head, seemingly in despair, Naomi did as her brother instructed and turned to leave the room. But when, smiling at his humour, Kate went to follow her out, he called her back.

Surprised, she turned to regard him. 'Yes?'

'Do you think you might have a go at persuading her to see sense?' he whispered. 'There's a greater chance she'll listen to you than to me.'

Unable to help it, Kate scoffed. 'Huh. I don't know about *that*.'

'Look, Kate, before I agreed to come here, I made it plain that I didn't want to cause a fuss. Please don't get me wrong, I'm grateful for the comforts that being here will bring . . . and for the company it will provide . . . but I don't need either of you to change your habits or, worse still, feel the need to keep up a constant presence at my bedside. I've come to accept that to get better, and to one day be up and about again, I have no choice but to lie here and let nature take its course. That's my lot and I'm reconciled to it, but there's no need for it to be anyone else's lot as well.'

She smiled down at him. 'I'll *try* to get her to reconsider. But you will have to let me go about it in my own way.'

'Well, I'm sure you know best how to — '

'Unker Ned! Unker Ned!'

Turning in the direction of the little voice, Kate saw Esme hopping about in the doorway, from one hand trailing her ragdoll, from the other, a book, its pages splayed open. 'Story, pease?' she asked, peering towards the bed.

With a smile, Kate went towards her. 'Well, lovey,' she said, bending to the little girl's height, 'Uncle Ned has to stay in bed and rest. So, how about you ask your mamma for a story?'

'"Not now, Esme",' the child mimicked her mother. 'Mamma too busy.'

Holding back laughter, Kate shook her head. 'Your mamma said she's busy?'

'Busy, busy, busy.'

Turning back to Ned, Kate grinned. 'Would you mind?'

'Read my favourite niece a story? Of course I wouldn't mind,' he said, rubbing his hands together.

'Shall I sit you up on this big seat then, lovey?' Kate asked the little girl, gesturing to the chair alongside the bed.

Venturing further into the room, the little girl nodded. 'Ess pease.'

'Can you *hold* a book comfortable enough to read?' she thought to ask Ned as she settled Esme onto the chair.

'It's actually one of the few things I *can* do,' he assured her. 'Which story is it anyway? What am I letting myself in for?'

Prying the book from between Esme's fingers, she closed the cover. 'It's her compendium of fairy tales,' she said, handing it to him. '*The*

71

Ugly Duckling always goes down well. She never seems to tire of that one. All the while you can bear to keep reading, she'll sit nice an' quiet.'

'Excellent. Then *The Ugly Duckling* it is.'

Hoping that Esme would behave, Kate started towards the door. Then, turning back, she said, 'Esme, you're to do as Uncle Ned tells you or else Nurse Hammond won't let you back in to see him again. Do you understand me?'

Her expression solemn, Esme nodded.

Once out on the landing, Kate paused to listen. Ned had begun reading: 'It was so beautiful out in the country, it was summer — the wheat fields were golden, the oats were green, and down among the meadows the hay was stacked.'

With a smile, she started down the stairs. Within a couple of days, it would probably seem as though Ned had always been there. And, hopefully, before too long, he would be free from that ghastly traction device and back on his feet. And yes, she would admit that to begin with she had been wary of Naomi's idea to remove him from the hospital. But she could see now that it was going to be all right. One way or another, they would find ways to cope with the upheaval; indeed, she would do everything she could to make sure of it.

★ ★ ★

'Ah, there you are, dear.'

Arriving in the kitchen a while later, Kate was greeted by Nurse Hammond coming through from the scullery. 'Nurse Hammond, did you need something?' she asked.

'In a way, dear, yes. I need a moment or two of your time to go over a few arrangements.'

Remembering her vow to make things work, Kate smiled. 'Arrangements. Yes, of course. How may I help you?'

'Well, firstly, there's the matter of the patient's meals. Ordinarily, I would discuss these with the family's cook. But, in this household, I imagine I should go through them with you. Would that be correct?'

Family cook? If only! 'Yes, that's right.'

'Good. Now, this won't take more than a minute or two, but shall we sit down?' Doing as Nurse Hammond suggested, Kate pulled a chair from under the table. She did hope Nurse was right about it not taking long — she had so much to get on with. 'Now, tell me, dear, when do you place your orders for meat and fish? Only, from the point of view of the patient, freshness is key.'

'Um . . . ' Suddenly, her practice of placing an order just twice a week seemed inadequate — remiss, even.

'I'll tell you what,' Nurse Hammond swept on, 'why don't I run through the whole thing with you and then, when you are next planning the patient's menus, you will be able to bear in mind what is required.'

For a moment, Kate simply sat staring ahead. Menus? Would Ned not eat the same things as they did, then? Last night, he'd had a few mouthfuls of the potato and leek soup without any bother. And this morning he'd eaten some toast.

Beside her, Nurse Hammond was turning the pages of a notebook.

'For your ease,' she said, 'I have noted everything down and organized it according to the various meals, starting with breakfast.'

Well, that didn't seem unreasonable. 'Breakfast,' she said. 'Yes.'

'Now, the patient will alternate between a porridge made from oatmeal and milk one morning, and a lightly boiled egg and toast the next. Needless to say, the milk should be from that day's delivery — the egg, the freshest available and boiled for no more than three minutes. The white should be only *just* set — not firm — and the accompanying toast should be of brown bread with the crusts *left on*. It should *not* be allowed to burn. In the event that it does, please do not attempt to scrape off the blackened areas and think it will suffice. It will not.'

Staring down at the handwritten instructions entitled *To Make Toast*, Kate frowned. Clearly, her usual habit of letting the bread catch and then scraping at it with a knife wouldn't measure up! 'No burnt bits, no,' she repeated, stilling an urge to laugh.

'Now, Lieutenant Russell tells me that he is fond of coffee — '

She looked back up. 'Yes.'

' — and I have no objection to him partaking of a single cup each day.'

'All right.'

'*But only if* the coffee can be made from beans

74

that are freshly ground and brewed in accordance with this recipe.'

Freshly ground beans every morning? Even the stuff Naomi brought from Clarence Square wouldn't fit that bill. 'And if it is not freshly ground . . . ?' she ventured, almost afraid of how Nurse Hammond would reply.

'Then the patient will have to go without, I'm afraid. All other forms of coffee, especially in these days of shortages and rationing, are, to a greater or lesser extent, little more than chicory, roasted until dark and then ground — the result of which not only lacks any nutritional value but has a taste bitter enough to taint the poor man's palate for all other foods.' As quietly as she could, Kate swallowed. 'If it is unavailable, then I suggest substituting beef tea.' When Nurse Hammond then flicked ahead through the pages of her notebook, Kate grimaced; by the look of it, there had to be three dozen recipes in there — maybe more. Surely, she couldn't be expected to tackle them all. When it came to preparing a straightforward meal she was reasonably sure of her abilities. Certainly, she had very few disasters. But if these were the expectations of her, then *panicked* didn't even begin to describe how she suddenly felt. 'As you will see,' Nurse Hammond went on, pointing to the appropriate page, 'at the back I have included recipes for puddings and drinks.'

'Yes.'

'So, here we are, beef tea. Now, from one pound of lean gravy-beef, a quart of water, and a salt spoon of salt, you will end up with a pint of

75

tea. If Lieutenant Russell's appetite is generally good, you might only need to make this up four times a week. But, if he is off his food for any reason, then he will need to take this tea three or four times a day, requiring a new batch to be made each morning.'

Clasping her hands in her lap, Kate noticed how clammy her palms felt. 'Each morning. I see.' Inadvertently meeting the nurse's look, she did her best to raise a smile.

'Don't worry, dear, once you become familiar with it, the whole recipe will take you less than an hour — possibly, with the right cut of the meat, even less than that.'

Feeling unexpectedly hot, Kate reached for the edge of the table. An hour. Every morning. And that was without the actual effort involved in procuring a supply of fresh beef each day.

To her despair, though, Nurse Hammond's requirements didn't end there. Flicking through the notebook, she came to a halt at a page headed *Rice-Milk Pudding*. 'Rice,' she said, 'boiled with a little finely-minced suet — and with a strip of lemon peel added to enhance the flavour — produces a most nourishing dish. Now, the instructions I've given here suggest boiling it in a saucepan but, in one house where I was employed for several months, the cook used to put it in the bottom of the oven while her other dishes were cooking. The result was more than acceptable.'

And on and on Nurse Hammond went: rabbit — preferably a very young one — stewed in milk; mutton chop, trimmed and boiled to a turn; calf's-foot broth, the main ingredient being *so fortuitously* now in season.

Eventually, her instructions seemingly exhausted, Nurse Hammond closed the notebook and offered it in her direction.

'Thank you,' Kate said, seeing no option but to accept it from her. 'I shall refer to it often and abide by it closely.'

'Of course you will, dear. Now, it just remains for me to ask you whether, once you have drawn up your first week's menus for Lieutenant Russell, I might take a little glance over them — just to satisfy myself as to the variety of dishes. Oh, which reminds me. We haven't discussed vegetable accompaniments. Not to worry — you will find guidance as to their preparation and cooking within.'

Of course I will, Kate thought.

'So, all it remains for me to mention for now, is presentation.'

Staring down at the cover of the notebook, her eyes wandering abstractedly along its title — *Guidance as to the Preparation and Cooking of Meals for Invalids* — she bit her bottom lip. Presentation? Presentation of what?

'Please, do advise me,' she said, trying not to sigh but nevertheless resigning herself to yet another lengthy set of instructions.

'Needless to say, cleanliness is key.'

'Of course.'

'Now . . . '

Separate set of utensils . . . hottest water available. Scour thoroughly . . . Good grief, Kate found herself thinking as she sat listening. Anyone overhearing this lecture could be

77

forgiven for assuming that she was a new girl, about to embark upon her first day in service.

Realizing then that she had allowed her thoughts to drift, she straightened her posture. 'Yes, of course,' she murmured when Nurse Hammond looked at her for confirmation of some or other point.

'And at no stage allow any food to slop over the side of the bowl or down the side of the cup or glass. Food dripping onto bedclothes or nightclothes necessitates that they be changed straight away, producing more work all round. A doily upon a charger beneath the plate, and another in the saucer of the cup, along with a napkin on the tray, all go a long way to avoiding such distress.'

Distress. The word rang in Kate's ears. *Doilies? Calves' feet?* How on earth was she going to manage all of this extra work when already, she struggled to keep on top of everything? Having a nurse to care for Ned's medical needs was one thing — but, by the seem of all this, it wasn't going to be nearly enough. Not *nearly* enough.

When Nurse Hammond got up from the table and left the kitchen, Kate didn't move. The notebook seemed almost to be defying her to ignore it. And how dearly she would love to. But where was the point in courting disaster? In any event, its purpose was to help poor Ned get better. And so, one way or another, she would ignore the colossal amount of extra work it was going to add to her days and make a friend of it

— do everything she could to ensure that, in no time at all, Ned would be up and about again, back on his feet and making a full recovery.

4

The Accident

Kate heaved a sigh of relief. At least Pamela Russell hadn't come alone; at least now, there was less likely to be *words*.

It was now more than a week since Ned had arrived from Manston Street and, just yesterday, Naomi had decided that extending an invitation to her mother could be put off no longer. Ned would have to grin and bear it, she had decreed; they all would. And so, to find that Mrs Russell had arrived in the company of Aunt Diana — the only person on earth ever able to reason with her — felt like a reprieve for all of them.

Having ventured less than two paces inside the front door, Pamela Russell was now teasing off her gloves and looking about the hallway as though distinctly uncomfortable at once again finding herself in such a small home. The uneasy set of her mouth made Kate want to giggle.

'Mamma,' Naomi greeted her mother.

'Naomi.'

Kate lowered her eyes; to witness such iciness made her bristle.

'If you don't mind, I should like to go straight up to your brother,' Pamela Russell announced, releasing her daughter from their frosty embrace. 'I have to be at the Ritz at twelve-thirty for

80

luncheon with Lady Ashwin, and so I am rather pressed for time.'

When Naomi affixed a smile, Kate thought it a very thin one. Hardly surprising: her mother showed not a glimmer of warmth whatsoever.

'As you wish. Kate, would you show Mamma up to Ned's room?'

But, as Kate made to step forward, Pamela Russell waved her away. 'No need to stir yourself on my account. There is precious little danger that I shall become lost.'

Affronted on Naomi's behalf, Kate stepped back again. The woman's manner was enough to make her pity Mr Russell for marrying her — and that was saying something.

Once Pamela Russell had started up the stairs, Kate saw Aunt Diana catch hold of her niece's arm and steer her into the drawing room. Since this usually signalled that the two of them were about to discuss something interesting, she decided to follow them in.

'I hope you don't mind my coming, dear,' Aunt Diana said. 'But, since the frostiness between you and your mother shows no signs of thawing, I thought it for the best.'

Watching the women take a couple of steps into the drawing room, Kate took up a position just inside the doorway.

'Frostiness. That's certainly apt.'

'Where your mother is concerned, you need to understand, darling,' Aunt Diana went on, her voice lowered. 'Having Ned brought *here*, instead of Clarence Square, was something of a blow for her.'

'Don't tell me she *still* feels slighted?'

'I'm rather afraid that she does.'

'Well, I can't help that,' Naomi replied. 'The only person of any consequence in all of this is Ned. And without a doubt, he is better off beyond her grasp.'

'And I don't dispute that. But perhaps, when you speak to her, try to show *some* consideration for her feelings — it might make for fewer upsets all round. Now, I suppose I really should go on up. Can't have her wearying the poor boy unnecessarily. But tell me, truthfully, dear, how is he?'

Listening to Naomi explaining the rather open-ended nature of Ned's continuing treatment, and the generally fair prognosis for his recovery, Kate stiffened: the rice-milk pudding! Christ almighty, she'd put one to simmer and forgotten all about it! Dear God, it would be ruined.

Mumbling an excuse, she bolted from the room and, praying that she hadn't left it too late, tore down the stairs. Half way down, though, the smell rising up to greet her was unmistakeably that of milk catching on the bottom of a saucepan. Damnation!

Hurtling across the kitchen, she grabbed a dry-ing cloth. Then, racing to the range, she pulled the saucepan off the heat and onto a trivet. Crossing to the sink, she leant towards the window and pushed it wide open. Curse it! Rice-milk pudding had been the only recipe in Nurse Hammond's notebook for which she'd been able to gather together all of the ingredients. But now, not only had she wasted the whole lot — a considerable quantity of valuable sugar included — she had probably ruined the saucepan as well. Damnation thrice over.

Tossing the cloth onto the table, she groaned in frustration. That she wasn't used to having something cooking away on the range so early in the morning was no excuse; she should never have allowed herself to become distracted. The only saving grace was that she hadn't told Nurse Hammond that she was trying out one of her recipes; talk about making herself look useless.

Staring down at the charred mess, she sighed heavily. All she could do now was clear away the evidence. And so, carrying the saucepan and the trivet through to the scullery, she set them down by the sink. There, she turned on the tap and reached to the shelf for the box of soda crystals. She would scrape out the contents and put the thing to soak. And, once Aunt Diana and Mrs Russell had left, she would do as Nurse Hammond had asked her to do in the first place and write out proper menus for the entire week. And *then* she would make a list of the groceries she would need. That way, she would always have the requisite ingredients to hand and wouldn't be tempted to do things willy-nilly. Yes, if she could find her way to becoming better organized, then she might avoid similar disasters in the future. In the meantime, she would see to it that this particular failure served as a lesson: slipshod and lackadaisical just wouldn't cut it any more. And yes, it might mean that she had to give up volunteering at St. Ursula's for a while.

But, well, so be it. In some ways, it would be a relief: one less direction for her to be pulled in. In any event, as Naomi was for ever saying, family came first. And rightly so, too.

★ ★ ★

'Heavens, Kate — that smells vile.'

It was one morning later that same week and, glancing across to where Naomi had arrived to stand in the doorway, Kate merely raised her eyebrows. With the greater part of her attention directed to the stock-pot, the contents of which had been bubbling away on the range for some time now, she couldn't afford to stop and chat. Instead, fanning with her hand at the steam billowing up from it, she withdrew a ladleful of the liquid, peered at its colour and, with a shrug of her shoulders, emptied it back into the pot. It was a *reasonably* close match to the description in Nurse Hammond's instructions.

Heaving the chicken carcass from the pan and lowering it onto a large plate, she stared down at it. 'Vile or not, I can do nothing about it,' she replied to Naomi's observation. 'I'm making clear chicken soup. And Nurse Hammond's recipe requires that the stock be prepared to a very particular method. And anyway, if *your* bones had been simmering for five hours, you'd probably smell vile, too. You can always push the window wider if you don't like it.' *Or go back upstairs and leave me to it*, being the reply she would have preferred to have given. Instead, she concentrated on fishing about for the little muslin bag that today, contained not only the requisite herbs — as was her usual custom — but also, in accordance with Nurse Hammond's detailed notes, four ounces of mild onions, previously softened in a little lard. They went into the bag, rather than into the pan with everything else; the recipe decreed, in order that they *not unduly colour the finished result.*

'Now it's done boiling,' she said, fully aware that she sounded tetchy, 'I've got to sieve all six quarts of the stuff. Not just the once, mind, as would suffice for us ordinary mortals, but three of four times 'until the stock is crystal-clear and of a pale amber colour'. Saints alive,' she muttered, standing back and mopping her forehead with a corner of her apron. 'It's only stock, for heaven's sake.'

'Careful,' Naomi quipped. 'Don't let Nurse Hammond hear you disparaging her culinary bible.'

When, from the corner of her eye, Kate spotted that Naomi was grinning, she let out a despairing sigh. 'Did you come down for anything in particular?' she called as Naomi made to head away.

'I *did*,' came the reply. 'But, since you're busy, it can wait for now.'

For now? Reaching for the tamis sieve, Kate rested it across the top of her largest bowl and shook her head in dismay. Did Naomi know something she didn't: was she, by some stroke of good fortune, destined to be less busy later on? Was there to be some respite from chasing her own tail? Only, it seemed highly unlikely, because, as soon as she had finished straining this stock and seen to all of the clearing up, she had that pile of smalls to get hung out on the washing line, and then the laundered towels to put through the mangle and put out before it was too late in the day for them to dry. And *then* she had all of the vegetables to prepare for luncheon.

Wearily, she sighed. In the two weeks since Ned had arrived at Hartland Street, Kate felt as though her work-load had trebled. If she wasn't boiling some or other part of an animal to produce a nourishing meal for him, then she was baking a cake for his visitors or clearing up after they'd been. And if it wasn't the preparation of food keeping her occupied, then she was taking the smoothing iron to a larger than usual pile of laundry. Or mopping the floors again. Or cleaning the bathroom and the lavatory — something she now felt duty-bound to do each and every day, not only on account of Nurse Hammond having a sixth sense for dirt, but also because of the continual trail of visitors, who called — often with little or no warning — to see Ned.

Last week, at Naomi's insistence, she had also somehow fitted in two afternoons at St. Ursula's but, for the first time ever, she'd had to force herself to go there. Indeed, on the second afternoon, the prospect of returning home to prepare three different dishes for supper — there being no way on earth to persuade Esme to eat liver and onions — had made her irritable and snappy, and seemingly unable to fill in one single form of application without making a mess of it.

Her distractedness hadn't escaped Marjorie Randolph's notice either, since, after a while, she had suggested — in her perfectly polite and serene way — that she put away her things and go home. 'I fear, my dear, that today your mind is elsewhere.' Had been her actual observation.

As if the sheer volume of work itself wasn't bad enough, this morning, she was also repeatedly beset by interruptions.

'There's Dundee cake left in the tin, they'll have to make do with that,' she said when Naomi returned later to remind her that at three o'clock, two officers from the RFC were coming to see Ned and check on his recovery. 'On the shelf above the sink in the scullery,' she answered Nurse Hammond when she arrived to request some blueing powder not ten minutes later. And, 'No, lovey, sorry,' she said, when, barely five minutes after *that*, Esme appeared, clutching two of her dolls. 'I can't make new capes for them at the moment. Why not go and ask your mamma to help you?'

Such was her morning that, when Naomi returned at ten o'clock to sit at the table and drink her mid-morning coffee, it was as much as Kate could do not to snap at her.

'Is everything all right?' Naomi enquired, fastening the lid back on the biscuit barrel. 'Only, forgive me for saying this but you don't seem terribly happy this morning.'

On the point of opening her mouth, Kate paused, careful not to look up and meet Naomi's enquiring look. 'I'm fine,' she lied.

'Are you certain?'

Gritting her teeth, she again waited a moment before answering. 'Certain. Though I do have a lot to be getting on with.'

'I know how you feel,' Naomi answered, moving to rinse her coffee cup and saucer under the tap before setting them down in the sink. 'There doesn't seem to be a minute to spare just lately, does there?'

Clearly, the woman had missed the irony of her own observation. A *minute* to spare? A minute would be a luxury; *she* didn't have a *second*. 'Not a single minute, no.'

'Oh, and on that note, would you be able to keep an eye on Esme for a moment? Garrett's have sent a card to say that my pearls are ready for collection — you remember, I took them there when the clasp broke. They've very kindly re-strung them as well, and I should like to go and get them back. I do hate being without them. They're by far my favourite string.'

In despair, Kate pressed her fingertips into her temples and moved them around in circles. 'Why not,' she said. 'Bring her down with a jigsaw or summat and she can sit at the table. It's not like I won't be here anyway.'

'Excellent. Then I'll go up and get ready. They're only in Burlington Arcade, so I shouldn't be gone long.'

Unsurprisingly, once Naomi had departed for the jeweller's, Esme quickly tired of sitting at the table.

'Why don't you finish your jigsaw, lovey?' Kate tried reasoning with her when she climbed down from her chair and started trailing about the kitchen.

'Finish.'

She glanced to the dozen pieces spread about the table. 'I don't think you have.'

'Want to help.'

Mindful of all that she still had to do, Kate gave a weary shake of her head. 'Well, it's real kind of you to offer, lovey, but you're not big enough yet.' Hoping that would be an end to it, she went through to the far end of the scullery and wheeled out the mangle. Positioning a bowl on the floor underneath it to catch the water, she turned the screw to close the rollers. At least today, her load shouldn't take too long — assuming she ever managed to make a start. 'No, leave it there,' she warned, spotting that Esme was reaching towards the bowl.

'Want to help.'

'I'm sure you do,' she said, picking out the top-most item from the pail of towels and feeding the end of it through the rollers. Lowering her voice, she muttered, 'Unlike your mother.'

When she then started to turn the handle, from beneath the mangle came the sound of giggling. 'Wet!'

Retrieving the squeezed towel, she folded it loosely and dropped it into the basket on the bench behind her. 'Please don't get in the water, lovey.'

Trundling a second towel through the rollers, she once again heard laughter.

'Wet!'

Sighing heavily, she stopped winding, went around to the other side of the mangle, and lifted Esme from the floor. Setting her back down a few feet away, she stared down at the front of the child's dress; unmissable on the front was damp patch the size of a dinner plate.

'Esme,' she scolded. The child stared up at her. 'I told you not to get in the water. Now look what you've done. Your mamma won't be happy.'

In truth, she didn't particularly care whether Naomi was happy or not — it was only a wet dress and would dry soon enough — it was more that Esme had disobeyed her. Naomi indulged the child, that was the problem; half the time, when Esme did something mischievous, Naomi merely laughed. All of which made her, Kate, seem like an ogre for raising her voice when the child did something wrong.

'Wet,' Esme said again, pressing her hand on the damp patch.

'Yes. And that's because you disobeyed me. So, wet you'll have to stay.'

'Want to help,' Esme started up again the moment Kate leant across for the next towel.

Reaching for the handle, Kate dropped her arm back to her side. At this rate, she was never going to get the job done. And it was no good taking Esme up to Ned and asking him to read her a story, because she'd have to keep going back up to check that she was behaving. Why Naomi had felt it necessary to go and collect her pearls this morning, she couldn't fathom. It wasn't as though she needed that particular string — not when she had so many others.

'Come on then,' she said, seeing little option but to relent. 'I'll fetch a stool and you can wind the handle.' After all, she thought, returning with the low step she used to reach things from the top shelves, at an age not much older than Esme was now, she herself had begun helping in the scullery at Woodicombe. And it hadn't done *her* any harm.

'Help.'

'Yes, that's right, lovey, you're going to help me with the mangling.'

With Esme now standing on the step, Kate fed the edge of a tea cloth between the rollers. Then, reaching for Esme's hand, she placed it on the wheel and, with her own over the top of it, turned the handle. Seeing the expression on the little girl's face, she allowed herself a smile. To be fair, the child was never properly naughty; like most children of her age she was just prone to fits of wilfulness. She was also naturally curious, a quality that struck her as worthy of being encouraged rather than crushed.

From the little step, Esme craned to look under the mangle. 'Water!' she exclaimed, pointing with her free hand.

Selecting another towel, Kate fed it through the rollers and listened to Esme giggling; only a child could find something amusing in mangling clothes.

'Mrs Channer? May I bother you for a moment?'

Hearing Nurse Hammond calling to her from the kitchen, she let go of Esme's hand. 'Stay there,' she said. 'I'll be back dreckly.'

'Sorry, dear,' Nurse Hammond said when she went through to see her, 'but is there a reliable chemist nearby? Only, I need some more — '

The scream that rang out from the scullery stopped Nurse Hammond mid-sentence and sent Kate lurching back across the room. What the devil . . . ? It was Nurse Hammond who spotted that Esme's fingers had become trapped in the mangle.

Darting across to support the little girl's arm, the nurse shouted instructions. 'Release the rollers. Quickly!'

Frantically, Kate opened the screw and then watched as Nurse Hammond eased Esme's fingers away from the mangle, laid them flat upon the palm of her own hand, and peered down at them.

'Are they . . . ?' In her state of panic, Kate couldn't bring herself to finish her question.

'Do you have any ice?'

She spun about, her first thought being *probably not*. But then, remembering the meat box, she lunged towards it, threw open the lid and hunted about inside. Just as she had expected, there was scarcely any there. Scooping up what there was, she carried it back to the scullery. 'This is all we have.'

'That will suffice. Pack it in a clean cloth, quick as you can.'

When she returned with the ice, wrapped as directed, Nurse Hammond gently pressed the fingers of Esme's hand onto the parcel and, seemingly from the shock of it, Esme broke off from sobbing to let out an ear-piercing howl.

Unable to stop shaking, Kate stared down at the little fingers. Just a few moments ago they had been plump and pink and perfect, but now they were purple and red and badly swollen. 'Are they b-broken?' she forced herself to ask.

'I won't be able to tell for a moment,' Nurse Hammond replied, folding the end of the cold cloth over the top of Esme's fingers. 'Right now, it would be unwise to distress the child further by trying to examine them. Of greatest importance is to get the swelling under control, which we do by keeping them on the ice. In a while, we'll move her upstairs to a sofa where she can be made comfortable. Then, once she's calmer, I'll try to determine whether any damage has been done.' Feeling sick, and with her heart beating fit to burst from her chest, Kate nodded. 'And then we will need a proper cold compress that can remain in place for an hour or so. After that, if one or more of her fingers is broken, I will apply splints and bandage them together to prevent her trying to use them.'

If one or more of her fingers is broken? Oh, dear Lord, what had she allowed to happen? Broken fingers? Naomi would be furious. No, she would be beyond furious — far beyond it.

'But . . . they'll be all right . . . eventually?' She sought to reassure herself, the mention of splints bringing to her mind a picture of Ned. He had splints — *and* traction — and yet despite all of that, the doctors still couldn't say whether he would ever walk unaided again. What if Esme grew up without the proper use of her fingers? Feeling suddenly faint, she doubled over and stared down at the tiled floor. What had she allowed to happen?

Nurse Hammond, though, sounded calm. 'She's young. Her bones are still forming. There's really no reason to think that, even should they prove to be fractured, they won't heal just fine. If I believe the situation warrants it, we'll take her to a hospital and get them set properly by a doctor so as to reduce the chance of them ending up crooked.'

'*Crooked?*' Flushing even hotter, she reached to the draining board. Naomi wouldn't just be cross, she would never forgive her. Feeling completely helpless, she turned back. 'What can I do? Should I go and hail a cab? Should we go to the hospital anyway? St. Mary's is close by . . . '

Although Esme was still howling, Nurse Hammond shook her head. 'No, not yet. There might be no need — '

But then, without warning, Esme fell silent, her head flopping backwards and her arms falling limply by her sides.

'Wh — What's happened?' Kate stammered, staring down at the little girl's lifeless form. 'She . . . she . . . she looks like she's . . . '

'It's all right,' Nurse Hammond reassured her, moving to support Esme's neck. 'She's simply cried herself into a faint. It happens more often than you might think, such prolonged sobbing more than capable of interrupting the breathing of a small child. Prolonged temper tantrums can give rise to the same thing.'

With that, Esme opened her eyes and, unblinking, stared ahead. Then she started to whimper, seemingly unaware that anything had happened.

'Oh, thank God!'

'She'll be all right now,' Nurse Hammond said, moving to lift Esme from the floor. 'Making this a good time for us to get her up to the drawing room. Once there, I'll give her something to make her sleep — something very mild. Then, as soon as she comes over drowsy, I shall examine her fingers and decide what needs to be done.'

'Can you manage her on your own?' Kate asked as Nurse Hammond started to carry Esme through the kitchen and towards the stairs.

'Just fine, dear. After Lieutenant Russell, she's as light as a feather.'

'Praise be to God you were here,' Kate mumbled, feeling light-headed from the surging of relief. 'Lord only knows how I should have managed had I been on my own.'

And heaven only knew what Naomi was going to say when she got home, either. But, for the moment, she wouldn't think about that. For now, she would only consider Esme — and how best to help Nurse Hammond ensure that she was all right.

★　★　★

'You let her do *what*?'

When Naomi returned from her trip to the jeweller's — her parcel wrapped and tied with satin ribbon — Esme was asleep on the sofa, the fingers of her left hand bound together, her eyelids swollen, her pale face blotched with pink.

Despite the myriad possible explanations that

95

had been running through her head for the last couple of hours, Kate knew that she had to be honest.

'I was letting her help me with the laundry.'

'You let her *play with the mangle?*'

'No, of course I didn't!' she hissed angrily, her voice lowered so as not to disturb the sleeping child. When she reached to take Naomi's arm, though, intending that they continue their conversation out in the hallway, Naomi shrank away from her.

'Then what, pray tell me, *were* you letting her do?'

'I . . . ' Oh, dear Lord, this was even worse than she had feared. 'I was holding her hand on the winder and we were turning it round. She was watching the water coming out and laughing at it. Then Nurse Hammond called to me about something. Next thing I know, Esme was screaming. Somehow, she'd got her fingers trapped between the rollers. I think she must have — '

'You *think?* You're telling me that you couldn't even *see* her — that you hadn't even kept your eye on her? For heaven's sake, Kate, she's a child. What did you think was going to happen — that she would just stand there like a statue and not move?'

'I didn't — '

'You didn't think! No, that much is plain. And now she's hurt. Scarred, possibly for the rest of her life.'

This time it was Kate's turn to shrink back. Scarred for the rest of her life? What on earth had put that idea into Naomi's head? 'Nurse

Hammond said it's likely just bruising — '

'But it might *not* be. The bones in her fingers might be *broken* — her tiny little bones! And that's before contemplating the agony . . . the pain . . . the distress she must have felt. Good God, Kate, what were you thinking? It was utterly irresponsible of you — not only to leave her alone with a mangle — but to allow her into the scullery in the first place!'

'*Allow her in?*' Despite having resolved to be open with Naomi and shoulder the blame she was due, Kate could hold back no longer. '*You* were the one who went out and left me to look after her — knowing full well I was already up to my eyes with everything else.' Freed now from having to anticipate how Naomi would respond, it felt to Kate as though something inside of her shot open, allowing all manner of pent up feelings to come rushing out. 'Which one of us already has a day that's full to bursting? I do. Which one of us takes care of all of the extra cooking needed for Ned's meals? I do. Which one of us does all the extra cleaning up afterwards — and behind all of his visitors — without so much as a word of complaint? I do — '

'For heaven's sake, don't try and change the subject,' Naomi snapped. 'This has nothing to do with Ned. This is about *you* not keeping an eye on Esme.'

'I think you'll find,' Kate rounded on Naomi, 'that *the subject*, as you call it, is one and the same. The extra work I don't mind — not for Ned's benefit, I don't. But it doesn't *stop* with Ned, does it? There's Nurse Hammond — she

97

needs feeding too. Then there's Aunt Diana and Mrs Russell coming to visit — and other folk calling all willy-nilly. For Ned, though, I do it with nary a complaint. But, *with* all that extra work don't come no more hours in the day, you know. No, I'm the one left with scarcely a chance to draw breath. I can't go to St. Ursula's. I can't look after Esme — let alone do something nice like take her to the park and play with her. In fact, do you know, apart from going down the garden path to hang laundry from the clothes line, some days just lately I haven't stepped outside of the house at all. I can't remember the last time I walked out through the front door and down Hartland Street. So, yes, you asked me to look after Esme and she got hurt. You can't know how sorry I am for her pain. But — and it grieves me to say this — I do think it was unreasonable of you to ask me to take care of her just so you could go to Garratt's.' Her feelings having poured out in a great torrent, Kate started to cry. But, despite her tears, she determined to make one final point. 'I'd do anything for Ned — you know that. I've given up my room for him. I work all of God's hours for him. But I can't do *everything* Naomi . . . try as I might. Nor do I think it fair of you to expect it of me, either.' With that, and feeling utterly drained, she spun away and rushed from the room.

Once out in the hallway, she ran down the stairs and bowled straight through the kitchen to the scullery, where she slammed her fists down onto the drainer and let out a growl of frustration. Catching sight of the pail of towels, she

98

turned stiffly about. Wet or not, they would have to wait. She had more important things to see to — one of them being to prepare Ned's luncheon and take it up to him before Nurse Hammond could grumble that she was late; tardiness, along with dirtiness, being the failing she tolerated the least.

As it happened, when Kate eventually made it upstairs with Ned's tray, it was to find that Nurse Hammond had gone out to fetch something — a minor reprieve, at least.

Setting Ned's tray on the trestle, she crossed to his bed and opened up the hinged flap that served as a makeshift table. 'Is that all right?' she enquired. Whatever happened, she mustn't be short with him. None of this was his fault.

'Just fine, thanks, Kate.'

Setting out his cutlery, she returned to the tray and, looking back over her shoulder, said, 'It's smoked haddock with mashed potato and griddled asparagus. Would you like some mustard sauce with it? I've made it quite mild.'

'Please.'

With no clue as to his preference in such matters, she again turned to ask, 'Over the fish or on the side?'

'On the side, please.' Pouring a small amount of sauce from the jug, she watched it pool on the plate. 'Smells good,' he remarked. 'I like smoked fish.'

'Me too.' Trying to relax her limbs, she returned the jug to her tray and then carried the plate across to him. Poor man: how on earth did he manage to eat from this awkward position?

His shoulders might be raised by those pillows, but it still looked a nigh on impossible feat. 'Would you like me to cut the fish into pieces for you?' she asked.

'Please. And then I can usually manage from there.'

'All right.'

Taking his knife and fork to the piece of fish, she could feel him watching her.

'I heard what happened to Esme.'

Her shoulders sagged. Naomi, it had to be. No doubt she had come straight up here and laid it on thick, painted her black.

'Oh?'

'Min told me.'

Just as she'd thought. 'Oh.'

When she laid down the cutlery, Ned wasted no time in picking up the fork, stabbing a piece of the fish and putting it in his mouth. 'Tasty,' he said, gesturing with the fork towards his plate.

'Is she *very* cross with me?'

With difficulty — given his unnatural position — he tilted his head, a slight smile creeping across his mouth as he chewed and then swallowed his food. 'Cross? You know Min. She's livid. I tried to tell her she's directing her anger at the wrong person but, well, she rather tore into me. At that precise moment, I would probably have been less afraid for my life had I been forced to bail out from a thousand feet above the sea. But then *you* would know as well as anyone how hard she is to reason with.'

Resignedly, Kate agreed. 'Yes.' She'd been hoping to learn that Naomi had calmed down

— even just a little. It seemed now, though, that she had been hoping in vain.

'Indeed, you know how *all* we Russells are,' Ned went on. 'Hot-headed, impulsive. Intemperate.'

Despite having never come across the word 'intemperate' before, she had a good sense of what it meant: unrestrained; prone to outbursts. In other words, in the image of Pamela Russell.

Reflecting upon Ned's observation, she smiled. 'That's true enough.'

'I was about to say it's a trait we inherited from Mamma — ' Her point precisely! ' — but, actually, the old man is the same. That said, I'm sure Min will calm down. Eventually.'

'Hm.' But what was she going to be like in the meantime, Kate wondered?

'Anyway,' he went on, 'this afternoon, Father is coming to visit — '

'Your father is coming *this afternoon?*'

— and there are some things I shall talk to him about — some changes that clearly need to be made. For instance — '

Astonished that no one should have thought to tell her that Hugh Russell was coming, the rest of what Ned went on to say missed her altogether. All she could think was that she most definitely did not want to bump into *Hugh Russell*.

'There's not much cake left,' she said, concerned as to how she might knock something up with so little time. A Victoria sandwich would be quickest — providing she had sufficient eggs. Oh, *why* had no one thought to tell her? Mr

101

Russell coming to call, *of all people*!

'Fond of cake though he is,' Ned said, setting his fork upon his plate. 'I doubt he will stay long enough to partake. He's probably only coming because someone — most likely Mamma or Aunt Diana — has pointed out to him that since I left hospital, he hasn't been to see me.'

'I'm sure that he's meant to.' The instant the words left her mouth, though, she wondered why she'd said them. What did *she* know of Hugh Russell and his intentions? She knew precious little about the man. She had certainly never come to think of him as her father, despite the fact he was. To her mind, Hugh Russell was best avoided — especially if, on this occasion, Naomi was going to tell him what she, Kate, had allowed to happen to his granddaughter. In fact, for the next few days, at least until it was plain that Esme was going to be all right, it was probably best that she keep her head down generally — pay thorough and proper attention to her work and stay out of everyone's way. Eventually, Naomi would have to start speaking to her again, wouldn't she? Surely even *she* couldn't hold one mishap against her for ever. Could she . . . ?

5

Repercussions

In dismay, Kate shook her head. No matter how much scouring powder she used, nor how hard she scrubbed, the stain in the bottom of the washbasin still refused to budge. She'd lost count of the number of times she'd told Naomi that the blessed tap needed fixing — the constant drip-drip-drip of it almost certainly the cause of the ugly brown mark — but her appeal only ever fell on deaf ears. Well, the basin would have to do as it was. If Nurse Hammond thought it unhygienic, then perhaps *she* would like to have a go at Naomi. And good luck to her with that!

Dropping her scourer into her cleaning pail and spotting a smudge on the wall-mirror, she leant across the basin to wipe it away. Then, taking a final glance about, she let out a weary sigh. No time to tarry: a long list of chores still awaited.

It was the morning after Esme's accident, a day that, to Kate's mind, was going to stick in her memory as her worst ever. But then, she could be wrong; today was only a few hours old and, with the atmosphere this morning, could yet turn out to be even worse. For a start, Naomi was still avoiding her; she'd even set off somewhere just now, Esme in tow, without the slightest mention of where she was going or when she would be back. For all that she could be thoughtless at times, such behaviour just wasn't like her.

Yesterday afternoon, deeply troubled by the way that Naomi was continuing to ignore her, she'd toyed with asking Ned to intervene. In the end, though, she hadn't. It hadn't seemed fair to expect him to take sides or, given his own problems, to expect him to act as some sort of peacemaker or referee in a matter that had nothing to do with him.

Exhaling a long sigh of resignation, she bent to pick up her pail of cleaning things and reached to open the door. From the other side of it came the sound of voices, one of them clearly Naomi's, the other, one she didn't recognize. Naomi was back then. But with whom? Keen to find out, she eased the door a little further and strained to hear.

'So, Mrs Colborne, the position you propose will be a full-time one.'

'That's correct.'

Position? What position? Puzzled, Kate pulled the door wider still.

'But not a live-in one?'

'No,' she heard Naomi reply. 'There *is* a perfectly adequate room on the second floor but, as you have seen for yourself, this house isn't overly large, and I'm not sure how my husband would feel about living in such close proximity to a stranger.'

'Then I'll make a note that you're seeking a day girl.'

A day girl? Perfectly acceptable room on the second floor? Who *was* this woman? Unsettled,

Kate backed away from the door. *Her* room on the second floor — was that the one Naomi was talking about? Since the only other room on that landing was a store room, it had to be.

Breathing more rapidly now, she hastened back to the door and peered through the crack. Bother — Naomi and the mystery woman were already part way down the stairs; she had missed seeing who it was. Disquiet mounting, she checked along the landing and then tiptoed across to peer over the balustrade. The stranger was wearing a navy-blue mackintosh and matching beret. From her shoulder hung a satchel-like bag, and in her hand was a leather-bound notebook. Who the devil was she? And what *was* Naomi up to?

Seeing the two women moving towards the drawing room, Kate crept down the first few stairs.

'If I understand correctly,' she heard Naomi say, 'day girls have become difficult to find.'

With a quick check back over her shoulder, Kate crouched behind the bannisters. It was wrong to eavesdrop — and Naomi would be appalled — but, had she not been ignoring her, had she told her what was going on, then there wouldn't be this need for her to sneak about in the first place. Naomi might be stubborn, but rarely was she secretive — in fact, quite the opposite. Since the accident with Esme, though, she seemed to be going out of her way to avoid her. Up until now, she had assumed it was because she was still cross with her. Now, though, she wasn't so sure — wasn't so sure something else wasn't afoot.

With the women moving further into the drawing room, and their conversation becoming harder to catch, she once again checked over her shoulder. Satisfied that she was still alone, she stole the rest of the way down the stairs, darted across the hallway and, edging as close to the door as she dared, pressed herself flat to the wall. Once there, she stood, breathing rapidly. How ridiculous to be sneaking about, eavesdropping on conversations. It was the sort of thing children did. Well, needs must. Besides, Naomi had only herself to blame.

'Day positions *are* hard to fill, yes,' the visitor was now saying. 'For a young girl in London these days, there is simply so much choice. From Mr Selfridge's stockroom, all the way down to a stall on a local market, hard-working young women are highly sought after — and trust me, they know it. That said, there is still a trickle of girls coming in from the countryside, trained in nothing but domestic work, and able to think no more imaginatively than to secure a position in service somewhere. Those same girls, though, also have need of a roof over their heads.'

'Which is why you find live-in positions easier to fill. Mm, now I understand.'

'Quite.'

In the hallway, Kate stood rigidly. The woman had to be from a domestic agency, which could mean only one thing: Naomi was looking to employ someone. Oh, dear God, she was going to replace her! Naomi was so cross about what she had allowed to happen to Esme that she was going to dismiss her. Trying to swallow down a lump in her throat, she reached to the half-moon table. Upon it, a Chinese vase stuffed with tulips rocked precariously back and forth. Just in time she shot out a hand, narrowly preventing it from crashing to the floor.

'I see. So — '

Desperate now to confirm her suspicion, she leant closer to the doorway. If only her heart would stop pounding; she could barely hear a word they were saying.

'But allow me to make enquiries, Mrs Colborne. You have a nice home — compact and modern — in a pleasant street. Leave it with me for a day or two. The moment my enquiries turn up with someone suitable, which I am confident they will, I shall send you a card.'

With the conversation seemingly drawing to a close, Kate glanced about. Where to hide? The lavatory; yes, she would slip in there.

Stealing silently across the hallway and taking care to ease the door quietly shut behind her, she stood, breathing heavily, her fists curled tightly and her nostrils filling with the smell of Jeyes Fluid from the drain beyond the window. Plainly, Naomi was planning to replace her. She was about to lose her job; this woman was proof of that. And all because of one little mishap that hadn't even been truly her fault. After all these years of housekeeping and drudgery — not to mention providing comfort and counsel in Naomi's many times of need — how unfair was that? Naomi might talk of them being family — when it suited her to — but the truth was that she only had this position at all because Naomi had felt sorry for her — because she had felt bad about her father's behaviour and what had happened with Ned.

Yes, when it came to loyalty, Naomi's would always lie, first and foremost, with her true family: with Ned, and Pamela and Hugh Russell and . . . Wait. Hugh Russell. What if it wasn't just coincidence that he had been to visit? What if *he* had been the one to suggest that she should be got rid of? *Be done with the girl; find yourself someone more reliable*, he could so easily have advised his daughter. Naomi did hang on his every word. And he did pay Naomi the allowance that, in turn, covered payment of her own little salary. But why? Why would he do that? What axe did he have to grind with *her* — Kate? He might be an odious man, but he had never seemed a vindictive one — certainly not the sort to bring hardship upon one of his own offspring, which, like it or not, she was. Latterly, he had even taken it upon himself to keep Edith — the woman he had seduced to bring her into this world in the first place — in a home and a job, when it might be argued that he had no obligation to her whatsoever. Oh, dear Lord, what if he was going to stop doing that as well? Coming over all hot and sticky, she flapped at her blouse. No, he wouldn't do that, would he? No, but his wife might. She had only ever shown complete scorn for her; to this day still referred to her as a farm girl. Oh, Naomi, what the devil were you up to?

Torn to know what to think, let alone know what to do about it, she sank back against the wall, tears blurring her vision. What on earth would she do without this job? Nowhere else would come even close to being the sort of home this one had been. Yes, she wouldn't deny that, sometimes, she did miss the peace and quiet of Woodicombe — but that didn't mean she wanted to go back there. Having to rub along without a proper salary would spell the end for her little bit of independence — not to mention be a considerable blow to her pride. Back in Woodicombe there would be no chance of earning anything like the money she earned here. The best she could hope for down there would be seasonal work in Westward Quay: a chambermaid for holiday makers or waiting on day trippers. Lord, what a come down that would be!

Leaning against the wall, she felt her insides twisting into knots. She had to make this right. And quickly. But how? How did she do that? She could hardly go behind Naomi's back to Aunt Diana and ask *her* to intervene. No, but perhaps, despite her reservations, she could try and talk to Ned. If anyone knew how to get Naomi to reconsider, it would be him. Yes, despite having previously decided against it, she would go and see what he knew, and then ask for his help.

Having first gone to splash her face and tidy her hair, she arrived outside the door to his room. But, even before she had raised her hand to knock, Nurse Hammond, coming from her own room next door, forbade her to disturb him. 'I'm afraid not, dear,' she replied to Kate's request to speak to him. 'The lieutenant passed an unusually disturbed night and, at my insistence, is making up for lost sleep.'

Damnation. Now she would have to confront Naomi directly, which would mean showing her hand. Well, either she had to admit to eavesdropping, or else let matters take their course and wait to see what Naomi did next. Not that she could just wait about; the worry alone would devour her from the insides out. No, she would have to go and see Naomi, have it out with her.

Feeling as though every inch of her body was on full alert, she made her way slowly back down the stairs. Arriving in the hallway, she paused to stand for a moment and inhale deeply. Although it did nothing to slow her breathing, she went in through the doors to the drawing room anyway, her question for Naomi ready on her lips. To her astonishment, the room was empty. Turning swiftly about, she went to check the dining room — no one there, either. So, where were they?

Making her way on down to the kitchen, she tried to remember whether Naomi had previously mentioned anything about going out. But then, as she went in through the door, she spotted a chit of paper on the table. Darting towards it, and recognizing Naomi's handwriting, she snatched it up.

Shan't need luncheon today. Esme likewise.
N.

That was it? No *Dear Kate*? No explanation as to where they had gone? No suggestion of when they would be back? Feeling her shoulders sinking, she hung her head. Such matter-of-factness. could only mean that Naomi was nowhere near close to forgiving her, and, in which case, her heart was thudding for good reason.

Despite putting the note back on the table, she nevertheless continued to stare down at it. Where could Naomi have gone with Esme such that neither of them would need luncheon? Presumably, to Clarence Square; had she been headed anywhere else, then she would have left Esme at home. Well, up until yesterday she would have. She would probably no more do that now than she would allow Esme to go out and play in the street. Dear God, this truly was an awful mess.

Heaving a long sigh, she turned away from the table. On the other hand, was it a mess? Was there a chance that she was just making a mountain out of a molehill? Was she, her judgement clouded by guilt, seeing trouble where none existed? No. No, sadly, she didn't believe that she was; the feeling in the pit of her stomach was there for a reason. She was in trouble.

Distractedly, she turned about. The thought of being dismissed from here made her feel sick. How she would miss Esme. How she would miss seeing her grow up. And Aunt Diana! How she would miss her dry humour, and the way she managed to dish out perfectly sound advice without ever sounding patronising or judgemental. And, despite how sorely mistreated she felt at that precise moment, how she would miss Naomi, too. Desperately so. Granted, Naomi and

111

Ned weren't family in the truest sense of the word — she was, after all, only a half-sibling, and one born out of wedlock, at that. Nevertheless, until now, she'd thought that the three of them had become close; Naomi and Ned were certainly the nearest things to siblings that *she* had. But perhaps she had misjudged things. Perhaps, when it came to the people Naomi considered to be family, she languished at the bottom of a very long list; despite Naomi's various protestations to the contrary over the last few years, perhaps she ranked closer to housekeeper than sister. It was certainly beginning to feel that way.

Sniffing loudly, she wiped a hand across her eyes.

And then there was what Luke would have to say when he came home to find that not only had she lost her job and a respectable salary, but that she had cost them their home, too. Disbelieving, that's what he would be. Utterly disbelieving. And bitterly disappointed in her, too. He would come home from the war, fully expecting to take up employment for Mr Lawrence, only to discover that Naomi no longer wanted them in her home. Oh, dear Lord, what a sorry mess she had made of things.

Reaching into her pocket for her handkerchief, she blew her nose. She had to pull herself together — if not for herself, then for Luke. She hadn't lost her job *yet*. There still existed the chance that she could get Naomi to reconsider — although only if she bucked herself up. Yes! And the only way to do that was to continue to make herself indispensable. And so, to that end, she would go and wash her face, tidy herself up, and then she would come back down and simply get on with her work. She would leave Ned out of it, wait for Naomi to come home, listen to whatever she had to say, apologize profusely for what had happened, and then beg her forgiveness — try to appeal to her sense of fairness. That done, there would be nothing more she could do. She would have tried her hardest. After that, what would be, would be.

★ ★ ★

'I'm afraid I've let her become over tired.'

When Naomi eventually did come through the front door, Esme whimpering in her arms, it was late — by normal standards, far too late for such a small child to still be up. Not that Kate had any intention of pointing that out. No, she was just relieved to see the two of them. The longer it had gone on without them coming home, the more her panic had driven her to imagine all manner of terrible things.

Closing the front door behind them, she stepped forward to help. 'Shall I — '

'Entirely my fault for keeping her out,' Naomi said, sweeping past on her way to the stairs.

'Shall I — '

'Oh, and I shan't need anything to eat. I dined with Mamma and Papa.'

Watching Naomi carry Esme up the stairs, Kate stood, rooted to the spot. At least Naomi was talking to her. And in a civilised tone — if not a rather cold and direct one — which had to count for something. That being the case, all she could do was wait to see what happened next.

For a while after that, she poked about in the kitchen, the hands on the wall-clock showing that it was approaching nine, and it being as much as she could do not to fall asleep standing up. After a truly horrible day, her eyes felt like squares and her skull felt as though she was wearing a tin hat that was several sizes too small. Worse still, having spent the afternoon with her insides twisted into knots, she'd been unable to face even a mouthful of the food she had put on a plate for herself, such that now, she didn't know whether to attribute her light-headedness to hunger or to fear.

The only chink of light was that Naomi hadn't — as she had spent all afternoon picturing — marched straight in and told her to pack her things. In fact, she had seemed strangely subdued. Was it too much to hope that she'd had second thoughts about getting rid of her?

Hearing Naomi's light tread on the stairs, she tensed. One way or another, she was about to find out — was about to be put out of her misery. Misery? Huh. If she was right about this, then her real misery was only just about to begin.

'Kate, I need to talk to you.'

She forced a swallow. This was it.

'Yes?' The only comfort she could draw was that Naomi looked similarly ill at ease, wringing her hands as was her habit when something was troubling her.

114

'Unfortunately, I cannot wind back time.'

'No.' *If only.*

'What happened cannot be undone.'

'No.'

'But apologies can be rendered.'

Apologies? Naomi wanted her to apologize again? Well, if that was all it was going to take to bring this business to an end and enable her to keep her job . . .

'I — '

'And so, in the hope that you can bring yourself to forgive me, I apologize, without reservation, for the way I spoke to you.'

Wait a minute . . . *what?*

'I don't — '

'When you told me what had happened,' Naomi pressed on. 'Naturally, I was upset — in shock even — but, as Ned was to point out to me, that was no excuse. Raising my voice to you was wrong. Wholly inexcusable.'

Unable to stop shaking, and wondering whether to trust her hearing, Kate pressed her hands upon the edge of the kitchen table. *Naomi* was *apologizing?* She was off the hook? Thrown by the possibility, she found herself unable to reply. 'Well . . . '

'No, please don't say that it doesn't matter. It matters greatly. I behaved in the manner of a . . . well, to put it plainly, in the manner of my mother.'

'Naomi — '

'No, Kate, please don't say that it's all right. It's *not* all right. It was *wrong. I* was wrong. Utterly. And all I can do now is repeat my

115

apology and trust that you will accept it.'

Warily, she raised her eyes to Naomi's face. She did look truly remorseful. But dare she hope that this was to be the end of it — that she wasn't still going to be dismissed anyway? There seemed only one way to find out. 'I do accept it. Thank you.' And then, steeling herself, she said, 'So . . .'

Naomi, though, seemed to have more to say. 'No matter the shock I felt in that moment, I should not have accused you of neglect.'

Overwhelmed by a mixture of regret and relief, Kate exhaled heavily. 'I wouldn't ever neglect Esme — '

'I know you wouldn't.'

' — and you should know that I'm truly sorry about what I let happen to her.' And it was the truth; while she still didn't think she had been wholly responsible, she *was* filled with remorse. 'I just had so much to think about all at once that I — '

'I know,' Naomi interrupted her to say. Then, heaving a sigh of her own, and rounding the end of the table, she went on, 'Things do seem to have rather overwhelmed us, don't they? Things with regard to Ned, I mean. Every day, you toil away down here, unaided and unseen, such that I failed to notice just how much I was expecting of you. Once Ned arrived, I naïvely assumed that having a full-time nurse would be all that was required — what with that and Papa's allowance for the additional costs. But I see now just how much more there is to it. And how all of it has fallen upon you. And for that, I am truly sorry.'

116

Slowly, Kate once again raised her eyes to meet Naomi's. 'And that's why I went to see Papa. You see, yesterday, Ned made a suggestion. But, because it involved asking Papa for help, I'm afraid to say that I rather summarily dismissed it.'

'Oh.'

Making a little scoffing noise, Naomi gestured airily. 'No married woman wants to ask her father for help, particularly not where money is involved. But, later, reflecting back upon Ned's suggestion, it occurred to me that I wouldn't be requesting assistance for myself, but for him. And, perhaps even more importantly, for you. Anyway, the long and the short of it is that Papa has kindly agreed to pay for domestic help of some sort — whatever we need until Ned is fully recovered. And I have accepted his offer.'

Having been holding her breath, Kate reached to the edge of the sink. *That* was what the visit from that woman had been about — getting *her* some *help?* Had she really spent the entire day, sick with guilt, all het up and fearing the worst — for *nothing?*

'So, you mean — '

'I even met with someone from the domestic agency on the High Street,' Naomi continued. 'The proprietress came here. You may well have seen her. Anyway, apparently, these days, staff are hard to come by. But she has gone away to see what she can do. Although, only now that I'm telling you this does it occur to me that perhaps it's not for *me* to determine what sort of help we need — that *you* need. No, I rather think that should be for *you* to decide.'

The sudden coursing of relief through her body made Kate feel faint. Against all the odds, it seemed that she was safe. She was not about to lose her job. She had simply misunderstood what Naomi had been up to. And the realization was making her feel giddy with relief.

'I thought you were going to replace me,' she whispered, surprised by a desire to giggle.

Wide-eyed, Naomi stared back at her. '*What?*'

'I thought you were so cross with me about Esme that you were going to give me my marching orders.' Her confession out in the open, she was surprised to find herself starting to cry.

'Oh, my dear Kate,' Naomi said, rushing to embrace her. 'You couldn't *be* more wrong!'

Despite feeling Naomi's arms fold about her, Kate could do nothing to stop her tears. It was as though with each gasping sob, all the horror of the last few days was flooding from her body. 'I . . . I . . .'

'My dear, dear Kate, I can't believe you would think such a thing.'

Feeling suddenly foolish, she fished about in her pocket for a handkerchief and blew her nose. Oddly, *she* couldn't believe it now, either. Now it just felt as though, in her own way, she had been as quick to judge as Naomi had. 'I thought it because . . . well, no, it don't matter.' And it didn't any more, either.

By her side, Naomi shook her head. 'I could never dismiss *you*. This is your home. Not only

118

that but I depend upon you far too much to be without you. Added to which, if you left, neither Ned nor Esme would ever forgive me. Nor Lawrence. Quite simply, without *you*, we would all fall apart. You are, well, to us, you are irreplaceable.'

Mortified by her own stupidity, and anxious now to change the subject, Kate dabbed her handkerchief at her eyes. She would say no more of it. She would forget all about it — attribute it to her general tiredness.

'So . . . so what do you propose for this help, then?' she asked, deciding that looking forward might be the best way to put the whole sorry affair behind her. 'What sort of person do you have in mind to take on?'

When Naomi moved to join her leaning against the edge of the sink, she, too, seemed to soften with relief. 'Well, what would be of greatest help to you — a kitchen maid? A cook? A parlour maid for odds and ends? You tell me what would be of greatest benefit to *you*, and I will go back to the agency and see whether they have anyone to suit.'

Still trying to picture how such an arrangement might be made to work, Kate let out a long sigh. There could be no denying that having some help would be a godsend — but precisely what sort of help did she need the most?

'Help in the kitchen,' she said. 'Although, someone to take care of cleaning would be handy, too.'

'Well, look,' Naomi said, reaching to touch her arm. 'There's no need to decide tonight. I've no

119

wish to make matters worse — too many cooks and all that!'

Unable to help it, Kate grinned. 'No, and while I've no wish to end up like Edith, I do understand why she fears that folk supposedly trying to help will do little more than get under her feet.'

'Yes. Unlike Clarence Square — or Woodicombe — this is not a house well-suited to many staff, is it?'

She shook her head. It was true. 'No.'

'Well, you look exhausted. And I know *I* am. So, I think I shall bid you goodnight. In the morning, you can let me know what you think.'

'I will. And thank you, Naomi.'

'No, thank *you*, Kate.'

Upstairs in her room shortly afterwards, almost too weary to even undress, Kate knew that falling asleep was going to be beyond her; there were just too many thoughts in her head, each and every one of them clamouring for attention — among them the mortification she still felt for having jumped to the wrong conclusion. But there in almost equal measure were relief and elation, both brought on by the realization that she had been wrong.

Taking off her petticoat and folding it over her arm, her eyes fell upon her most recent letter from Luke. It had arrived a couple of weeks ago and she had long since written back to him. But, perhaps, if she sat down now and penned him another note, it would help to bring some order to her thoughts. If, when she read it back in the morning, it turned out that she had written a lot of nonsense — or, through sheer fatigue had expressed herself poorly — then she needn't send it. She could screw it up and start again on a day when she felt less muddle-headed. Given how her head was buzzing with thoughts, it had to be worth a try.

Naomi told me tonight me that Mr Russell has offered to pay for some domestic help, she wrote on the uppermost sheet of her pad. She would not, she had decided, bother him with the matter of their falling out, nor with what she had subsequently gone on to assume: he would consider it a trifling business of no consequence. 'Women always patch up their differences,' he had once said to her. 'And men?' she recalled asking him. 'Men don't fall out so much in the first place,' had been his reply. No, she would stick to the point.

She is leaving it to me to decide what sort of help she should hire, she went on to write. But here is the thing; I don't know what to tell her. I suppose I could have a cook, but you will no doubt recall how the kitchen here is small, and anyway, it is hard to imagine any cook worth her salt wanting such a job — especially when they see Nurse Hammond's devilish requirements for Ned! I shouldn't mind a parlour maid — someone to clean the lav and the floors and the windows and so on. The coal smuts here, winter and summer alike, are far worse than anything from the fireplaces at Woodicombe.

When she broke off from writing and looked up, it was to find that the room had grown quite dark. Not wanting to bother with the gas light, she struck a match and lit her candle. Woodicombe. Yes, what she really needed was staff like Edith and Mabel — Edith to take care of all of the cooking, especially since she liked to stick to a tried and tested recipe and would, therefore, relish following Nurse Hammond's instructions to the letter — and Mabel to take charge of a day girl and keep things ship-shape generally. But she doubted such people existed in London. Even Aunt Diana had said that these days, it was as much the prospective employee who interviewed and scrutinized the employer than the other way around. 'It seems one must be grateful for whomever one can get,' Aunt Diana had recently remarked, bemoaning the trials of having to fill a vacancy on her own staff. 'And then simply trust that it will work out all right.' And if Aunt Diana struggled to find staff for her opulent home — to quote Naomi's description of it — then what hope was there for the needs of the rather more modest number twelve, Hartland Street?

Mabel and Edith: her grandmother and her mother; her other family. Yes, she really should write to them, too. It must be so dreary and soulless, rattling around in that big empty house, Mr Russell seeming to have no immediate plans for it. Poor Woodicombe — what a waste of it. But wait: *Woodicombe*. Perhaps they should all decamp there! They could do a lot worse.

Fighting to keep her eyes open, she laid her

pen on her blotter, screwed the cap back on her bottle of ink and stared down at her letter. She would finish it tomorrow. And, while at this precise moment she was no clearer about the sort of help she was going to ask Naomi to employ, perhaps the answer would come to her in her sleep. Stranger things had happened.

★ ★ ★

Poached eggs? Goodness, there was a welcome surprise.

Despite it being 'porridge day', word had arrived in the kitchen that Ned had voiced a craving for poached eggs on toast, which could only mean, Kate reflected as she filled a pan with water, that he was regaining his appetite. She did hope so because, later that morning, he was due to be examined by a doctor from Queen Alexandra's, and they were all keeping their fingers crossed for a good prognosis.

It wasn't until almost eleven o'clock, though, when Naomi came down to the kitchen, Esme in tow, when she had the chance to find out how he had fared.

'Well, how did it go?' she asked, reaching for the kettle in the expectation that Naomi had come down for a belated morning coffee.

'Very well.'

Lighting the gas on the range, Kate nodded. 'The doctor was pleased?'

'Better than that — tomorrow, he is coming back to remove Ned from traction.'

The gas lit under the kettle, she spun about.

123

'*Really?* He'll be able to get up?'

'Not able to get up *just* yet, no. The idea in the first instance seems to be to remove the traction rods but leave the splints. Then, after a further couple of days, Nurse Hammond will remove the splints as well and commence a regime of gentle exercises to start to re-build his muscles. Apparently, they will have wasted away through lack of use.'

While a pleasing thing to hear, it seemed clear that Ned still had a long way to go. Nevertheless, she found herself smiling warmly. 'He must be over the moon.'

'You should have seen his face! You know, I do believe he had started to think the day would never come. The doctor warned him not to expect a miracle. Apparently, progress will be slow and frustrating, and a great deal of regular exercising will be needed before he will even countenance letting Ned try to actually walk. He also took great pains to stress that these things must not be rushed — not that Nurse Hammond would permit that anyway.'

'So, Nurse Hammond will stay on, then?' she said. 'She can do these exercises with him?'

'Apparently, yes. The doctor seemed impressed by her knowledge of bones and joints and *recuperative therapies*, as he called them.'

'That's all good then,' she said, her delight genuine.

'Not only that but, before he left, I asked the doctor to look at Esme's hand.'

At the mention of Esme, Kate stiffened. Hearing the kettle start to whistle, she reached to lift it from the ring. 'And . . . ?'

'And he said that there are no broken bones — no long-term damage done as far as he could tell. He bandaged her fingers again — largely to prevent her from accidentally knocking them and doing further harm — and said that Nurse Hammond should look at them again in four or five days, by which time all should be well. Perhaps still a little bruised and tender, but otherwise fine.'

Unwittingly, Kate let out a sigh of relief. In a way, that was better than the news about Ned. 'Good,' she said. 'Then let me make you your coffee.'

'Thank you. And I'll pour Esme some milk. Then, if you can spare a moment to sit down, perhaps you can tell me your thoughts about the extra help.'

Despite not having had time to give it any further thought this morning, Kate knew what she wanted. If, shortly now, Ned was no longer going to be confined to his bed, then what she had first thought to be the answer no longer seemed appropriate. Instead, coming together in her mind was another idea. The trick, though, would be to convince Naomi that not only could her plan be made to work, but that it would be to the benefit of all of them.

★　★　★

'So, let me see whether I understand the pair of you.'

It was after luncheon that same day and,

125

having discussed with Naomi her idea to help the next few months pass more smoothly, Kate had accompanied her up to Ned's bedside, where they were both now trying to convince him of the same thing. To put it plainly, he looked bemused.

'Go on.'

'You would pack up here,' he said, looking between their faces, 'and take everything we need — this bed, for instance, and all of Nurse Hammond's equipment — down to Woodicombe because you think . . . well, no, I'm not entirely sure what it is you do think. I'm afraid you will have to spell it out.'

'We think,' Kate began, suddenly seeing her idea as she realized he might be doing — in other words, as mazed — 'that once you start to get up and about again, you're going to find this place real cramped.'

'There's the stairs, for a start,' Naomi chipped in.

'Unless memory deceives,' Ned responded, 'Woodicombe also has stairs.'

'Yes,' Naomi continued. 'It does. But, as Kate reminded me, it also has several rooms on the ground floor that could, with only minimal effort, be set up for your use — Uncle Sidney's study, for a start. You wouldn't believe how much space there is in there now that all of his books and that enormous desk are gone. And just across the hallway is the lavatory.'

'And, on nice days, you would be able to sit outside,' Kate hurried on to say, 'which you can hardly do here since from either of the doors you would have to negotiate a flight of steps.'

'Hm.'

Although he appeared to be considering the idea, she could tell that he was far from convinced. 'Better still,' she said, eager that he should see the whole picture, 'your father wouldn't need to pay for more staff — as he's proposing to do here — because we would have Mabel and Edith. I know that Edith, for one, would be thrilled to have reason to cook again, and for certain Mabel would be willing to keep on top of everything else. At worst, we might need a girl from the village to do a couple of hours of cleaning each morning. But that would cost Mr Russell a good deal less than having to find someone through an agency here.'

When she was forced to pause for breath, Naomi picked up.

'In addition to which, it would be a good reason to open up the house — make use of it through the summer, rather than let it sit there mouldering away.'

'And there would be the fresh air,' Kate added. 'Everyone feels better for some fresh air.'

'And *this* place?' Ned wanted to know, gesturing about the room.

'Oh, we'd just throw dust sheets over everything,' Naomi replied, waving her hand dismissively, 'and ask Mamma to send someone from Clarence Square once a week to give it the *quick once over* — as Kate would say. We've done it before.'

'Hm.' Still Ned seemed unconvinced.

'Truly,' Naomi continued, 'this place is the

127

least of our concerns.'

With that, Kate saw him frown.

'All right, forgetting about this place, what about *you*, Min? Am I to believe that you could put up with being in Devon? Only, you know how desperately quiet it is there.'

'I won't deny that it's quiet,' Naomi admitted. 'But, to be honest, it's not terribly lively *here* at the moment either — not *sans* spouse, it isn't.'

Still, Ned hesitated. 'I do see why you think it a good idea. But we could only undertake it with the blessing of the doctor and the agreement of Nurse Hammond.'

''Course.'

'Absolutely,' Naomi agreed. 'We would discuss it with Doctor Ramsey. And, assuming he raised no objections, we would ask Nurse Hammond whether she wished to join us — because, if she didn't, we would have to make certain that we could replace her.'

'And we really ought to ask Father,' Ned pointed out. 'Not just assume that he will go along with the idea. It's only good manners.'

'Don't worry about Papa. You can leave *him* to me.'

Flicking her eyes back and forth between the two of them as she followed their exchange, Kate felt encouraged.

'And you're sure you're all right with these arrangements?' Ned turned to her to ask.

Looking back at him, she nodded. 'I think it will be easier all round.'

After a further moment's reflection, he too nodded. 'Very well then. Let us see whether we can bring it about. Although, I do have a favour to ask.'

Beside her, Naomi shook her head, a gesture Kate read as being one of mock dismay.

'Go on then. What are you after?'

'See if you can get hold of my chap Rowley, would you? A while back, Mamma brought me a letter he'd sent care of Clarence Square and so, now, I do at least know where he is.'

'Tell him where you're going to be?' Naomi asked. 'Is that what you mean?'

'Actually, no,' he said, starting to grin. 'I rather meant you to get hold of him and see whether he would like to come with us — so that we might do our convalescing together . . . '

When Naomi shook her head, on her lips was a smile. 'What do you say, Kate?'

'He writes that any day now he should be ambulant again.' Ned seemed to think it helpful to clarify. 'Fortunate to smash just the one leg,' he said. 'A rather simple break', is how he actually described it.'

Noticing Ned's animation, Kate knew it would be mean to refuse him. Having company while they recovered would surely be of benefit to both men. Besides which, having more people at Woodicombe might go some way to bringing the place back to life — maybe even make it feel a little like the old days again. 'Why not?' she said with a shrug.

'The more the merrier?' Naomi turned to her to ask.

'Something like that, yes.'

6

Woodicombe

'I do hope this hasn't all been too much work for you, Mrs Bratton.'

'Not at all, ma'am. To tell you the truth, we've rather enjoyed it.'

Watching Naomi talking to Mabel, Kate smiled. This was only her second day back in Woodicombe but, even accounting for the tiring railway journey down from London, made alone, and a full day yesterday spent getting things up together, she felt better than she had in a long time. And she suspected the same was true for Mabel and Edith. And now, even Naomi, who had just arrived with Esme, seemed brighter, too.

'Well, I must say, Mrs Bratton, everywhere looks spick and span as always,' Naomi picked up again, looking about and taking everything in. 'And what lovely flowers. Did you do them yourself?'

'I did, ma'am.'

From a couple of steps away, Kate watched Naomi inspect the crystal vase crammed with peonies, their shades of burgundy, soft pink and rich cream all set off by dazzling sprigs of yellow-lime spurge — *chartreuse*, as she'd once heard Naomi refer to the vibrant colour. In a way, she envied Mabel her eye; when it came to anything even remotely artistic, she herself was utterly hopeless.

With a relaxed smile, Naomi glanced at her wristwatch. 'Well, I suppose we should get these few belongings unpacked before the delivery van arrives with everything else. Oh, and you say that for Nurse Hammond, you've readied a room downstairs?'

Relieved that, together, they'd got everything so organized, Kate nodded. 'We've made up the old butler's room — you remember, next to the housekeeper's parlour. Should Ned ring for help during the night, Nurse Hammond will hear the bell. Come with me and I'll show you.'

'I'm sure Nurse Hammond will have no complaints,' Naomi remarked moments later, her inspection of the little room complete. 'I'm sure she has put up with far more spartan conditions in her time.' Lowering her voice, she then went on, 'My greater concern is how Mabel and Edith will cope with us all descending like this — Edith especially. It's years since they've had to look after more than the odd visitor and I worry that they will be overwhelmed. Are you still certain they will be able to manage?'

Pleased by Naomi's concern for them, Kate nodded. 'Edith won't fret. Always seemed to me she preferred to work on her own anyway — you know, with no one to get under her feet or do something wrong and cause a confloption. For certain she'll find it hard going these first few days, but I'll wager she'd rather be worn out than bored. If nothing else, it will make a change from endless hours sat knitting.'

'Knitting?'

Recalling the cardboard box labelled with the

name of the local depot of the VAD, Kate grinned. 'You should see the mountain of socks and scarves she's got waiting to be sent off again.'

'And what about Mabel, you mentioned that she's brought in a girl?'

Kate nodded. 'Winnie Dodd from up at Woodicombe Cross.'

'And she'll be reliable, this Winnie?'

'Mabel wouldn't have taken her on otherwise.'

'Very well then.'

'But I did make a point of saying — to both Mabel *and* Edith — that if they need help, they're to ask you straightaway and not wait until they're on their knees.'

'Well done,' Naomi said, looking along the empty corridor. 'Now, I'm not expecting Ned and Nurse Hammond to be here until quite late this evening. And this fellow Rowley isn't due until Friday, by which time I'm rather hoping the rest of us will have settled in.'

Following Naomi out of the little room, Kate smiled. 'If Nurse Hammond has anything to do with it, we will have. Mark my words, once she and Ned arrive it will be just as though we'd always been here.'

Watching Naomi heading back along the corridor, Kate gave a contented sigh; it felt good to be back in the wide open spaces of Woodicombe and away from the cramped and dirty conditions of London. Of course, it also helped that she wasn't up to her knees in drudgery — or constantly chasing her tail. Yes, for the first time in a good many months, she felt calm.

Following in Naomi's footsteps, she headed

back towards the stairs. She rather liked having time to just stand and breathe — to have so little depending upon her. And so, she would try to enjoy every moment of it — because, in these times of uncertainty, who knew how long it would last, or what lay in wait for them around the corner?

★ ★ ★

Fancy her, occupying the Rose Room — the room on the ladies' landing named for the huge cabbage roses on its wallpaper. In varying shades of pink, they were complete with little green leaves, and stems with vicious-looking thorns. Although it had always struck her as a nice room, she'd never thought to one day sleep in it. In fact, Kate reflected, as she stood looking about, it was definitely the nicest room she had ever slept in. From its windows it had a view across the front gardens and down the drive and, over the years, had been used by many visiting ladies, the last of which had probably been Aunt Diana. Granted, in the winter, it did tend to chilliness, facing, as it did, to the northeast. But, in warmer months, that same aspect ensured that it never became unbearably sticky like those on the other side of the house. Travelling down on the train, and thinking about what lay ahead, she'd been expecting to find herself back in the attic — in the same room she'd always occupied — and so it had come as a surprise to discover that she had been put in a room on the main landing. Perhaps Mabel hadn't known quite what to make of her station now — perhaps, being unable to work out whether she was now more family than staff, she had erred on the side of caution. On the other hand, her decision might simply have been down to common sense; with so few people in residence, why spread them out over more than one floor?

A little earlier, seeing Ned arrive, Kate had slipped into the study to welcome him. After his lengthy journey he had looked pale and tired, and she had quickly left Nurse Hammond to get him settled. After that, she had come upstairs intending to retire for the night but, deciding it too early to go to sleep, had attempted instead to write to Luke. Seated at the dressing table — the little armchair and side table proving too low for the task — she had written the first few lines easily enough, letting him know that they were now safely installed at Woodicombe. But after that, as was often the case, she could think of little else that might be of interest to him.

Hoping for inspiration, she stared out into the dimpsy. She had already written that she had seen his parents, and that they were both well. She had also written that she had unpacked most of the things brought from Hartland Street by Mr Russell's delivery men. So, what to say next? There had to be *something* of interest that she could tell him.

Turning away from the window, she crossed back to the dressing table. Then, sitting down and picking up the pen, she somewhat hesitantly wrote,

Mabel looks a good deal older. To my eyes, she seems smaller and thinner, though perhaps that's just my memory playing tricks. Edith looks the same as she ever did, though she does seem glad to be busy again and proper pleased to see us. She does seem to have hit it off with Nurse Hammond, too.

With her words beginning to flow, she got up and reached to turn on the electric light. Then, wriggling herself comfortable upon the stool, she carried on,

Since last time Naomi and I were here, all of the rooms save one or two have stayed shut up. It is a sad sight to see. Outside has fared little better. Though your Pa still keeps the lawns neat, it is the fruit and vegetables that take up all his time, and so the flower borders are mostly gone to pot. It breaks my heart to see it all like it, but what is to be done? Even down here, young folk these days, well, those that are left, don't want to go into service no more. Mabel was fortunate to persuade Winnie Dodd to come down as a day girl for the duration of our stay. Do you remember her? She would have been about fourteen when you joined up. Sadly, her chap was killed two years back, in that terrible slaughter on the Somme. And now she says she won't never marry.

Now in the swing of it, Kate continued.

Yesterday afternoon, when Naomi arrived, Mabel and Edith were quick to fuss over Esme. Ned came separate with Nurse Hammond in an ambulance train from Waterloo to Exeter, from where Cousin Elizabeth had arranged for them to be collected and driven here by someone from the local VAD. Since it was all my thought that we should come down here, I do hope the effort and upheaval proves worth it.

I am put in the Rose Room on the ladies' landing. You would laugh to see me in here. There is so much space I do rattle around somewhat. All told, I find I don't mind being back here again as much as I might have supposed. The air is certainly nicer to breathe, and we shan't be afraid to light the lamps come dimmet for fear of drawing the attention of the Zeppelins. Nor do I think there will be any bombs. So that will all be good. Indeed, the war seems very far away, like I have left it behind in London. Mabel even said that down here, few folk bother to change their clocks for this new Summer Time, most of them being unable to see the point of it and it making not one jot of a difference to their days.

Deciding then that her eyes were growing too tired to keep going, she carefully set her pen on her blotter and determined to write the last bit in the morning. Then she went across to the switch, extinguished the light, and got into bed.

Staring up into the darkness, she had a feeling

136

that from tomorrow, the days would start to take on some sort of routine. Although, without the preparation of meals to worry about, and with very little by way of cleaning to see to, she had no idea of what her part in that would be. But, in comparison to the frenzied days of the last few weeks, not knowing what she would be doing from one moment to the next felt like an agreeable problem to have. *Delicious*, in fact, as Naomi so often said of nice things.

★ ★ ★

'If you ask me, 'tis all one unholy muddle.'

Edith's observation, made as she stood scraping new potatoes for lunch, made Kate laugh. ''Tis only a muddle because we're all still settling in,' she replied, watching Edith taking her paring knife to the last of the potatoes. Smooth and evenly shaped, they smelled fresh and earthy and appetising. 'Give it a day or two and we'll be proper sorted.'

'Nice to have folk about, though,' Edith went on. 'Can't recall the last time I heard a child's laugh about the place. 'Course, once you all go back up to London, it'll seem quieter than ever.'

Inwardly, Kate groaned; only Edith could manage to summon gloom in the midst of discussing something she professed to find cheering. 'No need to go thinking about that yet,' she said, frustrated but not entirely surprised. 'And anyway, come wintertime, maybe keep one or two more rooms open this time round. Use them yourselves. Be more cosy.'

Then, recalling the sight of the woodshed stacked to bursting with seasoned logs, she said, 'It's not as though firewood is in short supply. Not that Mr Russell would mind if you burnt a bit more coal — not if it meant plenty of hot water and a bit of warmth when you needed it.'

Edith's response to that was to scoff. 'Happen *he* wouldn't, but *I* would. I'm already beholden enough to that man — ' Beholden? Now what was the woman on about? 'What you seem to forget is that with as little as a stroke of his pen, or one word from his mouth, me an' Ma could be out on our ears.'

'Edith!' Honestly, the woman hadn't changed a bit: still a doom-monger. And still someone she never would think of as her mother, let alone feel moved to address as 'Ma'. 'Mr Russell wouldn't do that to you. Think about it, why go to all the bother and the cost of keeping this place going these last years just to throw you out now?' No, as she had only recently had cause to reflect, of all the things that man might be, vindictive wasn't one of them. In fact, from what she knew of Russell family matters, as time went on, he even seemed to be softening a little.

'Huh.'

Exasperated to the point of wishing she could grab Edith and shake her, Kate turned and walked away. No sense getting into an argument with her so soon after arriving. *Pick your battles*, Aunt Diana always advised, and this did seem a bit of a daft thing to fall out over. If Edith wanted to be bitter, let her be — that was her choice.

Arriving back up in the hallway, though, she decided that Edith was right about one thing: the house *was* a muddle. For a start, piled up alongside the door to the study were several empty crates and a number of boxes stuffed with paper — the debris from Nurse Hammond's unpacking of her equipment. And she knew for a fact that on the landing were Naomi's empty trunks, along with her leather travelling bags, and the small chest in which Esme's toys had been transported. The trouble was, short of fetching in poor old Pa Channer to take them up to the trunk room, they looked likely to stay there. Although, why did they? Why couldn't she just drag them out of sight somewhere? It wasn't as though they were short on empty rooms. It would also show Edith that she had meant what she had said about them getting sorted out.

Realizing that in no time at all she had gone from having far too much work in Hartland Street, to having none whatsoever down here, she crossed the hall and surveyed the items outside of the study. She would take it all down to the butler's pantry. She knew from being down there the other day that it was empty. And it had to be easier to drag things *down* a staircase than up. Yes, she would make herself useful.

Stacked one inside the other, she soon had the boxes condensed in number and carried away. The crates, although not overly heavy, proved rather more cumbersome — especially when it came to the staircase. But, somehow, cursing when she clouted her shins with one of them, and then having to stop off in the scullery to dig out a splinter gained from another, she eventually achieved what she had set out to. Then, fetching a broom and dustpan from the closet, she swept the floor.

'Did Winnie not make a thorough job of it?'

In response to Mabel's enquiry, she spun about. 'What? Oh, no,' she replied with a shake of her head. 'No, I've just moved all of the crates and boxes that had been left here and now I'm cleaning up.'

To that piece of news, she felt certain Mabel raised an eyebrow. All she said, though, was, 'Well for heaven's sake, don't go putting your back out.'

By the time she noticed that it was almost one o'clock, Kate felt as though she'd been of some use. But, on her way to get cleaned up and see whether she could help fetch and carry for luncheon, the bell in the porch rang. Glancing towards it, she saw a man with what appeared to be an oversized envelope under his arm. Opening the door to him, she also noticed that out on the gravel were two motorcars, one of them small and sporty, and the brightest of yellow colours.

'Mrs Lawrence Colborne?' the man enquired.

She shook her head. 'No, but if you will tell me your business, I'll go and fetch her for you.'

'My name is Roberts, from Roberts and Brown Motors on the Barnstaple Road. I have a delivery for her.'

She glanced again at the two motorcars. Alongside the larger of the two stood a second man, dressed similarly to the first in dark trousers and a checked jacket. In his hand he was holding a cap, and what appeared to be goggles.

'Is she expecting you?'

'I'm afraid I couldn't say, ma'am.'

'Please,' she said, frowning. 'Do come in. Mrs Colborne is about to sit down to luncheon, but I'll go and tell her that you're here.'

'A delivery?' Naomi said when Kate found her and explained about the caller. 'A delivery of what? Did he say?'

'No, he didn't.' Following Naomi along the corridor, she decided not to mention what was standing on the drive.

'Oh well,' Naomi said with a sigh, 'as long as he's quick.'

When Naomi went across the hall and introduced herself, Kate hung back. After shaking Naomi's hand, the man called Brown gestured towards the driveway but, although she strained to hear what he was saying, the only words she caught were 'papers' and 'receipt'. But papers for what?

In her eagerness to learn what was going on, Kate went towards them, surprised to overhear the man remark, 'I assure you, most sincerely, ma'am, this is not a prank.'

Growing slightly concerned — but mainly taken by curiosity — she followed them out onto the drive. 'Is everything all right?' she asked, arriving at Naomi's side.

Naomi's face, when she turned to regard her, was one of amusement. 'It would seem that Papa has bought me a motorcar.'

Without meaning to, Kate laughed. 'A motorcar?'

'That natty little yellow one, apparently.'

With no idea what to say, Kate took a few steps towards it. With its folded down roof, polished brass lamps and yellow-rimmed wheels, it looked absurdly racy. She could only think that Mr Russell had taken leave of his senses. 'Heavens,' she eventually said, lost for a more suitable remark.

'Quite,' Naomi agreed, arriving to peer in at the tan buttoned-leather interior.

'Um, forgive me asking, madam,' the man ventured, drawing alongside them, his demeanour uneasy. 'But do you know how to *drive* a motor-car?'

'In London I drive an ambulance,' Naomi was quick to reply. 'And so I don't imagine this little thing will present me with too many problems.'

'Nevertheless, madam,' the man persisted, 'perhaps you would allow me to explain a few of the features to you.'

'By all means,' Naomi said, nudging Kate in the ribs. 'Please, do go ahead.'

'Yes. Well. Mrs Colborne, may I present to you the Humber Humberette, with its V-twin, 996cc shaft-drive engine, which you will quickly discover produces a more than respectable eight horsepower. Now, here you will see — '

'It's perfect, don't you think?' Naomi whispered. 'And typical of Papa to provide a solution to a problem I didn't yet know I had!' Problem she didn't know she had? What *was* Naomi on about? 'The small matter of how on earth we were going to get about while we're down here,' Naomi went on to explain. 'I confess I hadn't

142

given it a moment's thought. But this is perfect. So clever of Papa. This afternoon, I must telephone him to say thank you.'

'Happen I'll go and ask Edith to hold luncheon for a moment,' Kate said, wondering as to Mr Russell's sanity. 'While you make sure to follow what the man says.' If Naomi was hell-bent on accepting her father's outrageous gift, then she might as well know how to operate it safely.

Going back in through the porch door, she gave a rueful shake of her head. It *was* thoughtful of Mr Russell, she'd give him that much. Now they would be able to take little trips into Westward Quay. What a sight they would make — the two of them whizzing about unaccompanied in a canary yellow motorcar! That would cause some jaws to drop. She just wished that Luke could see them nipping about like it. Although, on second thoughts, perhaps not. Either way, at least now she had something to write and tell him. Yes, and maybe now, this summer wouldn't turn out to be quite so dull after all.

★   ★   ★

'Is it Rowley?'

From the window that looked out over the drive, Kate watched as a young man in uniform stepped down from the driver's seat of a large black motorcar, went around to open the rear door, and then assisted another young man who was clearly struggling to use one of his legs. 'Yes,'

143

she answered Ned's enquiry. 'I think it must be.'

'Do go out and greet him,' he urged her. 'I know without a moment's hesitation that you'll like him.'

Out in the hallway, Kate discovered that Naomi had beaten her to it, and was already greeting the new arrival. 'I am so very pleased to finally meet you, Lieutenant Rowley-King,' she was saying. 'Would you like me to bring you a chair?'

The young man shook his head. 'No, thank you, Mrs Colborne. If it's all the same to you, I should prefer to stand for a moment. I find that if I stay in one position for too long, my leg seizes up. And please, do call me Rowley — absolutely everyone does, even our squadron commander.' With that, Ellis Rowley-King turned back to his driver, now waiting in the porch.

'Shall I fetch in your luggage, sir?'

'Yes please, Private West.'

'Very well,' Naomi said. 'Rowley it is. And may I introduce to you my sister, Kate.'

'How do you do,' Lieutenant Rowley-King said, deftly switching the walking stick upon which he was leaning to his left hand and extending his right. 'Ned spoke about both of you — rather often, actually.'

Accepting Rowley's hand, Kate felt herself blushing. 'How do you do,' she confined herself to replying.

'Now, first things first,' Naomi went on. 'If I don't take you straight in to say hello to Ned, he will never forgive me. So, Kate, while I do that, would you offer the lieutenant's driver some refreshments? I'm sure he wouldn't say no to a

144

cup of tea and a piece of cake — or possibly something hot if it's not too late for Edith to rustle something up.'

'Yes, of course. I'll see to it.'

'Don't be afraid to tell him to take my luggage all the way to wherever it is to go,' Rowley said to her, before turning awkwardly to follow Naomi across the hall.

It wasn't until later, though, when their new guest had taken supper with Ned and she had gone into the study to clear the small table set up for them, that Kate had a proper chance to study Rowley's appearance. Her first thought upon meeting him had been that he was neatly-proportioned; neither short nor overly-tall, everything about him seeming in keeping. Now, with his airman's cap removed, she could see that his hair was an exceptionally dark brown and — today at least — unoiled and slightly curly. His eyebrows were particularly heavy, his face clean shaven — apart from a moustache of neat and modest proportions — and his eyes a true shade of brown. Earnest. Yes, if she had to sum up his appearance in just one word, that would be the one she would choose.

'I'm afraid I'm going to have to head for an early night,' the young man himself chose that moment to remark.

'Shan't think any the less of you for that,' Ned replied.

'Jolly good thing the drive up from Exeter was scenic, because it felt to be never ending.'

'You'll pretty soon discover,' Ned remarked, 'that there isn't a straight route from A to B in the whole of the county.'

'Not unlike Oxfordshire, then — except this seems a good deal more hilly.'

'And rather less civilised. Sorry, Kate.'

Catching his eye, she grinned. 'God's own country, this is. Ask anyone.'

'Anyway,' Rowley said. To Kate, he appeared to be trying to stifle a yawn. 'After so long in the motor this afternoon, I must at least take a few steps — perhaps outside if I may?'

When he struggled to get up from the chair, Kate fought back the urge to go to his aid. Was it the done thing, she wondered, or would he be offended? Would he ask for help if he needed it? Since it wasn't in her nature to watch anyone struggle with anything, perhaps, tomorrow, she should ask Nurse Hammond. She would know the right way to go about these things. With Ned, it had been different: that first day he had lowered his feet down from his bed, Nurse Hammond had already shown her how to stand the other side of him and take his weight as he leant on their arms. To see him shuffle even just that one step — ignoring that he had winced in pain and borne heavily down upon them — had been so reassuring. It was such a shame then, that even with the aid of two sticks and the exercises he did with Nurse Hammond every morning and evening, more than a week later, he could still only manage just that same single step. And, though she would never admit it to anyone, in her heart, she wasn't even sure that it was a proper step; she wasn't sure that his foot actually ever left the ground. Still, she reminded herself, it was early days yet — very early days. He would get there; one only had to look at Lieutenant Rowley-King to see what was possible.

'You might find the grass a bit wet,' she cautioned now, opening the French doors for him. 'But if you keep to this path,' she added, gesturing down to the ground, 'you can follow it all the way around the house.'

'Thank you,' he acknowledged her suggestion. 'But while I should dearly love to make a circuit of the house, I am nowhere close to managing that sort of distance yet. A couple of dozen steps is about all I shall manage, especially after all that travelling.'

Cursing her foolishness, Kate blushed. 'Forgive me. When I saw you walking from the car I thought — '

'Don't worry about it,' he said. 'Coming into the house under my own steam was a matter of pride. Two dozen steps is more than I could do a week ago. And if, every day that I am here, I add even just one further step to my total, I shall be more than pleased.'

'And if *I* ever manage even *half* a dozen,' Ned called after him. 'I can tell you now that I'll take them straight towards Father's best cognac in celebration.'

After that first evening, it felt to Kate as though Lieutenant Ellis Rowley-King — Rowley to everyone from Esme upwards — had always been there. Refined, nicely mannered, and quiet — but not so much that his presence could be overlooked — he seemed content to spend long spells sitting with Ned at the little table by the French doors in the study, their conversations wide-ranging, his influence upon Ned's spirits beyond doubt.

He also shared with Ned a determination to get better. Though it might take him several minutes — and a couple of stops on the way — he was soon able to negotiate without help, the staircase to the first floor followed by the short distance along the bachelors' corridor to his room. Downstairs, he was able to make his way about even better, albeit the effort required left him close to exhaustion. Moreover, in the following days, while Ned failed to increase the number of steps *he* was able to take, Rowley added first two or three to any attempt, and then five or six.

'Do you know much about birds, Kate?' he asked her one morning when she arrived bearing a tray containing a jug of fresh coffee and the barrel of biscuits. Setting it down, she waited for him to go on. 'Only, something keeps flitting about, catching insects and then darting into the grass at the base of that far hedge — small and brown and speckled. I rather imagine it to be feeding young.'

When he indicated where he meant, she followed the line of his finger. 'Meadow pipit?' she ventured. 'They like to hop about on the lawns. And they do build their nests on the ground.' Somehow, she sensed that her answer surprised him. That being the case, she redirected her attention to her tray.

'Meadow pipit, hm. That could be it.'

148

'Venture the other side of that hedge, where the land runs to the clifftop,' she said, 'and you'll likely see rock pipits, too.' Kate arranged their cups and saucers on the table.

'Really?'

To Kate, he now seemed genuinely interested. 'Yes. Though they might be larger than meadow pipits, they're also a good bit duller — a sort of light grey-brown. Less pretty, I think.'

'I've never seen one, though, I should very much like to.'

'There's not much Kate can't tell you about the flora and fauna down here,' Ned chipped in.

Bother him! Now she could feel Rowley eyeing her.

'Really?'

'I tell you no lies,' Ned went on, winking at her as she looked up. 'Go on, ask her something.'

Dismayed, Kate shook her head at him. 'If you're going to be mean, then tomorrow I shan't bring biscuits. Either that, or I shall leave them beyond your reach.'

'I meant it as a compliment,' he said. 'And anyway, you forget that Rowley can walk quite the distance now — especially if biscuits are involved.'

'But I doubt he'd want to walk all the way down to the pantry for them — especially not just so that you could wolf them all.'

To that, Ned roared with laughter. 'No, I daresay you're right.'

Being the centre of their attention was beginning to make Kate feel hot but, when she went to say something to deflect their interest in her, Rowley beat her to it.

'Choughs.'

'Choughs?' Ned repeated as they both turned to look at him.

'You told me to ask Kate something. So, my question is this — do you ever see choughs here?'

Slowly, she shook her head. 'Not no more, no. Pa Channer remembers them, but no one hereabouts has seen one for years.'

'Shame.'

'I've heard tell there's some in Cornwall.'

Their exchange about birds giving her an idea, she excused herself and went to the kitchen porch where she rummaged about in the boot cupboard. When that failed to throw up what she was seeking, she went to search about in the attic. Returning to the study later that afternoon, the item in question concealed behind her back, she found it difficult not to smile.

'Not seen any choughs yet, I suppose?' Ned greeted her arrival.

Still trying not to smile, she answered lightly. 'Sadly not. But I have found these.' Onto the table she placed an ancient set of field glasses. Then she stood back. 'Now maybe you'll spot some for yourself. At the very least, you should be able to study whatever it is that's nested by that hedge.'

Glancing to Rowley, she saw his face brighten.

'Golly,' Ned said, craning towards them. 'They look as though they saw the Boer War — the first one.'

'Doesn't matter,' Rowley remarked, lifting

150

them from the table. 'If they're not damaged then they'll do the job just fine. Thank you, Kate. These are quite brilliant. I shall enjoy seeing what I can spot.'

And in which case, Kate reflected, crawling about in the attic, getting covered in dust, had been worth it.

Over the following days, Ellis Rowley-King surprised everyone with his increasing mobility. On the stretch of path outside of the French windows, he walked with more and more confidence. He even announced that he felt ready to attempt a circuit of the house.

'But you're to do that only if you take someone with you,' Nurse Hammond instructed upon learning of his intention. 'A fall now would set you back weeks. And I'm sure you don't want that.'

'No, Nurse Hammond,' Rowley was quick to agree.

'I might not be responsible for your well-being, but I almost certainly would become so were you to injure yourself further. And I already have my hands full with your colleague here.'

'Yes, Nurse Hammond.' This time when he answered her, it was with a grin.

'Kate, will you go with him?'

Since it sounded rather more like a command than a request, Kate felt obliged to comply. 'If you're sure you're up to it,' she said, watching Rowley getting slowly to his feet.

'Certain of it,' he said. To Kate's mind, he seemed to be leaning too heavily on his stick to be ready to take on anything even close to the distance involved. On the other hand, she also knew just how many times he had walked back and forth along the same stretch of path. Moreover, this morning, there also seemed to be a new purpose about him. Belief — that was what she saw in his eyes. 'I have decided that today is the day. *Try and fail but never fail to try.*'

'John Quincy Adams,' Ned observed.

'That's right.'

'Very well,' she said, with not the least idea of who John Quincy Adams was. 'Then I shall come with you.'

When she reached to open back the door, he made his way towards it and then stepped carefully over the threshold and down onto the path.

'Nice afternoon,' he said as they set off.

'Yes,' she replied.

'I say, thank you for coming with me. It is my fervent hope that I don't need to lean upon you for support. For this to count for anything, I have to do it on my own.'

Despite his good intention their progress was ponderous, his limp pronounced and his need for his stick beyond doubt. In places along their route, foliage spilled from the border to almost completely obscure the little brick path and render it barely wide enough for them to walk side by side: circular leaves of lady's mantle sprouted from between the cracks; un-pruned lavender bushes, their centres grown ancient and woody, sent pale and flimsy new stems reaching towards the light; three-foot high delphiniums in need of staking teetered towards them, their spires of dark and perfectly round buds on the point of bursting open.

'Perhaps this isn't the best of paths for you,' she said, reaching to hold aside the wayward tendrils of a clematis.

'My mother loves these,' he said, nodding to it as they passed underneath, presumably ignoring her observation about the state of the path because he disagreed with it. 'When I was quite young, she planted a couple to scramble up through the apple trees in the orchard. A couple of years on, Father got really cross, claiming that her clematis were strangling his trees. One day, when she was out, he got the gardener to cut them down — her clematis, I mean — and dig out every last trace of the roots.'

'Goodness.' Not only did it sound a draconian thing to do, it also seemed underhand of him to go behind his wife's back. 'What did she say?'

He shook his head, his dismay apparent. 'They had the most awful row. It went on for days, neither of them speaking to the other. It was long vacs and I remember wishing I could go back to school. It was horrible.' Despite the slowness of their pace, he came to a halt and arched his back. 'Trouble with a stick,' he said, briefly lifting his cane and waving it in front of him, 'is that you start to lean on it.'

Unable to help it, she laughed. 'I should have thought that was the point of it.'

He sighed. 'Well, yes. But what I mean is that after a while, when my leg stiffens and tires and doesn't want to go any further, the whole

153

business of walking becomes so very wearying that I start to double over. And Nurse Hammond says I must try to remain upright at all times.'

She glanced ahead of them; they had yet to reach the first corner of the house. 'Should we turn back?' she said. 'Or rest up a moment?'

'No, thank you. Shortly now I'll find my rhythm.'

Eventually reaching the first corner, they followed the path around, the steps up onto the terrace appearing ahead of them. At the sight of them, he came to a halt.

'We could cross onto the lawn and take a longer route — miss the terrace altogether,' she suggested.

'No, if you don't mind me resting upon your arm, I think I can manage them,' he replied. 'After all, I manage the stairs.'

She nodded and, offering her arm, felt him bear heavily upon it. 'There's only five of them anyway,' she said. 'And they're quite shallow.'

At the top of the short flight, they paused again. 'I've lost my bearings,' he said, looking up to the sky. 'Which way are we facing?'

'This side of the house gives south,' she said.

'Towards Cornwall?'

'That's right.'

'But the sea . . . ' he began, turning about. 'Is that way?'

'To the west of us, yes.'

'I find something about being on the north coast disorienting,' he remarked.

She smiled. 'I suppose I'm used to it.'

Once again straightening up, he looked along

the terrace. 'Right-ho then. Onward we go.'

'Where is home for you?' she asked as they set off again. 'What I mean is, where is your family?'

'Just outside of Oxford.' Realizing that he was still resting upon her arm, and since it seemed important to him that he did this without help, she very slowly lowered it such that he let go. 'My father lectures in government and politics. The university is where he met my mother.'

'Oh.'

'At the time, she was a junior research assistant and, one day, coming across her in the library, he asked her to go to the opera with him. She said no. He kept asking though until, one day, she relented. Then, of course, they married, and she had us.'

'Us?'

'Oh, yes, I have two sisters, both older than me. Both married.'

'Oh.'

Looking ahead, she realized that they were now approaching the end of the terrace and another short flight of steps, this time back down to the path.

'I'll take these on my own,' he said to her. 'Going down is rather easier than going up.'

From there, they walked through the gravelled courtyard, the stables and workshops away to their right.

'Big place this, isn't it?' he remarked, seeming to take it all in.

Watching the slow movement of his feet, she shrugged. 'Since I grew up here, I suppose I don't really notice.'

'But now you're in London.'

She nodded. 'Yes.'

'Quite the change.'

'Yes.'

'Forgive me. I'm interrogating you.'

With a smile, she shook her head. 'No, it's all right. My . . . situation is a bit . . . odd.'

'And not mine to probe,' he replied. At the next corner, they stood for a moment and looked along the front of the house. 'Almost three-quarters of the way.'

'Almost.'

From there, they walked on in silence, passing the front porch, then the window to the study. Turning the final corner, they arrived back at the French doors.

'I was on the point of mounting a search party,' Ned greeted their return.

'No need,' Rowley said, tossing aside his stick and collapsing into a chair. 'It might have taken me an inordinately long time — given the relatively short distance, but at least I made it.'

'Well done. Good for you. At this rate, you'll be back in the air in no time.'

Watching for Rowley's response, Kate saw him shrug. 'Won't be down to me, will it? That will be down to some desk-bound sort, some fellow whose feet have never left the ground and who has no idea whatsoever of what being up there entails.'

'Even so,' Ned said, his tone solemn. 'You'll be back in the air weeks before I am. Maybe even months.'

To hear them talking about returning to flying made Kate stiffen. Given what had happened to the pair of them, she didn't like to think of them having to go back at all. If it was Luke, hearing him talk of returning would fill her with dread. She couldn't bear to think about it even now — and Luke hadn't even been injured.

Inwardly, she sighed. In truth, she should be grateful that young men like these were prepared to *go* back — that they didn't want to take the cosy way out, remain at home and leave the task to someone else. After all, from what she was able to understand of it, this war was still some way off being won.

Yes, and until it *was* won, Luke would *never* be back where he belonged. And she would never properly know marriage — or motherhood. So, tonight, when she said her prayers, she would offer up thanks for the continued courage and the bravery of young men everywhere — Luke and Mr Lawrence, and Ned and this nice man Rowley included.

7

Rowley

'Blessed with this weather, aren't we?'

In response to Rowley's observation, Kate cast her eyes to the sky: forget-me-not blue, and unbroken by even the merest wisp of cloud. It was the sort of day when poplin dresses replaced skirts and blouses, and straw hats became necessary to take just a few steps out of doors. Even Rowley had jettisoned his pullover and rolled back the cuffs of his shirt sleeves.

'We are,' she replied. 'I hope it holds a while longer.'

It was after luncheon one afternoon and the two of them were crossing the lawn beneath the terrace, Rowley hobbling and still reliant upon his stick but nevertheless keeping up with her gentle pace. With a week now having passed since his first *sortie* around the house — as he referred back to it — she suspected that he no longer needed someone to accompany him 'just in case', but she went with him anyway and resisted pointing it out.

'You know, I'd give anything to have this house in *my* family,' he said, gesturing towards it as they walked on.

With his comment seeming to come from nowhere, she wondered what had spurred it. 'You would?'

'Goodness, yes. Beautiful gardens, rolling countryside — '

'And you say that without even having been down to the cove yet!'

' — wildlife to observe. It's such a shame I don't have my notebook. It was with my kit where we were billeted in Sussex, which hasn't caught up with me yet — despite my writing to request that they send it on to me.'

She offered him a sympathetic smile. 'That's a shame. Where were you taken to hospital — after the crash, I mean?'

'Folkestone. It wasn't too bad. Couple of other RFC chaps there. By comparison to them I was lucky — just one clean fracture to the bottom of my shin bone. I felt it crack as I hit the ground. I remember the pain, and laying there trying to get my wits together. Eventually, I started to crawl towards where Ned was in the wreckage — you know, to see how he'd fared and try to help him, but others got to him first. Apparently, the farmer's boy had seen us coming down and had gone for help.'

Knowing *precisely* how Ned had fared, she tried to stop herself from picturing the scene. 'He was proper lucky. You both were.'

'Lucky or unlucky? Depends on your view. We were barely three miles from an airfield. When she first started to splutter, we both thought she had it in her to stay up just long enough for us to make it there. But then she started to drop too quickly,' he said with a shrug of his shoulders. 'Anyway, as our squadron commander is forever pointing out, any landing you

159

can make is a good landing.'

'Yes,' she said. 'I suppose it is.'

'And, since we both survived to tell the tale, then he must be right.'

'Yes,' she agreed again.

'And your husband?' he asked after a while. 'Where is he serving at the moment?'

'France.' Oddly, on that bright afternoon in early summer, she felt closer to him than she had in a long time. Perhaps it was because she was back in Woodicombe, where her memories of him were strongest anyway. 'He's been there throughout. 'Course, I only have his word for it. As Naomi pointed out a while back, they could be almost anywhere. As family, we'd be the last to know.'

They walked on, the copse ahead of them filled with birdsong, from among which she could pick out the warbling of a chaffinch.

'What does he do?' he asked.

'He's a driver. Being able to drive something — anything, I think — was what made him so eager to join up. Mr Lawrence — Naomi's husband — spoke for him. They went out there together.'

'That's good.'

'It is, yes. It made it — '

'I say, listen . . . '

Stopping in her tracks, she fell still. 'Cuckoo,' she said, the sound of it on the warm air lazy and muffled.

'Calling quite slowly, too,' he observed, straightening up to listen.

'Not surprising,' she said. 'We *are* in June now.'

'Good heavens, yes, I forget that. Being laid up has completely thrown my sense of the seasons.'

'*The cuckoo comes in April, Sings his song in May, He changes his tune in the middle of June* — '

'*And then he flies away.*'

'You know it, too,' she said, regarding him with surprise. 'I always thought it was just one of Ma Channer's old rhymes. Confess to being a-fret over something and she's certain to have some or other piece of lore to cheer you up.'

'*Ne'er cast a clout*, and all that?'

She smiled. 'For certain that's one of them, yes.' Close now to the edge of the copse, they drew to a halt. 'As soon as you're up to it, you should make a point of following this path down to the cove,' she said, gazing through the birch trees into the sun-dappled green of the woodland. 'If you like it up here, you're bound to like it down there.'

'Are there rockpools?'

'At low tide, right down by the water line there are. Above that, though, it's sand.'

'I hope to be here long enough to see it,' he said, his eagerness apparently genuine.

When they had stood for a while, listening to birdsong and soaking up the warmth, she turned to look back at the house. 'We've been gone quite a while,' she felt moved to point out. 'And you've still got to walk all the way back.'

The sigh he gave was a wistful one. 'Shame I can't manage a little further. The woods look lovely.'

In that moment, Kate felt a sort of ache in her

chest: a pining; a melancholy. It caught her off-guard. 'The woods *are* lovely,' she said softly. 'There's deer and badgers — if you know where to look for them. And squirrels. And the nests of just about every woodland bird you can think of.'

'Sounds enchanting.'

'It is. Though happen I didn't realize it until now.'

With his head held at an angle, he stood for a moment, appearing to reflect. 'I fear it is all too common a failing of human nature not to appreciate a thing until we no longer have it.'

'Yes,' she agreed but, not wanting to spoil such a fine afternoon with maudlin thoughts, she gestured back across the lawn. 'Shall we?'

'Given the distance we've covered, I suppose it would be wise.'

As they retraced their path, their original footsteps through the grass still visible, his progress was more laboured than when they had set out. Indeed, by the time they reached the house, his pace had slowed considerably, his injured leg struggling to even drag his foot over the flagstones. And, when the doors to the study — flung wide for the air — came into view, he stopped altogether and turned towards her.

'I hope you're not over tired,' she said, thinking him about to confess to that very fact.

'I will admit to being rather weary. Glorious though it is, this heat doesn't help.'

Puzzled that he seemed reluctant to take what had to be less than a dozen paces back to the doors, she agreed. 'No, I'll warrant it doesn't.'

'Look, Kate,' he said, leaning so heavily upon

his stick that he appeared lopsided — one of his shoulders a lot lower than the other and a look of discomfort on his face. 'I hope you won't think this a terrible imposition, but do you think I might ask a favour of you?'

'Of course.'

'Do you think you might acquire for me a notebook and pencil? There are so many unusual things to see here that it seems a crime not to jot some of them down — make a few sketches, even.'

'I can do that,' she replied, flattered that she should be the one he asked. 'If there's not already a notepad in the house somewhere, I'll fetch you one from the stationers in the village. You might have to wait a few days, but I won't forget.'

'Thank you. Being able to note down some sightings would be great.'

'Then I'll see what I can do.'

★ ★ ★

As luck would have it, the following day, Naomi proposed going into the village. 'I've a *stack* of letters to send,' she complained. Seated at the breakfast table, she had been trying to coax Esme to eat her boiled egg. 'No, not like that, darling. Dip the soldiers in nicely,' she urged, pushing her daughter's plate closer to the edge of the table. 'Just lately, I've fallen terribly behind with my correspondence. But, these last few days, with some time on my hands, I've finally been able to catch up.'

163

'In which case, I hope you're feeling wealthy,' Kate replied.

'Wealthy?'

'Price of a stamp has gone up — from a penny to a penny-ha'penny.'

'It has? Oh well, like the rising cost of everything else, there's not much we can do about it, is there? Letters must be written. Anyway, is there anything you would like me to bring back for you? Or would you like to come with me?'

'If it's all right, I'll come with you.'

'Very well. I shall aim to leave around ten.'

For Kate, whizzing along in the little yellow motorcar proved both exhilarating and terrifying at the same time. The weather still being fine and warm, Naomi had insisted on folding down the roof, the sensation of the air rushing past only adding to the petrifying sensation of speed. And, despite having secured her straw hat with a scarf tied under her chin, she felt obliged to keep it pressed to her head with her hand — just in case.

'This isn't an ambulance, you know,' she shouted at one point, the hedgerows feeling precariously close to her arm. 'We're not making one of your emergency dashes!'

'I've never driven an ambulance at anywhere near this speed!' Naomi shouted back. 'Too much traffic always. This is much more fun!'

Watching Naomi tug on the steering wheel to avoid a particularly treacherous rut, Kate found herself drawing away from the door. If Naomi struck one of the hedge-banks, they would have

164

need of an ambulance themselves.

On the outskirts of the village, Naomi finally slowed the little motor to a more sedate pace, and Kate dared to remove her hand from where she had been clutching at her hat. 'No doubt we will cause quite the stir anyway — without having to speed past,' she said as they trundled along by Church Green. 'Two women out alone in a bright yellow motorcar.' And she wasn't wrong. Despite it not yet being the height of the holiday season, the village was busy and, from the pavement, everyone who noticed them seemed to do the same thing — turn back for a second look as though witnessing something that couldn't possibly be. 'Do you think Mr Russell chose this colour on purpose,' she turned to ask Naomi as they continued on towards the quayside, the body of the little car rattling over the cobbles. She couldn't make up her mind what she felt most — pride at being out unescorted, or embarrassment at drawing such attention. Judging by the expressions on the faces of some of the pedestrians, their *London ways* — as they would no doubt be denounced — were already beyond the pale.

'He told me he left that to the man at the garage,' Naomi replied. To Kate, she couldn't have looked less concerned by all the attention, appearing girlish and carefree. Light-hearted. 'I'm rather pleased he chose this colour, especially since the alternatives were apparently maroon, tan or dark blue.'

Maroon and tan sounded masculine and unremarkable. But the dark blue, well, she imagined that would look refined: 'understated', to use one of Naomi's own expressions; everything, in fact, that this yellow — a match for the colour of yarrow, or the flash on the wing of a goldfinch — most definitely wasn't.

'Dull,' she said, deciding not to disagree.

'Quite.'

When Naomi eventually brought the vehicle to a halt across the street from the post office, and they both climbed down, Kate realized that the looks they were drawing divided into type according to the sex of the onlooker. While the women frowned and hurried on past — or avoided looking altogether — the men made no attempt to disguise their fascination, their expressions betraying one of several things: astonishment that the little vehicle should have no male driver; downright envy; or something altogether more lascivious.

'The men all think you're fast,' she whispered as they crossed the street; *fast* being a word she had read in one of Naomi's cast-off magazines.

'The men can all think what they like,' Naomi replied, bowling in through the door of the post office to send the little bell into a frenzied tinkling and bring stares from the half-dozen faces within. 'Bother,' she said as her eyes fell on the queue of people ahead of her. 'We'll be here for ever. And I want to go to the chemist after this.'

'Well,' Kate said, counting five people already in the queue and determining to head off any unnecessarily loud moaning about 'country ways', 'if you can just wait a moment while I pick out a notebook for Rowley and a packet of envelopes for myself, I'll queue for your stamps while you go on to the chemist. How many do you need?'

'A dozen,' Naomi said, opening her purse and fishing about for coins. 'Although, if it's always like this in here, you might as well make it two dozen and be done with.'

The notebook chosen — a pocket-sized moleskin one with narrow-ruled pages — Kate resigned herself to waiting. As it turned out, the delay was no more than ten minutes and when she went back out onto the street, it was to find Naomi already back at the motor, staring out across the harbour, her pale grey skirt flapping about her legs and her flowery blouse rippling in the breeze.

'All done,' she said, arriving alongside her.

'You would think, wouldn't you, that with all the changes this war has brought on, people would be a little harder to shock.' Naomi remarked, turning to look at her.

Deciding not to ask her what Naomi had done to raise eyebrows, she opened the passenger door and climbed up onto the seat. 'This is Devon,' she said drily. '*North* Devon, at that. Most folk up here will never journey beyond Barnstaple — if they even get *that* far. Truly,' she said, when, climbing up beside her, Naomi frowned, 'they believe everyone beyond here — especially down in places like Torquay — is racy. So, the sight of a lady getting down from a motorcar, having driven it here on her own, let alone cranking it started all by herself — '

167

'Well how else is one supposed to start it?' Naomi wanted to know, reaching to let off the brake lever and then squeezing the bulb horn to signal to the crowded quayside that she was pulling away.

Dismayed that Naomi had so little grasp of just how backward attitudes in North Devon really were — the true extent of which she herself had only come to discover upon moving to London — she shook her head. 'Folk down here would maintain that *you're* not supposed to be starting it at all.'

'Preposterous,' Naomi countered, turning the little motor in a large circle and then pointing it in the direction from whence they had come. 'What on earth would they say if they knew that in town, I drive an ambulance.'

Hastily throwing her scarf over her hat and then tying it under her chin, Kate again shook her head, her cause a lost one. 'But folk here *don't* know that.'

'Then the next time someone stares at me, I shall tell them.'

Determined not to rise to Naomi's bait, Kate sat staring ahead. 'As you wish.'

Once they had driven back past Church Green, and were heading away up the hill, Naomi turned briefly towards her. 'What do you think of Rowley?'

For some reason, Kate felt herself blushing. 'He seems very nice,' she said, wondering at Naomi's reason for asking.

'I think so too. Nicely mannered. But then I suppose with academics for parents, he would

168

be. That said, I have come across some terribly opinionated and boorish sorts from those scholarly families.'

'Oh?'

'He's doing well, though, isn't he — Rowley, I mean? He seems able to walk quite the distance now.'

'Yes,' she agreed, raising her voice to be heard as they gathered speed. 'He seems very determined.'

'Unfortunately, determination alone would appear to be no guarantee of success,' Naomi replied, slowing a little as the lane narrowed to pass between two cottages. 'The single-mindedness on Ned's face when he is helped to his feet is unmissable, and yet he still doesn't seem able to take more than a single step.'

No, that much she'd seen for herself. 'I suppose it's going to take time,' she said.

With the lane in front of them opening out once again, Naomi changed gear and the little motor began to regain speed. 'I suppose.'

'We have to remember that his legs were in that traction device for ages. Nurse Hammond says it is going to take a while to build them up again. She says all he needs is nourishment, exercise and patience.'

'I know. I also know that she's seen this before, and so I do try not to worry.'

'But you worry anyway.' It was only natural, she reminded herself; she worried too, not that it would help Naomi to know that.

'I do. Although I try not to show it in front of Ned.'

'No. We must have a care to always sound encouraging.'

'That's right,' Naomi agreed.

Yes, Kate thought as, ahead of them, and between a blur of green hedgerows, the dip down into Woodicombe came into sight. Worries that Ned might never walk again were something she would be best advised to keep to herself. And, while doing so, hope to be proved wrong.

★ ★ ★

A letter from Luke!

Back at home after their bone-jarring ride, the sight of an envelope on the hall table had made Kate gasp with delight. Having snatched it up from the salver, and grinning with joy at the discovery, she had stolen into the drawing room, crossed to the window seat at the far end and torn open the flimsy brown envelope to scan his words. Then, satisfied that it didn't start with news that would confirm her greatest fears, such as *I have been injured* or *I am in hospital,* she relaxed her arms, sat down, and read on at a more sedate speed.

My Dearest Kate.

Thank you so much for your last letter. It arrived here today. You can't imagine how pleased it made me to learn that you are safely back at Woodicombe. Though we are the ones out here fighting this war, we seldom get told much of how it is going. But we do hear of when something happens in

London, and I don't mind saying how shook we always are to learn of Zeppelin raids and bombs upon our capital city and of ordinary folk getting hurt. So I shall rest more easy now, knowing that you are back home in Devon and out of harm's way. Besides, it is easier for me to picture you there, since I know what it all looks like and the sort of things you will be doing.

I am going along fine enough. A few days back, we met up with a battalion of Americans. They don't half talk funny, and have the cheek to say the same of us! They all seemed like nice lads, though.

Reading his words, Kate smiled. Dear Luke. He could make friends with anyone.

Word came the other day for my pal, Sam. A while back he had some home leave and now his wife writes to him that he is to be a father. I cannot begin to tell you how joyed he is. The babe is due in the autumn, another reason, as he said, for this sorry shambles to be over, and for us all to return home. You know me, Kate, I'm not one for envy but his news fair turned me green. I miss you so much and although I want nothing more than to be home with you again, I also long for us to know happiness like Sam's. When we talked of children one time, you said you would like two boys and two girls. I pray that one day soon we will be so richly blessed.

171

Lowering the sheet of paper, Kate frowned. *Four* children? She didn't remember saying *that*! The prospect of such a thing nevertheless making her smile, she read on.

Anyhow. I must end here. Please write back soon. May God keep you safe and well. Your loving husband Luke.

Feeling how her throat had tightened, she bit on her bottom lip. But it did no good whatsoever, tears still reducing everything in front of her to a blurry mess.

In despair at her own foolishness, she shook her head. How daft to get upset by the news that her husband wanted nothing more than to come home and start a family! Given the amount of suffering and loss and hardship there was these days, it was a ridiculous thing to cry over, especially since the very thought of such a thing left her brimful of happiness.

* * *

'Thank you again for going to the trouble of getting me the notebook.'

It was later that afternoon, and Kate was once again accompanying Rowley as they took their now customary route across the lawn.

'Glad to be of help,' she replied.

'Fortunately, my mother finally sent on my spare spectacles.'

She smiled. 'That's good.'

'I really only need them for maps — or things

where the writing is tiny or faint.'

'I see.'

'Golly, it's good to be able to get out,' he went on, drawing a deep breath down into his chest. 'I have no idea how Ned manages — stuck inside all the time.'

'Nor do I,' she replied, her earlier conversation with Naomi coming back to mind. 'It must be awful for him.'

'I'd be climbing the walls.'

At the thought of him trying to do just that, she smiled. She knew what he meant, though. 'Me too.'

'He is dreadfully frustrated, you know.'

When he turned to look at her, she nodded. 'It must be real hard for him, seeing you up and about again, and making such strong progress.'

'It is, I know it for a fact. I might be hobbling, and I might still find it enormously tiring, but at least every day I do seem to manage a little further — or to walk a little more easily. Whereas Ned . . . '

'He mustn't get angry with himself,' she said, picturing her twice-daily attempts with Nurse Hammond to get him on his feet. Each time they helped him move from the side of his bed into a standing position, his face twisted with the effort of willing his legs to move. But then, when his feet did nothing but remain rooted to the floor, his look of determination quickly faded to one of frustration, hotly followed by despair — and, increasingly, she had noticed these last few times, by the stirrings of anger.

'Do you have time enough to keep going as far

as those birch trees?' Rowley asked, lifting his walking cane just high enough from the ground to gesture ahead of them to the edge of the copse.

On his forehead, she noticed, were tiny beads of perspiration. 'Of course,' she said. 'If you think you can manage it. It is rather warm.'

'It is rather. But if we could make it over there,' he said, gesturing again. 'We could perch a moment on one of those stumps. I could catch my breath, sit a while with these field glasses and see — although, no, you won't want to wait around. You'll want to get back. Of course you will.'

With a smile, she shook her head. 'Truth to tell, I wouldn't mind sitting out here a while — unless you'd prefer to be by yourself.'

From his expression, she read genuine surprise.

'Good God, no. I've had quite enough of my own company. Please, do stay. With any luck, I might spot something I need you to identify for me.'

And so, having helped him to lower himself onto the largest of several tree stumps, she chose one of the others and, brushing at its surface, sat down. A couple of feet away from her, he raised the field glasses to his eyes and then scanned slowly from left to right.

'Anything?' she asked after a moment.

'Not a thing,' he said, lowering the glasses to his lap.

'Wrong time of day,' she surmised. 'Warmest part of the afternoon, when all but the hungriest

174

of souls are hidden away, dozing, their heads tucked under their wings.'

'Either that,' he said, his face breaking into a grin, 'or word went around that some fool was out with a pair of field glasses and that, just for devilment, all birds should take cover.'

'That's also possible,' she agreed with a laugh.

And so they sat for a while, the dappled shade making the heat a little less unbearable, the silence between them comfortable.

With the glorious spell of warmth persisting into the following days, though, taking his daily stroll seemed to leave Rowley even more weary than usual. And so it was that on one afternoon later that week, after idly noticing the pool of blue shadow cast on the front lawn by the cedar tree, Kate persuaded Mr Channer to unearth from the stables some lawn chairs, along with a couple of little round tables and the two remaining steamer chairs that had once belonged to Mrs Latimer. From indoors, she then brought cushions, and dragged the whole lot into something resembling a circle.

'There,' she said when she had finished. Despite having been working in the shade, she felt a good deal hotter and stickier than when she had started.

'I feel such a cad,' Rowley replied, having watched her at work. 'Seeing you puffing like that makes me feel utterly useless.'

'I doubt you will feel that way for much longer,' she said, plumping a cushion and setting it on one of the chairs for him. 'You'll be back to normal soon, mark my words. Even so, you might find these seats too uncomfortable to sit for any real length of time.'

'To be out here, I'll put up with it,' he said, lowering himself cautiously onto one of them. 'In any event, being banged up like this has taught me the true meaning of discomfort, not to mention about the goodness of other people — and how there is always someone worse off than oneself — no matter how much one might not think so.'

Satisfied that he was genuinely comfortable, and noticing how, almost the moment he settled, his eyes started to close, Kate reached into her wicker basket and set out her writing materials on the adjacent table. Then she unscrewed the lid to her bottle of ink and opened her notepad, this being her first chance to write back to Luke.

My Dearest Husband, she wrote.

Thank you for your letter. If I have been a mite neglectful with my own of late, please do forgive me. Though I am rarely needed in the kitchen — except to wash up — and need only do a small amount of the cleaning, somehow, I am still kept real busy. Apart from the study for Lt. Russell, and bedrooms for each of us, the only other room we have opened up is the drawing room, though hardly do no one have the time to make use of it. Also, and this will make you smile, we take our meals all together in the staff hall. That is Naomi's doing. Sometimes, with all of the dust sheets everywhere, it do feel like we are camping inside the house but, as Naomi says, it makes for less work.

Today is the finest day of summer yet. It is so warm that to walk across the grass is to grow sticky in no more than a half-dozen strides and to imagine you can see a pond shimmering on the old croquet lawn. This very moment, I am sitting under the cedar tree. Lt. Rowley-King has brought out field glasses and a notebook to keep his Nature Notes but has fallen asleep. Esme is indoors having a nap and I think Naomi is reading to Ned. Unlike Lt. Rowley-King, Ned does not make good progress at all. But I am sure it is just a matter of time.

Dipping the nib of her pen into the ink, she paused. Then, seeing Naomi looking out through the French doors, she decided to bring her letter to a close.

I hope the weather is good where you are and that you are safe. I have not read so much news of the war lately. Down here it do still seem very distant. Either way, I hope it is nearly won now and that, as you say, you will soon be coming home. It was indeed good news for your friend, Sam. And yes, I hope that we shall one day know that joy too. God bless for now. Your loving wife, Kate.

'Well, this all looks very civilised.'
Setting aside her pen, Kate looked up to see

Naomi standing with her hands on her hips as she surveyed the arrangement of the chairs.

She smiled. 'It seemed the shadiest place within easy reach of the house.'

'Well done. Quite brilliant.'

Across from them, Rowley stirred. Sitting up and looking about, he grimaced. 'Please tell me I haven't been asleep.'

Neither woman wanting to embarrass him, both simply smiled.

'Shame there is no way to get Ned out here,' Naomi remarked, glancing back towards the windows of the study. 'He looks so terribly pale — ' But then, as though struck by an idea, she threw up her hands. 'But of course! If he's not ready to come out here under his own steam yet, then we should get him a wheelchair!'

With some difficulty, Rowley was now raising himself up from where he had become slumped into his seat. 'Would he use it, do you think? He can be terribly stubborn.'

'To be able to get out here, I think he might,' Naomi replied, and she started to retrace her steps across the lawn. 'I'm going to telephone Cousin Elizabeth,' she announced over her shoulder. 'See if she can tell me how to go about acquiring one.'

* * *

Cousin Elizabeth being endlessly resourceful, no one was in the least surprised when, two days later, a van arrived and, from the back, a wheelchair was unloaded.

'Through here, please,' Naomi instructed the driver as Kate stood looking on.

Even Nurse Hammond was impressed. 'Nice and sturdy,' she said, looking it over. 'Unused, I would say.'

But Kate couldn't help thinking that more than anything, Ned looked disheartened.

'Thanks, Min. You didn't also happen to requisition two new legs while you were at it, did you?'

'It's only to get you outside while the weather's nice,' Naomi replied, her tone the one she adopted when she was not in the mood to be thwarted.

'Daylight and a little sunshine can only aid recovery,' Nurse Hammond supported her remark. 'Hard though it might be to credit, sunlight has vitamins that help the growth and repair of bones.'

'Vitamin D,' Naomi piped up.

Nurse Hammond seemed surprised. 'Vitamin D, that's right.'

'The only drawback, I'm afraid,' Naomi went on, 'is that when you want to wheel him out, you will have to come along the hallway and out through the porch. It's the only doorway without a step.'

'So, Lieutenant Russell,' Nurse Hammond turned to him to say, 'how about, after luncheon, we try it out? I see that some chairs have been set up on the lawn. Now you will be able to join in.'

'If you truly think it will help,' Ned said with a dismayed shake of his head. 'Then I will sit in all the sunshine I can get.'

By mid-afternoon, the lawn had become home to quite a gathering. Having carried out even more cushions from the drawing room, and with the steamer chair eventually padded to her liking, Naomi lay reclined upon it. Kate occupied a chair nearby, and alongside her sat Rowley. To his left was Ned, his wheelchair just in the sunshine, while in the shade sat Nurse Hammond with her knitting. Having wheeled Ned across the gravel, she had been going to return indoors, but Naomi had bid her stay.

'Truly, Nurse Hammond,' she had said, 'place a chair somewhere of your choosing if you would prefer not to be part of this little circle. But I would venture that *you* could do with some daylight almost as much as Ned.'

With a smile, Nurse Hammond had complied. And, on a rug in front of everyone, sat Esme, keeping up a soft but continual conversation with several of her dolls.

It was an arrangement that was to be repeated the following afternoon, and again the day after that. Sometimes, soporific from the heat, they would all simply sit making the odd observation; other times, they would read or write letters. Sometimes, Ned would tell Esme a story, it never occurring to the little girl to ask why he didn't sit in the spare chair or join her down on the rug. For the most part, Rowley kept up a vigil for birds, occasionally exclaiming at something he had seen, or making notes in his book.

'Aha,' he chose that moment to announce, and

with which Kate turned to see where he was indicating. 'A jay. In that leaf litter under those trees. Do you see it?'

She nodded. Not so long ago, leaf litter on the lawn would have been unheard of, the leaves being swept up almost before they'd had the chance to touch the ground. Staring across there now, though, she could see that no one had been out with a broom since last autumn at least, the boy who had once worked the grounds having long since received his call-up papers.

'Whenever I hear a jay calling,' she said, bringing her mind back to the matter of the bird, 'I always think it sounds as though a jackdaw and a seagull had raised a half-breed. You know, a sort of cackle-cackle followed by a long wail.'

'Can't say I've been lucky enough to hear one,' he said. 'But I'll write that down, if I may.'

Feeling herself blushing, she shrugged. 'Hear one for yourself and you might disagree with me.'

His reply came without him even looking up from his notebook. 'I highly doubt it.'

From thereon, and while the weather continued to permit, it seemed quite natural that, once out under the cedar tree, they remain there to take their afternoon tea: Kate wheeling a trolley containing everything they needed as far as the front door and Naomi helping her to ferry the contents to the tables.

'What on earth would your mother say?' Kate whispered one afternoon as they made their way across the lawn, each carrying plates of sandwiches and cake. 'Salmon and cucumber, and egg and cress,' she announced as she set down the first of hers.

'Lemon Madeira,' Naomi said of her cargo, 'and scones. Jam to follow.'

'Along with napkins and cutlery,' Kate added as they turned back towards the house. Catching Ned's eye, she went on, 'So don't nobody help themselves yet.'

'Mamma would turn white,' Naomi replied to her question from earlier. 'She would affect to feel faint and accuse me of having taken complete leave of my senses.'

'Leave of your senses about what in particular?' she asked as they reached the porch and she lifted from the trolley the tray containing the plates, cups and saucers. At Mabel's advice, they had left the Royal Worcester indoors and had brought instead the rather sturdier stoneware from the staff parlour. 'With this war on,' Mabel had opined, 'who knows if we would ever be able to match the pattern were there to be a mishap.'

'What?' Naomi asked.

'What would bother your mother the most — our choice of chinaware? Our inviting Nurse Hammond to join us? Or our leaving the crusts on the sandwiches — '

'I've told you, I won't have us wasting bread,' Naomi remarked, picking up the basket of cutlery and napkins. 'Not when the flour to make it is so hard to come by. I especially don't want Esme to grow up thinking it acceptable to be wasteful.'

' — or would it be the sight of her daughter

having to fill in for a butler that would drain the colour from her cheeks?'

At that, Naomi erupted into laughter. 'That, and the fact that her daughter has been inappropriately dressed in her tea gown since breakfast, I should think.'

'Well, that too, yes.'

'And anyway, if I am the butler, you must be the footman.'

'For certain,' she said as they made their way back to the circle of chairs. '*Senior* footman, of course. Wouldn't raise a single eyebrow round here, though — *my* folk are used to seeing me scurrying about with a tray of crockery.'

Their tea taken, the individuals in the little gathering fell into a state of gentle contemplation. Rowley, Kate noticed, was still staring across to where he had earlier seen the jay. In comparison to Ned, he seemed such an intense young man, his frown often so deep that his dark brows appeared almost to join in the middle. And, when he was wearing his spectacles, a very bookish air came over him.

She glanced again to his face. One day, purely to satisfy her curiosity — and no more — she would try to find out how old he was. From his appearance alone it was hard to tell, almost anything above twenty and less than thirty seeming possible.

When she came across him the next afternoon, he was seated in the same chair, this time reading the *Telegraph*.

'Ned not come out yet?' she asked when, looking up and seeing her, he struggled to get to his feet. She did wish he wouldn't bother getting up on her account. But, by now, she knew that politeness was in his bones, and that he would simply ignore any and all suggestions from her that he not get up.

'He asked Nurse Hammond to do some extra exercises with him,' he said. 'Won't you take a seat?'

With a smile, she sat down. 'And you?' she asked, tidying the fabric of her frock over her legs. 'Have you been for your walk?'

He gave his newspaper a shake. 'I have. I had intended trying to go a little further today. But, when it came down to it, I didn't feel I had it in me. I think I made it there and back quicker, though. I do miss my proper wristwatch — the one with the second hand. I could do with it to time myself. Unfortunately, it got smashed when we crash landed.' Reading from his face his disappointment, she sensed that the watch had been important to him. 'It was a present from my Godfather upon my twenty-first birthday,' he explained. 'I do still have it but fear it will be beyond repair.'

She pressed her lips into a sympathetic smile. 'That's a shame.'

'Who knows, once this war is over and it doesn't seem such a trifling thing, perhaps I shall see what can be done for it.'

When he looked at her somewhat sadly, she again smiled. 'I think you should do that. You should at least *try* to get it fixed.' At that moment glimpsing large lettering across one of the pages of his newspaper, she nodded towards it. 'Any news worth hearing of?'

'About the war?'

She nodded. 'No sign that victory is in the offing I suppose?'

Though she had said it largely in jest, he let out a long sigh. 'While I wouldn't want to raise anyone's hopes, reading some of the opinions expressed here today, I am led to thinking that perhaps we are closer than we have ever been.'

Startled, she drew a quick breath. 'You mean . . . it could all be over soon?'

Suddenly, he looked less certain — uneasy, even. 'I suppose what I really meant is that for the best part of a year now, and with the situation in stalemate, the Germans do seem to be losing their appetite for it.'

'Oh.' Not *quite* so hopeful, then.

'You see, some time back, the Kaiser decreed that if they couldn't crush the British Army, then they would crush the spirit of her people.'

'*Us*? They would crush *our* spirit? How did they mean to do that?'

'Well,' he said, the deep furrow once again back to his brow, 'the actual words of the Kaiser were something along the lines of, 'we will starve the British people, who have refused peace, until they kneel and plea for it'. So, for some time now, the German plan has been to use their submarine U-boats to sink merchant ships bringing in our supplies of food. British ships have long blockaded German ports, but these U-boats, well, they have terrified people just as the Kaiser had hoped — not to mention caused all manner of problems to our supply of foodstuffs.'

'And *that's* why we have rationing,' she said. Suddenly, and for the first time, it made sense to her. 'Until now, I thought we had to make do with less food because it was needed to feed our army — '

'And that *is* partly the case.'

— whereas more truthfully, we have less food because the Germans are stopping us from getting it.'

'To an extent that is also true, yes.'

'So, their plan is working.' How odd, that after almost four years of war — and six months of rationing — she was only now seeing what was behind all their hardships. 'Will they be able to keep it up — these blockades, I mean? Will they really bring us to our knees?' Despite asking the question, she wasn't really sure that she wanted to know the answer.

'The Germans obviously think so. I mean, for how long now have flour and sugar been in short supply?'

She screwed up her face in thought. 'Since late last summer, I should say.'

'So, in part, they *are* succeeding, yes. But, to its credit, our government has us doing everything we can to get by. Pass any farm these days, and you're as likely to see German POWs put to work, or women in the fields, as you are a farmer. And then there's what the newspapers call *allotment-itis* — everyone doing their little bit.'

'But going to all of that effort still hasn't been enough, has it?' she said. 'I mean, we still have to suffer rationing. We've had it since after Christmas.'

'That's true. But it is the rationing that has made the difference. It has meant that everyone can provide their family with enough — the same amount, regardless of where they live — whether or not they are able to grow their own food.'

'Hm.' His explanation made her stop and think. 'I hadn't ever looked at it like that.' Fifteen ounces of meat, five ounces of bacon, four ounces of margarine, half a pound of sugar: at first, to last one person for a whole week, it hadn't seemed much. But now she could see how it was helping everyone to get by.

'Some see it as bringing the war home to the people,' he went on. 'It's where we got the expression 'Home Front'. People at home are involved in this war — not just the men fighting battles in foreign lands.'

To Kate, it seemed an incredible thing to suddenly understand. But there was still one thing she was struggling to get straight in her mind. 'So, why did you say just now that you think the war might be over soon? If the Germans are succeeding in stopping our food . . . '

'Because, the Germans are going to all that bother but it's not breaking our spirit, is it? We're getting less food, yes — but we're learning to manage with less. Women like Edith in the kitchen are coming up with new ways to make it go further. People are digging up their gardens and growing their own vegetables, and keeping chickens and so on. That very resolve of ours not to be beaten — the very spirit the Germans set out to break — is still strong, which means that the Germans' plans have backfired. Only the other day I was reading that the people of Germany have even less food than we do. Conditions are far worse for them than they are for us, the result being that, increasingly, they are no longer behind their own government — they're losing their stomach for the whole business.'

Goodness. In that moment, her thoughts seemed to be running in all directions. Moreover, she had never heard Rowley talk for so long or sound so impassioned — she didn't think anyone had. How well informed he seemed — how much in that respect did he remind her of Ned. Even more striking, though, was the idea that the war might soon be over. Finished once and for all. *Won.* Soon, Luke might be able to come home. They would be able to get on with their lives. Have children: two, three, or even, yes, four of them!

With a shake of her head, she allowed herself a rueful smile: the very thing she had once told Luke she didn't want and yet now, here she was, almost unable to contain her excitement at the prospect. *Dear Luke.* Soon now he could be coming home. Soon now she could become a proper wife and a mother. And oh, how that made her feel as though she might burst with happiness!

8

News from the Front

'Good Lord, Kate, wherever did you find that thing? It's ancient.'

'Ignore him, Kate. It's brilliant. Thank you.'

Witnessing the delight on Rowley's face, and ignoring Ned's disparaging assessment of her find, Kate smiled. 'I remembered Ned once telling me that for you, photography isn't just what you do from an aeroplane — it's a hobby, too. So, I thought you might be able to make use of it. Although happen it don't work no more — I couldn't say.'

Examining the camera she had just handed to him, Rowley nodded enthusiastically. 'It has always been an interest of mine, yes.'

'But where *did* you find it?' Ned asked, straining to see as Rowley continued to examine the rather dusty piece of equipment.

'In a box in the attic,' she said. 'I supposed it to have once belonged to Mr Latimer. Although it might just as easily have been left here by one of his guests.'

'Any film in it?' Ned wanted to know, still craning across from his wheelchair.

Opening a flap on the back, Rowley shook his head. 'No,' he said. 'And actually, it's not as old as you might think — just in need of a good clean up. I know for a fact that Kodak didn't start making this model until about ten years ago. I say, Kate, if I were to write down the name of the film it uses, do you think that next time you go into the village you might see whether you could get some for me?'

Pleased by how delighted he seemed, Kate nodded. She'd had a suspicion he might like it. 'Not much good to be had from a camera with no film, I shouldn't think.'

'Great. Thanks. This will be brilliant.'

It was now the last day of June, and still the weather showed no signs of breaking. Afternoons remained sticky, nights even more so, the shade of the cedar tree a welcome refuge sought out by all.

But the heat wasn't the only thing that showed no sign of changing: despite Rowley's optimistic prediction, the war continued to rumble on, there being few indications from anywhere that an end really was in sight. From the front, Naomi received a much-delayed field postcard from Mr Lawrence, the edited statements reading, *I have received your letter dated . . . /telegram/parcel.* But, from Luke, there had been nothing for a couple of weeks. Not that she was unduly troubled; it wasn't out of the ordinary for a month or more to pass without word from him, only for two letters to then arrive within days of each other.

And it wasn't as though she wanted for company. The requisite rolls of film procured for Rowley, she continued to accompany him on his strolls, accepting his cane and watching as he supported himself against a tree or a wall to capture images of the house and its grounds.

'I wish you could have seen it before the war,' she said on one such occasion, as he stood, apparently trying to frame a picture of the long border. 'Both Mr Latimer and his wife were real fond of their flowers. There were always great bunches of them in the house.'

'I can picture it in my mind,' he said, and with which she heard the lazy double-click of the camera's shutter. 'Though I rather like that it looks slightly forlorn — a metaphor for our time, don't you think?'

Although he wasn't looking at her, she shrugged. Metaphor? Not knowing what the word meant, she opted for sounding non-committal. 'Mm.'

'I'm sure it will return to its former glory eventually,' he went on to say, reaching to relieve her of his walking stick. 'And anyway, aren't these thistles just as worthy of a place here as any of these delphiniums? The bees would seem to think so.'

'True. And the finches love how these get left,' she said, reaching to finger the airy heads of a clump of oat grass. 'They love to peck out the seeds.'

'Which is rather my point.'

'Yes, I suppose so.'

When, soon after that, the warmth became too much for him, they began to make their way slowly back to the chairs on the front lawn.

'Another day,' he said, lowering his voice and glancing ahead to where Ned was amusing Esme with her puppets, 'if you don't think it out of order, I should rather like to take *your* photograph.' When she stumbled — over nothing in particular — he reached for her arm, his touch sending a flash of heat racing up her throat and over her cheeks. 'Forgive me,' he said, quickly withdrawing his hand. 'But I thought you were going to fall.'

'You want to take a photograph of *me?*' Unable now to look at him, she went on to ask, 'Why?'

'Quite simply, because I believe it would be remiss of me not to.' To Kate, his tone sounded warm without being overly familiar. Sincere, too. 'This summer is turning out to be a most singular one. Through becoming injured, I find myself without . . . well, without commitments, I suppose you could say. Instead, here I am, welcomed into a family with whom I was not previously acquainted, and into surroundings that — almost by accident — are quite enchanting. By rights, given that I am an officer in what is now the Royal Air Force, and that we are fighting a war, I *should* be somewhere else altogether. But when, in the fullness of time, I am indeed back in that place, I should hate for all of this to fade from my recollection. Thankfully, since you have so kindly furnished me with a camera and some film, I have the means to prevent that from happening. Moreover, to my delight, I find that the camera has a timer device, and so I shall be able to capture all of us in a single photograph. But, since you in particular have given up so much of your time to my recovery — and so much of your patience especially — it feels only right that as well as the house, and the gardens and the views, I have at least one picture of *you*. When I am gone from here, I should very much like it to remember you by, if you wouldn't mind.'

Shocked to feel tears welling, she bit down hard on the side of her tongue. Why on earth should someone wanting to take her photograph move her to tears?

'If that is what you would like,' she said a moment later, struggling to think of a way to refuse his request. 'Then I shall agree to it.'

'Tomorrow, on our walk then,' he said, a newfound purpose about him. 'At the edge of the copse where the light is soft. With your permission I shall take two — just in case the exposure should be wrong and one of them turns out to be no good.'

Grateful to be arriving back at the circle of lawn chairs, and hearing someone coming across the gravel, she turned to see who it was.

'Lend a hand?' Naomi called towards her, the tray she was carrying stacked with crockery.

''Course,' she called back and, hastily excusing herself to Rowley, headed away to the porch.

Heavens, what a muddle her thoughts had suddenly become! And how embarrassingly flushed she must look! Was it wrong of her to agree to let Rowley take her photograph? How could it be; his request was made in all innocence, wasn't it? Yes, of course it was: he was a gentleman if ever there was one. He was respectful. So, why, now, with hindsight, did she feel so uncomfortable? Why, of all the feelings she had at that moment, did the foremost of them seem to be guilt? Perhaps she should have told him no. Perhaps she still should. Perhaps she should say that upon further reflection, the idea made her feel uncomfortable. Or would that just make her look foolish?

Stepping into the porch, she reached to the kitchen trolley for the basket of cutlery and picked up the stack of napkins. Yes, of course she was being foolish. What harm could a photograph do — especially if . . . yes! Especially if she were to ask him for a copy of it, saying that she would like to send one to her husband. Not only would it reinforce to him that she was married, and that any ideas he might have in that respect were out of order, it would also be the perfect opportunity for her to send a picture to Luke.

Heading back across the gravel, her shoulders softening with relief, she smiled warmly at Naomi, coming in the opposite direction. What a daft woman she could be at times — of course there was nothing wrong in letting him take her picture!

Later, over tea, the topic of conversation remained that of photography — only this time it was because Ned and Rowley were recalling some of the missions they had flown.

'Do you remember that first time we thought we weren't going to make it back?' Ned asked, his grin suggesting that he found the memory amusing.

'Shan't ever forget it,' Rowley answered emphatically. 'Never been so scared in all my life.'

'We'd been reconnoitring over Belgium — '

'We had.'

— when all of a sudden the engine started to

splutter, and it felt as though at any moment she was going to cut out.'

'We flew the entire way home lurching and jerking along. But, somehow, she stayed up, and we got down quite safely.'

'And then there was the time we were struck by that enormous bird.'

'Over Belgium. Again.'

'Canada goose, you told me.'

'Huge thing. Damaged the rudder.'

'Spent the entire homeward leg flying pretty much sideways.'

'And we were still finding feathers weeks later.'

'It's a good job Mamma doesn't know any of this,' Naomi said, looking at her brother over the rim of her teacup. 'Or she would write one of her intemperate letters to the RFC and demand — '

'It's the RAF now, not the RFC.'

'Yes, apologies,' Naomi corrected herself. 'She would write to the RAF and demand that they find you a job on the ground.'

Sitting alongside Naomi, Kate stared down into her lap. The more weeks that passed with Ned doing no more than stand, supported on either side but unable to take a single step, the more she was coming to think it unlikely he would fly again anyway. And, though no one else might be saying anything, they all had to be thinking as she did — that for Ned, this war was over.

'Mamma! Motorcar come!'

When, from the rug on the ground in front of them, Esme scrabbled to her feet and pointed across the lawns, Kate turned to see that coming

195

through the gates was the station taxi.

'Please don't tell me that by simply talking about her, we've somehow managed to summon Mamma,' Ned remarked, laughing as he did so.

Beside him, Naomi got to her feet. And, as the taxi continued to make its way up the drive, it was clear that, from inside, someone was waving. 'Good heavens,' she said, reaching for Esme's hand and setting off with her towards the porch. 'It's Lawrence!'

'You didn't tell me he was due leave,' Ned called after her.

Dropping Esme's hand and starting to run, Naomi called back. 'I didn't know he was!'

Instinctively, Kate rose from her chair. Was Mr Lawrence on his own — or was anyone else with him? In her head, something cautioned against getting her hopes up: just because Mr Lawrence had been granted leave, didn't mean that Luke would have been too, even though they *had* come home together before — several times.

Watching the taxi turn on the gravel and then lumber to a halt in front of the porch, she hardly dared to breathe. Seemingly fixed to the ground, her feet wouldn't allow her to move, but, when just a single door to the taxi swung open, and only one uniform-clad figure stepped out, her heart plummeted far enough to join them on the grass. Shoulders sagging, she exhaled her disappointment in a long stream of breath. How cruel was that? Mr Lawrence had been granted leave to come home but not Luke.

Unable to think what else to do, but with no

196

desire to watch Lawrence and Naomi embracing, she bent to pick up her plate and put it on the tray. Then, in mechanical fashion, she started to gather up the rest of their tea things. Reaching for the cup and saucer on the table alongside Ned, she was prevented from doing so by the feel of his fingers closing about her wrist.

'Next time,' he said softly. 'His turn will come. Just you see.'

'Of course,' she said, feeling him let go, and feigning a brightness she didn't feel.

'And Lawrence is sure to have news of him for you.'

'Sure to,' she repeated, nodding in supposed agreement as she bent to lift the tray and then carry it away.

Reaching the front door, and dispensing with the use of the trolley, she continued straight on across the hall and down the stairs. But, walking the length of the corridor towards the scullery, she had to fight to hold back tears. She must not engage in pitiful weeping. She *must not* feel sorry for herself. Mr Lawrence had been given some leave and she should be happy for him — for him and Naomi both. It was as Ned had said, Luke's turn would come, and then it would be Naomi envying *her* good fortune.

Depositing the tray on the side, she sniffed loudly and then reached into the sleeve of her dress for a handkerchief to blow her nose. There. Better.

Passing Mabel's parlour on the way back, she came to a halt, retraced her last steps, and stuck her head around the door. 'Mr Lawrence is here,' she said, surprised by how pleased she managed to sound. Even so, preferring not to get drawn into conversation, she quickly ducked back out again.

'Lord, then I'd best see about stretching supper a bit further . . . ' she heard Edith remark, followed by the sound of chairs scraping back across the floor.

'And I daresay they'll be a-wanting the dining room tonight,' Mabel went on to observe.

Already several paces back along the corridor, Kate slowed her pace. The dining room was still covered in dust sheets and would be in a terrible state. 'I'll be there in a minute to lend a hand,' she called back towards them. Opening up the dining room was just the sort of job to keep her thoughts from Luke. 'I'll go an' fetch in the rest of the tea things and then I'll go in and open up the windows — get the place aired.'

Arriving back up in the hallway, though, she was surprised to see Naomi standing alone in the porch, shielding her eyes against the light and staring out across the lawn. Behind her, just inside the door, was Lawrence's kitbag. At the very least, she would have expected them to be unpacking his things . . .

'Oh, Kate. There you are.'

The thing that struck her first was the paleness of Naomi's face.

'Everything all right?' Kate asked, continuing towards her.

'You need to come through to the drawing room a moment. Only . . . well, no, just come through, would you.'

'For supper tonight,' she said, dutifully turning about, 'we're going to open up the dining room. And Edith is going to magic up another helping.'

But from Naomi there came no response, and, when she trailed behind her into the drawing room, it was to see Mr Lawrence standing stiffly in front of the fireplace, his only concession to having arrived home seeming to be the removal of his cap, now lying on one of the side tables. Her immediate impression was that from his collar down he looked immaculate, whereas, above it, his face looked grey with exhaustion and shockingly thin, his nose prominent and his eyes sunken. It was as much as she could do not to gasp.

'Captain Colborne,' she said, concentrating upon swallowing down her unease at his appearance. 'Good afternoon to you. Welcome back.'

'Kate.'

His manner, she noticed, was twitchy. She supposed it stemmed from the constant need to be on alert. And there was something about his eyes, too. They seemed darker than she remembered them — nearly black, and with a glassiness that almost certainly hadn't been there before.

Feeling a hand on her arm, she turned to see Naomi gesturing to one of the sofas. 'Kate, come and sit down for a moment.'

With a perplexed shrug and a light shake of her head, she did so, Naomi immediately sitting closely beside her. 'W-What is it?' she asked, looking from Naomi back to Mr Lawrence.

'What can I do for you?'

Having not moved from the empty fireplace, Lawrence cleared his throat. 'Kate, though I've searched my mind all the way home for a better way to do this, I have been unable to find one. I'm afraid I've come to tell you that Luke has been killed.'

When she tried so many times later to recall that moment, she was sure she remembered there being a thud, though she was also sure that it had come from within her body rather than from without. All she ever seemed able to remember with any clarity was finding herself on the sofa, her feet raised up on a couple of cushions, Naomi fanning at her face, and voices that sounded as though they were coming from under water. Incredibly, it was only when she had raised her head and had seen Mr Lawrence standing stiffly over her, that she understood what he had just said. And then she had felt as though something inside of her had broken: a deep and unbearable ache seemed to have spread throughout every inch of her, from the tight dryness in the back of her throat all the way down through her chest to her abdomen. Luke was dead. Mr Lawrence had said that Luke was *dead*. He had promised her he would look after him but, instead, he had let him be killed and then he had come home to tell her about it. Not wanting to look at him, she turned away, drew up her legs, and buried her face.

Through the fabric of her dress, she felt a hand press lightly upon her back and then start to move in circles as though in consolation. But, for her, there could be none. Luke had been killed. Her dearest husband was dead.

★ ★ ★

'Oh, my dear, I am so sorry. So very sorry.'

To Kate, it seemed to be all that anyone could say to her. Several hours later, and with dusk falling, all anyone seemed able to do was keep saying those same few words, over and over. Already fed up with hearing them, she begged them, in turn, to leave her alone. But would they do that? No, even once she had taken to her bed, people kept coming and going, offering their sympathy; Naomi in particular stubbornly choosing to keep vigil at her bedside.

Raising her eyes to stare up at the ceiling, she wished that her limbs didn't feel so leaden and useless, a state presumably brought on by the sizeable measure of brandy Mr Lawrence had encouraged her to drink. 'For the shock,' he had said, pouring some from the decanter into one of the crystal balloons and handing it to her before pouring an even larger measure for himself. Brandy, she knew, was what you gave people so they wouldn't feel pain. But what if she *wanted* to feel pain? Who was anyone else to deny her that right? Her husband was dead. She was a widow. And here she was, 'three sheets to the wind', as dear Nell, back at St. Ursula's, was so fond of saying about the men who staggered along the towpath considerably the worse for drink. Picturing Nell made her giggle — presumably another effect of the brandy. But then,

201

abruptly, she stopped; Luke would wonder what had come over her — would urge her to behave with some dignity. 'For heaven's sake, Kate,' he would whisper, 'someone has just died.'

Luke. Poor, poor Luke. Never again would he have to despair of her wilful ways.

★ ★ ★

'I wasn't sure what you would feel like eating.'

Raising her head an inch or two from the pillow, Kate struggled to focus her eyes and work out where she was. She recognized the voice as belonging to Edith but, all around her, the room was in darkness. With difficulty, she turned her head. Edith was setting a tray on the occasional table, which, for some reason was now standing alongside her bed. Hearing the chink of the china, she strained to see what was going on. From what she could just make out, the tray bore a bowl, the contents of which were steaming, a basket wrapped in a napkin, and an egg cup in which stood a boiled egg. Breakfast? Then whatever time was it? Turning to look at the window, she could see that beyond the curtain was daylight. Then why on earth had no one woken her until now?

Opening her mouth, and feeling how dry it was, she flexed her jaw a couple of times. It felt oddly stiff, and the inside of her mouth horribly parched.

Evidently seeing what she was doing, Edith went around to the other side of the bed and, putting a hand under her shoulders, helped her to sit up. Plumping the pillows behind her, she then eased her back against them and handed her the glass of water from the nightstand.

Raising the glass to her lips, she took a mouthful and swallowed it. 'Ugh.'

'Sip it,' Edith instructed, refusing to accept the glass back from her. 'You needs water inside you to counter the effects of the brandy. Leaves you dry, that stuff does.' Dutifully, Kate took several more sips, but the water tasted as though it had been laced with brass polish. And, although she could feel it trickling down her throat, it seemed to be doing nothing to alleviate the dryness of her mouth. 'Go on, keep going.'

The glass eventually empty, she reached to replace it on the nightstand. 'What time is it?' she wanted to know, turning again towards the curtained window.

'Never you mind the time,' Edith replied, refilling the glass from the jug. 'You've nowhere to be.'

And then she remembered: Luke was dead. Mr Lawrence had come to tell her. And in which case Edith was right: she had nowhere to be; nowhere to go. No one to wait for any more.

'How long did I sleep?' she asked. Inside her head, it felt as though someone was refusing to stop hammering. And in one of her ears there seemed to be an angry bluebottle.

'You went through the night. Shall I draw back the curtains a little?'

She nodded, the effect upon her head dizzying. 'Please,' she mumbled, pressing the tips of her fingers to her temples. 'Draw them wide. I want the light in.'

'If you say so.'

As the room brightened, Kate screwed up her eyes. Edith was in her mourning uniform; the last time that had seen light of day must have been when Mrs Latimer died. Against her pale skin such utter blackness made her look ill. She supposed they would expect *her* to adopt mourning as well. *Widows weeds.* Oh, dear God, this was awful. Luke was dead. And *she* was a widow. How could that possibly be?

Once Edith had sat and watched her try to swallow a few mouthfuls of porridge — the toast looking too dry for her throat and the thought of the egg turning her stomach — she agreed that she might drink some tea, and Edith had gone to make her some. In the moments of quiet that followed, she lay, propped up like an invalid, trying to make sense of her feelings, only to discover that she didn't seem to have any. Worse still, having been desperate for Edith to stop fussing, she now found that she couldn't wait for her to come back. Left alone, it was impossible to distract her thoughts from the fact that, if she felt anything at all, it was guilt — guilt at feeling nothing.

The person who subsequently returned with her tea, though, was Naomi.

'Here you are,' she said, her tone neither overly gloomy nor artificially bright. 'It's been brewing a while, so I'll pour it.' That done, she repositioned the chair and sat down. 'At least you managed to sleep.'

'From the feel of my head, I'd say *that* was down to the brandy. Never was no good with spirits — with drink of any sort, for that matter.'

'Me neither,' Naomi replied, and then, after a moment, went on. 'Look, Kate, I just want you to know — '

'*Please*, Naomi,' she begged, 'don't say how sorry you are — not again. I know you are sorry, truly I do. But it don't do me no good to keep hearing it from everyone.'

'No, I don't suppose it does.'

'Makes *me* feel bad that folk feel the need to keep apologizing . . . especially when it won't bring him back.'

'No, I know. But what I was going to say — and I know this probably isn't the time, given all the things that must be going through your head right now — is that you're not to worry about anything. Not money, nor about having a roof over your head, nor anything else for that matter. You have a home and a family. And, between us, we will take care of you.'

Kate summoned a watery smile. Despite what she had just urged about repeated apologies, it was a reassuring thing to hear. 'Thank you.'

'I want you to know that however long it is before you feel able to . . . well, before . . . you know, before you feel able to pick up the threads of your life again, I will be here to help you. Lawrence too.'

'Can you help me know how to feel?' she asked, her voice beginning to tremble as she did so. 'Only, though I would have thought to know, I find that I don't. All the times I feared something would happen to him, all the times I pictured my grief were he to be lost, and all the times I've seen this happen to other women, you'd think that come the day, I'd know what to feel — that I'd feel sadness or loss. Or even anger. But I don't feel none of them. I just feel . . . numb.'

'I think,' Naomi said, reaching to clasp her hand, 'that the numbness *is* part of your grief. When my uncle died — quite suddenly — I remember Mamma being the same — overcome by a sort of numbness. Her physician said it was normal. He said that grief and mourning take on a pattern and that the numbness — caused by the shock — would eventually be overtaken by disbelief, denial, anger even. All of those, he told her, are perfectly normal things to feel. Of no comfort to you, I know,' Naomi went on, and squeezed her hand. 'But I do think that once the news sinks in, and the shock wears off, sadness and grief will follow.'

Although having no reason to doubt what Naomi said, Kate shook her head. 'Do Mr Lawrence know what happened to him?' she asked. 'I should like to know.'

Naomi nodded. 'Yes. And he said that as soon as you want him to, he will come up and talk to you.'

'No,' she said, beginning to pull herself more upright. 'I think I should like to get up and be dressed for that. I don't think this bed is the proper place to hear of Luke's final moments on this earth.'

Gently, Naomi let go of her hand. 'I understand. Then I'll go along and run you a bath. And we'll wash your hair and make you feel fresher. By the time you're dry, Mabel will have finished your dress. When I came up just now, she was just seeing to the hem.'

'My *dress?*' Why did she know nothing of a dress?

'For your mourning.' Her mourning. Yes, of course. 'Last night,' Naomi went on, 'Mabel asked me whether I thought you had anything suitable with you — to wear that is — and I said I thought not. I suggested — solely for ease — that we buy you one, but she didn't like the thought of you wearing something ready-made — not for Luke. She insisted upon making you one. By the look of it, she's been up all night sewing.'

Yes, she thought, that would be Mabel — always there in times of trouble. And thoughtful, too.

'Fortunate you always make me pack *yours*,' she said, wondering why it had taken her until now to notice Naomi's plain black shift. ''Queen Mary never travels anywhere without a mourning outfit, and so neither do I', that's what you always said.'

She sighed heavily. Mourning. Widowhood. What dreadful things to be thinking about. Dare she even wonder how long she would be expected to swathe herself in black and grieve? Dare she contemplate how long she was to be confined to that state of limbo? Edith had once told her that when Thomas had died, Mabel had observed two years — and then six months of half mourning after that. These days, with so many young men dying on the battlefield, such

207

strict observance seemed to have fallen by the wayside, a slightly more practical approach seeming to have come to prevail — in London, at least. At St. Ursula's, Marjorie had once told her that with so many women left needing to remarry, among the labouring classes a period of six months was now deemed more than enough. By her account, some of those same women never even wore black to start with — there being no money spare to buy the cloth. Instead, for the service of remembrance at the church, they fashioned a black veil for their hat, or borrowed a black blouse or skirt to receive callers who came to offer their condolences. But where did any of that leave *her*? She might have been brought up in service, but she had become part of a family who were most definitely middle-class — had adopted most of their ways and observed their social niceties.

Perhaps, she thought numbly, swinging her legs down over the side of the bed and sliding her feet into her slippers, those were considerations for another day. Her most pressing desire at that moment was to get up and do something — anything that would allow her to move about and be rid of the feeling of numbness. Better still, she hoped to find something to occupy her mind, at least until — as Naomi had put it — the shock wore off and the grief set in.

★ ★ ★

'He was a terrific chap.'

Seated on the sofa in the drawing room, across

the table from Mr Lawrence, Kate tried not to stare. He looked so different from when he had last come home on leave, the flesh on his face seeming to have shrunk so much that it now clung to his skull like little more than a covering of gossamer. On his left temple was a purple vein, prominent and knotted, and in his left eye was a tic.

'There weren't nothing much he feared, even as a lad,' she said, directing her thoughts away from Mr Lawrence and back to Luke. 'Bowl headlong into anything, he would. 'Specially if someone were in danger.'

'I'm not surprised to learn that about him,' Lawrence replied.

'No.'

'No matter the peril, he was always the same — concerned only for others — right to the very end. And I trust that when I tell you what happened, you will be able to draw comfort from that thought.'

In her lap, Kate clasped her hands together. This might be something she needed to know but that wasn't going to make it any easier to hear. 'Yes,' she said.

'You see, we'd been camped in the same village since the spring, and so he knew the roads and routes around us well. On the day in question, a call came to say that a new attack was to be launched and that there were urgent documents to be collected from field HQ. Of our two other drivers, one was already out, the other laid up with dysentery. So, despite being on a rest break, your husband volunteered to make the run. Under reasonable conditions, the journey should have taken him about two hours each way. But when, by dusk, he hadn't returned, I imagined only that he had needed to take cover against an attack, or that his route had been blocked, necessitating that he find another way back.

'Many hours later, word reached us that there had been heavy shelling on the road to . . . well, let us just say *on the road*, and that there had been casualties. It wasn't until the following morning, when further details came in, that I felt certain Luke was safe. You see, when I saw the report of the attack, specifically its time and location, I thought it unlikely that Corporal Channer would have been caught up in it — '

Corporal Channer. Goodness, it made him sound so important. ' — since I didn't think he could have made it so far back in the time. However, when word reached me that he was one of the casualties, his vehicle hit by an enemy shell, I realized otherwise. Sadly, by making good progress on that day, your husband had ended up in the wrong place at the wrong time.'

Wrong place at the wrong time. How unfair, especially since, by the sound of it, it shouldn't have been him making the trip in the first place. But for his eagerness . . .

In that moment, seated on the sofa, the light in the drawing room greyer than it had been in ages, the reality of Luke's death struck her like a blow to her stomach, a blow so hard and so unexpected that she doubled over. With it, came the sensation that she was about to be sick.

210

Forcing herself to swallow back a nasty taste, she looked down into her lap. Her hands, resting on the unfamiliar black crepe of her mourning dress, looked as though they belonged to someone else. 'Would it have been . . . would it have been . . . '

'Would it have been quick?' Lawrence finished her question. 'Without a doubt. The report I received from a nearby unit stated that it was a direct hit, and so I have no doubt whatsoever that he would have been gone in a flash.'

'Small mercy,' she whispered. In her lap, the fingernails of her right hand were pressing into the palm of her left. She pressed them harder. The pain was a good deal less than she would have liked.

'Small mercy, yes.'

'So . . . may I ask when to expect him to be brought back?'

The frown that crossed Lawrence's brow drew her to looking at him more closely. He really didn't look at all well.

'Back?'

'His . . . remains,' she said, it being a word she had heard Marjorie Randolph use. 'Only, I should like him to be buried here, in Woodicombe, in the churchyard alongside all the other Channers gone before him. So, when do I tell his Ma and Pa that he will be back?'

'I — '

'And his belongings,' she went on. 'I shouldn't imagine there will be much, but it would be a comfort to me to have his signet ring . . . and anything else he had with him.'

'Yes, yes,' Lawrence said quickly. 'I will arrange for his belongings to be sent on to you. And his medals.'

'Medals,' she said. She felt so weary, so tired, every thought a labour to make. 'He never mentioned receiving no medals.'

'In my experience, men rarely do.'

'Well, thank you for telling me what happened,' she said, getting up from the sofa. 'Though I doubt it is your first time having to impart news of such tragedy, I don't suppose it comes easy to you.'

In an instant, Lawrence too was on his feet. 'No,' he said. 'It does not.'

'No.'

'Look, Kate,' he picked up again. 'You should know that your husband was a model soldier. Never one to shirk a task, he was most diligent in his duties. Reliable. Popular with the other men, too. Well-liked. Trusted. The whole company will miss him. *I* shall miss him.'

Slowly, and as though watching herself doing so from on high, she turned towards the door. 'He was a good man all round, took before he'd even led a life. That's what he was.'

'He was indeed. And my condolences, again, for your loss.'

⋆ ⋆ ⋆

She had seen the rain coming. She had watched it on the far horizon, falling in slanting lines from leaden clouds above a slate-coloured sea. And now it was falling upon her, flattening her hair to her head and starting to soak through the crepe of her dress. Rivulets of it trickled down her forehead, dropping from her eyebrows onto her cheeks to curve around the outside of her lips and drop from her jawline onto her chest. After the heat of the last few weeks it felt cold. And miserable. And yet utterly just. Finally, soaked to the skin and chilled through to her bones, she felt proper pain. And it came as a relief.

When she had left Mr Lawrence in the drawing room, she'd had no idea where she was headed. Waiting for her on one of the hard chairs in the hallway had been Naomi, ready to comfort her. But she had been in no mood for comforting words, no matter how kindly intended. Instead, watching Naomi get to her feet, she had raised a hand, gesturing vaguely that she didn't want to talk and hurrying on past. And now, here she was, down in the cove, the high tide sending waves lolloping onto the sands, the wind whipping about her ears, and the rain coming down in great torrents. Luke was dead. Never again would he set foot on this shore, or indeed upon any other. His life had been taken from him by a stupid war in a foreign land. And from *her* had been taken the husband she had yet to properly know, and whose children she would never now bear.

Turning slowly about, she stared back up the beach to where the path made its way through the boulders, her eyelashes clumped with tears and rain, the view before her blurred and grey. Just as slowly, she collapsed down onto the sand, its soft dampness sucking at her knees while, behind her, the waves continued to rush at the shore. And then she cried. She cried until her ribs ached and her head felt so heavy that she could do nothing but double over and bring it to rest on the sand.

Gone. Luke was gone. And with him were gone all of her hopes and dreams.

9

Grief

'Kate, you must promise me.'

Feeling overly-warm and sticky, but not daring to throw back the bedcovers, Kate looked up at Naomi and nodded. At least the delirium seemed to have passed. At least she no longer seemed to switch from being boiling hot one moment to freezing cold the next. Now she just seemed perpetually hot.

'I promise I won't go out without telling someone where I'm going.'

In truth, given the fuggy state of her head, she was just uttering words. But it seemed important to Naomi that she say them. And, from the ashen tone to her complexion and the grey-green bags under her eyes, this morning, Naomi looked like a woman who could do without any more worries. Perhaps *she* wasn't well either, Kate thought, her attention already drifting away.

A couple of days had now passed since Mr Lawrence had arrived to break the news about Luke. As to what had happened more recently — specifically, to confine her to her bed — she was rather less certain. She recalled going down to the cove to get away from the sympathetic expressions everyone affixed each and every time they saw her, and to escape their repeated condolences. She could even remember that the beach had been grey and blowy and welcoming in its freshness. But then it had started to rain, and the next thing she knew was that she had been in bed, in this room, shivering violently, giant shadows stalking the ceiling, and the walls — with their oversized cabbage roses — taking on a life of their own: one moment threatening to suffocate her, the next, drawing far away to leave her quaking, vulnerable and afraid. And now, here she was, apparently two days on from all of that, having awoken from what she guessed to have been a tincture-induced slumber that had apparently consumed an entire day and the two nights on either side of it.

'I have thanked Lieutenant Rowley-King for his quick thinking,' Naomi was now saying. 'But, as soon as you are up and about again, I would urge you to make a point of thanking him for yourself.'

Ah, yes, and that was another thing she didn't recall: apparently, she was only here at all because, finding her on the beach, soaked to the skin and blue with cold, Ellis Rowley-King had somehow carried her all the way home. How on earth he had managed to get her back up the path through the woods she couldn't imagine. He had to be stronger than he looked. And yes, Naomi was right: she really should thank him.

'I will,' she said.

With a shake of her head, Naomi exhaled a long sigh. 'Right. Well, thankfully, you seem to be over the worst of it. Even so, I shall leave you to get some more rest. You are not to get out of bed. If you need anything, ring the bell.

216

Otherwise, please, stay where you are. I assure you, it is the best place for you. I shall come back and see you later.'

In frustration, Kate gave a little sigh. But she didn't have it in her to make a fuss. She felt too tired — exhausted, in fact — and far too weak. But she *could* just check that Naomi was all right.

'Are you — ' But Naomi was already halfway across the room and didn't turn back. Oh well, she would ask her later.

Out on the landing, someone was hovering. Dressed in black, and with grey hair, it had to be Mabel.

'She's awake, you say? Well, that's a relief an' no mistake.'

From her bed, Kate strained to hear.

'Yes. I do believe she's over the worst of it.'

'Once her fever broke, I knew she was out of the woods. You can always rely on Loveday Channer to know what to prescribe.'

Ma Channer had been to see her? Well, she had no recollection of *that* happening. Eager now to learn what else had been going on, she tried to raise herself up from her pillow, but even as she began to do so, it felt as though the insides of her head had come loose and were bobbing about in her skull like corks on the flood tide.

'Yes. Well, I've told her to stay where she is. And I suggest that for the moment at least, we don't answer any questions from her about — '

Bother. Naomi had pulled the door closed. Answer any questions from her about what? What was it they were planning to keep from her? She must try to think what it might be. And then, the next time someone came through the door, she would wheedle it out of them. In the meantime, she would just close her eyes for a while — maybe even have a little sleep. Just for a few minutes, that was all.

★ ★ ★

'There you are then, Kate, love, all dressed.'

'Yes,' Kate agreed with Mabel's observation. 'All dressed.' *All dressed for mourning.*

'Let me help you to your feet. Slowly, mind. Only, you said just now you felt woozy again.'

'I did. But that was just the first time I stood up. I feel better now.'

The truth of it was that she didn't feel better at all; she still felt dizzy — horribly so. An hour back, she had opened her eyes to find that, rather than snoozing for just a few minutes as she had intended, she had slept all through the morning and into the afternoon, to be awoken only by a ravenous hunger. Sitting up in bed, she had then devoured a bowl of chicken soup, a bread roll with a pat of butter, and a slice of Edith's rhubarb and custard cake. And now, here she was, with Mabel's help, bathed and dressed and about to venture downstairs.

'You haven't missed out on any sunshine,' Mabel said to her as they processed slowly along the landing towards the stairs. 'If it hasn't been raining, it's been threatening to. That spell of nice weather has well and truly broken. Distant memory, that is. If reports in the newspapers are

218

to be believed, it's been the same everywhere. Most rainfall in parts of London in the month of July for more than a hundred years they're saying.'

Rainfall. Tears. Oddly, since she had woken up from her fever, she hadn't cried once. Perhaps she was all cried out. Perhaps that was it now; perhaps she was done with crying.

At the bottom of the stairs, the two women turned towards the drawing room. Ahead of them, the French doors to the terrace were letting in the greyest and bleakest of lights.

'Everyone's been asking after you,' Mabel said as they walked on. 'Ready to go in and see them?'

She closed her fingers more tightly over Mabel's sleeve. 'No,' she said. 'Wait a moment. There's summat I want to ask you.'

'Yes love? And what would that be, then?'

Very slowly, she turned to study Mabel's face. She might be smiling but she looked tired — her complexion as pale as the outdoor light. 'Has there been any word yet about . . . about Luke's remains.' Noticing Mabel's smile slowly dissolve, she determined not to be fobbed off. 'About when he will be brought home, I mean. Only, I should like for him to be buried soonest. No doubt that's what his Ma and Pa would want, too. Tedn't right for him to be left lying about in some foreign land.'

'No word yet, love, no. Least, not that *I'm* aware of.'

As a rule, Mabel never lied to anyone. But, this afternoon, she was definitely concealing *something*. And, the more Kate thought about it,

the more she was convinced that it was connected to what she had heard her discussing with
Naomi earlier. Perhaps she should try asking
Naomi herself; if nothing else, *she* might be able
to ask Mr Lawrence for news of Luke's remains.

Going in through the doors to the living room,
the person she saw first was Ned, in his wheelchair, sitting at a table newly positioned alongside
one of the pairs of French windows — presumably for the light, such as it was. Across from him
sat Rowley, and, between them, standing on a
chair and straining to reach something, was Esme.

From one of the sofas, Naomi got to her feet.
'Kate,' she said, smiling and coming towards
them. 'I'm so glad you felt well enough to come
down. Would you like to come and sit with me?
As you can see, the boys already have help with
their jigsaw. Well, when I say *help* . . . '

'Yes,' she said.

Grateful not to have to talk to everyone all at
once, she allowed Naomi to lead her around to
the sofa. To her surprise, in the fireplace, a couple
of logs were crackling.

'Shameful, I know,' Naomi conceded, evidently seeing her notice it. 'But it's such an awful
afternoon again and without the cheeriness of a
fire the room felt so utterly dismal.'

Slowly, Kate lowered herself onto the sofa.
Although it was only a few days since she had sat
in this very spot — Mr Lawrence standing at the
fireplace telling her about Luke — it felt like a
couple of weeks.

'Mr Lawrence gone out?' she said, noting his
absence.

220

'Lawrence?'

'Yes, has he gone out somewhere?'

Reaching across to Kate's lap, Naomi caught hold of her hand. 'Oh, my dear Kate, he had to go back. He only had sufficient leave to stay just that one night.'

'Just the one night? So where is he now then?'

'I should imagine that by now, he'll be back at the front — back in France,' Naomi replied.

Back at the front? Already? Well that hardly seemed fair; it was only a couple of days since the poor man had arrived. And he'd looked so badly in need of a decent night's sleep, too, not to mention some proper food. 'So . . . '

'He asked me to apologize to you for having to depart so soon — '

'Apologize to me?' What reason did Mr Lawrence have to apologize to *her*? It didn't make any sense.

'I think he feels guilty about what happened to Luke — doubly so for having to go back without being able to talk to you again . . . '

Puzzled that Mr Lawrence should feel to blame, Kate shook her head. 'It weren't his doing that got Luke killed.'

Beside her, Naomi gave the slightest shrug. 'No. But given that he was the one who encouraged Luke to join the Wiltshires in the first place, I suppose it only natural that he should feel *some* responsibility.'

Kate continued to shake her head. 'It's not right for him to blame himself,' she said. 'Luke would have joined up anyway. With or without Mr Lawrence to speak for him, he would have

221

been one of the first to volunteer. That was his way. So Mr Lawrence shouldn't feel bad. Oh, I do wish he hadn't left so soon, then I could have told him as much for myself. I can't believe I didn't have the chance to speak to him again before he went.'

'Next time I write to him,' Naomi began, her voice soft, 'I will convey to him what you have just said. Or, if you prefer, you could write a note yourself and put it in the envelope with mine.'

This time, Kate nodded. 'Yes,' she said. 'I'll do that. Only, I can't bear to think of him fretting over it . . . not when it's not his fault. Such a shame he's had to go back so soon. He can barely have had time for a decent meal.'

Giving Kate's hand a squeeze, Naomi smiled. 'Oh, my dear Kate. Trust you to be concerned for *his* well-being! Lawrence's visit might have been brief but, knowing him as I do, the inconvenience would not have entered into his mind. Not for a moment.'

She glanced to Naomi's face. 'No?'

'No,' Naomi said. 'He told me himself that the moment he learned what had happened to Luke, he went straight to request a leave of absence in order to be the one to come and tell you. He said he couldn't bear to think of you learning of the news by letter, which, apparently, with enlisted men, is what usually happens. His commanding officer granted his request but said he could only be spared for four days, which is why he had to go straight back.'

Slowly, Kate turned away. Learning of Mr Lawrence's selflessness made her feel dreadful. 'I didn't realize,' she whispered. 'If I'd known that, I would have shown more gratitude for the trouble he went to. But I didn't know. I wish he'd said.'

Unable to bear it, she started to cry.

'Dear Kate. Please don't upset yourself on Lawrence's account. He'll know you were grateful, truly he will. And before too much longer he's bound to be back again, on proper leave next time . . . '

'Yes,' she said between sobs. 'I suppose he will.'

' . . . and then you can talk to him all you like.'

Sniffing loudly, Kate did her best to nod her agreement. 'Yes,' she said. 'Next time he's home here, I'll do that. I'll make sure to thank him proper for his trouble.'

★　★　★

Who knew that having nothing to do all day would make time pass so slowly?

Having been up and about again for a couple of days now, Kate no longer felt nearly so weak nor so wobbly. Instead, the problem seemed to have moved from her body to her mind, being confined indoors making her feel as though she had become trapped inside her own head with no chance of escape, her thoughts all of a muddle one moment, benumbed by grief the next. The fact that no one would let her help with any of the chores didn't help. Rather than obey everyone's instructions to *rest up*, what she really needed to be doing was filling her hours with activity. That way, her days might not feel so long and so empty . . . and so utterly pointless.

Distractedly, she went to the window and stared up the drive towards the lane, her eyes roving the myriad greens of the trees and the lawns. The tranquillity of the scene in the soft evening light gave her a thought. Uncertainly, she glanced over her shoulder towards the door: surely, no one could take issue with her going for a walk?

Wrapping about her shoulders the black woollen shawl loaned to her by Edith, she crept down the stairs, let herself out through the front door, and headed away. At the far corner of the lawn, a little-used path led through the rhododendrons to the lane, emerging near the lodge houses at the entrance to the old manor. Reaching the start of it, and without looking back, she plunged through the shrubbery, the leathery leaves, still wet from the rain, drenching the front of her skirt. She would go and see her mother-in-law; she was bound to have something helpful to say.

Arriving under the porch to the lodge house, she raised a hand to knock on the door. But, before she'd even had the chance to announce her presence, the door opened back.

'Come on in, girl,' Loveday Channer said, her expression devoid of surprise. 'I been expecting you.'

Lowering her hand, Kate stepped inside. 'Hello, Ma Channer.'

'Been expecting that dreadful news of the boy, too, truth to tell. Come on, sit down with you. I'll make us a brew.'

'If you're sure it's no trouble.'

'Trouble? Pah. Stuff and nonsense. Make yourself at home.'

Pulling a chair from under the table and lowering herself onto it, Kate was unsurprised to feel the tightness to her head beginning to ease. She should have come sooner — for so many reasons. But at least she was there now.

Glancing about the kitchen, her eyes came to rest upon the door to the parlour — closed, as always. In fact, the only time she had ever seen it open — and had actually stepped inside — was the day she had married Luke.

'Pa Channer not about?' she asked.

'Gone up The Fox.'

Goodness, she really *had* lost track of time — had over-looked that it was Wednesday and therefore Pa Channer's night for dominoes with the Braund brothers. ''Course, yes.'

'So, what in particular brings you up here this late on? Not that you need reason to call, you know that.'

Catching the heady scent of the June roses arranged in the vase on the table in front of her, Kate shrugged her shoulders. 'Oh, you know.'

'Aye, love. I do,' Loveday Channer replied, setting the kettle on the stove. 'I suppose that poor Captain Colborne has gone back now?'

Slowly, Kate nodded her head. 'He has, yes.'

'Nice feller. Handsome, I shouldn't wonder — before this blessed war drained all the life from him. Said some lovely things about young Luke. Good of him to come up here, what with him having so little leave. An' I made a point of

225

saying so. 'Thank you', I said to him, 'for taking the time.''

'Yes,' Kate agreed. 'He is nice. He an' Luke got along well together.'

'Aye. But then that boy got along with just about everyone.'

She smiled. It was true; he'd had that way about him. 'He did.'

Sitting at the Channers' table, Kate felt calmer than she had in a while. Clearly, being able to talk to someone who had known Luke for who he really was — without the conversation being heavy with sadness and regret about his passing — was what she had needed. Here was someone who would help keep the memory of him alive — with whom she could make sure that he never came to be forgotten — and yet who didn't feel the need to keep apologizing.

'Happen you'll find it hard, you know — what with there being no remains.'

Looking swiftly up from her lap, Kate watched as Loveday Channer took a teaspoon to her aged teapot and gave it a stir.

'There's . . . there's no remains?'

'Didn't no one tell you, love?'

With her heart beginning to thud in her chest, and a wave of heat engulfing her body, she responded with a shake of her head. 'No . . . '

'That infernal thing he was driving was hit square on. Boom! Went straight up in flames.'

She cast her mind back, trying to remember precisely what Mr Lawrence had told her of the incident. Seemingly, in his bid to spare her the grislier details, he had been economical with the truth, something she was only now realizing. Ma Channer, on the other hand, had clearly been possessed of the wherewithal to press for the whole story. And then there had been those whispers in the doorway to her bedroom; pound to a penny, concealing the matter of Luke's remains was what Mabel and Naomi had been discussing that day. Gripping the edge of the table, she stared down at her fingernails, watching as, before her eyes, they blurred into a flesh-coloured mass. 'No,' she said softly. 'No one told me.'

'Aye,' Loveday Channer continued, lifting the pot and filling two cups with dark tea. 'Like the time your Mabel lost her boy when he set out with the lifeboat to rescue that pleasure yacht. The poor lad's body never did wash up. Aye, *she'll* know what you're feeling. I remember distinctly her clinging to hope, long after all was proper gone.'

Clinging to hope? Was that what she would find herself doing — holding out for her husband to still be alive just because there were no remains? She didn't think so. It was true that she couldn't believe he was gone, but not because she thought him still alive.

'I — '

'You know, he wrote often that the thing keeping him going through all the madness and the waste over there was the thought of getting home to you.'

Feeling tears welling, Kate bowed her head. If Ma Channer thought that telling her such things would make her feel better, she was wrong.

Things like that just made her feel worse. 'But it's my fault he's gone.'

When Loveday Channer reached across the table to take hold of her hand, Kate let her. '*Your* fault, girl? How so do you reckon that then?'

Slowly, she looked back up. 'I dallied,' she said, noticing that although Ma Channer was dry-eyed, she had clearly been weeping at some point recently because her eyelids were rimmed with pink. 'He asked me to wed him, over and over — so many times I couldn't tell you. But I dithered, and I dallied . . . '

'No harm in wanting to be certain of your own mind, girl. This cursed war aside, *till death us do part* is a long time. Fearful long time. No sense anyone ever rushing headlong into a thing like marriage.'

' . . . but had I took him first time around, had I not let myself get distracted by . . . other ideas then, well, happen we wouldn't have got caught up with the Russells and the Colbornes and the whole business of going up to London in the first place. Happen Luke wouldn't have gone off with Mr Lawrence to join the Wiltshires . . . and been in the wrong place at the wrong time . . . '

'Or happen he might have been took all the sooner, girl,' Loveday Channer remarked. 'In one of them big slaughters a few years back. Can't none of us know for sure. That said, one thing I do know is that the boy was common-sensical. More than anything, he'd want you to get on with your life. Grieve for him by all means. Wear your widow's weeds. But don't spend the rest of your life mouldering away in them. It's not what he would have wanted for you. He'd think it a waste. An' so would I.'

'But if I were to just carry on as normal,' Kate said, 'just get on with my life . . . well, I couldn't do it. I'd feel terrible.' It was, she realized, the truth. 'I'd feel deceitful and disrespectful and . . . and just plain wrong.'

'I'm not saying go out and find yourself a new feller tomorrow,' Loveday Channer replied. ''Course I'm not.' When she then tightened her hold on her hand and chuckled, Kate noticed that her laugh had a chesty rasp to it. 'But don't spend the rest of your days a widow, neither,' she finished up. 'Do you understand me?'

While not what she had been expecting her mother-in-law to espouse, Kate nevertheless nodded. 'I'll think on what you've said.'

When the two women then fell to quiet reflection, Kate finished her tea. Then, noticing with a start that dusk was falling, she moved to get up from the table.

'For as long as I draw breath,' Loveday Channer remarked, getting to her feet and reaching to catch hold of her arm. 'I shall forever lament that things didn't work out as they should have for the pair of you. But I stand by my advice. Grieve for as long as it takes, but then find a way to start over — while you're still young enough to make another life for yourself. It's what the boy would have wanted.'

Grieve? Yes, she would do that — was doing that now. But start over? She didn't think so. It felt wrong to be even considering it.

Thanking her mother-in-law for the tea, Kate let herself out through the front door and started back along the lane. It was when she reached the rhododendron wood, and was carefully picking her way through the gnarly growth, that she realized she hadn't come away from her mother-in-law's feeling as settled as she would have liked: for certain she felt no less guilty for the way she had treated Luke that summer the Russells had arrived to stay. Yes, it had all worked out all right in the end. But she still felt guilty for taunting him for not wanting more from life — for craving nothing more than to be wed and to raise a family. Looking back now, she could see that he had simply been a couple of years ahead of her — a couple of years more mature — it being only in the last year or so that she, too, had come to crave those same things. As fate would have it, now that Luke was gone, she would give anything to be back in that summer, with the chance to be less evasive — to be quicker to accept him and choose the right path.

Arriving at the edge of the lawn to see lights showing from several of the downstairs windows of the house, she realized with a jolt that she had broken her promise to Naomi; she had gone out without telling anyone where she was going. Well, there was nothing she could do about that now other than hope to creep back in unnoticed and avoid upsetting everyone. Besides, she had only been to see her own mother-in-law. Surely, no one could reasonably take issue with that.

★ ★ ★

230

'Whatever are you up to, love?'

In response to Mabel's enquiry, Kate sighed. Already, she had been awake for several hours. But, reluctant to go downstairs and face the usual well-intentioned enquiries from everyone about how she had slept, and how she felt 'this fine morning', she had been struck by the idea to find the box of belongings Luke had brought there after their wedding. Thus, when Mabel had arrived, she had been kneeling on the floor, the box in question fetched from the attic, its contents already sorted into piles on the rug.

'Just going through a few things,' she said, a quick glance in Mabel's direction revealing that she was bearing a tray containing a pot of tea and a rack of toast.

'Been up long, have you?'

Deciding to be truthful but nevertheless refraining from looking up, she sat back on her heels. 'Quite a while, yes.'

'Good job I brought you this, then,' Mabel said, moving to set down her tray on the side table. 'If you've been about a while, you'll likely be in need of something to eat.'

Kate stifled a yawn. 'Believe it or not,' she said, eager to stave off disapproval of the fact that she hadn't stayed in bed and tried to get back to sleep. 'I had a reasonably restful night. Best for a while, actually.'

'And what is it you've got there, then?'

Thinking it obvious, she nevertheless fought back her frustration to explain. 'I went to fetch the box Luke brought for safekeeping before he went off to join up. I thought I should see what was in it. As you see before you, it's mostly his old clothes, which I was thinking I shall give to the church.'

From the corner of her eye, she saw the bottom of Mabel's skirt drawing nearer. Still she refrained from looking up. 'There's no rush, you know, love.'

She shrugged her shoulders. 'There's a couple of things I thought his Ma might like — his prayer book, for instance. And one or two things I might keep myself. But these clothes ought to be passed on to the needy, do someone else a good turn.'

'If you think so, love.'

'I do.'

'All right, well, I'll leave you to it then. Just don't let your toast get cold.'

'No. Thank you. I won't.'

Only when Mabel's skirt had disappeared from her sight, and she had heard the door click shut, did Kate get to her feet and cross to the table. She hadn't realized how hungry she was — nor, until Mabel had arrived, that it was after half-past seven. Lifting the cosy from the teapot, she removed the lid, stirred the contents, and then poured herself a cup. Settling into the easy chair, she buttered some toast and, eschewing the marmalade, bit into it. To her surprise, and for the first time in a while, she could taste the nuttiness of the bread and the creaminess of the butter. She helped herself to a second slice.

Chewing thoughtfully, she stared down at the collection of belongings on the rug; not much to show for a man in the prime of his life. But then, to be fair, Luke wasn't one for possessions. If he'd come into a fortune, the only thing he would have gone out and bought was a motorcar. And, probably, to make him feel the part, a new tweed cap and a pair of driving gloves. The rest of his fortune he would have squirrelled away. *A nest egg*, he would have said of it. *For our old age and our children's weddings.*

Wiping her fingers on the napkin, she dabbed it at the corner of her eyes. She'd been going along all right until that point, so why, now, was she tormenting herself with such thoughts? What was she doing, making herself feel all teary again over something that, in any event, was the mere product of her imagination? In dismay at her own foolishness, she shook her head. Then, staring down at the pile of Luke's clothing, she decided that later this morning she would ask Naomi to drive her to the church so that she might donate all of it to the poor.

To that end, and crouching back down on the floor, she picked up an old wool jacket and, recognizing it as the one Luke had worn almost every day, offered it to her nose. If she had been hoping to detect some trace of him, she had been hoping in vain; the garment yielded nothing, smelling only of the cardboard box in which it had been languishing these last years. She ran her hand through the pockets, checking for anything that might have been left there: nothing in either of the flapped ones on the front. In the breast pocket inside though, her fingers met with something that felt like a small square of card. Opening back the front of the jacket, she carefully pulled it out. What she saw caught her breath. Soft with damp, its corners rubbed to fuzziness, it was a valentine's card. Immediately, she recognized it — the illustration that of a cherubic cupid aiming his arrow at a heart-shaped cloud, the tiny image set inside a wreath of entwined forget-me-nots. She swallowed hard, recalling so clearly the words she had written on the back but reluctant now, after all that had happened, to turn it over and read them. Doing so anyway, she felt her throat tighten.

Won't You be Mine, Sweet Valentine?

The February of 1914, that would have been. She knew it for certain because, later that same year, once they had wed, they had agreed that valentine cards were daft. Instead, failing at the time to spot the equivalent soppiness of their idea, they had decided that from then on, on February the fourteenth each year, they would simply promise one another to remain true. After all, by the exchanging of their wedding vows, they had both secured their valentine for the rest of their lives. And, in the few short years that had followed, they had kept to their promises to swear their ongoing fidelity, even if Luke's subsequent going to war *had* required that their proclamations be committed to paper and entrusted to the post office.

Exhaling a long and shaky sigh, she turned the card back and studied the picture. Four years ago, before anyone had known that war was coming, Luke must have put it in his pocket so as to carry around with him, only to then leave the jacket behind. Well, she would keep it. She would put it with his letters.

Getting to her feet and crossing to the dressing table, she opened the lid of the walnut box where she had taken to keeping them. It was something he had brought back for her on one of his spells of leave that first year he had been in France. She remembered him telling her that he'd been given it by an old lady in a village, who had been grateful for something he had done for her. She could no longer recall the precise deed, and it didn't matter; the patterns on the wood were beautiful and she had loved it at first sight.

On the point of placing the valentine's card on top of the uppermost envelope, she stopped, moved to pull one of them from the bundle. Smiling at the wayward nature of his handwriting on the front, she tugged out the sheet of paper from inside.

My Darling Wife. She glanced to the date. January 1915; the war would barely have got going.

I can't put into words how much I enjoyed being on leave with you. Tearing myself away to return to this place was the hardest thing I ever had to do. I felt so proud to be walking around London with you on my arm, seeing the sights. It made all of this business over here seem unreal. How I wish that it was.

I know every husband swears he has the best wife in the world, but I truly do. There isn't a moment in the day when I don't think of you, and it keeps me going to know that you think of me, too. Not long, I am sure, and I will be back with you, making a new life with you and raising our family. Every night I pray that if there is to be no ending to this war just yet, then I shall at least have more leave again soon. Keep me in your prayers, as I will you, Your loving husband, Luke.

Spotting that a tear had fallen from her cheek and landed, directly upon the spot where he had written his name, smudging the ink and spreading it out across the bottom of the page, she let out a low moan. Then, clutching his letter to her chest, she doubled over, the pain searing through her insides too much to bear. She had thought she was getting over it. She had thought she had made peace with the fact that he was gone. But it was clear now that she hadn't. At that precise moment, she couldn't see how she would ever get over it. Without Luke, life would never be the same again.

10

Lawrence

For early July, it wasn't very summery. It had been pleasant enough to start with — fine and warm and sunny. But, over the last few days, it had turned cooler and unsettled, such that everyone seemed at a loss to know how to amuse themselves.

'I miss our picnics on the lawn,' Naomi opined on this particular afternoon, as she stood, staring out from the dining room towards the cedar tree. On the buffet behind her lay the remains of a Victoria sponge, and a solitary scone; the remnants of an afternoon tea that had, by force of necessity, again been taken indoors.

Peering out at the grey sky, Kate knew how she felt. The change to the weather meant that the last couple of days seemed to have passed as little more than a succession of meals interspersed with forlorn attempts to fill the hours between them.

'I miss them too,' she said, turning back into the room and, in the absence of anything better to do, setting about the clearing up. 'Sitting out there with everyone had become the nicest part of the day.'

At the window, Naomi moved. 'Look,' she said. 'Who do you think this could be?'

Putting down the stack of plates, Kate turned

about. Lumbering up the drive was a military staff car. 'No idea,' she said, crossing to the window and straining to try and make out its occupants. 'They don't look to be RAF, so I doubt they've come about Rowley or Ned.'

'No . . . ' Naomi replied, darting away from the window and hastening across the room. 'They look to be from the army.'

A dozen possibilities rushing into her head, Kate reached to a chair for support. *Oh, please, dear God*, she willed, gathering her wits and starting after Naomi, *please don't let this be more bad news*.

Arriving in the hallway to see her standing in the porch, Kate watched the staff car come to a halt, and then saw the driver, in army uniform, get out and go around to open one of the rear doors. Heavens. It was *Mr Lawrence*. He was back — and without so much as a word by way of warning, either.

Continuing on to the front door, she heard Naomi exclaiming in surprise.

'Darling! How wonderful! But why didn't you send word?'

Whatever Mr Lawrence said in response, Kate was unable to hear it. But she did notice that when Naomi threw her arms about his neck, he stood stiffly, making little effort to return her embrace.

'Mr Lawrence,' she greeted him when, taking his arm, Naomi led him in through the porch. 'Good day to you, and welcome back.'

The single nod he gave her in return struck her as the sort of acknowledgment one might

238

make to an acquaintance when passing them in the street, the blankness to his expression leading her to think he wasn't entirely sure where he was.

Naomi, though, was chattering on regardless, her smile girlish, her manner effusive. 'What a delightful surprise *this* is. Absolutely wonderful. Come, let's go through to the drawing room and see who's there for you to greet. Oh, and Kate,' she said, turning over her shoulder as she led Lawrence further along the hall, 'would you mind seeing to it for me that Lawrence's things are brought in?'

Behind her, in the porch, the driver already had matters in hand. 'All right there, ma'am?' he looked up at her to ask as he deposited Mr Lawrence's kitbag on the tiled floor.

Giving him a light smile, she nodded. 'Yes. Thank you.' But then, unable to ignore the nagging of unease, she said, 'Tell me, corporal, if you would, from where has Captain Colborne just come?'

'Regimental HQ, ma'am.'

'In Wiltshire.'

'That's right, ma'am.'

Curiouser and curiouser. 'Thank you,' she said.

'Will there be anything else, ma'am?'

She shook her head. 'No, thank you. Unless, of course, you'd like some refreshments.'

The young driver smiled. 'Thank you for the kind offer, ma'am, but I was instructed to make good time and head straight back.'

'Yes, of course. Well, good day to you then.'

239

'Good day to you, ma'am.'

Watching as the driver climbed into the motorcar and then proceeded to navigate it away over the gravel, Kate gave a puzzled shake of her head. What had Mr Lawrence been doing at Regimental HQ? She had assumed — *they* had assumed — that he was in France. He had given them no reason not to.

Closing the door to the porch, and noticing that a light drizzle was setting in, she turned back into the hallway. Then, determining that clearing away the tea things was less important than finding out what was going on with Mr Lawrence, she went through to the drawing room. When she arrived, it was to find him seated on the sofa, Naomi close beside him and Ned wheeling himself across from the window to join them.

'So, how many days' leave do you have?'

Ned's question seemed to catch Lawrence off-guard.

'Uh . . . a few.'

'A few?' Naomi pounced upon his reply. 'Good gracious, darling, for an army captain, that really is the vaguest of answers!'

'They're going to let me know . . . let me know when I'm due back, that is.'

Drawing closer, Kate couldn't help but notice that both Naomi and Ned were frowning. Indeed, at that moment pulling away from him to regard his face, Naomi went on to say, 'Forgive me, Lawrence, but I don't understand. *Who* will let you know?'

When Lawrence cleared his throat and then

240

proceeded to straighten the knot of his tie, Kate wondered why he was being so evasive. The question put to him hadn't been an unreasonable one. So was he, for some reason, unable to tell them what was going on? Goodness, what if he was on some sort of secret mission? Luke had once hinted that such things did exist — that it wasn't just the stuff of story books.

'HQ,' Lawrence eventually said. '*They* will tell me.'

Carefully, Kate sat down on the opposite sofa. Mr Lawrence looked truly terrible. In fact, he looked even worse than when he had come to tell her about Luke, his face haggard well beyond anything that a hot bath and some nourishing meals would remedy this time — beyond even being put right with a couple of good nights' sleep, by the look of him. Poor man. What on earth could have happened to make him look so ill?

'HQ,' Naomi repeated her husband's answer. 'I see.' To Kate, though, it was plain that she didn't see at all. 'Well, putting that aside for now, how about I go and draw you a bath so that you can have a lovely long soak? I'm sure it would make you feel fresher. And then perhaps we'll all have a drink before supper . . . '

Lawrence didn't reply. Nor did he make any move to.

Concerned by how this was unfolding, Kate glanced to Ned. Catching her look, he gave her the slightest of shrugs.

'Drinks, yes,' Lawrence eventually mumbled his agreement.

Watching him then follow his wife from the room, Kate, too, got up. 'Mr Lawrence doesn't seem very well,' she said to Ned.

'I expect he's just exhausted,' he said, turning his wheelchair about and wheeling himself back towards the French windows. 'One shouldn't underestimate how wearying the travelling can be. Making that arduous trip for the second time in a few weeks would be enough to exhaust any man . . . '

'Yes, for certain that'll be it,' Kate agreed. In truth, she thought Ned wrong but, since this was Mr Lawrence they were talking about, and since it wasn't her place to pry, she couldn't really press the matter. Perhaps it *was* as Ned said. Perhaps, once the poor man had got cleaned up and had a hot meal inside him, he would be more like his old self.

Not sure what to do for the best, she crossed to the window at the far end of the room. On the window seat, Rowley was reading.

'I think the weather's lifting,' he said, glancing up at her from the pages of his book.

Leaning across, she looked out. 'It does seem to be, yes.'

'To the extent that I was just thinking about making the effort to take a turn outside — you know, strike while the iron is hot and all that? Just because it's dry now, doesn't mean it will be later.'

Desperate for some air, Kate jumped at the suggestion. 'Would you like some company?' But then, realizing that he might not, but might feel unable to say so, she quickly went on: 'Although, if you'd thought to go alone, please do say.'

As it turned out, Rowley seemed glad that she had offered.

'Thank you for coming out with me,' he said as they set off around the side of the house. 'I've been itching to get out for some air all day.'

Noticing the earnestness on his expression, she reciprocated with a smile. 'I was growing desperate too. These last few days, I've thought the rain was *never* going to let up.'

'No, being stuck indoors has been truly awful, hasn't it?'

'For so many reasons, yes.'

'Tell me,' he continued, his manner as gentle as ever. 'How are you feeling now?'

'Me?' His question taking her by surprise, she realized that it was a while since anyone had thought to enquire. Not that she minded. In fact, she preferred it that way. Uncertain how to reply, though, she let out a sigh. 'In truth, I'm not altogether sure I know how to answer that. For certain, grief isn't how I thought it would be.'

'No?'

She shook her head. 'No. Though I don't know what I was expecting, I suppose I'd always thought that being in mourning would mean endless tears and pain. And I *have* cried. Quite often. And I have felt pain, too. But mostly I find that I feel nothing. Sometimes, I don't even remember that Luke's gone. And then, other times, I don't feel as though he was ever here to start with. 'Though we might have been married going on four years, the number of days we spent at home together can't hardly have amounted to more than a couple of dozen. So, it seems to me that constantly dissolving into floods of tears would make me a fraud, since, in truth, I'd be mourning something I'd never truly had.'

'Mourning the loss of an ideal as much as an actual entity,' Rowley observed.

Walking along beside him, she realized that it was the sort of observation she had been expecting, but hadn't got, from Ma Channer. 'Yes!' she said. 'Yes, that's it. That's it precisely. I hadn't thought anyone else would understand — '

'You explained yourself very clearly.'

'I did? Only, until now, I'm not certain I even saw it for myself.'

With that, they both turned their eyes to the sky. Bother. It was starting to rain and there was something she had wanted to ask him, something she didn't feel comfortable discussing indoors.

'We should probably turn back,' he said. 'I shouldn't want to get you into trouble for being out in the rain.'

On his face as he spoke was a wry smile, which she returned with one of her own.

Raining or not, she would ask him now, while they were still some way from the house. 'What do you think about Mr Lawrence?'

Initially, he didn't reply. When he eventually did, it was to say, 'To be truthful, I'm not sure what to think.'

Oddly, his response came as a comfort because it meant that she hadn't been alone in noticing; there *was* something amiss with the poor man. 'Me neither,' she said.

'Clearly, for him to arrive so unexpectedly, something must have happened. But I shouldn't care to guess what that might be.'

'He doesn't look at all well,' she remarked, picturing the sickly tint of his complexion.

'He doesn't, no. But then who among us would, had we witnessed the horrors he must have.'

'Perhaps he has been sent home for some rest,' she suggested. Sadly, no matter how badly she wanted to believe it, it felt unlikely.

'Perhaps.'

Noticing that their quickened pace seemed to be leaving him short of breath, she glanced to his face. 'Are we walking too fast for you?'

He shook his head. 'No, it's fine. More important that we get indoors.'

'You think me wrong about Mr Lawrence, though, don't you?' she said. 'You don't think he's just been sent home to rest at all.'

Continuing to retrace their steps across the lawn, the distance they covered before he replied this time was considerable.

'I'm not sure it's my place to speculate. If there is something Captain Colborne feels able to tell us — about where he has been and what he has been doing there — then I'm sure that he will.'

'Yes,' she said. 'Of course. You're right.'

Arriving back indoors, Kate left Rowley staring out at the passing clouds and made her way up to her room to get dry. If the weather was better later, then perhaps she could suggest that

Naomi take Mr Lawrence for an evening stroll — perhaps down to the cove. After all, everyone slept better for a few breaths of sea air.

Over dinner, though, it became apparent that Naomi and Lawrence wouldn't be walking anywhere. Their meal finished, Nurse Hammond arrived with Esme. Wrapped in her dressing gown and ready for bed, the little girl squealed with delight and scampered around the table to climb onto her mother's lap.

'Mamma! Mamma! Story! Story!'

'Darling, hush,' Naomi urged, nevertheless lifting the little girl onto her knee. 'Do try not to be so loud.' Turning to Nurse Hammond, she went on, 'Thank you for seeing to her, Nurse Hammond. I'll bring her up in a moment. Esme, say goodnight.'

Gurgling with laughter, Esme waved to the nurse's departing back. 'Nighty-night,' she shouted after her. 'Sleep tight.'

'Christ almighty!'

Taking everyone by surprise, Lawrence slammed his fist upon the table, rattling the dinner service and bringing each of them to turn in his direction.

From her mother's lap Esme started to cry.

'In the name of God, whose child *is* that?' Lawrence demanded, his eyes bulging, his face crimson.

Shrinking back against her chair with Esme clutched to her chest, Naomi's expression was one of incomprehension. 'She's . . . ours,' she whispered. 'Lawrence, this is Esme — our daughter. Surely you can see that.'

With that, Lawrence craned across the table. Under his stare, Esme squirmed and wriggled, her wailing growing louder.

'*Daughter? What* daughter? I don't have a daughter! Why do you lie to me, woman? Where's that nurse gone? Someone go and fetch her and have her take this child to its mother.' When, in their shock, no one moved, Lawrence pushed at his chair and sent it hurtling backwards. 'Do none of you hear me? Now, I say!'

In the disbelieving silence, Rowley cleared his throat. And, when everyone except Lawrence turned to look at him, he rose to his feet. 'Captain Colborne, sir,' he said, struggling upright and then standing as though to attention. 'Might you accompany me outside, sir? You . . . uh . . . that is to say . . . a most urgent matter requires your presence.'

With no idea what Rowley was doing, Kate held her breath and turned back to Lawrence. At least his attention was now directed away from Naomi and Esme.

'*Lieutenant* . . . ?'

'Rowley-King, sir. On assignment here from RAF Chittenham.'

'I'm needed outside, you say?'

'Yes, sir. Something spotted on approach from the south, sir. Thought you might be able to advise.'

'Enemy?' Lawrence asked, casting about as though for his cap but then, evidently deciding that he could do without it, rounding the end of the table.

'Uncertain, sir.'

'Number?'

'Also uncertain, sir.'

'Come on, then, man. Don't dally. Show me.'

With Rowley going ahead of Lawrence into the hallway, those left at the table finally dared to breathe out.

In his wheelchair, Ned sat slowly shaking his head. 'Well done, Rowley, old chap. Quick thinking.' Then, turning to his sister, he said, 'Look, Min, now might be a good time to take Esme upstairs and settle her into bed. In the meantime, I'll see if I can find some smokes to take out — see if, between us, Rowley and I can calm the man's nerves.'

Setting Esme down on the floor, and wiping a hand across her cheek, Naomi stared back at her brother. 'Is that what . . . is that what this is — his nerves?'

Ned's first response was to shrug. 'Clearly I'm no doctor, but, if pressed for an opinion, then I'd say that yes, this is almost certainly down to his nerves — most likely shot to pieces by what he's been through.'

Holding tightly onto Esme's hand, Naomi went to stand in front of him. 'And what *has* he been through? Tell me, what could possibly do this to a man such that he doesn't even recognize his own daughter? And to make him think . . . make him think that his own wife would lie to him? What could do that? Tell me, please, because I am at a loss. I'm at a loss to even recognize my own husband.'

'What would do this? I wouldn't even try to guess.'

'But it is why he's come home, isn't it?' Naomi went on. 'He's been sent back here because he's — what's the term — 'no longer fit for duty'? That's what this is all about, isn't it?'

Again, Ned shrugged. 'Min, I couldn't say. Only he can tell you that.'

'Yes, yes, I know. But, assuming for a moment that *is* why he's been sent home, what is it the army would have us do with him? Is there a treatment? Is there something to be done for him?'

In a gesture of helplessness, Ned raised his hands. 'I'm sorry, Min, I can't answer that. I can only suggest that you have a word with Nurse Hammond — '

'I don't think Nurse Hammond is the right person to be involved in this — '

'Trust me, she might not be a doctor but, were you to hear her talk, you would appreciate that she has the knowledge of one. At the very least, she might advise you how best to approach him — how to avoid angering him, or how to calm him down — '

'*Calm him down?* Why should that even fall to me? I'm his wife. I'm not the one who put him in this . . . in this state . . . and then . . . and then just . . . just sent him home.'

'I know that, Min. We all do. Nevertheless, I still say speak to Nurse Hammond. I'm sure she will know what can be done — in the longer term, I mean.'

'In the longer term? But what about *now*?' Naomi wanted to know.

Pained to see her looking so lost, Kate got to

her feet and went towards her.

'Now?' Ned replied.

'Yes. Now. Tonight. What am I supposed to do with him right this very minute?'

Exhaling a long breath, Ned shook his head. 'Well — '

'I certainly don't want him anywhere near Esme.'

'Tell me,' Ned said, looking up at his sister, 'which would he be most likely to reach for to steady his nerves — whisky or brandy?'

Still holding tightly to Esme, Naomi looked pale and lost, the gesture she gave one of despair. 'He's not much of a one for either. Of the two, brandy, I suppose.'

'Then I'll get Rowley to help me ply him with some. It's not the right answer, I realize that but perhaps, if we can get him drowsy enough, he'll fall asleep.'

'Well . . . '

'That does sound sensible,' Kate said. Her aim being to ensure that Naomi didn't ignore what seemed to be practical advice. 'And then, in the morning, we can talk to Nurse Hammond and see what light she can shed upon Mr Lawrence's . . . condition — see what she recommends we do to help him.'

'I suppose we have little choice,' Naomi conceded. 'In the absence of any other ideas, I suppose it has to be better than doing nothing.'

When Naomi then departed to take Esme upstairs, Kate was left to stand and look about. What did she do? Did she go with her — try to offer some words of comfort? Huh. What comfort could *she* offer? Of what help could *she* be? Besides, after what had just happened, it would surely be better for Naomi and Mr Lawrence to be left alone to talk. There would be apologies to be made, and explanations to be given. And, no doubt, tears to be shed, too. No, if she could be of any use, it would be in the morning, once Mr Lawrence had explained himself, and Naomi better understood what was going on. And so, although it was still early, and since, on this occasion, she could be of no real use, she would retire for the night.

★ ★ ★

Arriving in her room, she sat on the side of her bed, forlorn, her mind picturing Naomi's puzzlement as Mr Lawrence had questioned her about Esme. She couldn't believe he had forgotten that they had adopted her — even allowing for the fact that he had been away at war. That first time he had come home to discover that Naomi had taken the little girl in, his reaction had been one of amusement; it wasn't even stretching the truth to say that he had been tickled pink, spending much of his leave doting on her. Once he had returned to the front, Naomi had even remarked that she couldn't have hoped for a better reaction from him. She also knew that Naomi wrote diligently, relaying to him news of the child's progress and antics, and that, on her birthday and at Christmas, she sent him photographs of her. So, what on carth had gone wrong? Ned had said

251

that Mr Lawrence's outburst stemmed from his nerves being frayed, but Mr Lawrence had always been such a solid and composed man — certainly never one for jumpiness or disquiet. Indeed, he had the very backbone — the very sense of correctness and duty — that his brother had so completely lacked, all of which just made the whole business so very much sadder.

With a defeated shake of her head, she sighed. She couldn't bear to think of there being something properly wrong with Mr Lawrence. Nor could she bear having to speculate about what might have brought on such a severe and pronounced change to him. But, as she had reminded herself earlier, it wasn't her place to pry. If, when Naomi and Lawrence had spent some time together, Naomi chose to share with her what her husband confided, that would be down to her. If she decided not to tell her, well, then she would have to hope to find out from Ned. And if *he* didn't know anything, then perhaps there was nothing to know. Perhaps it really was just Mr Lawrence's exhaustion making him so fractious and forgetful.

Once washed and undressed and in her nightgown, she knelt at the side of her bed and tried to apply her mind to saying her prayers, asking, as usual, that God look after all of the people most dear to her. Then, switching out the lamp on her night table, she climbed into bed. With any luck, it would turn out that all Mr Lawrence really needed *was* just a good night's sleep. Indeed, perhaps tomorrow, after a nice rest, he would be back to his former self.

Although happen it would be wise to add one last request to her prayers and ask the dear Lord to see to it — just in case.

★ ★ ★

'How is Mr Lawrence this morning?'

Wandering into the drawing room before breakfast the following morning, Kate came across Naomi staring out of the window. Since waking, she'd been hoping that her prayers had been answered and that Mr Lawrence would be feeling better.

Catching hold of her arm, Naomi drew her to the far corner of the room. 'I tell you, Kate, he's definitely not well.'

'No?' Oh dear. Precisely what she'd been hoping *not* to hear.

'Far from it.'

'Naomi,' she said, looking quickly about, 'last night, I felt it wasn't my place to . . . well, to involve myself in your business. But please know that you can tell me. Whatever it is, you can tell me and I will help you, no matter what.'

Naomi exhaled heavily. To Kate's mind, she still seemed reluctant to say much.

'Well, last night,' Naomi eventually began again, 'after all the to-do, and despite having several inside him, once Lawrence came to bed, all he did was toss and turn and mutter — mutter things that made no sense, made no sense to me, that is. Then, after a while like that he seemed to settle. He became quieter and still. At one point, I even thought that he had fallen asleep . . . and thought that I might, too. But then, with no warning whatsoever, he railed into the darkness that it was too quiet. With that, the tossing and turning started up again. And then he got up and started pacing about the room. Despite me asking, several times, what was wrong, he ignored me. Or didn't hear me. Either way, it was as though I wasn't there. At that point, I even wondered whether he was sleep-walking.'

Realizing that she had been holding her breath, Kate exhaled. Alone in the dark with such behaviour, Naomi must have been beside herself with worry. 'And then what happened?'

'Shortly after that, he left the room. At first, I thought he had probably just gone to use the lavatory. But when, after a while, he didn't come back, I got out of bed to look for him. There was no sign of him along the corridor, so I went to the window . . . and there he was, down on the lawn, just standing there, not moving.'

'What did you do?'

'I didn't know *what* to do — to leave him to his own devices or go and fetch him. In the end, fearing he might stray to the cliff edge, I went down to him. And, do you know, he came like a lamb. 'I'm so terribly cold,' was all he said.'

Unexpectedly, Kate shivered. 'And then did he sleep?'

'He did. And I think that for a while, I did, too, because the next thing I knew it was daylight, and Mrs Bratton was at the door with our tray. Besides tea and the *Telegraph*, she'd brought the first post, including a letter addressed to Lawrence.'

'At least you managed *some* sleep, both of you,' Kate observed. 'And did he seem better — when he awoke?'

Naomi shook her head. 'Only for the briefest of moments, really just while he worked out where he was. After that, he started complaining about everything — the brightness of the light coming in through the window, the slipperiness of the eiderdown, that the pages of the newspaper were making too much noise — whereupon he demanded I see to it that they 'stopped rustling so much'.' Noticing tears in Naomi's eyes, Kate reached for her hand and clasped it between her own. 'And then, when he saw the letter and read it, well . . . it was like a red rag to a bull — he simply blew up. He leapt out of bed, threw it to the floor and stormed from the room.'

Although alarmed by this turn of events, Kate continued to hold Naomi's hand and nod encouragement. There was more to be learned, she was sure of it. 'I see,' she said softly. 'And then what?'

'Once he'd gone, I picked up the letter and read it.'

'*You did?* But wasn't that taking a chance?'

'Very possibly.'

'I mean, what if he'd come back and caught you with it?'

'At the time I thought only that it might be my one opportunity to discover what's been going on — what's making him like this. Besides, he didn't seem to care that he'd left it behind. To be honest, he was so cross, I'm not sure he knew *what* he was doing. I've never seen him so enraged. It was as frightening to witness as his outburst last night. Truly, Kate, his behaviour has me on tenterhooks. I'm nothing but a bag of nerves.'

'So, this letter,' Kate said, her concern being to piece things together. 'Does it, as he suggested it would, say how long he is on leave — when he must return to the front?'

Beside her, Naomi pressed her lips together. 'No,' she said, her voice little more than a whisper. 'To the contrary. It states that he has been placed on a period of medical leave, the duration of which — and I quote — 'is to be determined following consultation with a regimental doctor, to take place at a date and location to be advised.''

'Medical leave?' She glanced at Naomi's expression for further clues. 'So . . . he's been injured then . . . or fallen sick?'

Lowering her head, Naomi seemed to be considering how best to reply. And, when she did, it was with her voice reduced further still. 'The letter makes no mention of either. In that regard, I'm none the wiser. And I don't feel inclined to ask him, either. Oh, Kate, what has it come to when I can't even ask my own husband what's troubling him for fear of how he might react? What has the army done to him? And how *dare* they? How *dare* they do this to my husband?'

Reflecting upon what Naomi had just told her, Kate had no idea how to answer that. It wasn't that Naomi's questions were unreasonable, just that she hadn't the least inkling of what to suggest. Mr Lawrence had always been one of the most easy-going men she knew. He liked things done in a certain way, yes, but only because he upheld standards. But he'd never been a difficult man. And he'd certainly never been an angry one.

'And how is he now?' she asked, the thought of Mr Lawrence rampaging about the house a worrying one; for a start, there was Esme and her safety to consider.

'That's the thing. When I came downstairs, I found him sitting in the morning room, dressed and reading the *Telegraph* as though everything was perfectly normal — as though nothing had happened.'

'And this letter that came — did it say *anything else?* Anything that might help us decide what to do?'

'The only other thing it said was that he is not to return to duty until passed as fit to do so by the medical board. Oh, Kate, I'm beside myself. I've even found myself biting my nails. And I haven't done that since I was at school.'

Still Kate couldn't think how to be of help. 'And for his part, he's offered you no explanation at all?'

Naomi gave a forlorn shake of her head. 'None whatsoever. Not a word about any of it. In a way, that's the part in all of this that worries me the most. I can't decide whether he already knew he was on medical leave and was deliberately keeping the fact from me, or whether he genuinely didn't realize it. I prefer to think it the latter, and that, perhaps, with what happened to

Lu — Well, no, it doesn't matter. I shouldn't be burdening *you* with all of this anyway.'

'You think Luke's death might have set this off?' Kate said, guessing at what Naomi had been going to say.

'It has gone through my mind.'

In a way, Kate reflected, letting go of Naomi's hand, it did make sense. Luke's death, while perhaps not solely to blame for Mr Lawrence's state of mind, might have been the straw that broke the camel's back.

'So, what are you going to do?' she asked.

In response to her question, Naomi exhaled heavily. 'I have no idea. I suppose all I can do is as Ned suggested last night — talk to Nurse Hammond.'

Relieved that Naomi should think it a good idea, Kate nodded. 'All right. Then straight after breakfast we'll go and see what she has to say.'

★   ★   ★

'Utter poppycock!'

Seated at the table in the morning room less than ten minutes later, Kate glanced warily in the direction of Mr Lawrence to see him staring down at his newspaper, his expression, thus far unremarkable, suddenly thunderous.

Across from him, Naomi looked up from her plate. When she spoke, her voice trembled. 'What's that, dear?'

'You people know nothing of this war. Nothing whatsoever. How could a man, who has done nothing but sit at a desk in Fleet Street, wielding

258

nothing more than an ink pen, profess to know even one-tenth of what is going on over there? Blind, that's what you all are. And precisely how this government likes it.'

'Darling — '

'And you — you women,' Lawrence pressed on, glancing about. 'Your sex are the worst, with your cooing and your sympathy and your — your platitudes. You couldn't possibly understand, not any single one of you. Not even that flying-boy brother of yours. None of you know — will ever know the sheer hell of it — the suffering. Can't possibly.'

As suddenly as he had started, Lawrence fell quiet, his attention given back to his newspaper. Afraid to make the least sound, Kate sat, motionless, wondering what to do for the best. Mr Lawrence's moods seemed beyond anyone to predict, it being impossible to know, from one moment to the next, how he would react to anything. When she had come in and taken her place at the table, although noticing that he was clearly still tired and strained, his manner had seemed lucid and straightforward. Within moments, though, he had started to ramble nonsensically, muttering about the army having set loose mad dogs. And she could see how his behaviour was affecting Naomi: she was sitting there now, jittery and pale-looking.

'What?' Lawrence chose that moment to look up and demand. No one answered. Instead, they exchanged glances that betrayed their bafflement. 'Dear God, tell me I can't hear that mewling child again?'

Naomi shot a glance towards the door. Before coming into breakfast, she had taken up Kate's suggestion that they take Esme into the study, telling her that, as a special treat for being a good girl, this morning she was to have her breakfast with her Uncle Ned. Even so, it only needed Ned to have become distracted for a few seconds for the child to have spotted her chance to slip from the room.

The hallway, though, appeared silent and, looking across at Naomi, Kate indicated her puzzlement at Lawrence's question with the slightest of shrugs: there had been no sound from anywhere. In fact, only moments earlier, she had been thinking how excruciating the silence was.

'No, there's no child in here,' Naomi replied to her husband's question. Her cheeks and throat, Kate noticed, were flushed to a high shade of pink. 'Would you like me to pour you some more coffee?'

'No, I do not want more coffee,' Lawrence snapped back. 'What I *want* is for that child to stop bawling. For God's sake, tell me, do you not hear it? Any of you?' With that, he clutched at his head as though in some terrible torment. Then, with his face screwed up in agony, seemingly of its own accord, his right arm shot sideways to send his coffee cup skittering across the table.

Rooted to her seat, Kate looked to Naomi. She appeared to be fighting back tears.

'Um . . . no. I can't hear anyone at all.'

Lawrence, though, was adamant. 'Imagining it, am I? Is that it?'

'No, dear, I'm not saying anything of the — '

'Think I don't know?' he went on. Even from a distance, Kate could see veins pulsing in his temples. 'Take me for a fool would you — telling me I have a daughter! I have no daughter. You, on the other hand, *do* seem to. Been busy with another man while I've been away, have you?'

'*What?*' In her disbelief, Naomi reeled backwards.

'Major Cameron, was it? His little bastard, is she? Wouldn't surprise me, the stubby little ginger weasel. Have Corporal Channer bring the motor round. I shall go over there now and have it out with the man. Never did trust the oily devil — '

'Lawrence, please — '

His condition was worse than they had thought, Kate reflected. Not only had he forgotten who Esme was, he seemed not to have registered that Luke was dead. Perhaps Naomi was right: perhaps his death *had* been the final straw.

'Or would you have me believe it an immaculate conception? Is that the lie you're peddling?'

'Lawrence, please, stop this,' Naomi pleaded. 'I told you. The child is Esme. She was orphaned. We took her in. We call her our daughter but in actual fact she's my niece. Surely you remember — '

'Ha! More lies. Well, we'll see about this.'

With that, from further along, Rowley pushed back his chair and got to his feet. 'Captain Colborne, sir, I was wondering about your orders for this morning . . . '

In despair, Kate hung her head and stared down into her lap. Surely Rowley couldn't

261

believe such a ruse would work a second time? Even if it got Mr Lawrence away from the table, they couldn't possibly ply him with alcohol at this hour of the morning.

As had been the case last night, though, Lawrence seemed to undergo a transformation. 'Orders,' he said, getting to his feet and throwing down his napkin. 'Time to inspect the lines, is it?'

'Yes, sir.'

'Very well. Then let's be getting out there Lieutenant . . . Lieutenant . . .'

'Rowley-King, sir.'

Moving around the table, Lawrence paused to peer at Rowley as though seeing him for the first time. 'New to the company, eh, lad?'

'Newly arrived, sir. Yes, sir.'

'Excellent. Come on then, man. At the double.'

The moment they left the room, Naomi sank heavily back onto her chair and, rushing to her side, Kate bent to grasp her hands.

'Oh, Kate, whatever am I to do? This is exhausting.'

'First,' she said, kneeling down beside her, 'we'll go and talk to Nurse Hammond. Ned is right — with all the soldiers she's nursed, she's bound to have seen something like this before. Then, whatever she advises, we follow her instructions to the letter.'

The sigh Naomi gave in response was a long and weary one. 'The worst thing is that when, last night, he left and didn't come back for a while, I felt relieved,' she began to say, shaking

262

her head in dismay. 'How dreadful is that?' When she then raised a hand to her face, and the sleeve of her blouse slid down her arm, Kate found herself staring at a reddish-purple welt just above her wrist. Unmistakeably, it was the shape of three long fingers.

In her shock, she pulled away. 'Did *he* do this?' she whispered, her own hand trembling as she reached to catch hold of Naomi's arm and take a closer look.

Hanging her head, Naomi seemed reluctant to reply. Eventually, though, she gave the tiniest of nods. 'But he didn't mean to.'

Didn't mean to? To leave such bruises would have required considerable force, certainly more than was required to simply take hold of somebody. 'Naomi, I think perhaps — '

'It happened after he'd been thrashing about as though in the throes of a bad dream. You have to remember that is was dark. He awoke in a panic . . . and when I leaned over to ask what was wrong, I suppose he thought me someone else.'

'Someone else?'

'Oh, I don't know,' Naomi said wearily. 'The enemy or someone, I suppose. All I know is that in his state of terror, he made a grab for me and clutched at my arm. That's all it was.'

That's all it was? Maybe. But how long before it was something other than her wrist that he grabbed? What if, in a state of confusion, he went for Naomi's throat?

'Then I think we should get another room made up for him,' she said. 'Along on the bachelors' landing. That way, you'll be able to sleep, safe from these night terrors of his.'

'But he's my husband, Kate. I shouldn't be banishing him . . . certainly not over a few nightmares — '

'But it's not just the nightmares, is it?' Kate said. 'He's hurt you. And he could do so again, lash out whether he means to or not. No, until we work out what's wrong with him, and get him some treatment — or some medication, or whatever it turns out that he needs, you have to think of your own well-being. For Esme's sake, you have to protect yourself.'

'Protect myself? From my own husband? But Kate, that's madness.'

'The thing that would be madness,' Kate said, 'would be to let this happen again. Just think for a moment. He could have injured you real bad. Maybe worse. No, we'll put him in another room. And then we need to get the doctor out to him.'

Sitting there, deflated, Naomi gave a despairing shake of her head. 'I don't understand it, Kate. He used to be such a gentle man — not this . . . this . . . stranger. Do you know, last night, alone in the darkness after he had gone, I even found myself wondering what I would do were it to turn out that this war has changed him for good — what I would do if he is never the same again. And then I thought, what if, deep down, and all along, he has always had this streak in him — the same cruel streak Aubrey had — and all it needed was for this war to trigger it, bring it out of him, if you will. What if this is how he's going to be from now on?'

The same thought having gone through her own head, Kate sighed. 'Naomi, look, why don't we — '

'If this is how he's going to be, all I can think to do is throw myself upon the mercy of Mamma and Papa — see whether they will have me back at Clarence Square. If this is who he is now, then I see no alternative but to leave him.'

Unable to think how to ease Naomi's distress, Kate got up, went to the French windows, and scanned the gardens: Rowley and Mr Lawrence were standing right at the edge of the lawn, looking over the hedge and out to sea.

'Come on,' she said, turning back into the room and determining not to take no for an answer. 'Like it or not, we owe it to Mr Lawrence to get him some help. And, since she would seem to be the only person we've got, we're going to start with Nurse Hammond.'

Thankfully, it turned out that Nurse Hammond had indeed witnessed such behaviour before.

'My dear,' she said, pulling a chair from under the table at the window and gesturing to Naomi to sit down. 'There is no doubt in my mind that your husband is suffering from a combination of frayed nerves and exhaustion. The term most often used to describe the condition is shellshock — although, more latterly, opinion would seem to be that in very few cases does it have anything to do with exposure to actual shelling.'

To Kate, Naomi's face seemed to be one of utter incomprehension. 'Shellshock?'

'For those of us who have never been to the front, the horror there is impossible to imagine.'

'It's true, Min,' Ned interjected.

'For days upon end,' Nurse Hammond picked up again. 'With no respite whatsoever, men on the front line are subjected to deafening noise and the most terrible of sights. But, hard though this will be for you to believe, it is the silence, when it does come, that they end up fearing the most. By contrast to the frantic noise, the stillness is eerie and unsettling and plays tricks on a man's mind. Then there is the carnage — the blood, the wounded, the dying. And that's without the narrow scrapes, the near misses, the constant terror and fear — the guilt, even, especially for an officer who has had to watch his men suffer, often unable to do anything for them. All that fear and terror, even the sustained courage and bravado, it builds up in a man and takes its toll. With no other outlet, the strain of it will eventually manifest itself as jumpiness, twitching, disorientation, delusions. Violence even.'

Delusions, yes, Mr Lawrence was certainly plagued by those. 'So, what do we do?' Kate took the chance to ask, Nurse Hammond having, to her mind, described quite enough. Picturing such conditions and afflictions was the last thing Naomi needed.

'I understand your husband has been sent home on medical leave,' Nurse Hammond turned to Naomi to say.

Naomi nodded. 'Yes. A letter came from his regiment. Not that he has told me it says that.

And, for my part, I've purposely avoided letting him know that I've seen it for fear of how he might react.'

'Well, even an army doctor will tell you that there is no quick remedy to be had. Indeed, opinion is divided as to the appropriate course of action. Some say that removing the man from the front is the worst thing that can be done. Others disagree, citing rest as the best treatment. Others still, well, the barbarism of *their* methods is best not spoken of. To my mind, what your husband needs most — initially, at least — is a spell of proper sleep — '

'But he *won't* sleep,' Naomi pointed out. 'Or at least, he *can't*. If last night is anything to go by, then it would seem that instead of sleeping, he tosses and turns and cries out. He gets up and wanders about. And in the darkness in the middle of the night . . . ' With this, Kate sent her a nod of encouragement. 'I am left fearing for what he might — do.'

'Sadly, it's not uncommon for getting rest and sleep to be the last thing a man with such difficulties is prepared to try. More often than not he sees it as giving in, or as cowardice, or letting his men down. But I still suggest that we try, by whatever means, to get him to sleep. Nothing is worse for either the nerves or the mind than exhaustion.'

'And then?' she ventured. 'If sleeping doesn't help him?'

'Well, what I was going to suggest anyway, Mrs Colborne, is that you ask Lieutenant Russell here to telephone the captain's regiment.

Though they won't talk to *you*, they might talk to *him*. If he can relay details of the captain's behaviour and request that, without delay, your husband is seen by the regimental doctor, it would be a step in the right direction. That does mean, of course, that you will need a pretext for getting him there, should he not be willing to go of his own volition. But that is a bridge we need only consider once it is in sight. In the meantime, I do have a couple of things I use to sedate a badly wounded patient. I suggest we try one of those.'

'But he isn't wounded,' Naomi pointed out.

'But he is, Min.'

'Your brother is right, Mrs Colborne,' Nurse Hammond went on. 'Captain Colborne might not have lost the use of a limb, nor be suffering the effect of, say, gas, but I assure you, he *is* wounded. The expression you'll often hear used for such troubles is 'wounded in mind.''

Wounded in mind. How on earth did you treat a wounded mind, Kate wondered? You couldn't apply a bandage to it or a splint. And, presumably, you couldn't exercise it to speed up its recovery like you could a broken limb. So, what the devil did you do — keep the man drugged? Cart him away and lock him up?

Watching Nurse Hammond pull from her pocket a tiny key to unlock her medicine chest, Kate gave a long sigh. This condition of Mr Lawrence's didn't sound good at all. And he had always been such a nice man, too. Many more outbursts from him, though, and Naomi could be forgiven for wishing he hadn't made it back from the front at all — that instead, he had been taken quickly and unexpectedly from them like poor Luke.

Dear Luke. At least *he* was no longer troubled by *any* earthly concern. Unlike poor Mr Lawrence, at least *he* was at peace. And, for that, she would perhaps one day be grateful.

11

Recoveries

'I wonder how Mr Lawrence is faring?'

It was after luncheon one afternoon, almost a week after the arrival of Mr Lawrence and, when Kate had announced that she was going to take Esme out into the garden so that she might let off some steam, Rowley had offered to keep them company. Now, with the little girl charging ahead of them, the breeze flapping at the hem of her dress and buffeting her bonnet on her head, the two adults walked companionably, their conversation relaxed.

Earlier that morning, accompanied by Naomi, Lawrence had left for his regiment in Wiltshire. By some stroke of good fortune, Ned had eventually managed to speak to someone there who had been sympathetic to Lawrence's plight, resulting in him jumping the queue for an interview with a panel of the regiment's medical staff. Together, Naomi and Ned had then concocted a story about him being called for an assessment of his fitness to return to duty. The news had pleased Lawrence, a degree of calmness subsequently coming over him. He hadn't even taken issue with the fact that Naomi was going with him, ostensibly simply for an outing — a two-night stay in a pleasant country hotel supposedly a welcome break. As a result, those left behind at Woodicombe also came to feel a certain calm, the constant need to be on alert receding with the departure of the station taxi.

'I should very much hope that he is receiving a sympathetic hearing,' Rowley replied to Kate's question. 'Some view shellshock as nothing more than malingering, and deal with it harshly. But Captain Colborne doesn't seem the type for that sort of behaviour. He seems a decent chap.'

'He is,' Kate replied, glancing up to where, some distance ahead of them, Esme was bent low, examining something in the grass. 'Don't pick it up, lovey,' she called towards her. 'Whatever it is, leave it be, there's a good girl. No,' she went on, 'Mr Lawrence is as sincere a man as I have ever met.'

'War shows no respect for character,' Rowley observed. 'It will take anyone — good, bad, ugly. Sincere or otherwise.'

Reflecting upon his remark, Kate sighed. 'It has certainly changed a lot of lives. Only the other night I was thinking how none of the three men sent from this family to go an' fight will have been left untouched by it — one way or another.'

'No.'

'Same goes for you,' she said as the realization dawned. 'What will happen to you now — once you're fully better, I mean?'

He shrugged his shoulders. 'I should very much like to continue flying.'

'Truly? Even after what happened to you?'

He laughed. 'Despite that, yes. Until you go

up there it's hard to comprehend but you see, there really is no feeling quite like it. The engine splutters to life, the prop whizzes round, you hare along over the grass and then, with no say in the matter, you're off the ground, gaining height and looking down upon everything from above, the wind whistling about you. Sadly, though, I doubt I shall be allowed back up again. For a start, the Royal Air Force has some very different ideas to those prevailing when I joined the RFC. Not only that, but the war itself has moved on. It requires something different now.'

'I suppose it won't be long before you have to return *somewhere*, though.' Unexpectedly, the idea of him leaving Woodicombe made her stomach twist: yet another wrench to deal with. By now she would have thought to be more practised at it — more used to having the things and the people around her constantly shifting.

'I am expecting to hear any day now, yes. In fact, I'm rather surprised that I haven't done so already. But Mother has been sending on my post, and I've yet to receive any orders.'

There was no news for Rowley the next day, either. And for her part Kate found that she was glad. She realized now that she had missed their afternoon strolls, the pattern of which had been interrupted by the abysmally poor weather and Mr Lawrence's illness. But, now that they had resumed, she was reminded of how interesting Rowley was, and how being in his company brought her a degree of calm.

It was while they were out walking that particular afternoon that they saw the station taxi pulling in through the gates, bringing Naomi and Mr Lawrence back from Wiltshire. Cutting short their stroll, they hastened to meet them.

'How did you fare?' Kate whispered to Naomi as the two of them embraced.

'Not too badly,' Naomi whispered back. 'Come up and help me unpack and I'll tell you.'

And so, with Rowley drawing Lawrence into conversation about their journey, Kate followed Naomi upstairs. 'I've never known you travel so light,' she observed when they reached Naomi's room and, unfastening Naomi's travelling bag, she reached inside.

'Needs must. It was only the two nights.'

'Was your hotel nice?' she asked, removing the purses containing Naomi's toiletries and cosmetics and putting them on top of the chest of drawers.

'It was. Small and quaint. Quiet. Of course, I had to make sure to slip the sleeping draft into Lawrence's drink both evenings — couldn't have him pacing about in the middle of the night, shouting and ranting and bothering the other guests.'

'No, of course. So, what's going to happen to him then?' Getting up from the floor, she took Naomi's mackintosh from the back of the chair and gave it a good shake. 'I'll try sponging this mark. It looks like smuts from the train.'

'Sorry.'

'No matter.'

'Well, obviously, I wasn't party to his actual examination — I was taken away to wait in an office while that was taking place. But, when it was over, and Lawrence popped his head round the door to tell me he had to go and sign some papers, I slipped out and, as luck would have it, came across a doctor.'

'And you were able to speak to him?'

'I was. At first, he refused to talk to me. But I begged him, explaining that we have a small child in our care and that, at times, I fear for her well-being.'

Unpacking Naomi's shoes, Kate set them aside to clean later. 'And?'

'And he said that the panel will now write to Lawrence to inform him of their decision.'

'Their decision about what?'

'About what they're going to do with him via-à-vis returning to duty. But this doctor did say that in his personal opinion, Lawrence is no longer fit to command a company of men — and that, in the longer term, he might be better suited to a job in some sort of administrative capacity.'

'So he won't have to go back and fight?'

'It would seem not.'

'And what about his . . . well, his moods? Can they do anything for those?'

'On the train coming back,' Naomi said, lowering her voice, 'Lawrence actually started to talk to me. He told me that the panel are minded to recommend him for some new form of treatment, and showed me some papers they'd given him, setting out some details. Apparently, in Exeter — of all places — there is a sort of hospital called Priory Glen, where a doctor is trying out a new approach to cure what he calls 'war neurosis'. Lawrence said that at first, he didn't like the sound of it, thinking it might be a lunatic asylum in disguise. But then, when he listened to what was involved, and read the details, he changed his mind.'

Lifting from the bag Naomi's little jewellery pouch, Kate took it across to the dressing table, where she proceeded to put the items back in her box. 'So, what do they do there then — in this place in Exeter?'

'It would seem that they fill the men's days with gentle but meaningful activity such as growing vegetables and walking. They give them a nourishing diet and plenty of exercise. They encourage the men to talk about their experience and the things that keep returning to bother them — to haunt them, if you will.'

'I see.' To Kate, it didn't sound like any more of a treatment than Mr Lawrence could get right there at Woodicombe if he was so inclined.

'The other thing this doctor does, is persuade the men that they *can* recover — gently bullies them into getting better, is how Lawrence described it.'

'And it works?' To Kate, it seemed unlikely.

'Apparently, some soldiers have been cured in less than seven days. But most stay for between two and four weeks.'

'And Mr Lawrence is keen to do this — go there to stay and be treated.'

'He does seem to be in favour of it, yes, although I do think that, in part at least, his eagerness stems from a notion that if this neurosis of his can be cured, he will be able to return to the front.'

'Whereas you think that's unlikely.'

'From the sound of it, yes, I do,' Naomi answered. 'Which, of course, pleases me no end. But if, by thinking he might be able to go back, Lawrence is encouraged to try this new treatment, then who am I to quash his enthusiasm?'

'Mm.'

'Oh, and they have also prescribed him something he can take to help him sleep, and something different he can take if he feels as though he's losing control of his thoughts.'

'And do you think he will take either of them?' she asked, glancing across to where Naomi had gone to stare out through the window.

'He has already started to. He took the first dose on the train on the way home.'

'Goodness.'

'Apparently, the doctor told him that he can either choose to help himself — by whatever means available — or else he can be committed to hospital, especially if he is perceived to be a danger to other people.'

'Such as to you and Esme.'

'To anyone at all, really.'

Looking at Naomi's face, Kate thought she looked better than she had in a while. 'If you don't mind me saying, you seem . . . relieved.'

'I suppose I am. All things considered, the whole thing went far better than I had dared hope. Now all we can do is pray that he can be accommodated at this Priory Glen place in Exeter, and that this unbelievably simple treatment will work.'

Lifting Naomi's empty bag from the floor she smiled. 'I shall pray hard for it.'

'Thank you. And what about you? How are you feeling today?'

'Not too bad,' she replied. 'All told.'

'Good. I'm glad.'

'Right, well, I'll just put these few things along the corridor with your trunks and what-not, and then I'll see you downstairs. There's a couple of slices of strawberry tart left — if you fancy. Go real nice with a cup of tea, they would.'

'Then I'll see you down there.'

Could it really be that simple, Kate wondered as she trailed along the corridor to the spare room. Was Mr Lawrence really to be so easily cured? She did hope so. As she had said to Rowley, this family had sent three men to war, and each of them had, in one way or another, lost the lives to which they had expected to return: Ned had been injured so badly that he would probably never walk again; Mr Lawrence had lost his mind and had, until now at least, been in danger of losing everything else along with it; and Luke, well, poor Luke had paid the biggest price of all. But, by the seem of it, there *was* now hope for Mr Lawrence — and thus for Naomi, too. Yes, at least *Naomi* might be able to look forward to having her husband back — and to going on to enjoy being married and raising a family. And that had to be better than both of them being left to wonder — and fear — for what lay ahead.

★　★　★

'Is it wrong that I feel better for that?'

''Course not, child, that's what funerals are for — even though it mightn't have been a funeral in the ordinary sense of the word.'

Reassured by her mother-in-law's response, Kate attempted a smile. Along with Mabel and Edith, and Naomi and Esme, they were returning from the service of remembrance held for Luke in Woodicombe church. In the days beforehand, the prospect of it had hung over her like a ghastly spectre, the gloom and the solemnity of the occasion filling her with a deep dread. But, as his widow, she knew there could be no avoiding it. She also knew that it was something Luke deserved, even though he himself would probably have pooh-poohed the whole thing as being nothing but a lot of unnecessary sadness. However, now that it was behind her, she saw it differently: she recognized it as something designed as much to comfort the bereaved as to celebrate the deceased, and a milestone in the journey that was their grief.

'Shall you come down for a cup of tea and a slice of cake?' she asked, glancing to Ma Channer walking by her side. Waiting for her to reply, she lifted her face to the warm sunshine. An hour or so back, the sky had been overcast and the air humid and flat. Sombre. But they had left the church to find the sun shining and the leaves in the hedgerow fidgeting in a light breeze.

'I won't, girl, if you don't mind. You'll no doubt remember how Pa's a stickler for having his dinner dished up on the dot of midday.'

Glancing over her shoulder, Kate noticed that some way behind them, having failed to utter a single word since arriving at the church, Pa Channer was walking by himself. It was hard to gauge how he was taking the loss of his son, he being someone whose countenance never changed — someone who only ever exhibited a sort of unvarying acceptance of whatever came his way, whether brought by fair wind or foul.

'No, I don't mind,' she said. 'Just remember that you'd be welcome any time.'

Back at the house, the little party went in through the porch and, as they each stood unpinning their hats, Naomi turned to regard her. 'How do you feel after that?'

'All right,' she replied, the surprise in her tone almost certainly down to her relief. 'Surprisingly, I feel a little better.'

Setting her hat on the hall table and staring down at it, she was glad she had resisted Mabel's desire to attach a veil to it; it would have been too much. There was nothing special about her loss of Luke: women everywhere were mourning their menfolk; it was just how it was. Drawing attention to grief or making a big display of it — as women had done before the war — had come to be frowned upon, widows now being expected to bear their grief with stoicism, a state seen as patriotic. And anyway, out here in the countryside, where death had always been treated rather more matter-of-factly, it had never been the done thing for ordinary folk to mount great or theatrical displays of mourning.

Heaving a long sigh, she felt a set of warm

little fingers curling around her hand and looked down to see Esme's clear eyes staring up at her.

'Aunty Kate?'

She smiled. 'Yes, lovey?'

'Would you like to play with Rabbit?'

'Well, I have to go and — '

'Mamma say Aunty Kate sad. Playing with Rabbit make you happy again.'

'Then thank you, yes,' she said, swallowing down a lump in her throat. 'I should very much like to play with Rabbit. If you're sure *you* don't need him.'

The little girl shook her head, her dark ringlets bobbing about her shoulders. 'No, you have him. I've got Mr Grumpy Bear.'

When Esme skipped away, humming brightly, Kate fingered the little toy, the nap of its felt rubbed almost bare. It was having Esme in the household that had first made her aware of her own broodiness — or, at least, how she had been burying it — and made her realize that she *was* looking forward to starting her own family. No, she checked herself: not *was* looking forward to starting her own family — *had been* looking forward to it. No point continuing to look forward to something she could no longer have.

'I should think they will be there by now.'

Brought from her thoughts by Naomi's remark, Kate turned to see her studying her reflection in the mirror.

'I'm sorry?'

'It's almost midday, so I should imagine Lawrence will be at Priory Glen by now.'

'Heavens, yes.'

'It was good of Rowley to go with him. I can quite understand why Lawrence didn't want me to see him being admitted to what is, to all intents and purposes, a hospital, and I know Ned was right to suggest that I stay here, but I couldn't have let him go alone.'

'No,' Kate replied. 'This way you'll know he arrived safe. And what the place is like.'

'I will, yes. Oh, Kate, I do hope they can cure him. Or, if not cure him completely, then at least ease his suffering. I can't bear to see him so broken.'

'Nor me,' she said. And it was true. Mr Lawrence was a good man — like Luke. Like Luke *had been*. Would she *never* get it into her head that he wasn't coming back? Presumably, eventually, she would. *Give it time*, Ma Channer had urged her this morning. In truth, she had no choice: with or without Luke, her life was going to carry on. It just wasn't going to be the same life she had spent the last four years dreaming about . . .

★   ★   ★

'If you're sure you don't mind. Only, my leg is so awfully stiff from the train and in desperate need of some exercise.'

It was after five o'clock when Rowley arrived back from accompanying Mr Lawrence to Exeter. His first task being to reassure Naomi that Priory Glen was a surprisingly pleasant place; he then announced that he was going to take a turn around the grounds, whereupon Kate

281

offered to accompany him.

'If your leg is bothering you, then it's better you don't venture out alone,' she said now, as they made their way out through the French doors.

Reaching the steps that led down from the terrace onto the lawn, he proceeded alongside her in somewhat lopsided fashion until, at the bottom, he turned to regard her. 'Captain Colborne asked me to apologize to you again for not being able to attend the service.'

Giving him a light smile, she nodded. 'More important that he gets well.'

'And I'm sorry *I* couldn't be there to honour your husband either.'

To put him at ease, she raised another smile. 'It's all right. It's not as though the two of you were acquainted.' *Nor*, she thought, reflecting upon how little the two men had in common, *were you ever likely to have been.*

'No,' he replied, limping on. 'But it is largely down to the kindness and generosity of this family — and *your* efforts in particular — that my recovery has been as it has. And, although I didn't know your husband, I *do* know *you*.'

Feeling suddenly uncomfortable to be discussing Luke with him, Kate opted to change the subject. 'So, Mr Lawrence is all settled at this Priory Glen place, then'

Awaiting his reply, she glanced about. From force of habit, they were taking their usual path across the lawn towards the copse.

'Well, I don't know about *settled*, but he's installed there, yes.'

'And it was nice, this place?'

'As I said to Mrs Colborne,' he replied, 'it struck me as a cross between a rambling manor house, a gentleman's country club and a make-shift army camp — in some ways all terribly informal, in others, highly regimented. And the staff I met seemed utterly dedicated — highly enthusiastic about what they do there.'

When he looked towards her, she nodded. 'That's good.'

'When they took Captain Colborne to be admitted, I got talking to a chap who is about to be discharged. It was he who told me that the proper name for the captain's condition is *neurasthenia*. He also said that the doctor there believes it occurs following a sudden or prolonged disturbance to one's emotions. Anyway, this chap gave me a tour of the place — couldn't speak highly enough of just about every aspect of it.'

The more he described it, the more Kate felt herself relaxing. It would be such a comfort to Naomi to know that Mr Lawrence was in good hands.

'And what about you?' she asked, their pace slowing as they neared the trees. 'Do you have any news yet?'

Coming to a halt and turning to look back at the house, he shook his head. 'None yet, no. But I shall try to telephone home this weekend — just in case Mother hasn't managed to forward on my most recent letters. She's always so busy that the more mundane things in life often escape her.' When, intrigued, she looked back at him, he took it upon himself to explain. 'She's a researcher on

283

a project trying to develop new types of radio communications for military use. Before the war, she worked on something similar at the university but, when the chap she worked for got drafted onto this project for the government, he took her with him. She's the only woman among about a hundred men. But she was the only woman at the university too, so, as these things go, she's used to it.'

'Goodness.'

'But, as I say, being so involved with her work does mean that sometimes, things at home do rather go to pot. Before the war, she had a housekeeper and a charwoman. But all we have now is a young girl who comes in each day to see to the dogs — we have two Lakeland terriers, Bertie and Charles.'

The thought of dogs being called Bertie and Charles made her laugh, while the thought of his mother doing something so important made her realize for the first time just how properly different his background was — even to that of Naomi and Ned.

'And your father?' she said, keen now to picture the whole of his family.

'Professor of physics at the university. I think I might have said to you it's where they met.' Remembering something to that effect, she nodded, hoping he would go on to tell her more. 'Obviously, for a long time after she had me and my sisters, my mother stayed at home. But the life of a housewife didn't suit her and, as soon as she could, she returned to a research post. Unheard of, really. But there you are. That's my mother. And, whenever something at home used to get overlooked — like the date for us to go back to school — my sisters and I used to joke that she was too busy saving the world to concern herself with mortal things like term times and exeats.'

'Didn't you mind that?' she asked, struggling to picture something so apparently haphazard.

'Being neglected, do you mean?' Side-stepping a dip in the lawn, he laughed. 'I didn't know any different. I thought it was how everyone lived. Well, until one day when my mother invited some of her colleagues around and one of them said to me that had my mother been a man, her work would have been nominated for all sorts of awards, and that she would have been recognized for her contribution — '

'But because she was a woman — '

'She could only be listed on scientific papers as somebody else's research assistant or, at best, as a co-author.'

Reflecting upon what he had just told her, she frowned. 'That hardly seems fair.'

'It isn't. But, when I asked my mother about it, she said that one day, things will probably change but that, in the meantime, the most important thing wasn't the sex of the person making the discoveries but that they were made at all. For *his* part, Father always made sure we understood how valuable her work was — forever telling us that we should be proud of her. And so we were.'

In the days that followed that afternoon, Kate continued to accompany Rowley on his same stroll around the gardens. Sometimes, he took the camera she had found for him, other times they just conversed as they went. On this particular day, spurred by something he had read in the *Telegraph*, their topic for discussion was aeroplanes and flying.

'They want to fly from America to England?' she said, wondering whether she had misheard him. 'But isn't that a very long way?'

He raised a smile. 'About three thousand miles across an ocean.'

'Three thousand miles across an ocean in an aeroplane?' As notions went, it was hard to credit.

Amused by her astonishment, he nodded. 'A group of American army pilots want to do just that, yes. They want to be the first to arrive at the battlefields of Europe by air.'

'And can they do it?' she asked. It had been bad enough when Ned had first told her about flying across the Channel and, from what she could recall, that wasn't even as far as the distance they covered by railway train from Woodicombe to London.

'Someone is bound to do it soon,' he said. 'The newspaper believes that by the end of this year, someone will succeed in making it non-stop. But, if it is to be the Americans, they will have to use English aeroplanes, shipped across especially for the purpose because they themselves don't have anything capable of covering that sort of distance, particularly in those conditions.'

On their subsequent walk, later that same afternoon, Rowley's topic of conversation had changed to that of the recent battles in France.

'The Germans simply weren't expecting the numbers,' he said of one particular skirmish. 'Weren't expecting the amount of forces we had on our side. Their attack at Marne was only ever meant to be a diversion from a series of others they had planned for Flanders, where their numbers are much stronger. But, having underestimated the combined strength of the allies, they suffered massive losses — by some estimates, in excess of one-hundred-and-fifty-thousand men. It's a real win for us, and a terrible blow for them. To my mind, it must surely mark the beginning of the end. I really do believe it. If nothing else, perhaps they will now listen to their Prince Wilhelm. As long as a year ago he was denouncing this war as senseless, and calling for peace.'

'But no one listened to him,' she remarked as they walked on.

'They didn't. Everyone else in Germany still thought they could win.'

'Think of all the deaths that need never have happened,' she said, realizing that Luke's could have been among them. It was a thought she quickly tried to push from her mind.

'Hundreds of thousands.'

'But even if it *is* nearly all over, you still want to go back and fly, if they'll let you?'

Glancing towards her, he briefly met her look. 'I do. If they'll let me.'

His return to service was something else she tried not to think about. On a warm and sunny afternoon, it was hard to even picture war, let alone understand how a young man from his background could want to return to it. There had to be something in a man's make up that a woman didn't have: given the chance to come home on leave, all Mr Lawrence had wanted to talk about was getting back to lead his men; and Ned, despite waking up one day to discover that he no longer had the use of his legs, had thought first to ask about his chances of returning to flying. And now, here was Rowley, itching to get back to it too. It was a difficult thing to understand. Oddly, though, it was also reassuring: the empire needed brave men like these, who were prepared to give up everyday life to go and fight for what was right — even if it did mean that a lot of women were left without husbands, without sons and brothers, and a lot of children without fathers. Not to mention all those children who would now never be born — like hers and Luke's.

On the morning following that particular discussion, the postman finally brought Rowley an envelope, from inside of which she watched him extract several smaller ones.

'Your mother's been catching up,' she said when he grinned at her and waved the contents.

'She has. This first one is from my elder sister, Eugenie. I recognize her handwriting.' He flicked on down through the pile. 'Then there's a mess bill — which should most surely stand at zero — a statement of account from my bank, and this,' he said of the last one, putting down the other envelopes and, with the letter opener, slitting along the top of it. 'Which must be about my return to service.'

Feeling as though something inside her chose that moment to shrivel up, and acutely aware that she was holding her breath, she watched him unfold a single sheet of heavy paper and scan the contents. In one way, she hoped that he *was* going to be able to return to flying — since it was, after all, what he wanted to do — but, on the other hand, she hoped there was also a chance that they would no longer want him.

'Well?' she said, unable to tell anything from his expression and unexpectedly desperate to know.

He looked up. 'I've been called to the old RFC central training school at Upavon for assessment and interview.'

'Soon?' she asked, forcing herself to swallow.

Raising his left hand, he looked at his wristwatch. 'Actually, yes. I have to report there on Thursday.' Examining the page more closely, he went on, 'I think this letter must have been sitting around at home for rather a while. God job it turned up when it did, otherwise I'd be in deep trouble. Well then, I suppose I had better see about trains — and find out whether I can bunk at the camp for a couple of nights.'

As it happened, a little earlier, Naomi had announced that she intended going into the village.

'If you can be ready in the next quarter of an hour,' she said upon learning of Rowley's news, 'I can take you to the railway station. I have a few things to attend to, after which I can bring you back again.'

'Thank you,' he said, shooting Kate a pleased look. 'And while I'm there I can send the rolls of

289

film from the camera for developing. And buy a couple of replacements, too. Good stuff.'

From that moment, Kate felt as though the rest of the week passed in a blur. Before she knew it, it was Thursday — the day of Rowley's assessment — and when she went into the dining room to set the table for breakfast, he was already down, the sight of him back in his uniform stopping her dead.

'Don't suppose I shall be able to wear this khaki for much longer,' he said, poking a finger behind his starched collar in an apparent attempt to relieve the discomfort of it against his neck. 'Now that we're the RAF, we have new pale blue kit.'

Never mind the colour, she was still struggling with the effect of his changed appearance: immaculate; business-like.

'Oh.'

'But, since we have to buy our own, we've been granted a period of 'wearing out' for these old ones. All the chaps I know prefer this one anyway — the pale blue is quite nasty — '

'Aunty Kate, Aunty Kate!'

She turned away from him. In the doorway stood Esme.

'Hello, lovey.' By way of apology for the interruption, she gave Rowley a smile and then went towards the door. Seeing no sign of Naomi, she bent down to the little girl's height. 'Where's your mamma?'

'Poorly sick.'

'She's poorly?'

'Mamma says Esme get Aunty Kate.'

Puzzled, she took hold of the child's hand. 'So, who got you all dressed then?'

'Mamma dress Esme.'

'And then she went back to bed?'

Looking terribly solemn, Esme nodded. 'Uh-huh. Mamma poorly sick.'

'All right. Well, let's you an' me go up and see her then.' Turning back into the room, she found that Rowley had been watching her. 'Hopefully,' she said, for some reason blushing, 'I'll be back in a moment or two to ready the table.'

Upstairs, Kate discovered that Naomi was indeed back in bed, her velvet sleep-mask over her eyes, the curtains drawn tightly across the window. 'Dreadful headache,' she murmured as Kate approached. 'Woke up with it.'

'Oh dear. Can I get you anything? Some feverfew and honey? Some ginger powder tea?'

Slowly, Naomi shook her head. 'Perhaps some of Mrs Channer's peppermint when you have a moment. That sometimes works.'

'All right,' she said. 'I'll go and brew you some.'

'And can you see to Esme's breakfast for me?'

'Of course.'

'Oh, and the other day, I said I'd take Rowley to catch his train. But I'm not sure I'm going to feel like driving — '

'No, I'll go and explain that he needs to telephone for the cab.'

'Better than that, borrow the Humberette and take him yourself.'

Despite being in a darkened room, Kate blinked as though dazzled. '*Me?*'

'Yes. You know how to drive.'

What Naomi was suggesting felt wrong in so many ways that she didn't know where to begin. 'Happen I do,' she ventured, wondering which of the reasons stood the best chance of getting her out of the task. 'But it's ages since I've driven anything.'

Unseen in the darkness, Naomi sounded exasperated. 'It's not something you forget.'

'But the roads around here — '

'Are far quieter than they are in town.'

'And you forget that I'm in mourning.'

With that, she made out that Naomi had lifted her head from the pillow and turned in her direction.

'I hardly think the sight of you running an officer of the RAF into the village to catch a train will have people branding you an *unfaithful widow*. If anyone passes comment, tell them he's a cousin. It's not *that* implausible — you do both have brown hair.'

'But — '

'Well,' Naomi said, lowering her head. 'It's down to you. Take him or don't take him. But if he misses his train . . . '

Not even certain why she felt so cross with Naomi for suggesting it, Kate shook her head in irritation. 'Oh, for goodness sake,' she snapped. 'I'll take Esme down and then I'll be back up with your peppermint tea.'

'Thank you. Oh, and you might like to bear in mind,' Naomi said, sounding suddenly less weary, 'that just lately, the motor has needed several cranks to get it going. But I'm sure

Rowley will see to it for you.'

As it turned out, not much more than half an hour later, Rowley — clearly surprised that she should be the one to take him at all — wouldn't even countenance letting her try to start the motor.

'No, I'm afraid I must insist,' he said, depositing his kit bag and pushing back his cuffs. As it happened, on the first turn of the crank, and with a *tickety-clack-clack-clack-clack*, the engine spluttered to life and, from where she had been standing a pace or so behind him, looking on, she didn't know whether to be relieved or disappointed. 'There,' he said, rubbing his palms and moving around to the driver's side to open the door. 'All set.'

All she could think in that moment, as he stood smiling back at her, was that the chances of her making a fool of herself were almost without limit.

'Yes. Thank you. All set.'

'Lovely little motor. Just right for running about. Dashing colour, too.'

But then, as he took a step back, apparently in readiness to assist her up, she was struck by an idea.

'Would you like to drive it down?'

He didn't hesitate. 'Very much. But are you sure?'

She had never been more sure of anything: suggesting that *he* drive did away with so many chances for her to embarrass herself. 'Yes,' she said, nodding eagerly. 'I can drive it any time.'

'Then may I help you up?' he asked, moving smartly around to the other side.

'Um . . . '

All she had done, she realized at that moment, was shift her discomfort from having to drive the thing with him as her passenger, to being forced to allow him to help her up and then still have to sit next to him. In any event, unable to bring herself to decline his request and risk causing *him* embarrassment, she placed her hand on top of the one he was proffering and, stepping first onto the running board, climbed up onto the seat. When he then closed the little door behind her, she mumbled her thanks and stared down into her lap.

Down on the ground, he went around to the other side and, picking up his bag and placing it on the seat between them, climbed in behind the wheel.

'You're sure Mrs Colborne won't mind me driving her?'

At that precise moment, what Naomi would or would not mind was the least of Kate's worries. But, this way, she would only have to drive back from the station, with few people to witness her mistakes — of which, no doubt, there would still be plenty.

'Not at all,' she eventually replied to his question.

'Then hold tight and off we go.'

'Yes. Off we go.'

When he reached outside of the door for the lever to disengage the brake, she gripped her fingers around the edge of the seat. With something of a lurch, they pulled away, trundling cautiously over the gravel of the driveway and onwards through the gates.

Along the track, the lodge houses to the old manor came into view and she wondered, rather too late, how she would explain to Ma Channer how she came to be in a motorcar with a young and unmarried man. Despite there being little point in her doing so, as they passed by, she reached for the narrow rim of her hat, as though to hold it in place, even though it was already secured against the wind with a scarf. Eventually, further along the lane, she brought her hand back to the edge of the seat.

Barely a foot from her right shoulder, she felt him turn towards her.

'Are you all right?' he asked above the noise of the little engine and the clatter of loose stones being thrown up from the lane.

She nodded. 'Yes, thank you.'

'Glorious morning,' he said above the din.

Above them, the canopy of ash and oak, and of horn-beam and willow, was filtering the bright sunlight such that when she looked back at him, a procession of shadows flicked across his face.

'Yes,' she raised her voice to answer him. Among the folds of her skirt, she slackened the grip of her fingers. It *was* glorious. But it was also unsettling. And not a little bewildering — in her chest a sensation of hurtling towards the unknown, and in her head a lightness, a giddiness almost.

Once out onto the lane proper, Rowley changed gear and the little motorcar quickened its pace.

'Do you mind this speed?' he asked, once

again glancing towards her.

She shook her head. 'No.'

The truth was that Naomi drove a good deal faster — and with rather more abandon and less consideration for the machine under her control. Rowley, she noticed, drove it as though he understood the workings of the engine, changing gear more often and conducting the motor with far greater sympathy.

At the top of the hill above Westward Quay, he slowed and pulled onto the verge. 'Goodness, what a view.'

Forcing a swallow, she nodded, fearful of what he might say or do next. But, after a moment spent staring out to sea, he pulled away again, using the gears to hold the motor back from hurtling down the hill; Naomi, at this same point, would simply be standing on the brake pedal. At the bottom of the hill, they motored past Church Green and, at the junction with Quay Street, turned right towards the station, where he brought the vehicle to a smooth halt alongside the entrance. 'Thank you for allowing me to drive her,' he said, opening back the door. 'Shall I leave her running for you?'

Relieved, but also feeling a peculiar tinge of disappointment, she nodded. 'Yes, please do.'

Leaving his bag on the seat, he went around to her side and opened the door. 'Take firm hold,' he said, reaching with his hand, 'and mind your skirt on the step.' Satisfied that she was safely on the ground, he reached for his bag. 'Well, thank you again. All being well, I shall see you in a couple of days.'

She nodded. 'Yes. I hope it all goes all right for you.'

'Me too,' he said, adjusting the angle his cap on his head. 'Do take care going back.'

Casting her eyes downwards, she moved around to the other side of the motorcar and, with one hand lifting the hem of her skirt, reached with the other to the back of the seat and climbed up. Then, careful not to meet the look of any of the people milling about the station forecourt, she closed the door, engaged the gears, let off the brake, and slowly edged the little car back out onto the road. With her heart beating nineteen to the dozen in her chest, she conducted the Humberette very slowly back towards the junction and turned left.

From there, unable to decide what was causing her the greatest distress, she pressed down on the accelerator pedal to gain more speed and make it up the hill. *Stay in low gear,* she recalled Naomi reminding herself on the first occasion they had made this trip. *Maintain sufficient speed.*

Under her stiff and terrified direction, the Humberette struggled up the incline, passing Bellevue House at the bend and lumbering on past Wennacott Farm just before the rise. Shortly after achieving the summit, she pulled over onto the grassy verge, peeled her hands away from the steering wheel to apply the brake and, while the engine sat chuckling away in front of her, brought her hands to her lap, where they lay trembling and pale against the black crepe of her mourning frock. She would take a minute to calm her thoughts — and perhaps try to work out quite why they were in such a tizzy to start with.

Peering through the windscreen, she took in the view. Ahead, the land dipped softly away before rising up again. Somewhere, down in the fold of the valley, concealed by the lush woodland, sat the house where she had spent almost all of her life. And then, hundreds of miles beyond that farthest ridge was London, home to her more recent years and her brief spell as a wife, albeit in little more than name only.

Leaning back against the seat, she recalled the afternoon Mr Lawrence had stood before the fireplace and told her of Luke's death — and how Naomi had been quick to reassure her that her life in London would still be there. But was that what she still wanted? Where, without Luke, did her future lie — surrounded by the busyness of town, or back here, in the peace and tranquillity of a landscape much less foreign? Did it even really matter? Without a husband, wherever she ended up, she would still be alone.

Although continuing to stare ahead, she stopped noticing the myriad greens of the pastures, the sunshine yellow of the specks of gorse, or the first glimpses of the lilac of the heathers. All she could see with any certainty was that wherever she ended up, she hoped not to spend the rest of her days like Edith — which meant that at some point, she would be faced with having to remarry. And that was a prospect as difficult to countenance at that moment as spinsterhood. Or, perhaps more correctly, as widowhood.

With a long sigh, she put the motor back into gear, reached to release the brake lever and, with a glance over her shoulder, pulled back out onto the lane. But, despite having sat for those few moments in the blustery air, she felt no calmer: as she pressed down on the pedal and the little car picked up speed, and the breeze began to lift the brim of her hat and flap at the end of the scarf tied under her chin, her earlier sense of being deeply unsettled still prickled at the back of her throat and nagged at her stomach. And it was going to keep doing so, too, because, while all of those other matters clamouring for her attention had rightly to be reconciled and dealt with, the thing unsettling her the most was the one she was trying so studiously to ignore — in part because, as feelings went, they had arrived so unexpectedly, but also because, deep down, she was fairly certain that for someone so freshly widowed, even simply entertaining them was a deeply unholy thing to do.

12

Surprises

'Please forgive the state of it, but Esme got to it first.'

Handing Rowley a dog-eared envelope that arrived by first post a few mornings later, Kate continued on around the table to pass a second one to Naomi.

'I do apologize,' Naomi looked across at Rowley to say. 'I've told her before that she mustn't open the post. I trust you will find the contents undamaged.'

Running a finger under the flap, Rowley shook his head. 'Wouldn't be the end of the world if they weren't — it's only from my squadron. Probably another demand for me to settle my mess account, which they seem unable to comprehend stands at zero.'

Despite having already finished her breakfast, Kate sat back down at the table; the writing on the envelope she had handed to Naomi was Lawrence's, and she was keen to hear how he was. Of even greater interest, though, was the one for Rowley, which she suspected not to be a mess bill at all. And one look at his face proved her suspicions correct. In fact, having taken no more than a cursory glance at the single sheet of paper contained therein, he got to his feet, excused himself, and left the room.

'Bad news, do you think?' Naomi enquired with the briefest of glances to his departing back.

Uncertainly, Kate shrugged her shoulders. For Rowley's sake she did hope not. 'Couldn't say. What about Mr Lawrence? He writes that he is well, I hope.'

When Naomi put down the first sheet of notepaper and, picking up the second, continued reading, Kate chanced the briefest of glances towards the door. She did hope Rowley was all right. The thought of him returning to flying might make *her* feel uneasy, but it seemed to be the thing upon which *he* had been pinning his hopes.

'He does indeed seem well,' Naomi eventually remarked of Lawrence, setting down her letter and picking up her coffee cup. 'He writes a great deal about working in the vegetable garden — waxes quite lyrical in fact.'

'That's good.' Despite trying to sound interested, she was finding it hard to sit still. Why hadn't Rowley come back and told them what his letter said? Could it be that he had received his orders? Could it be that, at this very moment, he was upstairs packing in readiness to leave? Unable to bear not knowing, she shot to her feet.

Across the table from her, Naomi looked up. 'Yes?'

Curling her fingers into the palms of her hands, Kate hesitated. 'I've . . . just realized that I can't hear Esme anywhere.'

'I expect she's with Ned.'

'Perhaps,' she said, edging away from the table and, in overly exaggerated fashion, peering towards the door. 'Happen I should go an' check.'

'As you wish.'

Out in the hallway, Kate looked quickly in both directions. Seeing no sign of anyone at all, she turned towards the porch. Ah, there he was — out on the drive, letter in hand. But, on the point of making her way towards him, she faltered. If it *was* bad news, would he want to share it? Knowing so very little about him, she had no idea. Had it been Ned receiving news he didn't like, he would have been waving his arms and cursing and muttering words like *gross unfairness, injustice* and *rotten luck.* Rowley, though, seemed markedly less effusive.

After a moment's indecision, she went towards the front door anyway. Worse than having him think her nosey would be for him to turn around, see her loitering, and think that she was spying upon him.

As it happened, she had made it all the way to the porch, and was stepping out onto the gravel, before he had even moved.

'Kate,' he said upon seeing her, his tone suggesting that he had been far away in his thoughts.

'Forgive me,' she said, 'but I wondered whether everything is all right?'

When he raised his hand and waved the letter, she read his gesture as one of disappointment. 'While I can't report that anything is actually *wrong*,' he said, holding her gaze. 'It's rotten news all the same.'

When he didn't then go on to elaborate, she

felt moved to prompt him to do so. In the event, all she could think to say, was, 'Oh.'

'It appears I am not to be granted my wish to fly again.'

This time, she replied with rather more feeling. 'Oh! Oh, I'm real sorry to hear that.'

'Thank you.'

'I know that wasn't what you were hoping for.'

The sinking of his shoulders alone conveyed the extent of his dismay. 'You're right. It wasn't. You know, I did keep reminding myself that this might happen. I even told myself that it wouldn't matter too much if it did. But now that it has, I find that it *does* matter. And rather more than I imagined. Once a flying man, always a flying man, I suppose.'

Lost for any words of consolation, she shifted her weight. 'Could you ask them to think again?'

In response to her question, he shook his head. 'No point. When I went before the medical board that day, I made sure to stress just how badly I wanted to go back up — to return to spotting. And I saw them noting down what I was saying. But, according to this letter, in recent months, operational needs have changed and, with only about a third of current sorties now being devoted to reconnaissance, what they need today isn't so much airborne observers and photographers as men on the ground, interpreting the information already coming in, and marking up the images.'

What did that mean, she wondered? Taking in the glumness of his expression, she decided not to ask. Instead, she said, 'So, do you know where you will be going?'

303

He glanced to the letter. 'Actually, I am to be offered a choice. I can either accept a secondment to a military department in Whitehall — ' *Whitehall.* That was in London. Well, unless there was more than one place with that same name. ' — or else I can volunteer for a new division being set up in Gloucestershire. Other than describing it as being classified secret, of this second choice they say nothing more. Well, apart from emphasising that it carries a promotion.'

Feeling the onset of panic, Kate drew her hands behind her back. 'And . . . which will you choose?'

'Well, I'm certainly in no rush to disappear down a Whitehall rabbit hole — for fear of never making it back out again.'

So he wasn't going to choose London then — unless his comments were meant as a joke. She couldn't really tell.

'No,' she said, hoping that her reply could be construed either way.

'But Gloucestershire might not be too bad.' Cautiously, she raised her eyes to look back at him. 'It's not so very far from my family home. And the work could be interesting — certainly worthwhile. And the promotion might go *part* way to making up for being stuck on the ground.'

Overcome by a gloominess she felt lost to understand, Kate started to turn away. She had come to find him in the hope of learning that the news was to his liking. But, clearly, it wasn't. And nothing *she* could say was going to change that.

'Would you like anything more for breakfast?' she asked. Heavens, how banal. 'Only, you didn't have the chance to finish your plate.'

He shook his head. 'Sorry about that. But no, thank you, I find I am no longer hungry. In fact, I might go for a stroll and . . . well, you know, see if the news sits any more easily once it sinks in. And then, I suppose, I shall weigh up my options.'

The smile she managed was a weak one. Ordinarily, she would have offered to go with him. On this occasion, though, she imagined he would prefer to be alone.

'Of course,' she replied. 'But if you change your mind, and find that later on you're hungry, just say.'

'Thank you, Kate. You're very kind.'

And you're *very sad*, she thought, turning away from him to head back indoors.

★　★　★

'Goodness. I can scarcely believe this. Lawrence is being discharged from Priory Glen. He's coming home!'

It was a grey and showery morning several days later. And, when Naomi had wandered in with their second post of the day, Kate had been sitting staring out through the French doors, lost to know what to do with herself.

Watching Naomi reading her letter, she got up and went towards her. 'So soon? Is he cured, then?' After barely ten days it seemed hardly likely.

'He writes that although not fit enough to return to service, the doctor has decided to allow him to come home and continue his regimen of activities here. Apparently, by doing that, not only will he benefit from being back with us, but his place at Priory Glen can be taken by someone who would otherwise be without what he describes as 'access to a suitable environment for recovery'.'

'Does he say when he'll be here?' she asked. For Naomi's sake, she did hope that he was properly better and not just being pushed out to make way for someone else.

Naomi scanned the letter afresh. 'Friday — '

'The day after tomorrow? *This* Friday?' Heavens, that *was* quick.

'It would seem so, yes. He writes that he hopes to catch the early afternoon train.'

She studied Naomi's face; it seemed to convey only disbelief. 'For certain you must be . . . pleased.'

'To be quite honest with you, Kate, I'm somewhat shocked. Two to four weeks — that's what they said when they admitted him.'

'Then in just ten days he must have made excellent progress.' She did hope he had. At the very least, she hoped they had managed to cure his rages, and cure the way he saw things that weren't there while, at the same time, failing to recognize those that were.

'Friday,' Naomi remarked, apparently deep in thought. 'Oh! You know what we should do — we should throw a party!'

'A party?' Had Naomi taken all leave of her

306

senses? Ignoring the fact that so many things were in short supply, there was the small matter of them being at Woodicombe — hundreds of miles from anyone who might reasonably accept an invitation to such a thing.

'Not a party on the scale my mother would hold,' Naomi rushed to clarify. 'I rather meant a tea party, out on the lawn, weather permitting of course. Sandwiches, cakes, parlour games. You know, put on a jolly welcome back for him.'

When, picturing such a thing, Kate exhaled a long sigh, Naomi turned sharply towards her. 'Oh, my dear Kate, forgive me. What was I thinking? You're in mourning. We're *all* in mourning. Oh, I'm so sorry — the last thing we should be doing is holding a party.'

'No,' she said, reaching for Naomi's hand. 'You're right. Mr Lawrence being well enough to come home is tremendous news. We *should* celebrate it. Without a shadow of a doubt Luke would want us to.'

Despite her reassurance, from Naomi's eyes she still read only uncertainty.

'Are you sure? You're not just saying that for my benefit? Only, I know that's how you can be.'

She shook her head. 'I'm sure of it. Luke's passing shouldn't stop everyone else from getting on with their lives. And he'd agree with me on that, I know it. He'd even be cross to see me wearing this . . . ' Reaching to her skirt, she fingered the crepe of her mourning gown. ' . . . this thing. He'd say it makes me look pale and miserable. And he'd be right.'

'Well, if you promise me you mean it — if you

promise you won't be offended or upset by the gaiety . . . '

Unable to help it, Kate shook with laughter, the sound of such merriment from her own lips an odd thing to hear. 'Offended by gaiety? Me? Never!'

'Then shall we go down and see what Edith thinks she might be able to scrape together for such a thing? No sense trying to organize something for which there wouldn't be any food.'

'We shan't go down and see her, no,' she said, still smiling. 'That task is yours alone. Me, I intend keeping well away. I have no desire to hear Edith bemoaning all the extra work.'

As it happened, Edith didn't complain at all; by Naomi's later reporting, both Edith and Mabel were more than happy to suggest fare to which the pantry's rather meagre contents might be stretched. Thus, unwilling to risk them changing their minds, Naomi wasted no time in driving straight to Wennacott Farm to procure two dozen eggs which were, according to the farmer's wife, two or three days old but perfectly fine for baking. From there, she drove in the other direction to Farmer Braund, who kept cows rather than sheep, returning this time with two irregularly-shaped pats of butter, a half-gallon of milk, a block of hard cheese, and a wedge of blue-vein that smelled to high heaven.

'I used my charms,' she said when her haul met with Edith's approval. 'And an overly-generous number of coins from my purse.'

'Ah, that's the Braunds for you,' was Edith's observation.

From that moment on, the hours seemed to fly and, almost before anyone thought it possible, Naomi was setting off for the railway station to meet Mr Lawrence; on her face an expression she said she hoped conveyed her delight at seeing him again, while giving away nothing of the surprise awaiting him back at the house.

Once she had left, Kate helped Mabel and Edith put the finishing touches to arrangements on the lawn.

'Could have done with a mite less breeze,' Mabel opined, securing the tablecloth to the trestle with yet another weight. 'But at least the sky seems set fair.'

'We shall have to hope it don't blow out the flame on this burner,' Kate remarked, striking a match to light it, only to have it immediately extinguished by a gust of wind.

'May I?' Turning about, she came face to face with Rowley. 'Only, when it's windy,' he said, 'there is something of a knack to it.' Stepping back from the table, she handed him the box of Cook's matches and watched, as, striking a new one, and shielding the little burner with his hand, he offered one to the other. 'There,' he said, adjusting the wick. 'Burning nicely.'

With a smile, she accepted back the matches. 'Thank you.'

'Pleased to be of assistance. And if there is anything else I can do, please, do feel free to put me to work.'

She glanced about, the wind causing her to reach for the brim of her straw hat even though she had secured it with an extra pin. 'Thank you

309

for your offer. But I think we're done for now.'

With a polite nod he withdrew, just as Mabel arrived.

'Not a bad spread, all things considered,' she remarked, setting down the handful of teaspoons she had been carrying.

Kate smiled warmly. It was good to see Mabel looking so much brighter. 'You've worked wonders,' she said. 'I mean it. Mr Lawrence will be delighted. And I know for a fact Naomi is.'

'It was a joy to be able to set about something cheery for once,' Mabel admitted. 'Like it's a joy to see you with a little more colour to your cheeks.'

Suspecting Mabel knew what had put it there, and feeling herself blushing, Kate stared down at the front of her flowery frock — something else that was giving her more colour. All day, she'd been in two minds about her decision to leave off her mourning gown in order to wear this one.

'You don't mind that I've shed my weeds?' she turned back to Mabel to ask. 'It *is* only for this one afternoon. And only then because, otherwise, I should feel such a poor influence on what is, after all, a joyous occasion.'

'Me? Mind? Not in the slightest, love. How you choose to observe your mourning is a matter for you alone to decide. Wearing black always did seem to me more about showing everyone else how dutiful and sorrowful you are. No, as I see it, 'tis more meaningful to have a sincere heart inside than a false display out.'

Reassured, Kate slipped her hand through Mabel's arm. 'And that's the truth.'

' 'Course it is. Now, while there's still time enough to bring about a remedy, can you spot anything we're missing?'

Although knowing perfectly well what Mabel meant, Kate laughed. 'I can hardly see that summat's missing if it's not here to start with!'

'Heavens, you daft child. You know what I mean.'

She looked along the trestle. Secured upon it was a tablecloth from the household's third-best set of linens. Examined closely, it was possible to see scorch marks left by a too-hot smoothing iron, and the tiniest of moth-holes. But, as Naomi had said, it was perfectly adequate for dining *al fresco* and infinitely preferable to getting grass stains on one of the better ones. Weighting it down were two butler's trays, one stacked with tea plates and cutlery, the other with cups and saucers. Wisely, Mabel had eschewed the porcelain tea services, remarking that despite this one being ironstone, it did a fair impression of being something smarter, aided as it was by its plain white colour and surprising overall delicacy. It was, she had supported her recommendation of it to Naomi, *robust*.

Taking it all in, Kate moved further along the trestle. If the late Mrs Latimer could see her Georgian teapot put to use in the garden, she would turn in her grave. But, along with the matching coffee pot, they were the only pieces of their kind that were both large enough and still sufficiently presentable. Side by side, waiting to be filled, they also happened to be from the same set as the two milk jugs — covered against the flies with little circles of mesh that forever

311

reminded her of hair nets — and the sugar basin with its matching tongs, the little crystal knob on its lid catching the sunlight.

Behind the arrangement of ostentatious silverware, the towering hot-water jug was now perched on the burner, the smell of methylated spirits strong enough to make her feel queasy. Heaven only knew where Mabel had found that particular jug; the last time that thing had seen light of day had to be more than decade ago. Same went for the length of Union Jack bunting, which could only have come from the party Mrs Latimer had held for the coronation of King George.

Exhaling a long sigh, she stood back. In relatively few years, Woodicombe, along with much of the world beyond it, had changed beyond all recognition. And oftentimes, today included, she found herself wishing that it hadn't.

Determining not to succumb to gloominess, she turned about, her eyes falling upon the Royal Worcester cake stands, their contents protected from flies by the draping of tea towels. With the provisions Naomi had procured, Edith had managed to produce a Victoria sponge, a cherry Madeira, and what had originally been intended as a Dundee cake, but which had, when blanched almonds had proven impossible to come by, been substituted with a tea loaf. Still to come up from the kitchen were plates of sandwiches: crab and cucumber, cheese and tomato, and egg and cress. Not bad for a spur of the moment thing.

Stepping back, she folded her arms across her waist. Had things been different, they could have been putting on this very spread to celebrate the

312

return of not just Mr Lawrence but Luke as well — both of them returning victorious from battle rather than, in Mr Lawrence's case, from an asylum, and in Luke's case, not at all. But perhaps it was best not to think in terms of *if only*.

At that moment, a flash of sunlight glinting on brass brought her back from her reverie: the Humberette was swinging in through the gates, Mr Lawrence at the wheel. Then he must truly be better, she thought, shielding her eyes to look across at him, otherwise Naomi would definitely not have allowed him to drive. Unless, of course, he *wasn't* better and had simply insisted; few men, even unwell ones, would *choose* to sit in the passenger seat.

When the motorcar came to a halt in front of the porch, and Mr Lawrence stepped down onto the drive, his amusement and surprise at the sight before him came as a relief. Perhaps he *was* better; for Naomi's sake she hoped so. But, as the afternoon progressed and, later, she found herself watching him reclined in one of the canvas chairs, his long legs stretched out in front of him, her delight began to give way to something else. She was joyed for him, of course she was — and relieved to see him looking so much less grey and harrowed. He even looked to have put on a little weight. But none of her early happiness softened the recognition that, for a second time, while Mr Lawrence had come home, Luke hadn't. It didn't alter the fact that she had gone from being a wife, full of hope, to a widow with none, all of the things she had spent four years waiting for snatched away to be replaced

313

by . . . to be replaced by what?

As the days slipped past, her picture of the life stretching ahead of her became no less fuzzy. As things stood, when Naomi returned to Hartland Street, she would, of course, go with her. But to do what? She couldn't spend the next five decades as Naomi's housekeeper-cum-companion. Yes, it was possible that Naomi might go on to have children of her own — *might* — even so, those children were unlikely to need *her*: they would have a nursemaid, then a governess, and then go away to school. And anyway, she couldn't live the rest of her life vicariously, no matter her fondness for the Colbornes. *Be kind to Aunt Kate, she was widowed in the war.* No, she was going to need something of her own to live for. But what, precisely?

Heaving another long sigh, she stared down at the cake crumbs on her plate. In truth, it wasn't the mystery she pretended. Deep inside, and cold-hearted though it might be, she knew precisely what she was going to need: she was going to need a new husband. And, preferably, in due course, children, too.

Realizing that she had slumped down in her chair — and that she felt to have a scowl on her face — she got to her feet and went to put her plate on one of the side tables. Behind her, Mr Lawrence was talking.

'Officers and men alike,' she heard him saying, 'are told by their commanding officers to repress their feelings. They are told that their suffering is not unique, and that to cope in silence, and without complaint, is every soldier's patriotic duty. But I can tell you now, that few men at the front see war as patriotic. Nor do they see it as manly — certainly not after all of this time, they don't. Any illusions in that regard have long since been ground out of them. By now, that they survive at all is only through getting by each day one stint at a time, and by shutting out the most gruesome of memories.'

'And that is what they helped you to realize,' Kate heard Ned remark.

Turning slowly about, she saw how, seated in his wheelchair, he was leaning towards Mr Lawrence, his expression keen.

'It was *part* of the treatment, yes. But each man is different — each man arrives there with his own particular history. And that's the beauty of the place — there's no misconception that one size fits all men. Each individual gets to speak of his experiences — as often and as much as he needs — gets to confess to his fears and his guilt without the worry that he will be judged, or tarred as a coward. It is from that start point of honesty and respect, that the doctor determines a regimen of suitable treatments and activities to set him on his way to recovery.'

'And clearly, it works,' Naomi commented. To her tone there was once again a brightness, and to her demeanour a new fluidity.

'Clearly it's work*ing*,' Lawrence cautioned his wife. 'I'm not out of the woods yet. But I have come away from there with the means by which to control and cope with certain of my feelings, yes.'

'And for that I shall forever be deeply grateful,'

Naomi replied, moving to place her hand on his arm. Seemingly not even aware that he was doing it, Lawrence took hold of it and held it between his own.

Grateful not to be part of the contented little huddle, Kate swung away and blinked back tears. How much longer before she could take her leave of the little gathering? She had welcomed Mr Lawrence back, she had enquired after his well-being, and she had agreed with Naomi that yes, he did indeed seem to be a changed man. But, with her face now aching from all the smiling, and a lump once again back in her throat, she longed to be alone or, at the very least, away from all the unrelenting jollity and unwitting displays of affection.

Perhaps she would slip away now; no one could chide her for it. Down in the scullery there would be a pile of washing up that needed doing, and the mindlessness of the task might be just the thing to dull the envy gnawing away at her insides.

Sadly, distracting herself from her more chronic pain — the pain brought on by the dashing to pieces of her future — was going to require something more than a mountain of washing up. To dull that pain was going to require renewed hope. Not to mention some sort of plan to get her through the rest of her life.

⋆　⋆　⋆

'I forget you haven't been down here before.'

It was early evening the following day and,

316

with Esme put to bed and Lawrence retiring exhausted, Kate was doing as she had once promised Rowley and was accompanying him down to the cove. Given that, to date, they hadn't ventured from walking upon relatively even ground, she wasn't surprised to find their progress over the tricky path slow and halting. Not that it mattered; Rowley had been saying for ages that he wanted to see the beach, and she had no intention of nannying him by questioning his readiness to tackle the rugged conditions.

'Actually,' he began, causing her to look over her shoulder and witness on his face a look of discomfort, 'I *have* been down here.'

'You have? When was that?' With their path then becoming partly obstructed by the whippy growth of a willow, she reached to hold aside its branches. 'Have a care here. Beneath this moss are boulders just a-waiting to catch your toe.'

'Yes,' he said, glancing down. 'I see them. It was that day you came down here alone.'

Coming to a halt, she looked back at him and frowned. '*When?*'

With no choice in the matter, he too came to a halt. 'On the day it was raining.'

Feeling her cheeks colouring up, she turned back. 'Ah. *Then.*'

'I told myself that I would never mention it unless you did. But — '

'But I did ask.'

'Yes.'

She shrugged her shoulders. Already, that day seemed so long ago. 'It's all right,' she said as lightly as she could. 'But I'm surprised you felt sure enough of your leg that day to venture down over this sort of ground. Especially on your own, and not knowing the way.'

'I didn't feel at all sure of it,' she heard him reply. 'But, mortified though I am to admit to it now, seeing you heading down here, I followed, for some reason sensing that you might come to harm.'

Blushing even more fiercely, she fixed her eyes on the way ahead and kept going, unable to risk letting him see the depth of her embarrassment. 'Then, I thank you again,' she said. 'For risking your own well-being.'

For some time after that, their concentration was given over to watching their step, their progress reaching a stretch of path where the ground fell away more steeply. In any other year, the vegetation at this point would have been less vigorous and the path more clearly visible but, with no one venturing down there for some time, Mother Nature had been busily recolonizing even the most inhospitable of sections.

Further on, hearing a sudden scuffling behind her, and feeling loose gravel striking the hem of her skirt, she turned swiftly, holding out her hands in the expectation that he was about to slip.

'Whoa!' he exclaimed, skidding to a halt, one hand reaching to the trunk of a nearby tree, the other clutching at her arm.

Under his weight, she braced herself. 'Are you all right?'

Regaining his balance, he released his hold on her. 'Nothing more than damage to my pride,' he said, his expression nevertheless one of relief. 'But that was close.'

Turning to face forwards again, she continued on, the path descending less steeply now and the vegetation around it thinning. Behind her, his footsteps sounded more assured. 'Nearly there,' she called over her shoulder. 'Look, you can just make out the boulders at the top of the beach.'

'Yes, I see them.'

'Once we reach them, it's best to squeeze between them rather than try to clamber over.'

'Duly noted.'

Without further incident, they arrived on the sand.

'There,' she said, gesturing broadly. 'Woodi-combe Cove.'

Having bent to dust off the front of his trousers, he straightened up and looked about. 'My word. Just look how far out the tide has gone.'

'It goes down for almost a half mile — even more just after the full moon.'

When he went ahead of her, making towards the water line, she turned away and bent to take off her shoes. Then, with a quick glance to check that he wasn't looking, she reached under her skirt, pulled off her stockings and stuffed them in her shoes. The trouble with the new fashion for shorter skirts, she had recently come to discover, was that you couldn't get away with going about bare-legged, as she had once been able to — not that it was something she would countenance doing in London anyway. But, down here, on a beach in the height of summer, well, anything other than bare feet felt faintly ridiculous.

'It's heavenly,' he called back towards her, his arms raised above his head as he turned full circle and looked all about. 'That day in the rain it was all terribly dramatic but now, in this soft evening light, well, I can't imagine why anyone in their right mind would ever want to be anywhere else.'

'Everyone says that,' she replied, catching up to him but mindful to maintain a respectable distance to his side. 'To which I always say that you should see it in the worst of the gales come January-time. Then, for all of its supposed spectacle, the wind is so strong that you can't stand up, the salt from the spray stings your eyes, and the swirling sands blast at the least patch of exposed skin.'

'That may well be,' he said, staring back up the hill-side. 'But I find its benevolence this evening utterly bewitching.'

Amid the silence while he took in their surroundings, she saw her chance to broach the matter of his return to duty. Since their brief discussion about his letter the other morning, he had volunteered nothing further — and she hadn't felt able to ask. But now, with no one to overhear them, she said, 'Have you decided what you're going to do yet?'

Very slowly   at least, that was how it seemed to her — he brought his attention back from the far horizon. Then, as though considering how best to reply, he slid his hands down into the pockets of his trousers.

'Not . . . entirely, no.'

320

This close, she could see that his eyes had as many patches of moss green as they did chestnut brown. It was an intimate thing to discover. 'No?'

'No. You see . . . ' She wanted to tell him that it was all right — that he needn't tell her if he didn't want to. But she knew that if she did, he might take her at her word, and she would never be any the wiser. And over the last few days she had found herself increasingly desperate to learn of his intentions. 'As decisions go,' he picked up. 'Well, let's just say that my situation has become rather more complicated.' With no idea why that should be, she pressed her lips together and waited; left unprompted, he might go on to explain. But, if she gave the appearance of prying, then he might clam up. 'Other considerations have come to the fore — considerations that I am wary of addressing.'

When he turned to stare back out to sea, she did likewise. Over the years, she had learned that if you refrained from meeting the other person's eyes, they were often inclined to be more forthcoming.

'Oh,' she said, hoping to sound only lightly interested. 'Do you not even lean more in one direction than the other?'

The speed with which he responded to that took her by surprise. 'I do. That said, I would willingly settle for the alternative, should the situation require — given the overall picture, I mean.'

Now he just seemed to be talking in riddles. What on earth was this other consideration that it could hold such sway over his decision?

'So — '

Without warning, and before she knew what was happening, he had turned towards her, reached for her hands, and taken them in his own. Despite flinching from the shock, she didn't pull them away.

'Please, Kate, don't be alarmed. I mean you no harm — quite the contrary. But I do wish to say something to you, and I should like very much that rather than yield to your first instinct, you at least give a moment's thought to what I have to say.'

'Rowley — '

'Kate, you are the loveliest person I have ever met. Your patience and kindness know no bounds. You are honest. And warm. And not at all shallow or vain even though you must know how pretty you are — '

What on earth was he doing? She was married — well, no, she wasn't any more, but she *was* a widow.

'And yes, I know that it is only a few weeks since I was first introduced to you. But, *in* those weeks, I have spent sufficient time in your company to feel that I have come to know you. And no, it does not escape me that you are newly widowed, nor that by surprising you like this I am being unbelievably gauche — wrong, even. But you see, very soon now I must decide where I am to be posted. And, once I do, then in no time at all I shall be gone from here. So, I hope you understand that although I am being utterly reprehensible, I have to do this.' In that moment, she felt a surge of terror so deep that she started to pull away from him. 'Kate, please would you do me the honour of becoming my wife?'

Was she going to faint? Things around her had certainly taken on a peculiar appearance. And in her ears was that funny rushing sound that usually came just before everything went dark. Breathing far too rapidly for comfort, she resisted her previous inclination to get away from him and grasped his hands as tightly as she could.

'I can't — '

'You've no need to give me your answer this moment,' he hastened to add. Despite her confusion, the earnestness of his tone was unmissable. 'But I have to ask. Before it is too late. You do see that, don't you?'

When she tried to swallow, it felt as though her tongue had become stuck to the roof of her mouth. And yet it was vital that she say what was on her mind. 'I do see it, yes. But . . . but you must surely see that for something of this . . . this . . . enormity, well, I can't just decide upon it, not just like that, not so sudden.'

Keeping hold of her hands, he took a small step backwards. 'No. I realize that. I expected that was how you would feel. Which is why I say that you need not answer me now. All I ask is that you think about it — perhaps think about what you would like to ask me — what you would like to know before you can reach your decision. Please know that I shall happily tell you anything. Anything at all.'

The sensation in her head was a disconcerting one: while a good part of her mind felt completely beyond making sense of anything at all, a small corner of it seemed to have a clarity like never before. And that was the part that felt to be connected to her tongue.

'You can't fail to have seen,' she began, wishing that her hands hadn't grown so sticky, 'that I have discarded my widow's weeds, even though by most folks' standards I shouldn't have. But I shouldn't want you to think that just because I have — '

'I don't,' he interrupted her. 'I respect that you are still in mourning. Which is all the more reason why blind-siding you like this makes me a cad — '

Unable to disagree more, she shook her head. 'You're not.'

'Well, thank you for saying so. But tell me that you at least see my dilemma.' Not entirely sure that she did, she simply stood looking back at him. 'Well, then permit me to explain. If there is any chance whatsoever, no matter how small, that you might accept me, then I shouldn't want to decide the path of my future employment without reference to you first. For instance, would you be happy to live in Gloucestershire, or would you only ever want to return to London?'

Suddenly, she understood what he meant about complications, and felt moved to at least help him on that score. 'I know not a single thing of Gloucestershire,' she said.

'But, if I decided against London, you wouldn't mind that?'

In the full knowledge that she was getting ahead of herself, she shook her head. 'I shouldn't

324

mind somewhere that wasn't London.'

'Then tomorrow, I shall write a letter stating that I wish to accept the promotion into the new intelligence unit.' Finally lowering her hands, he gently let them go. 'And then, without mentioning the matter to you again unless you first raise it with me, I shall await your response — be that weeks from now . . . or months. Or even years. Yes, I shall wait years, if that's what it takes for you to be certain.'

Fearing that her eyes were about to fill with tears, and biting down on the side of her tongue in a bid to stem them, she watched him take several steps backwards.

'I give you my word that I shall think on this carefully,' she said. 'And I thank you for understanding my situation . . . for not pressing me to answer, for in all conscience, I couldn't.'

His response was to give her a single nod. 'If I leave you alone now with your thoughts, will you be all right making your way back up by yourself? Or would you prefer that I wait — back up on the path, I mean — until you are ready to return?'

Knowing how close she was to crying — and that once she started, she might not easily stop — she shook her head. 'No, please, you go on. I know the way back up better than anyone.'

'You will be quite all right? Only, if I should have to come to your rescue twice in the space of a few short weeks, people might talk . . . '

To her own surprise, she laughed. 'Go on with you,' she urged. 'I give you my word, I'll be back up dreckly.'

And anyway, she thought as he turned away and she watched his progress back across the sand, unlike that last time she was here, it wasn't pouring with rain; at least this time when she sank to her knees and started to cry, she was unlikely to catch her death of cold: death from heartbreak, yes, *that* might be her fate. After all, no matter the life he was offering her, and no matter how much she might want to accept him, she knew in her heart that she could do no such thing.

13

Dilemmas

She couldn't do it. By rights, she shouldn't even be considering it. And yet, she found that she was. Indeed, it was the only thing on her mind from the moment she opened her eyes in the morning until she closed them again at night — the *only* thing.

It was now several days since Rowley's proposal and, every time Kate recalled what had happened down in the cove, she was engulfed by a wave of guilt powerful enough to make her feel sick. Indeed, immediately after the incident, she had gone straight to bed, feigning a severe headache and refusing all remedies, insisting instead that all she needed was a good night's sleep. Not surprisingly, she hadn't got it; once in her room, with daylight still showing through the curtains, she'd got up again and paced about. Even when she had felt weary beyond all belief and had finally climbed back into bed, all she had done was toss and turn until, eventually, the light of the new morning had started to brighten the room. But, reluctant to face anyone for fear she would be unable to conceal the scale of her guilt, she had remained in bed, accepting only tea and toast from a concerned Naomi.

Eventually, she'd had no choice but to get up. Going to great lengths to avoid everyone, she had busied herself with clearing away meals, washing up in the scullery, and then, later, slipping out to scurry away across the lawn and take a walk under the cover of the wooded lanes. None of it was sufficient to take her mind from Rowley, though. Moreover, all the while the matter between them remained unresolved, she knew that nothing would.

Clearly, she couldn't marry him. But neither could she bring herself to tell him that, which had to be why she felt such guilt. It was tensing her limbs. It was strangling her throat. And it was contorting her insides to the point where she couldn't have eaten anything even had she wanted to. In addition, there was the guilt she felt at having accompanied him down to the beach in the first place. And the guilt she felt for having let him take her hands. And for having stood there and heard him out — led him to think that she might just say yes. Layer upon layer upon layer of guilt.

Most of all, there was the guilt she felt for agreeing to consider him when she wasn't free to do so. She was in mourning, for heaven's sake. And there was *another* thing: what sort of woman cast off her mourning gown simply because she was fed up with it making her look miserable? She was *supposed* to be miserable — her husband had been blown to pieces on the battlefield. He deserved to be mourned — properly — for his sacrifice.

Yes, hers was a blanket of guilt that showed no signs of lifting. In fact, when, having somehow made it through the day, she opened her eyes the *following* morning, it felt as though under cover of darkness, her guilt had simply doubled its weight. Completely worn down by it — crippled by it — she didn't even attempt to get out of bed. Instead, she curled into a ball and stayed there, completely lost to know what to do.

The first person to come in search of her was Naomi.

'What can I get you?' she asked, perching on the side of the bed, her voice gentle.

'Nothing.'

'You're not hungry? You wouldn't like a nice cup of tea to get you going?'

'I don't want to get going. I don't see the point.' Feeling Naomi's hand coming to rest upon the eiderdown, she felt mean for sounding ungrateful. But she didn't want to be coaxed from her mood. What she wanted was to unravel everything that had happened down on the beach, such that she might be freed from her shame: to have a clear conscience; to be facing some sort of life on her own, perhaps here, in Woodicombe, where no one would expect anything of her and there would be a natural order to things — an order she understood.

'I know how it must feel — '

'No,' she said from under the covers. 'You don't.'

'No. You're right,' she heard Naomi reply. 'I don't know at all. I know how I felt when Lawrence came back, so different to the man I knew — so brutally changed and unreachable. But at least he *came* back. And he *is* getting better. Going forward from here, things between us will be different to how I once imagined them

— less certain. But, while he might no longer be the steady and competent man I married, neither is he quite so stiff and so buttoned-up. And that can only be a good thing. So, no, I can't imagine what you must be going through. What's worse, I don't know how to help you, either. I *could* say something trite, like Mamma would, about time being the best healer, but I wouldn't insult you. Aunt Diana would know what to say. But she's not here.'

'Please, Naomi,' Kate said, folding back the cover for just long enough to look at her. 'Go and take care of Mr Lawrence . . . and Esme and Ned. Ain't nothing you can do for *me*, but you can see to it they're all right.'

From Naomi she heard a long sigh. And then she felt her get up from the bed.

'Well, I'll look back in on you later. In the meantime, try to get some sleep — I can see that you haven't had any.'

The next person to arrive — after what seemed to Kate to be an interval of about twenty minutes — was Mabel.

'It's the shock, love,' she said, setting a tray on the occasional table and then, clearing a space on the nightstand first, bringing across a cup of tea. 'Does strange things to a person, shock does. The moment you think you've seen the worst of it, and think you're getting back to normal, you realize there's no such thing as normal any more. And that's when it hits you all over again.'

Slowly, Kate pushed back her covers. Even more slowly, she raised herself up. Mabel was right. She *had* thought she was getting over it.

330

Perhaps then, she reflected, brushing back handfuls of her hair, what she was feeling had as much to do with losing Luke as it did with Rowley's proposal. Perhaps, with Rowley offering her a way to move on with her life, it was forcing her to accept that Luke truly wasn't coming back. Perhaps, as much as feeling guilt, her feelings were down to shock — were more muddled than she had realized.

'I just wish . . . ' But, having started, she felt unable to finish.

'I know, love,' Mabel said, reaching for her hand. 'It's terrible, terrible hard. But, take it from me, it does get better.'

She looked back at Mabel's face. 'Does it?'

'I lost a son and I lost a husband. Not a day doesn't go by when I don't think about one or other of them — oftentimes both. But, not only are you a good deal younger than I was, with a chance to one day start over, you've a good many folk who care about you, and who won't let you struggle on alone.'

Slowly, she nodded. 'I know. And I feel selfish for wallowing like this, truly I do.'

Picking up her hand, Mabel gave it a squeeze. 'There's no need to feel selfish.'

'It's not just that, it's . . . ' But, with Mabel looking back at her, Kate knew she couldn't say what was really on her mind, which was, in essence, that someone had already proposed a way for her to start over — but that she felt guilty for even entertaining the idea, no matter how briefly.

'Go on, love. It's not just what?'

In a wave of panic at realizing how close she had come to confessing the true reason why she was unable to drag herself out of bed and get on with things, she shook her head and stared down at the bedspread. 'No,' she mumbled, 'it's nothing.'

'All right, then. Well, drink your tea, and I'll pop up later and see if you want something to eat.'

Once Mabel had left, though, Kate felt even worse: now she had added lying to her list of transgressions. Whatever was she going to do? These feelings wouldn't go away on their own: to be rid of them was going to require action on her part. But, what to do?

Swinging her legs down to the floor, she padded across to the window and drew back the curtains. The vibrancy of the colours beyond them came as a shock. Rather than being the sort of grey and dreary day that befitted her mood, the sky was the most summery of turquoises, the newly-mown lawns bore emerald stripes, and the mid-morning sunshine was picking out a flash of ruby-red among the rhododendrons: Pa Channer's neckerchief; rain or shine, he never set to work without it.

Watching as he moved about in the dark foliage, she felt the stirrings of an idea: she would go and see Ma Channer again. Not only did she listen without judgement, she was discreet. And, given that there wasn't much she didn't know about a woman's nature, she might have some advice.

★ ★ ★

'Very well,' Ma Channer indeed commented once Kate had confessed to being in a turmoil over *a proposal she had received*. 'What troubles you most about it? That you felt obliged to turn it down? Or that you're minded not to?'

Once again seated at the Channer's kitchen table, Kate realized that she felt less tense than she had in days. By rights, she ought to feel haunted — ought to feel as though within these walls, Luke was able to hear what she was saying. Maybe that was even what she had been hoping for when she had thought to come here — that she would get some sign of approval from him. But the truth was that she felt nothing of him at all. The smells were familiar enough: lavender drying in bunches on the rack; lamb stewing in the pot; a faint dampness from beneath the floorboards. And the sounds were familiar too — sparrows chirping in the yard and the slow ticking of the clock on the mantel. But, of Luke, she sensed no presence whatsoever.

'Neither of them things,' she replied.

'No?'

'No. I just feel immense guilt to even be considering marrying someone else so soon after Luke's passing — '

'Natural.'

' — and at how upset Ro — *the person who proposed to me* is going to be when I must say no.'

'Tell me, love,' Ma Channer said, looking directly at her. 'Why it is that you feel bound to say no.'

'Well, Luke and my obvious state of widowhood aside,' she said, the fact striking her as

333

sufficient reason by itself. 'Because . . . the person in question . . . and his folks . . . are far above my station. They're *academics*.' Once uttered, the word seemed to hang accusingly. Belatedly, she hoped it meant what she had come to suppose it did.

'Look, love, purely for the ease of it, what say you we give this poor fellow a name — save us skirting the matter of who he is? What say you we call him . . . Frank?'

Having until then been pressing her lips together in thought, her amusement burst from between them with unexpected force. 'All right,' she said, unable to stop giggling. 'I've had a proposal of marriage from Frank. And not only do I feel guilty that he should think of me like that and want to wed me, I feel guilty that I've yet to turn him down.'

'Aye, girl,' Loveday Channer said. 'But what I'm more interested to know is why you think you should? Turn him down, that is.'

'Because I promised I would be true to Luke — '

'And you were.'

'And he promised to be true to me.'

'He did. And, so far as I know, you both kept your promises. But now he's not coming back. So, tell me, what else is going on in that head of yours? Is this supposed matter of your folks being so different of concern to *him*, as well as to you? Did he say, 'I *would* ask you to marry me, but our folks are too different'?'

She shook her head. 'No, of course not. Nothing like that.'

'So, if the differences between your family and his are of no concern to *him*, then why do they trouble *you*?'

'Because I just can't see me being a part of his sort of a life — '

'Pah! I doubt you've even tried seeing it — else you'd be telling me just what it is in particular that you can't see. Do you like this feller — this Frank?'

At the mention of Frank, Kate still couldn't help laughing. If ever there was someone who didn't look, sound, or act like a Frank, it had to be Rowley. 'I don't know him well enough to answer that.'

'Stuff and nonsense! When you look upon him, do your breath catch in your chest?'

'Ye-es . . . '

'And before all this business with his proposal, did you lay in your bed come nightfall a-thinking of him?'

'I tried my best not to.'

'And when he asked you to wed him, was your instinct — your very first thought deep inside of you, not the one in your head — to say yes to him?'

She forced herself to swallow. How to answer that? 'Um . . . '

'I'll take that as more properly being a yes.'

Ma Channer was right. Her first instinct had been to wish that she felt able to accept him; his advance, although wildly unexpected, had made her feel warm and thrilled and delighted. And wanting to say yes. But had that just been down to relief — a way out of her situation, or even a

335

sort of balm to her grief over Luke?

'Yes,' she whispered nonetheless. 'I wanted to say yes.'

'Then you must fathom what stopped you, and find a way to accept this young man. For surely 'tis better to marry someone you're drawn to liking now, than to one day marry out of necessity, and risk ending up with a pig in a poke.'

Laughing yet again, Kate felt as though her load was lightening. And when, almost an hour later, she was back in her room, her guilt felt to be giving way to a sense of purpose. Ma Channer had helped her to see that the question ahead of her had nothing to do with Luke. Luke was gone; he couldn't be offended or upset by what she chose to do next. In fact, as Loveday Channer — his own mother — had pointed out to her, he would want only that she should find a way to be happy. Were he able to give it, she would have his blessing to move on with her life rather than waste it or spend it living with regret. According to Ma Channer, she should confine herself to considering only whether 'this Frank fellow' was the man to whom she truly wanted to pledge the rest of her life. That, she had said, was the only decision she now faced. And the truth was that eventually, and despite Naomi's assurances about her being able to continue living with them for as long as she wanted, she was going to need a life of her own. And for her, as an unskilled young woman without private means, that meant finding a husband. On that score, Ma Channer was right again: better a man she liked and respected. But that didn't mean she should just go into it willy-nilly. Surely, she should only consider the idea if she could more properly acquaint herself with Rowley's thoughts and views — and get to know him a good deal better than she did at the moment. 'Tell him,' Ma Channer in her wisdom had urged, 'that you need to know more about what it is he's offering you. And tell him also that, in return for his honesty and his patience, you will consider him on the same basis.'

Crossing to the window, she stared out over the gardens. Pa Channer had gone now, but she could just pick out where he had left his mattock leaning against the trunk of a tree. Now he would be eating the lamb stew that had been simmering on the stove, with potatoes, and carrots fresh from the kitchen garden.

With a thoughtful sigh, she turned back into the room. She had been right to go and see Ma Channer. She talked sense. It was a Channer trait.

Glancing about, her eyes came to rest upon the floral dress she had worn for Mr Lawrence's tea party. She wouldn't wear it again yet; she would remain in her mourning, the feel of the stiff crepe reminding her not to act in a manner that she might later come to regard as foolish or rash. That said, she *would* find a way to talk to Rowley — but not down on the beach, or indeed, anywhere else that was out of sight of other people. No, she would ask him, in a plain and straightforward manner, to tell her more about himself. And then she would try to work out whether or not she should accept his proposal.

★　★　★

'So, now we just have to wait. And hope for the best.'

Listening to Naomi speaking, Kate shifted her weight upon her chair. How selfish to have become so wrapped up with her own affairs that she hadn't noticed what had been going on elsewhere in the house. Mr Lawrence had been called before a medical board and, just yesterday, had travelled to Exeter to have his fitness assessed for return to duty — and she hadn't known a thing about it. And now, probably at this very moment, the panel before whom he had appeared were discussing his fate. No wonder Naomi had asked her to join her for coffee — the poor woman had to be worried half to death: Mr Lawrence could be heading back to the front.

'I didn't realize,' she said, rueing that she hadn't known earlier.

Beside her, Naomi replaced her cup on its saucer. 'Why would you have?' Thankfully, her tone contained neither judgement nor recrimination. 'You've had quite enough on your mind without having me bend your ear with *my* concerns. Truly, I had no intention of adding to your woes. Besides, by comparison, my fears are far more modest.' *I haven't lost my husband*, was the inference Kate drew from her words.

It was the morning after Kate had been to see Loveday Channer and, sitting on the terrace with

338

Naomi, she was growing more and more unsettled to discover just how much she had missed. Without her realizing it, Rowley had also gone somewhere — and had yet to return. According to Naomi, he had ' . . . said something about having to go somewhere to see somebody about something'. What on earth use was *that* to her? Could Naomi *be* any more vague? The only thing she could think was that he had gone to see someone in the RAF regarding the letter he'd received about his next post. Perhaps he had gone to try and find out more about the job in Gloucestershire. Perhaps he had gone to accept it. Being only able to presume — knowing nothing for certain about a matter of such importance — made her feel restless and fidgety. The only thing she could think to do — just as soon as she could get away from Naomi — was to go and see Ned. He might know what Rowley was up to.

For now, she must turn her mind back to Mr Lawrence.

'So, where does Mr Lawrence think he'll be sent, then?' she asked Naomi, recalling what they had been more properly discussing.

'He has no idea. I've asked him over and over whether they gave any clue as to their leanings, but he says only that they gave no hint whatsoever. The only comfort I can draw from any of this is that when he was first assessed — you remember, when I went with him to Wiltshire — it seemed they did at least consider him unfit to return to the front. There was, I believe, talk of desk jobs with no downward

339

chain of command. Were that to be the outcome, I shouldn't mind at all. The trouble is, Lawrence *would*. He'd mind terribly. If it transpires that he's headed for an office, he'll fight tooth and nail to get them to change their minds.'

Listening to Naomi talking, Kate was inclined to agree. Since his return from Priory Glen, Mr Lawrence seemed lively and purposeful — at times possibly even overly so. But, equally, he had moments of reflection, too, talking often of how he hoped to be allowed to return to his men. As Ned had separately remarked, though, how many of the men Lawrence had in mind would still be there? Either way, being informed that he was to remain in England, especially behind a desk, would devastate him. Poor Naomi; for her, both possible outcomes had the makings of a disaster.

'How long before you find out what's to happen?' she asked.

Across from her, Naomi shrugged her shoulders. 'I haven't the faintest idea. I can't continually press him for information. He has already asked me to stop nannying him, so I have to tread carefully — not let it seem as though I'm prying. All he will say is that he should hear something 'any day now'.'

Able to understand Naomi's difficulty, she gave a short sigh. 'You must be on tenterhooks all over again.'

'I am. But only another woman could appreciate that.'

'It would seem so.'

'But what about you? How are you feeling

today?' Naomi asked.

'I — '

'Only, I notice you're wearing your mourning again.'

Slowly, she nodded. 'Yes. Though it felt all right to be out of it for Mr Lawrence's party, more generally it felt too soon.'

'Well, only you can know what feels right.'

To her relief, with Naomi then muttering something about needing to go in and check that Esme wasn't getting up to mischief, and taking her leave, Kate spotted her opportunity to go and see Ned. Indeed, when she followed the path around the side of the house to where the French doors from the study gave onto the terrace, she found him in his wheelchair, a book open upon his lap but his attention directed out across the lawn.

'Pied wagtails,' he said as she drew near.

When he nodded in the general direction of them, she turned to look. Bobbing about at the edge of the lawn were two slender birds with long tails, their light plumage striped with grey and black. 'I didn't know you could identify birds,' she said, turning back to look at him.

'For want of anything better to do, I've been reading Rowley's field guide.'

She smiled; here was her chance. 'Where *is* Rowley? I haven't seen him about this morning.'

'Shot off to see about his next posting.'

Well, it was a start. But, clearly, to find out what she wanted to know, she was going to have to be more devious. 'Oh. So he knows where he's being sent?'

'They've given him two options. But he's not keen on one of them and the other is something of an unknown. So he's gone to try and find out more about it.'

Now she needed to keep up the pretence. 'Does either of them involve flying?'

He shook his head. 'Sadly, no.'

'Oh.'

'As it stands, neither of us will be back in the air.'

Inevitably, her eyes fell upon his wheelchair. 'And how are *you* doing?' In a way, it was an insensitive thing to ask: it was quite plain how he was. But he would surely know that she meant it kindly.

'Struggling to accept that, despite Nurse Hammond's valiant efforts, I shan't ever walk again.'

Without thinking about what she was doing, she reached for one of his hands. It felt surprisingly cool. 'You can't be certain of that.'

Slowly, he turned to look directly at her. His poor body might be horribly damaged, but his eyes were as warm as ever. 'Kate, while I applaud your optimism, I *do* know it. If my legs were ever going to heal, they would have done so by now. The last doctor who came said that in all probability, my shin bones haven't knitted back together as had been hoped. Apparently, with the degree of damage they suffered, the odds were against me anyway. It was always a long shot — though only now has someone thought to tell me that. Apparently, the best I can hope for is that I am able to build up the muscles in my shoulders and arms such that I will be able to haul myself around on crutches. But where's the point in that? If I'm not going to be able to walk without aid, then I might as well stay in this chair.'

All too sadly, she could see his point. 'So . . . '

'So, any day now, I'm expecting to have to undergo yet another examination and assessment, after which I'm certain the RAF will have no alternative but to pension me off.'

Put like that, it sounded so final. But then it *was* final. Without the use of his legs, what good was he to the Royal Air Force?

Carefully, so as not to draw attention to what she was doing, she relinquished her hold on his hand. Then, even more slowly, she took a couple of steps away from him. 'I see.'

His belief about what would happen to him raised so many questions — like where would he live, and how would he manage? Presumably, arrangements would be made for him back at Clarence Square.

'You know, Kate, earlier, when I was sitting here, I had a vision of that party Mamma held. Must be four years ago now. Do you remember it?'

Remember it? It was an event she would never forget. She could picture it as though it was yesterday — but there was no need for him to know that. 'I do, yes.'

'She had entertainers. Oh, and a fortune teller.'

'I think she called herself a mystic — no, a prophetess.'

343

'That's right! She did. Madame Something-or-other — '

'Madame Sybil.'

' — and I got you in to see her.'

Surprised not to be blushing, she smiled. 'You did, yes.'

'Say, has anything she told you that night come true? Or definitely *not* come true?'

'If memory serves,' she said, no intention of disclosing anything from that particular encounter, 'the things she foretold were so vague they could have been taken to mean almost anything.'

'And therein lay her skill.'

'Yes,' she agreed. Then, changing the subject, went on, 'Well, I suppose you must be looking forward to having Rowley back — for some company, I mean.' It was a remark she hoped would lead him to divulging something of his friend's movements.

'He hopes to be back late this evening.'

'Good. Well, I suppose I'd best get on — go and lend a hand with luncheon.'

'All right,' he said, directing his eyes back out across the lawn.

'But I might see you later.'

'I shall be here.'

Once she had rounded the corner of the house and was certain that she was out of his sight, she paused. It was a long time since she had thought about the night of Pamela Russell's party. In those four short years, life had changed for all of them. And, from what she could tell, more change was yet to come. Especially, it seemed, for her.

344

Heaving a long sigh, and with a light shake of her head, she continued on her way. Rowley was due back tonight. Therefore, tomorrow, she must make a point of talking to him — if only to bring an end to her state of indecision. And, presumably, even though he'd said he wouldn't press for an answer, he would need *some sort* of indication from her before he had to leave to take up his new post. And so, for both of their sakes, she had better get on and make up her mind.

★ ★ ★

'I hope it was all right of me to tell you that.'

'Yes, of course it was.'

'Only, I thought you would want to know what I've decided to do — you know, on the basis that it might help you to reach your own decision.'

It was late that evening and Kate had been in the dining room, putting away the silverware, when Rowley had come through the door. Explaining that he had just arrived back from his trip, he had asked if she would accompany him on a stroll around the gardens. Initially hesitant — in particular because dusk was falling — she was glad now that she had agreed, because he had just been explaining how he had been to Gloucestershire to see for himself the RAF's new intelligence unit.

'It might help, yes,' she replied now to his observation. And it was true: deep down, it *was* a help to know where he had decided upon, possibly even helping her to narrow down the steadily lengthening list of questions she had for him.

'I wasn't sure whether or not to tell you,' he went on, his tone betraying a degree of wariness. 'You know, given that I had promised not to pester you for an answer. But I didn't think telling you of my decision would qualify as pestering. I say, it doesn't does it?'

Unable to help smiling, she shook her head. 'No, I don't see it as pestering.'

'Good. Because I'm still happy to wait for you to decide in your own time.'

'Thank you.'

'Though I do hope that doesn't mean I must entirely ignore you while you do.'

'It doesn't.'

'Only, naturally, I'm inclined to try to support my proposal — you know, make sure that you view it in the best possible light. Well, I should be a fool not to. Only an idiot would sit back and take his chance at the hands of fate.'

Glancing about to see where they had reached, she drew to a halt and turned to face him. If the speed with which he had been talking was anything to go by, he was as apprehensive about all of this as she was.

In the hope of calming her own nerves, she paused to think for a moment. Then, she said, 'I have been thinking about what you asked me.' In that moment, she felt certain that he tensed. 'Been thinking about it real careful and — '

'Oh, God, you're going to turn me down.'

The desperation on his face brought a huge smile to her own. 'No,' she said with a shake of her head. 'No, I've not yet decided it — '

'Thank heavens for that!'

' — because there are things I should like to ask you — things I feel I ought to know.'

Instantly, he straightened up. 'Oh! Well, yes, of course. Ask away. As I said, whatever you want to know, I shall be happy to tell you. Anything at all.'

And so, as they resumed their walk, their progress somewhat erratic, she came to learn that his mother and father were called Rufus and Virginia, that his sisters were Eugenie and Viola, that his parents still lived in the village where he had been born, and, incidentally, what he had both enjoyed and disliked about being away at school. Seemingly more at ease now, he then went on to tell her, unprompted, about his hopes and plans for the future.

'So you would like to stay in the RAF — even when this war is over and done with?' she asked when he seemed to have run out of things to tell her, and largely to check that she had understood him.

He nodded. 'I truly believe that we are only just beginning to understand what can be achieved through the power of flight. I mean to say, when the steam engine was first invented, no one could much see the point of *that*. But look how it went on to change our lives — just think of all the uses for it that we now take for granted. And the same will happen with manned flight, I'm sure of it. Once flying machines are no longer an instrument for waging war, all manner of new opportunities will open up. And I should like to be at the forefront of some of them.'

'By remaining in the RAF.'

'For the moment, yes. But not to the exclusion of having my own home, and a wife and a family, of course. No, I should very much like to have children — children that will live to see the great advances that are almost certainly upon us — and to be able to raise them such that they might play their own part in what is to come.'

Put like that, the life he was offering her sounded to be one of purpose and meaning. And, no doubt, one of creature comforts, too — certainly more so than she would have had with Luke. Oddly, she wasn't sure how she felt about that: did she truly deserve a life of privilege and luxury? And if she didn't, then *why* didn't she? When she one day had children, wouldn't she want them to have the benefit of proper schooling — wouldn't she want them to go out into the world, just as he had described, and do something meaningful with their lives?

'Would you send your children away to school?' she asked. It wasn't something she had wondered about until then but, with him having been the one to mention children, it struck her as something she ought to know.

'Well, ignoring for the moment the issue of being able to afford the fees,' he said, glancing briefly towards her. 'I should only want them to go away if it was the right thing for them as individuals. A decent grammar school in a good city — such as, say, Cheltenham — might be better than having them not fit in at boarding school. I suppose it would be something we would agree upon at the time. I certainly wouldn't mandate that they board. *My* parents didn't. At the appropriate age, they asked each of us how we felt and then respected our wishes.'

Goodness. She'd never come across a parent anywhere who listened to the wishes of their children. Quite the opposite.

Reflecting upon what he had just said, she gave a little sigh. He had been honest with her and so, perhaps, the time had come for her to be the same — to admit to the deepest of her concerns.

To that end, she drew a short breath. 'Thank you for being so forthcoming — '

'Not at all.'

'It helps me to picture . . . well, to picture the sort of life you hope for, I suppose . . . '

'But for any of those things to have meaning,' he rushed to add, 'I should want only to share them with you — once you felt entirely ready, of course.'

When she felt her insides tensing, she knew why it was. If he was going to profess to having feelings like that for her, then she had to tell him how she felt. She couldn't let him go about thinking that his chances were greater than they were.

'I worry that I would let you down.' There — she had said it. She had confessed to what she saw as the biggest obstacle to accepting him, which was, in essence, that she was well beneath his station.

'That you would *let me down?*'

Seeing just how taken aback he looked, she hurried to elaborate. 'You must already have noticed that I'm poorly taught. And, apart from Hartland Street, I know little of the world beyond Woodicombe. Indeed, I only know which knives and forks to use for the various courses of a meal because I grew up laying them on the tables of gentry folk. Truly, I am a nobody. And I worry that in your . . . sort of class, everyone would see that.'

'You're not a nobody,' he snatched the opportunity to correct her.

But the little noise she gave in response signified her disagreement. ' 'Tis kind of you to say so, but there can be no altering the truth. Many would be the time I wouldn't know how to act. Like in the company of your mother, for instance. With her being a person of learning, how would I ever — '

'She *is* learned, yes. But she wouldn't expect *you* to be. My sisters aren't.'

'Maybe not. But I'll warrant they're well-schooled.' *Certainly better than I am*; they couldn't fail to be.

'Reasonably well, yes. But the thing you have yet to discover about my mother is, her belief that every woman should be able to do whatever she wants with her own life. If that means being a wife and mother — as my sisters have chosen to be — then that's fine by her, just as long as it is by their own choosing. On the other hand, if a woman wants to fly aeroplanes or . . . or become a doctor rather than a nurse, then according to her, that should be all right, too.'

'But I wouldn't know how to talk to her . . . '

When he began to laugh, she blushed.

'I venture you would do as the rest of us do and use your mouth.'

'Please don't tease me,' she said, removing her eyes from his and turning them to the ground. 'You know what I mean.'

'I do,' he said.

At the periphery of her vision, she saw him move closer. 'Then please don't belittle my concerns. To me, they are most real.'

His hands, she noticed in that moment, twitched as though about to reach for her own, just as he had down in the cove. In the event, though, he thrust them behind his back. Thank goodness she was wearing her mourning gown; if nothing else, it felt like a sort of barrier — a shield.

'Kate, please, I would never belittle your fears. Indeed, I am grateful that you feel you can be honest with me. If I know of your concerns, then I can help you to overcome them. But, I assure you, you have absolutely no need to fear my mother. Or my father. Or my sisters. As a family, we don't judge people by where they come from. We just don't.'

'I fear she would look upon me with disdain — '

'She wouldn't.'

'I should feel unfit to be her parlour maid, let alone her daughter-in-law.'

'Oh, Kate, no — '

'Yes.'

'Then you must meet her — '

'What? No!'

'Yes, I mean it. There are clearly things about

351

which you need to be sure before committing to my proposal. And that's good. A desire to be certain tells me that you are your own person. I respect that. So, let me take you to meet my mother — '

'No. I couldn't — '

' — and allow you to see for yourself that the quality she values most in a person is sincerity.'

'Rowley, please — '

'Not for a luncheon, not if that would make you feel uncomfortable — just for an afternoon tea in a little café somewhere — neutral territory. I could introduce you to her as a dear acquaintance, so that on neither side would there be any expectations.'

Feeling the rate at which her heart was beating, she shook her head in dismay. His suggestion was a sensible one — she just couldn't see herself mustering the confidence to go through with it, especially not without enlisting some form of help and tutoring from Naomi beforehand. But, as things stood at that moment, she wanted to keep *her* — and everyone else, for that matter — as far away from all of this as she possibly could. So, what to do?

'I'll think about it,' she said, finally raising her head and meeting his look.

His expression was one of immense relief. 'Good. Please, do remember that it is just a suggestion. If you decide not to take up the offer to witness for yourself that what I say about my family is true, I shall think no less of you for it.'

'All right. And, howsoever I decide upon the matter, you stand by your promise that you won't rush me for an answer?'

'Kate, I give you my word. Look at it from my perspective — I want you to say yes, not send you running scared. And I mean what I say about being prepared to wait. Indeed, please know that you can say yes to me now without any expectation on my part that we shall rush to marry. It will be enough to know that you have agreed.'

When, at her request, he took his leave of her and started back towards the house, his form quickly lost to her in the dusk, she remained where she was, the night-air like a velvety cape about her gown.

Alone, but no less unsettled, she sighed. She had hoped that by doing as Ma Channer had suggested and drawing him into conversation about himself, she would now be leaning more in one direction than the other — more inclined to accept him or not. As it turned out, she simply felt more confused than ever. She couldn't deny that he was a considerate man. Nor could she deny that the more she came to know about him, the more she warmed to him. She even suspected that, were she to let down her guard and allow herself to, she might fall in love with him. True, it might not be the sort of flaming passion she'd had difficulty keeping under control when she had first been courted by Luke, but perhaps that was no bad thing. And anyway, the flame Luke had ignited within her was the sort to burn fast and hot, while somehow still being prone to flickering alarmingly in even the lightest of draughts. By contrast, Rowley seemed to be offering something that, while less passionate, felt more mature

— more of a gentle and soothing warmth than a fiery flame. Given her age, there was nothing wrong with that; in its own way, it was just as appealing. Besides, the stark reality of her position made it unlikely that she would get a better offer; in turning him down, she ran the very real risk of ending up like Edith.

Realizing that the last of the light had now completely gone, she lifted the hem of her skirt and started back across the grass. Already damp with dew, it quickly soaked through the fabric of her little mourning slippers — footwear clearly never intended for outdoor trysts of the dewy summer night variety. Struck by the inappropriateness of her thought, she giggled: was not every inch of her mourning outfit designed to ward off all possibility of *any* type of tryst at all?

Nearing the house, and spotting that all but the French doors of the drawing room stood in complete darkness, she slowed her pace. Perhaps her disrespectful behaviour told her something. Perhaps, deep down, she did know what she wanted to do. But, if that was true, then why was she continuing to hesitate? Was it simply because dear Rowley's proposal had come so soon after Luke's death? Did her concern centre more upon what people would think of her? Or did she still have genuine concerns about how she would fit into his very different life? Yes, the changes required of her would be greater than anything she had known before; even contemplating such upheaval made her jittery. On the other hand, what he appeared to be offering was the very thing she had once so badly craved — a life with a purpose and the chance of real fulfilment. So, yes, just why *was* she hesitating? If, as she had just thought, she knew how she felt, then shouldn't she just get on with it and give him her answer?

Shivering, and rueing her lack of a shawl, she resumed walking. Yes, tomorrow she would tell him what she had decided — and then all she could do after that was hope that she didn't live to regret it.

14

Shock

'Well, that *is* a surprise, I must say.'

Seated at the table, Kate turned to study Ned's face. Not only did he *sound* pleased, he looked it too.

'Isn't it?' Naomi replied to her brother's observation with a warm smile.

'I wasn't expecting to come to breakfast this morning to be told *that*.'

Yes, Kate thought, the news had come as a surprise to everyone: on account of him having been assessed unfit to return to active duty, Captain Lawrence Colborne was being discharged from the army — and on a full military pension, too. Finally, Naomi had something to smile about.

Seemingly becoming aware that all eyes were upon him, Lawrence straightened his shoulders and cleared his throat. 'Well, one would have preferred, of course, that this decision had not been necessary in the first place. No officer wants his service to king and empire cut short — not on medical grounds or any other. That said, nor does one ever wish to be a liability. As an officer, the decisions one makes and the commands one gives can mean the difference between life and death to the men who follow them . . . and if, well . . . '

To Kate, he seemed as though he was struggling to hold back tears; for him, the news was clearly a mixed blessing. Picking up the letter from the table, he gave it another glance and shook his head as if still unable to believe it. ' . . . if the army have deemed that I am no longer fit for such a responsibility, then I must respect their decision — find a way to come to terms with it. Almighty blow to one's pride, all the same.'

'But darling,' Naomi said, slipping her arm through his, 'you're bound to go on and do something just as meaningful and worthwhile. Just because you've been ruled unfit to serve in the army doesn't mean that you will be left unemployed.' Looking to her brother for support, she went on, 'Tell him I'm right, Ned. Tell him it's true.'

'It is true,' Ned replied. 'It will just be a matter of taking stock and finding the right profession, that's all.'

'A man with your record will soon be snatched up,' Rowley agreed. 'Trust me. Private companies — indeed, a large part of Whitehall — are crying out for men with your background — men with your record of being in command and your experience of being on the front line.'

'Well, thank you, all of you, for your faith in me,' Lawrence said, looking quickly about the table. 'Once the news has sunk in, I shall consider how best to set about building a new future . . . for myself and my family.'

Without making it obvious that she was doing so, Kate glanced to Rowley. Looking across at Mr Lawrence, he appeared relaxed and contented. They all did. And in which case, perhaps, once breakfast was finished, it might be a nice moment to give him her answer to his proposal of marriage. What could be finer than two pieces of good news in one day? Coming together, they might even be deemed worthy of a little celebration later on.

Mulling the wisdom of it, she looked down into her lap. First, of course, she would have to change out of her mourning gown, and then cease wearing it altogether. A few days ago, such a thing would have felt unthinkable and been something for which she hadn't been ready. But now, it felt like just another step along the road towards her new life. But then she remembered that last night, in bed, she had made herself a promise: she had vowed that this morning, no matter how certain she felt, she would make herself wait one more day to give Rowley her answer. Better to be safe than sorry after all. Besides, if the decision she had reached was the right one, then another four-and-twenty hours were neither here nor there. And so, for now, she wouldn't allow herself to get swept up in all the warmth of Mr Lawrence's news. Instead, she would sit on her hands, and force herself to wait one more day.

It wasn't until the menfolk had finally left the dining room, and the two of them were clearing the table of the debris from breakfast, that Naomi spoke to her directly. 'You know, I can hardly believe my good fortune.'

'I daresay,' Kate replied, carrying the little galleried tray of condiments across to the buffet. 'It's a real blessing for you. Just what you prayed for.'

'It is. I know it isn't what Lawrence wanted. I know he wanted to return to the front. And, had that come about, then, somehow, I should have found a way to bear it. But I can't *tell* you how enormously glad I am that I shan't have to! I can't *begin* to describe the relief.'

Gathering up the crumpled napkins scattered about the table, Kate nodded her agreement. 'I think I can imagine.'

'Finally, we shall be able to get on with our lives.'

'Yes,' she replied. But, despite smiling broadly, she was unable to bury the feeling that she was being horribly treacherous. Naomi would be deeply hurt if she knew about Rowley's proposal — not that she was intending to accept him, but because she had kept the whole thing a secret from her in the first place. Well, regrettable though that was, not everything was Naomi's business. And perhaps the time *had* come for her to live a little more independently — to find her own way in life.

'Of course, he still isn't fully recovered,' Naomi went on to say, forcing Kate to return her attention. 'He still struggles to sleep properly. And he's still jumpy. And frighteningly short with Esme at times. But, well, he is so very much better than he was.'

'I'm pleased for you,' Kate said, her mind back on Mr Lawrence.

'My priority now must surely be to prevent him from rushing, willy-nilly, into something new — you know, grasping the first thing that fires his imagination.'

Gathering up the corners of the tablecloth, Kate nodded. 'Yes.'

'And, in that respect, once we're back in town, I might need to call upon you to be another pair of eyes and ears for me.'

'Yes, of course.' Oh dear, now this was becoming tricky; she did so hate deceit.

'In any event,' Naomi continued, 'I have an idea, and I should like you to tell me what you think of it.' About to carry the cloth out onto the terrace and shake off the crumbs, she instead remained where she was and waited for Naomi to elaborate. 'Part of Lawrence's treatment requires that he be involved in various activities out of doors. So, I am minded to suggest to him, in a very roundabout way, of course, that, rather than go straight back to London, we see out the rest of the summer here. My hope is that, away from ordinary life, he might feel less inclined to start making plans. He has already said that in the short term at least, we can manage on his pension. My other hope is that with no real demands upon him here, he will spend time getting to know Esme.'

'I think your idea to stay down here is a good one,' she said, finally carrying the tablecloth out through the French doors and giving it a good shake. Calling back over her shoulder, she went on, 'It might help Mr Lawrence settle back into family life.' Yes, she thought, it might be good for all of you. *Whereas I, on the other hand,* she found herself thinking, *will have things of my own to settle into. And, that being the case, I could do without the upheaval of returning to*

London, with all the upside down-ness that would bring.

And no, the fact that she was being selfish wasn't lost on her. For the first time, she was putting her own needs first. And it was causing her no qualms whatsoever.

★ ★ ★

Goodness, she was cross. And how typical that it should be Naomi who was to blame for her frustration!

In a state of exasperation, Kate shook her head. Just when she'd had an idea about how to tell everyone her news, Naomi had gone and decreed that, this afternoon, tea should once again be taken out on the lawn, it being her desire to hold a small celebration in honour of Mr Lawrence's retirement from the army — as she had taken to calling it. A pleasant enough thing by itself, it nevertheless meant that tomorrow, when she made her own announcement — when *they* made *their* announcement — she couldn't really expect there to be an appetite for yet *another* celebration. And anyway, a party with the leftover halves of today's cakes wouldn't be a party at all. Moreover, by remaining true to her vow to wait a further day before telling Rowley of her decision, even *were* there to be a second tea party, it would surely lack all sense of occasion — would amount to nothing special at all.

To be fair, there had been no way for Naomi to have known what she had been planning to do — after all, out of necessity, she had been keeping it a secret. But that didn't make her any less annoyed. No, the upset was, she reflected, recalling something Aunt Diana had once said, 'an unintended consequence' of her decision not to take Naomi into her confidence. Well, then so be it. For the last four years, women had been announcing their engagements and getting married with next to nothing by way of celebrations at all. So, why should she be any different? It wasn't even as though her wedding to Rowley would be her first.

Seeing no option but to try to bury her disappointment, she gave a long sigh. On the up side, this afternoon's gathering did at least give her genuine cause to abandon her mourning dress and wear one of her pretty frocks. Then, tomorrow, when she again appeared in ordinary dress, this time in readiness for her — for *their* — announcement, it ought hardly to draw comment at all.

What she *hadn't* bargained on, though, as she sat under the cedar tree with the little family group, was just how twitchy the prospect of waiting another day would cause her to feel. She had always been hopeless at keeping secrets and, with all the bonhomie surrounding Mr Lawrence's news, she was simply itching to be free from the burden of concealing her own. Thankfully, despite knocking over a tea cup and spilling the contents, and despite being unable to sit still for more than a single moment at a time, no one — even Rowley — seemed to have noticed anything amiss with her, or had even enquired whether she was all right.

In an effort to distract her thoughts, she got up and helped herself to a slice of gooseberry tart. And then, for good measure, she spooned over it a generous dollop of clotted cream.

Eventually, though, when she got up again to return her empty plate to the trestle, she drew the attention of Naomi, who raised a hand and gestured to her to come and join her on the bench. 'Bring another cushion,' she called across.

Seeing no way to do otherwise, Kate took the remaining seat in the circle of mismatched garden furniture and glanced about. Mr Lawrence was stretched out on a steamer chair, his panama over his face and looking to all the world as though he were asleep. A couple of feet away from him, in his wheelchair, Ned was reading to Esme from what she recognized to be Rudyard Kipling's *How the Leopard Got His Spots*. Then came Rowley. And then, some distance from him, Nurse Hammond was sat knitting something very tiny from a skein of pale blue wool.

Once Kate sat down, Naomi turned towards her. 'Are you all right? Only, you've seemed rather distant today. And I shouldn't want you to think that just because Lawrence is back, we can't do things together — or talk to one another.'

Recognizing Naomi's sentiments as genuine, she raised a smile. 'No. I know.'

'I shouldn't want you to think that . . . ' Her statement unfinished, Naomi paused to sit more upright.

Curious to discover what could have caught her attention, she followed the line of her gaze across the lawn. Pedalling furiously up the drive was the postman, a slim mail bag across his body. 'Bit late for him to be all the way out *here*,' Kate remarked of his arrival.

Evidently spotting them gathered under the cedar tree, and applying screeching brakes, the uniformed official brought his bicycle to a barely controlled halt at the edge of the lawn. Then, attempting to affect a speedy dismount, he caught one leg of his trousers in the chain, cursed heartily, freed himself and finally, smoothing down the front of his uniform, came trotting towards them.

'Bring this 'un up special, postmaster says to me,' he announced, panting heavily.

Together, Kate and Naomi rose from the bench. Disturbed from his slumber, Lawrence, too, got slowly to his feet.

'To whom do you bring this very special delivery?' Naomi enquired, starting towards the postman.

Wresting a single envelope from his bag, the delivery boy peered at the address. 'Mrs Luke Channer. Express delivery all the way from some place in Wiltshire.'

She froze. Mrs Luke Channer? Was that even the correct form of address for her now that she was widowed? More importantly, why was someone from Wiltshire sending *her* a letter? And why had the postman come cycling all the way out here this late in the day to deliver it? At least it couldn't be word of Luke. Luke was already dead; Mr Lawrence had already brought her *that* news. So, since he couldn't have been killed a second time, what on earth was it about?

'For you, evidently,' Naomi said, handing her the slender envelope.

Taking it from her, Kate stared down at it. Despite the smudge to the franking mark, she could clearly read the word Wiltshire.

Her senses on alert, she sat back down on the bench and tried to slide her finger under the flap.

'Here,' Ned said, holding towards her one of their used tea knives.

Accepting it from him, she slit along the top of the envelope. Then, setting the knife down on the table in front of her, she tugged out the contents.

Confronted by a page of handwriting embellished with more loops and swirls than seemed strictly necessary, she tried to focus her eyes, but they ran ahead of her brain, tripping over certain words and alighting on others as they caught her attention.

Corporal Driver Channer, L. Accident. Injured. Medical Leave.

Unexpectedly short of breath, she let the second of the two sheets of paper slip from her fingers and fall into her lap. 'Please,' she whispered, holding the first page towards Naomi, 'can you tell me what this is about?'

When Naomi reached for the letter, Kate forced herself to look up and watch as her eyes sped along the lines of writing. Why was the army writing to her about Luke? Luke was dead.

Without saying anything, Naomi crossed quickly to Lawrence.

'What is it, darling?'

'It's . . . well, no. I think you had better read it. Just to be sure.' Handing her husband the letter, Naomi returned to sit alongside Kate.

Why did Naomi look so pale? How could a letter — that wasn't even addressed to her — instantly drain so much colour from her cheeks?

And then, just as she reached to grab the arm of the bench, Mr Lawrence came across and squatted down beside her. And Naomi was taking her hands and holding them tightly. Dear God, whatever was this?

'This letter, has been sent from Regimental HQ to inform you that there has been . . . ' Lawrence began, and with which she had to force herself to pay attention. 'Well, that there has been a mistake.' He too, she noticed abstractedly, seemed short of colour all of a sudden, his former glow, hard won from working outside, replaced by a sort of sickly pallor. 'Kate, it seems that your husband is still alive.'

For a moment, she felt certain he had said that Luke was alive. But, obviously, he couldn't have. Luke was dead. His vehicle had been hit by a shell. They had held a service of remembrance for him. She had worn her widow's weeds.

Feeling Naomi grasping her hands tighter still, she pulled them away from her. No. This made no sense. None at all. 'So . . . ' But she couldn't even think what to ask. Luke was *alive*? 'So . . . '

'It would seem,' Lawrence continued, and with which she saw him glance briefly to Naomi, 'that although his vehicle was hit by a shell, he

366

was not the soldier driving it. On the day in question, his own vehicle wouldn't start and, since his mission was an urgent one, unbeknown to me, he commandeered a motorcar. Later, when the problem with his usual vehicle was fixed, it was taken out by someone else. And that is when it was hit by a shell.'

'So . . . ' But still she couldn't make sense of this. If Luke hadn't been dead all these weeks, then where had he been? And where was he now?

Still squatting beside her, Lawrence glanced back to the letter. 'Apparently, on the return leg of his journey, he found the way ahead blocked by a skirmish. So he took a different road, whereupon he became lost, ending up behind enemy lines and forced to hide out on a farm. Some days later, when one of our battalions was trying to re-take the area in question, there was a protracted battle and, as your husband was helping families to find cover, he took a rifle shot to the thigh. Once the village had been regained by our chaps, and he was being treated for his injury, the matter of his earlier mis-identification came to light. Kate, as soon as he is well enough to travel,' Lawrence said, pausing to look up at her and smile, 'he will be on his way back to you. He's being sent home on medical leave.'

With that, Kate felt her ears fill with a familiar rushing noise. And then everything went dark.

★ ★ ★

'Please, Kate, just take a sip. Mabel put plenty of sugar in it for the shock.'

367

No matter how much Naomi pleaded, Kate didn't want to sip sweet tea. Yes, she was almost certainly in shock. And, yes, she didn't seem able to stop crying. But the reason behind her tears wasn't — as Naomi clearly supposed — relief: it was guilt. It was guilt at how close she had come to accepting Rowley's proposal of marriage, and it was guilt at the thought of how he must feel now, knowing that Luke was alive. Worse still, there was the guilt she felt for not leaping up and down with joy at the news, or for offering up thanks that Luke wasn't dead after all. But the truth was that before she could celebrate Luke's survival, she had to make her peace with Rowley. She had to apologize to him. No matter how distressing that might prove, he deserved more than to be simply forgotten about. And then, after that, she somehow had to bury what she felt certain was regret. Not that her decision to marry again had been easily taken. It hadn't. All along she'd had a nagging suspicion that it was too soon to be considering remarrying — although not, she had to admit, because she had believed Luke was really still alive. *Luke was alive*. No matter how hard she tried, she couldn't believe it. Daren't believe it. They had told her he was dead. But all the time he had been alive. Oh, the relief of it! But oh, poor, decent Rowley; he didn't deserve to have his hopes dashed in this way.

Lifting her face from where it had been buried in the eiderdown, she reached into her sleeve for her handkerchief and blew her nose. She had to speak to him; although she could never have foreseen how things would turn out, she had to ask for his forgiveness. Only when she had done that would she be able to rest — and begin to come to terms with the news that Luke was coming home. *Luke was coming home!*

'If you don't mind,' she said, stuffing her handkerchief back into her sleeve and glancing at Naomi's face. 'I should like to just sit quiet for a moment. On my own.'

Uncertainly, Naomi got to her feet. 'Well . . . if you are sure you will be all right.'

She nodded. 'Perfectly sure.'

'Only, I've seen how shock can affect people — cause them to misjudge things . . . have accidents.'

Slowly, Kate shook her head. 'You've no need to worry. I'm not going anywhere. I just need to . . . well . . . '

'Yes,' Naomi replied, smoothing a hand down the front of her dress. 'You're wary of becoming too excited until you can be completely certain that Luke really is alive and coming back to you.'

'Yes!' she said, exhaling with relief at spotting a perfectly credible reason for her singular reaction to the news. 'Yes,' she said again, taking care this time to measure her tone. 'That's it. I worry about getting my hopes up . . . '

'Before you have more certain proof.'

'Yes.'

'Well, on your behalf, Lawrence has already telephoned Wiltshire and, as we speak, is standing by for a return call from a Major Somebody-or-other. The moment he hears from him, and we have it from the horse's mouth, so to speak, I shall come and get you.'

In furtherance of her charade, Kate swung her stockinged feet back up onto her bed and reclined against her pillow. 'Before you go,' she said, 'do you think you might draw the curtains across?'

One day, she would be called to account for all of this deceit. In the meantime, it couldn't be helped. To stand any chance of speaking to Rowley, she had first to get rid of Naomi.

With the room in darkness and Naomi having finally left, she lowered her feet back down to the floor, poked them into her shoes, and tiptoed across to the window. Tweaking apart the curtains, she scanned the gardens. Beneath the cedar tree, Mabel and Edith were clearing away the remnants of the tea party. Of anyone else, there was no sign. Pulling the curtains back one over the other, she crossed the room, eased open the door, and then peered out onto the landing. Good — no one in either direction.

Holding her breath, she slipped out into the corridor and, very carefully, closed the door behind her. Rowley had been occupying a room on the bachelors' landing, which led off the far side of the stairwell. And so, drawing a deep breath, she stole towards it. Arriving at the staircase, she stopped to peer over the balustrade. The only voices she could hear seemed to be coming from some distance away — at least as far as the drawing room — and so she continued on around the semi-circular gallery and, at the far side, went up the couple of steps onto the bachelors' landing. Breathing heavily now, she paused. So far, so good.

Ahead of her, the door to one of the rooms on the left was showing a crack of light. Good — if the door was ajar, then presumably he was in there. Feeling her heart thudding, she went towards it. Then, careful not to knock too loudly, she tapped three times. For a while, there was no sound from the other side. But, as she raised her hand to knock again, the door opened back and there he stood, his collar unfastened, his shirt sleeves rolled up, the dishevelled state of his hair suggesting he had been repeatedly clutching at it.

'Kate.'

At least he didn't seem angry. At least he hadn't slammed the door on her.

Relieved, she unfurled her hands. 'May I come in? Only, I need to talk to you, and I can't really do that from out here.' When he shrugged his shoulders and stood aside, she mumbled her thanks. But, once inside, she stayed close to the door and directed her eyes to the floor. To venture any further felt wrong, to look around at his possessions even more so — an invasion of his privacy.

'I'm so sorry,' she said without looking up from the rug.

'Perhaps not as sorry as I am.' She heard him reply.

'If I'd thought for a moment . . . I would never even have entertained — '

'If I'd thought for a moment that your husband was still alive, I wouldn't have asked you.'

'No.'

'Cruel fate.'

'Yes.'

371

Seeing his feet coming nearer, she looked sharply up. He looked utterly broken.

'You were going to say yes, weren't you?'

Feeling tears welling, she bit hard on the side of her tongue. But, on this occasion, the dull pain did nothing to stop her eyes from brimming over. Fumbling in her sleeve, she drew out her handkerchief and dabbed with it at her face. 'I would prefer not to say.'

'But you were, I know it. Watching you earlier today, I could tell. You had a . . . you had a . . . a sort of glow.'

Again, she bit on her tongue, this time harder, to stop herself from answering him. Admitting that she had indeed been going to accept him would do nothing to help either of them.

'What will you do now?' she asked. Though she knew it shouldn't matter to her, she found that it did; if nothing else, she couldn't bear to think of him ending up somewhere he didn't want to be.

Letting out a long sigh, he thrust his hands into his pockets. 'Well, I was going to look for a cottage for us to rent in a village close to my new posting but, clearly, I shan't be needing that now. So, I suppose that instead, I shall take a room in a house, and hope for a landlady whose cooking is at least tolerable.' She swallowed hard. It was precisely what she had hoped *not* to learn. 'Kate,' he said, reaching for her hands and taking tight hold of them, 'Come with me. It's not too late.'

When, in her alarm, she shrank away from him, he let her go. 'Rowley, I can't. And you know that.'

By way of response, he gave an exaggerated shrug. 'Forgive me,' he said. 'This war has wreaked havoc with my sense of humour.'

She frowned. He hadn't mean it as a joke; she knew he hadn't.

'I ought to go,' she said, growing uncomfortable. But, before turning away from him, something made her go on to ask, 'When will you leave?'

'On the first train tomorrow morning. I shall depart early — before breakfast. I *had* thought to go tonight — take a room in Westward Quay, but I didn't want to leave you in a fix — you know, have people drawing conclusions about the timing of your news and my sudden departure.'

Oh, dear God. Considerate to the end. And now that she was stood here with him, the prospect of his leaving made something in her chest feel as though it was splitting in two. 'Thank you.' She somehow managed to reply.

Oddly, having determined to take her leave of him, she found that her feet wouldn't let her turn away. But she had to; this was it. This dear man, to whom in different circumstances she might have become married, had to leave. He had to. This was goodbye. She would never see him again.

Quickly taking the single step needed to close the gap between them, she leant across and kissed his cheek. 'You're a fine man,' she whispered. 'And I'm so truly sorry. I really am.'

Somehow, from there, she managed to make it all the way back to her room, close the door and turn the key in the lock, before all of the tears she had been holding back came streaming down her face. Blinded by them, she kicked off her shoes, climbed onto her bed, and curled into a ball.

Flooding out with her tears came feelings she could share with no one: deep, deep sadness for Rowley, and the excruciating guilt she felt for allowing herself to be the cause of his pain. And, yes, there was regret, too. But all of those things, she knew for certain, would pass. And she knew it because the other feeling welling up from deep within her, was one of the most intense relief: her dearest Luke was alive. And he was coming home.

★ ★ ★

More unbearable than she could ever have imagined; that was how it felt to be forced to spend one day after another in limbo — one day after another with little to do but wait.

It was now ten days since Kate had received the news of Luke, and yet still she'd had no word from him — just a type-written letter from the army confirming that, in due course, Corporal Channer would be arriving home on medical leave. At the bottom of that single-page missive, a handwritten postscript had been added to say that no doubt Corporal Channer would get word to her, *through the usual channels* — whatever *they* were — just as soon as he was in a position to do so.

On this particular afternoon, she was sitting in the drawing room — the weather too uninviting for her to want to venture out of doors — half listening to Ned reading Esme the story of *Thumbelina*. Eventually, unable to sit still any longer, she got to her feet.

'You do know, don't you, that you're wearing out the rug,' Ned observed, breaking off from the fairy tale and glancing up. 'Not to mention the soles of your shoes.'

'I'm wearing out my nerves more,' she replied, returning to sit heavily back in her chair.

'You don't fancy a stroll?'

She glanced to the window. 'It's threatening rain.'

'Ah. Then you will just have to sit quietly like Esme is doing and find out what happens to *Thumbelina* now that she's met her flower-fairy prince.'

'Yes, Aunty Kate,' Esme agreed, the look on her face a stern one. 'Be quiet for story.'

With that, and seeing Naomi appear in the doorway, she sighed yet again; someone else to try and coax her into doing something.

'Kate, I think you might want to come through.'

Just as she had suspected: *now* what had Naomi dreamt up for her to do? Only, whatever it was, and no matter how well-meant, she just wanted to be left alone to wait in peace. For anything else, her mind was completely useless — distracted in the extreme. 'No, thank you, I'm fine.'

'Let me put that to you another way,' Naomi persisted.

Hearing her coming further into the room, Kate turned more fully to look at her. On her face was the broadest of smiles.

'*What*? Is he here?' Feeling suddenly short of breath, she scrabbled to her feet. 'He never is!'

'The station taxi is just coming up the drive.'

'Lord alive,' she breathed. 'And here's me without so much as a comb dragged through my hair. Just like him to turn up when I'm not fit to be seen.'

'Come on,' Naomi coaxed, extending a hand. 'I can't imagine he'll be the least bit concerned by a few stray hairs.'

With her heart pounding in her chest, Kate skirted the end of the sofa and accepted Naomi's hand. Sure enough, beyond the porch stood the station taxi, its nearside door opening back. Hardly daring to believe her eyes, she tried to gulp down her disbelief. From inside the motor, a khaki-clad leg appeared, followed, with some difficulty, by an arm and then a head bearing a cap. Heavens. It really was him. He was home. Her husband was back!

Dropping Naomi's hand, she ran the length of the hallway and darted straight out through the porch and onto the drive.

Rounding the side of the taxi was the driver, carrying in his hand a crutch.

'Here,' she said, reaching to take it from him. 'I'm his wife. Let me.'

When Luke eventually lowered his other foot down to the gravel and slowly eased himself upright, she caught her first look at his face. His complexion was grey and his cheeks hollow. But there, in his eyes, was that unmistakeable glint, and on his lips, that mischievous grin.

'Hello, Mrs Channer,' he greeted her.

Almost buckling under the weight of him leaning on her shoulder, she fiddled to position his crutch. 'Back from the dead then, I see.'

His grin grew wider still. 'Aye,' he replied, 'you're not the only one who can be obstinate, you know.'

★ ★ ★

'So, here we are then, the two of us. Mr and Mrs Channer.'

It was later that same evening and, despite the fact that it had long since grown dark, Kate and Luke hadn't moved from where they had been seated together on one of the benches under the cedar tree. In front of them, silhouetted against the indigo twilight, a dozen pipistrelles flitted back and forth, zig-zagging through the dusk in their search for supper.

Exhaling a long and contented sigh, Kate angled her head to better see her husband's face. 'Yes,' she replied, reassured by the familiarity of his profile, her voice little more than a warm murmur. 'Here we are. Mr and Mrs Channer. And I can scarce believe it.'

'When I found out they'd wrongly told you I'd been took, I tell you now, I was livid. All I could think about was what hearing of my demise would have done to you — how it would have changed everything for you. And I wanted to swing for the dolt who hadn't thought to proper check the identity of the poor feller who'd really bought it.'

She snuggled back against his shoulder. It was

comforting to hear that his first thought had been for her. 'To listen to you earlier, telling of what happened over there, I do see how it happened,' she said. 'The confusing of you with some other poor soul, I mean.'

Beneath her weight, Luke shifted his position. 'Don't suppose it was the first time there's been such a mix up. And I daresay it won't be the last, either.'

'But you're here now,' she went on, feeling the warmth of his shoulder through the cloth of his shirt. 'Home where you belong. Safe.'

'And, if fate is on my side, I shan't have to go back out there again, either,' he remarked. 'With a fair wind, the last of it will be over before I'm anywhere near fit enough to be sent back — '

'You most certainly *won't* be fit enough,' she said, giggling. 'Rest assured I shall see to that myself.'

Pulling away to look at her face, he grinned. 'Is that right?'

'Trust me,' she said, grinning back at him. 'I know a good deal about getting legs to heal and, more importantly, the myriad reasons why they don't. Quite the expert I've become. Not that I'd thought to have further use for it, all that knowledge I've picked up from Nurse Hammond. I certainly hadn't thought I might one day make use of it to keep my own husband at home.'

'Handy,' Luke remarked, the mischief in his tone precisely as she remembered it. 'And what other skills have you picked up while I've been gone? What else have you been up to that I should know about?'

She knew straight away that he wasn't expecting an answer to that — she could tell from his tone that he was pulling her leg. He'd already remarked, more than once, that they were where they were, four years down the road, and that all he wanted now was to make a proper start on married life. Even so, she couldn't help herself. 'I've learned more things than I've time to tell you tonight, that's for sure,' she replied in similar vein. 'You wouldn't believe the half of it.'

'No?'

'No. But you know what? Now that you're back, not one single jot of it matters in the least.'

'No?'

Against his shoulder, she shook her head. 'No. I'm not saying it'll be easy, mind. The girl you wed was airy-headed and restless — '

He squeezed her closer. 'You won't hear me take issue with that.'

' — but in the same way that this war has changed all of you men, it's changed us women, too.'

'For certain it has.'

'We've grown up,' she said. 'Learned to stand on our own two feet. Looked out for each other. We've a taste for what it means to be independent — '

'And I'm proud of you, truly — '

'But you're back now. And to me, this feels like the chance we never had in the first place. A chance to be together, husband and wife at last. Proper wed.'

And it was true. A lot might have happened to

her in Luke's absence, but now was the time to draw a line under all of it and start over. Nothing that had happened before this afternoon mattered. It was all water under the bridge. She would look forward, not back. Her soldier had returned. And tomorrow, together, they would start afresh. *She* would start afresh. Her long and wearying search for her place in the world was over. And yes, she might be back exactly where she had started, but she knew now that it was precisely where she was supposed to be. And, for that, she couldn't be more grateful.

Epilogue

October 1918

The good weather that year continued, unabated, throughout August and well into September, with morning mists quickly evaporating to bring warm days that faded softly into dewy evenings. Sadly, the war also continued. But, as the month drew to a close, it became clear to those who understood these things that following recent counter-attacks from France and Britain, Germany was losing the initiative and that, within her ranks, disillusionment was spreading. Indeed, at Woodicombe House, Lawrence, Ned and Luke all agreed that negotiations for Germany's surrender were now unavoidable.

For everyone at Woodicombe, but for Kate in particular, the coming of victory would bring to an end an eventful period in their lives. Gone was the guilt she had felt about what she had come to think of as her *haste* with Rowley: she had believed herself widowed and, in her grief, had sought only to secure for herself a future. Looking back, her actions had been both understandable and forgivable. One day, some years from now, when she and Luke were looking back and reminiscing, she would probably even tell him about it. She had no reason not to.

Seated alongside her on the terrace, on this particular afternoon was Naomi, and when she shifted her weight in a bid to get more comfortable, Kate stole a glance at her face. 'All right?' she enquired.

'Never better,' Naomi assured her.

Despite the pleasant sunshine, about their shoulders they each wore a shawl against the breeze, because, as Mabel repeatedly insisted, neither of them could risk catching a chill — not with both of them having babies on the way.

It was Naomi who had first become aware of her condition, and whose baby, according to Dr. Hatherleigh, was due as early as Easter. Mindful of Naomi's previous misfortune, and her family's medical history, Lawrence had decreed that before the month was out, they would be returning to London to be close to the doctor in Harley Street. In any event, Kate knew it was where Naomi needed to be: it was where she belonged; where she would be happiest; neither Naomi nor Mr Lawrence having a country bone in their body.

Not like herself and Luke, she thought, glancing indoors to where her husband was sitting with Ned and Mr Lawrence, the former gesturing with his hands as he appeared to explain something about either aeroplanes or flying. Yes, Naomi might not be a country girl, but she, Kate, would never be anything else. She had tried London — and hadn't altogether disliked it — but the truth was that this was where she belonged, here, in this sleepy part of Devon. And that was why the offer that Naomi had made to her and Luke was so utterly perfect. Woodicombe House, she had said, needed returning to habitable standards. And her father — *their father* — agreed with her. And so, to that end, Kate and Luke were going to stay on, alongside Mabel and Edith, to oversee what Naomi had taken to calling the 'necessary updating works' that would turn the place into somewhere comfortable for them to bring their children during the holidays. At Ned's own request, plans for the modernisation included the creation of a self-contained suite of rooms on the ground floor, specially equipped, such that he might remain at Woodicombe — in the short term at least — to undergo some newly-emerging therapies and continue his convalescence not only in the clean air of North Devon, but among family.

Sitting there, contentedly, the irony of this state of affairs wasn't wasted on Kate; all those years ago, Luke had been right. Woodicombe really was going to be the perfect place to raise a family.

Acknowledgements

With grateful thanks to everyone who played a part in turning the nub of an idea into a fully-fledged saga.